NOVELS OF THOMAS LOVE PEACOCK

Thomas Love Peacock was born at Weymouth, the only child of a glass merchant. From the age of 13 he was self-educated, but nevertheless became a learned scholar. In 1819 he entered the service of the East India Company, and rose to be Chief Examiner from 1837 to 1856. He was the author of several satirical novels full of humour, paradox and learning, with witty dialogue and occasional poems interspersed. Among them are *Headlong Hall* (1816), *Nightmare Abbey* (1818), *Maid Marian* (1822), *Misfortunes of Elphin* (1829), *Crotchet Castle* (1831) and *Gryll Grange* (1860). He was the intimate friend of Shelley, and contributed memoirs of him to *Fraser's Magazine*.

D1215903

A Pan Classic

Novels of
Thomas Love Peacock

Headlong Hall   Nightmare Abbey
The Misfortunes of Elphin
Crotchet Castle

Introduction by
J. B. PRIESTLEY

Notes by
BARBARA LLOYD EVANS

UNABRIDGED

PAN BOOKS LTD : LONDON

wasted at a High Table and in some Senior Common Room. And it might be said that in his novels of talk he created superb imaginary High Tables and Senior Common Rooms, where the port and Madeira were riper, the wit brighter, than in any to be found in reality.

Apart from two brief spells of work, as a very junior clerk in the City and later as a naval secretary, Peacock spent most of his youth and young manhood reading and writing verse, falling in love, walking and wandering. From 1812 onwards, he saw much of Shelley and they became close friends. Peacock was not an idealist romantic himself – and could mock the type, as he did in *Nightmare Abbey* – but was genuinely attached to Shelley as his *Memoirs* prove. Indeed, he early understood and appreciated all the romantic poets. But they – and especially Shelley – did much to check a certain romantic and sentimental strain in himself and encouraged his sense of absurdity. He liked them, we might say, but they overdid it, so he laughed at them later in his novels, but always with something like affection, reserving his more malicious wit for very different types, political economists and the like.

In 1818, when Peacock was in his thirties and still unmarried, he probably suffered some financial loss that made him look for a reasonably well-paid job. He found it in the Examiner's Department of the East India Company, where, after succeeding in a competitive examination, he was appointed an Assistant Examiner at £600 a year. He rose steadily in this easy and comfortable service – the hours were from ten to four – and became Chief Examiner, holding this enviable post until he retired in 1856. Incidentally, he was sandwiched as Chief Examiner between the sour and sweet philosophical Mills, because sour James Mill the father was his predecessor and sweet John Stuart Mill the son was his successor. Peacock didn't care for either of them, having no regard for the solemn professors of the new science of political economy. Moreover, the Mills were not convivial men. Of James Mill, a friend of Peacock said, 'Will he like what I like and hate what I hate?', to which Peacock characteristically replied, 'No, he will hate what you hate and hate everything you like.'

Nothing could have suited Peacock better than this East India Company job. He enjoyed a good income and had plenty of time for reading and writing. And as soon as he felt

secure he decided it was time to marry. In 1811, during his
walking and wandering days, he had met a tall and handsome
Welsh girl, Jane Gryffydh, with whom he must have had at
least a lively flirtation. Now in 1819, without having set eyes
on her for eight years, and apparently without exchanging a
single letter, he wrote to her out of the blue – actually on East
India Company paper and perhaps during office hours – coolly
proposing marriage, just as if he were one of his own eccentric
characters. She accepted him.

They appeared to be well-matched, but their family life
brought them misfortunes. They lost their favourite daughter,
Margaret, while she was still a small child. Peacock wrote for
her tombstone the most moving of all his poems, beginning
Long night succeeds thy little day. It was said that Jane Peacock
never recovered from this blow, soon turning into one of
those (to us) rather mysterious Victorian invalids. This
suggests to my mind that the marriage itself was not really
successful, for happy wives can recover even from the death
of a favourite child. However, there is nothing to indicate that
Peacock was anything but a kind and considerate husband,
even though he may have been over-fond of convivial and
scholarly male company.

For reasons that will soon be made clear, I cannot leave
Peacock's family life without saying something about his elder
daughter, Mary Ellen. A brilliant and attractive girl, she
married in 1844 a young naval officer, Edward Nicolls, who
died at sea a few months after their marriage. She bore him a
daughter, Edith, to whom Peacock was greatly attached.
Years later, Edith kept house for him at Lower Halliford, and
it is to Edith Nicolls we owe any intimate accounts we possess
of Peacock in his old age.

In 1848 Mary Ellen was one of the contributors to a manuscript magazine, and among her fellow contributors was a
young articled clerk, several years younger than herself, poor,
clever, handsome, and very ambitious, George Meredith.
After refusing him (very sensibly) more than once, she was
finally swept away by his impetuosity, and they were married
in 1849. The marriage was disastrous, and nine years later she
left the country with the painter, Henry Wallis, but returned
the following year, a sick and miserably unhappy woman, and
died in 1861, unforgiven and unvisited by her husband. (It is
this marriage that is the subject of Meredith's magnificent

narrative, *Modern Love*, a poem which seems to belong more to our century than to mid-Victorian England.)

There is evidence to suggest that Peacock never liked Meredith, but even so they must have seen a good deal of each other for several years, when Meredith was still young and impressionable, was not certain what he was going to do, and had a genuine admiration for Peacock's work. The result was that Peacock's influence was far more important than it is generally supposed to be. It is not simply that a character like Dr Middleton in *The Egoist* must have been based on Peacock himself. It is not – though this is more important – that Peacock's women characters, though lightly sketched, at least suggest the outlines of the heroines that were later so much admired in Meredith's fiction. No, it is what Peacock probably did to influence Meredith in shaping the whole course of his future work. When they first met, Meredith was a vaguely romantic poet. Shortly after they parted he became the creator of a new kind of fiction, in which romantic narrative is fused with intellectual comedy. What was it that turned his attention to Comedy, which he created in his best novels and criticized so admirably in his *Essay*? Undoubtedly, it was in part the influence of that close and enthusiastic student of Comedy, that indefatigable servant of the Comic Spirit, Thomas Love Peacock.

All but one of Peacock's novels, *Gryll Grange* written in his old age, had appeared long before he met Meredith. They came out at odd irregular intervals. After all, Peacock was essentially an amateur author, a man who wrote for fun, to enjoy himself without caring much about literary opinion of his work and the taste of the reading public. Three of his novels were published not long before he joined the East India Company: they are *Headlong Hall* (1816), *Melincourt* (1817), and *Nightmare Abbey* (1818). There was now a four-year gap, during which he was probably settling down with his marriage and his East India office work. In 1822 he published *Maid Marian* and then waited seven years before bringing out his *Misfortunes of Elphin*. These were tales of the past with a peculiar Peacockian twist to them, but in 1831 he returned triumphantly to his earlier formula of talk-at-a-houseparty in *Crotchet Castle*, generally considered to be the best of his novels. Then there was a very long gap indeed, until 1860, when the fruits of his retirement and serene old age were gathered in *Gryll Grange*. That excellent editor and critic of Peacock, Mr David Garnett, declares that *Gryll Grange* is his favourite, but while it certainly has a smiling charm of its own, it has always seemed to me overloaded with classical scholarship and to come too close in some of its talk to *Notes And Queries*.

When we remember how little narrative there is in Peacock's novels, how few their concessions to the taste of the novel-reading public, how largely topical their satire was, it is surprising how often they have been reprinted.

Prince Seithenyn is a character – and the best character – in *The Misfortunes of Elphin*. Through his wife Peacock developed a keen interest in ancient Welsh legends and poetry. Though no master of narrative he did contrive with some skill to fuse together three different legends into one fairly compact tale. But his treatment of this romantic material is sardonic, filled with smooth irony but sometimes exploding into rich humour. I admit that as a literary form this really does not work. Romance and satire belong to two different worlds. A writer cannot do justice to Celtic legends and their poetry if at the same time he is busy poking fun at power, politics, education: he is trying to ride off in two different directions. Peacock tried first to mix romantic story-telling with satire and irony in his *Maid Marian*, and he failed: it is his weakest attempt at fiction. Though *The Misfortunes of Elphin* is stronger all through, I doubt if he would have succeeded there had he not created Prince Seithenyn, who, as Mr Garnett says, is 'one of the immortal drunkards in the literature of the world'. True, the level of blandly ironical report and comment is high:

> They had no steam-engines, with fires as eternal as those of the nether world, wherein the squalid many, from infancy to age, might be turned into component parts of machinery for the benefit of the purple-faced few . . .

> Of moral science they had little; but morals, without science, they had about the same as we have. They had a number of fine precepts, partly from their religion, partly from their bards, which they remembered in their liquor, and forgot in their business . . .

> In physical science, they supplied the place of knowledge by converting conjectures into dogmas; an art which is not yet lost . . .

Medicine was cultivated by the Druids, and it was just as much a science with them as with us; but they had not the wit or the means to make it a flourishing trade; the principal means to that end being women with nothing to do, articles which especially belong to a high state of civilization . . .

And of the office of Lord High Commissioner of Royal Embankment, he tells us:

He executed it as a personage so dominated might be expected to do; he drank the profits, and left the embankment to his deputies, who left it to their assistants, who left it to itself . . .

This High Commissioner of Royal Embankment is none other than Prince Seithenyn, the immortal drunkard. *Gwin o eur* – 'Wine from gold' – is his great cry, and he is always begging his guests to take a little more: 'Wine is my medicine; and my quantity is a little more.' He is not, like Falstaff, a wonderful wit in his cups; he is a little further on, in the argumentative and dialectical state of intoxication that tempts a man to talk as a metaphysician writes. He is a kind of daft logician. In the wonderful scene, too long to quote here, in which he replies to the charge that the embankment is rotten, declaring in effect that it is better if it is rotten, there are three different levels of satire and humour. The first is political and was also topical in 1829, being a burlesque of Canning's speeches defending the British Constitution against Reform. The second level is satire against stupid conservatism in general. The third level belongs to humour itself, not to satire, showing how Seithenyn tries to make his reason serve his idleness, his intellect minister to his thirst, and cheerfully sacrifices duty, security, commonsense, to uproarious good fellowship. He vanishes in the flood, after the embankment crumbles, but then, to our delight, turns up again (all great comic characters turn up again) when Taliesin visits King Melvas and the drunken butler tells him that he is Seithenyn:

'Seithenyn,' said Taliesin, 'has slept twenty years under the waves of the western sea, as King Gwythno's Lamentations have made known to all Britain.'

'They have not made it known to me,' said Seithenyn, 'for the best of all reasons, that one can only know the truth; for, if that which we think we know is not truth, it is something which we do not know. A man cannot know his own death; for, while he knows anything, he is alive; at least, I never heard of a dead man who knew anything, or pretended to know anything; if he had so pretended, I should have told him to his face he was no dead man.'

He is still in the same maze of syllogisms, the reeling philosopher. And as far as I am concerned, it is chiefly for his sake that *The Misfortunes of Elphin* can be found here.

Headlong Hall, *Nightmare Abbey*, and *Crotchet Castle*, though different in scene and tone, all roughly follow the same plan. They are novels not of action but of talk. A number of odd characters meet in or near a country house, eat and drink heartily, and talk away. Some of them are satirical sketches of real persons, as for example Shelley, Byron, Coleridge in *Nightmare Abbey*, while others merely represent a philosophy or a point of view. They are not quite characters, as we expect to find characters in a good novel; and yet they are also not quite so many talking dummies. They are something in between, and tend to take on a little more humanity in each successive novel, which is one reason why *Nightmare Abbey* is better than *Headlong Hall*; and *Crotchet Castle*, with its rich and ripe Dr Folliott and its charming Lady Clarinda, is better still. This device of assembling representative characters to debate their philosophies and respective points of view seems easy enough, with the result that it has been used by several clever writers interested in ideas. But the fact remains that they have never succeeded as Peacock did.

There are two reasons why he is read and remembered while the others have been forgotten. The first comes out of his character as a man. Thomas Love Peacock was an extremely unusual and paradoxical man. No familiar category will hold him. He was a deep-dyed Tory with strong radical feelings. Or he was a Radical with ultra-conservative prejudices. He was an epicurean humorist, yet he was a close friend of Shelley. He was both in front of his age and behind it. He was full of common sense and yet didn't despise ideas but delighted in them. Part of him seems to be lingering in the eighteenth century and the Enlightenment, yet another part appears to us to be closer to our own times and outlook than most of his contemporaries. He is a witty diner-out, with a cultivated taste in food and wine, who is yet ready to be sympathetic to the idea of a simple life in a cottage. He laughs at crackpots and yet has an almost tender regard for them. Most clever men interested in ideas – Peacock's potential rivals – tend to be narrow in their sympathies and, sooner or later, harsh in their judgements. Peacock's breadth, together with his opposing quirks of temperament, keeps him free of this narrowness and harshness and leaves him tolerant and good-humoured.

This tolerance and good-humour turn him into a very rare kind of satirist. During the last few years we have heard and read a great deal about satire. It looked for a time as if we were about to enter a new age of satire. Remembering a number of late Saturday-night television programmes, we might say that satire was both on the air and in the air. But among the many writers who contributed to such programmes or sharpened and flung their barbs elsewhere, no rival to Peacock emerged.

Nobody at first sight could seem more unlike George Bernard Shaw, the ascetic, than Peacock, the lover of wine and rich food and conviviality. (Peacock once cured Shelley, who was drooping on a thin vegetarian diet, by insisting upon his eating 'three chops well-peppered'.) But Shaw and Peacock are alike in being able to create this rare atmosphere of witty and humorous good-nature, in which true comedy flourishes. Indeed, if Peacock had ever become involved with the Theatre – though his particular time and his style of life were both against this – then, once he had mastered theatrical construction and acquired a technique, he might have written some superb stage comedies. And not only because he possessed the necessary tolerance and good-humour but also – and this brings us to the second reason why he is read and remembered – because he possessed a unique style, especially for dialogue. (It is significant that when the talk really gets going, Peacock stops being a narrator and, like a dramatist, depends entirely on dialogue.) His novels may be mostly talk, but what talk it is! If any reader, not himself a writer, imagines that it is easy to produce dialogue of this quality, I can only implore him either to change his mind or give us something equally good.

It is nearly forty years since I first wrote about Peacock and his style. On this particular subject I think now what I thought then and can only repeat what I wrote then. I pointed out that almost all Peacock's characters talk in the same way, like members of one closely united family. They all talk in crisp phrases, delicately balanced and full of anti-theses, and with a precision that is admirable and yet some-how droll. However wild their opinions and arguments may be, their actual statements of them are all given an epi-grammatic brevity and ring. Thus the maddest of them is something of a stylist and a wit. But this very fact gives all their speeches, which usually put forward some ridiculous notion, a curious undercurrent of irony. They explain them-selves, as it were, only too well; there is mockery in the very precision of their language and the crisp rhythm of their phrases.

Let us take a quick dip into these three novels of talk, to find some brief examples of their quality. In *Headlong Hall* Mr Milestone, the landscape gardener, is discussing the laying out of grounds:

'Sir,' said Mr Milestone, 'you will have the goodness to make a distinction between the picturesque and the beautiful.'

'Will I?' said Sir Patrick, 'och! but I won't. For what is beautiful? That what pleases the eye. And what pleases the eye? Tints variously broken and blended. Now, tints variously broken and blended constitute the picturesque.'

'Allow me,' said Mr Gall. 'I distinguish the picturesque and the beautiful, and I add to them, in the laying out of grounds, a third and distinct character, which I call *un-expectedness*.'

'Pray, sir,' said Mr Milestone, 'by what name do you distinguish this character, when a person walks round the grounds for the second time?'

And Peacock, as he tells us in a footnote, based this talk on a solemn controversy in the *Edinburgh Review*; but then, of course, gave it his own crispness, salt and flavour.

In *Nightmare Abbey*, when the men are filling bumpers of old wine, there is some talk against going abroad, to which Mr Cypress (Byron) replies:

'Sir, I have quarrelled with my wife; and a man who has quarrelled with his wife is absolved from all duty to his country. I have written an ode to tell the people as much, and they may take it as they list.'

He is then compelled to paraphrase his elaborate lamentations from *Childe Harold* into pithy Peacockian prose and deliver them over the bottle with a good dinner inside him:

'I have no hope for myself or for others. Our life is a false nature; it is not in the harmony of things; it is an all-blasting upas, whose root is earth, and whose leaves are the skies which rain their poison-dews upon mankind . . .'

This makes such affected pessimism sound very foolish, especially as Mr Cypress, like the others, is always ready for a bottle of Madeira and a chorus. And it is worth pointing out here that Shelley, who as Scythrop Glowry is the central figure of the absurd tale, never resented but enjoyed this caricature, composed out of one side of his mind and then mixed with the general stuff of Peacockian humanity, for ever dining, drinking, and arguing. Shelley always understood what Peacock was up to; after all, they had been close friends.

A last dip, very quick, into *Crotchet Castle*. The ripest of its characters, the Reverend Doctor Folliott, out for a walk, is questioned by a stranger:

THE STRANGER

I beg your pardon, sir: do I understand this place to be your property?

THE REV. DR FOLLIOTT

It is not mine, sir: the more is the pity; yet it is so far well, that the owner is my good friend, and a highly respectable gentleman.

THE STRANGER

Good and respectable, sir, I take it, mean rich?

THE REV. DR FOLLIOTT

That is their meaning, sir.

The crudely satirical questioner is dished; the wind has been blandly removed from his sails; and I can recommend the Folliott method – I have used it myself.

Even towards the end of an Introduction to him, I am not going to pretend that these odd but delicious novels of his will please all readers. He is a rather eccentric minor novelist, occupying a little corner all his own. But I shall certainly make no apologies for a man who was admired by Shelley in his youth, by Thackeray and Macaulay in his middle-age, by George Meredith in his old age. And it is not true, as some critics have suggested, that he cannot be really enjoyed if you are not acquainted with the notions and the persons he satirized, though no doubt some knowledge of his times does heighten the comedy. (Hence the notes.) There are, of course, obvious absurdities in him that anybody can enjoy, but what must not be missed is the constant undercurrent of irony in him, the faint mockery in the very neatness and crispness of his dialogue, the grave mischief in the style itself, a style like an old dry wine. Readers whose sense of humour and literary palate are equally blunted will find little refreshment in Peacock. But if you bring to his table a keen sense of humour and a fine palate, you can dine with him happily for years.

J. B. PRIESTLEY

THE NOTES

Throughout the text the author's notes are placed at the foot of the page, and followed by [P]. The editor's notes will be found at the end of the text, beginning on p. 361.

PREFACE

containing *Headlong Hall*, *Nightmare Abbey*, *Maid Marian* and
Crotchet Castle

ALL THESE LITTLE publications appeared originally without
prefaces. I left them to speak for themselves; and I thought I
might very fitly preserve my own impersonality, having never
intruded on the personality of others, nor taken any liberties
but with public conduct and public opinions. But an old friend
assures me, that to publish a book without a preface is like
entering a drawing-room without making a bow. In deference
to this opinion, though I am not quite clear of its soundness,
I make my prefatory bow at this eleventh hour.

'Headlong Hall' was written in 1815; 'Nightmare Abbey'
in 1817; 'Maid Marian', with the exception of the last three
chapters, in 1818; 'Crotchet Castle' in 1830. I am desirous to
note the intervals, because, at each of those periods, things
were true, in great matters and in small, which are true no
longer. 'Headlong Hall' begins with the Holyhead mail, and
'Crotchet Castle' ends with a rotten borough. The Holyhead
mail no longer keeps the same hours, nor stops at the Capel
Cerig Inn, which the progress of improvement has thrown
out of the road; and the rotten boroughs of 1830 have ceased
to exist, though there are some very pretty pocket properties,
which are their worthy successors. But the classes of tastes,
feelings, and opinions, which were successively brought into
play in these little tales, remain substantially the same. Per-
fectibilians, deteriorationists, statu-quo-ites, phrenologists,
transcendentalists, political economists, theorists in all sciences,
projectors in all arts, morbid visionaries, romantic enthusiasts,
lovers of music, lovers of the picturesque, and lovers of good
dinners, march, and will march for ever, *pari passu* with the
march of mechanics, which some facetiously call the march of
intellect. The fastidious in old wine are a race that does not
decay. Literary violators of the confidences of private life still
gain a disreputable livelihood and an unenviable notoriety.
Match-makers from interest, and the disappointed in love and
in friendship, are varieties of which specimens are extant.

The great principle of the Right of Might is as flourishing now as in the days of Maid Marian: the array of false pretensions, moral, political, and literary, is as imposing as ever: the rulers of the world still feel things in their effects, and never foresee them in their causes; and political mountebanks continue, and will continue, to puff nostrums and practise legerdemain under the eyes of the multitude; following, like the 'learned friend' of Crotchet Castle, a course as tortuous as that of a river, but in a reverse process; beginning by being dark and deep, and ending by being transparent.

THE AUTHOR OF 'HEADLONG HALL'

March 4, 1837

HEADLONG
HALL

All philosophers, who find
Some favourite system to their mind
In every point to make it fit,
Will force all nature to submit.

Headlong Hall was first published in 1816

Contents of
Headlong Hall

THE MAIL

THE AMBIGUOUS LIGHT of a December morning, peeping through the windows of the Holyhead mail, dispelled the soft visions of the four insides, who had slept, or seemed to sleep, through the first seventy miles of the road, with as much comfort as may be supposed consistent with the jolting of the vehicle, and an occasional admonition to *remember the coachman*, thundered through the open door, accompanied by the gentle breath of Boreas, into the ears of the drowsy traveller.

A lively remark, that *the day was none of the finest*, having elicited a repartee of *quite the contrary*, the various knotty points of meteorology, which usually form the exordium of an English conversation, were successively discussed and exhausted; and, the ice being thus broken, the colloquy rambled to other topics, in the course of which it appeared, to the surprise of everyone, that all four, though perfect strangers to each other, were actually bound to the same point, namely, Headlong Hall, the seat of the ancient and honourable family of the Headlongs, of the vale of Llanberris, in Caernarvonshire. This name may appear at first sight not to be truly Cambrian, like those of the Rices, and Prices, and Morgans, and Owens, and Williamses, and Evanses, and Parrys, and Joneses; but, nevertheless, the Headlongs claim to be not less genuine derivatives from the antique branch of Cadwallader than any of the last-named multiramified families. They claim, indeed, by one account, superior antiquity to all of them, and even to Cadwallader himself; a tradition having been handed down in Headlong Hall for some few thousand years, that the founder of the family was preserved in the deluge on the summit of Snowdon, and took the name of Rhaiader, which signifies a *waterfall*, in consequence of his having accompanied the water in its descent or diminution, till he found himself comfortably seated on the rocks of Llanberris. But, in later days, when commercial bagsmen began to scour the country, the ambiguity of the sound induced his descendants to drop the suspicious denomination of *Riders*, and translate the word into English; when, not being well pleased with the sound of the *thing*, they

substituted that of the *quality*, and accordingly adopted the
name *Headlong*, the appropriate epithet of waterfall.

> I cannot tell how the truth may be:
> I say the tale as 'twas said to me.[1]

The present representative of this ancient and dignified
house, Harry Headlong, Esquire, was, like all other Welsh
squires, fond of shooting, hunting, racing, drinking, and other
such innocent amusements, μειζονος δ' αλλον τινος,[2] as
Menander expresses it. But, unlike other Welsh squires, he had
actually suffered certain phenomena, called books, to find their
way into his house; and, by dint of lounging over them after
dinner, on those occasions when he was compelled to take his
bottle alone, he became seized with a violent passion to be
thought a philosopher and a man of taste; and accordingly set
off on an expedition to Oxford, to inquire for other varieties of
the same genera, namely, men of taste and philosophers; but,
being assured by a learned professor that there were no such
things in the University, he proceeded to London, where, after
beating up in several booksellers' shops, theatres, exhibition-
rooms, and other resorts of literature and taste, he formed as
extensive an acquaintance with philosophers and dilettanti as
his utmost ambition could desire; and it now became his chief
wish to have them all together in Headlong Hall, arguing,
over his old Port and Burgundy, the various knotty points
which had puzzled his pericranium. He had, therefore, sent
them invitations in due form to pass their Christmas at Headlong Hall; which invitations the extensive fame of his kitchen
fire had induced the greater part of them to accept; and four of
the chosen guests had, from different parts of the metropolis,
ensconced themselves in the four corners of the Holyhead
mail.

These four persons were, Mr Foster,* the perfectibilian;
Mr Escot,† the deteriorationist; Mr Jenkison,‡ the statu-

---

* Foster, quasi *Φωστηρ* – from *φαος* and *τηρεω*, lucem servo, conservo,
observo, custodio – one who watches over and guards the light; a sense
in which the word is often used amongst us, when we speak of *fostering* a
flame. [P.]

† Escot, quasi *ες σκοτον, in tenebras*, scilicet, intuens; one who is always
looking into the dark side of the question. [P.]

‡ Jenkison: This name may be derived from *αιεν εξ ισων, semper ex
aequalibus* – scilicet, mensuris, omnia metiens: one who from equal
measures divides and distributes all things: one who from equal measures

quo-ite;[3] and the Reverend Doctor Gaster,* who, though of course neither a philosopher nor a man of taste, had so won on the Squire's fancy, by a learned dissertation on the art of stuffing a turkey, that he concluded no Christmas party would be complete without him.

The conversation among these illuminati soon became animated; and Mr Foster, who, we must observe, was a thin gentleman, about thirty years of age, with an aquiline nose, black eyes, white teeth, and black hair – took occasion to panegyrize the vehicle in which they were then travelling, and observed what remarkable improvements had been made in the means of facilitating intercourse between distant parts of the kingdom: he held forth with great energy on the subject of roads and railways, canals and tunnels, manufactures and machinery: 'In short,' said he, 'everything we look on attests the progress of mankind in all the arts of life, and demonstrates their gradual advancement towards a state of unlimited perfection.'

Mr Escot, who was somewhat younger than Mr Foster, but rather more pale and saturnine in his aspect, here took up the thread of the discourse, observing, that the proposition just advanced seemed to him perfectly contrary to the true state of the case: 'for,' said he, 'these improvements, as you call them, appear to me only so many links in the great chain of corruption, which will soon fetter the whole human race in irreparable slavery and incurable wretchedness: your improvements proceed in a simple ratio, while the factitious wants and unnatural appetites they engender proceed in a compound one; and thus one generation acquires fifty wants, and fifty means of supplying them are invented, which each in its turn engenders two new ones; so that the next generation has a hundred, the next two hundred, the next four hundred, till every human being becomes such a helpless compound of perverted inclinations, that he is altogether at the mercy of external

---

can always produce arguments on both sides of a question, with so much nicety and exactness, as to keep the said question eternally pending, and the balance of the controversy perpetually *in statu quo*. By an aphaeresis of the α, an elision of the second ε, and an easy and natural mutation of ξ into κ, the derivation of this name proceeds according to the strictest principles of etymology: αιεν εξ ισων – Ιεν εξ ισων – Ιεν εκ ισων – Ιεν ʼκ ισων – Ιενκισων – Ienkison – Jenkison. [P.]

* Gaster: scilicet Γαστηρ – Venter – et praeterea nihil.[P.]

circumstances, loses all independence and singleness of character, and degenerates so rapidly from the primitive dignity of his sylvan origin, that it is scarcely possible to indulge in any other expectation, than that the whole species must at length be exterminated by its own infinite imbecility and vileness.'

'Your opinions,' said Mr Jenkison, a round-faced little gentleman of about forty-five, 'seem to differ *toto coelo*. I have often debated the matter in my own mind, *pro* and *con*, and have at length arrived at this conclusion – that there is not in the human race a tendency either to moral perfectibility or deterioration; but that the quantities of each are so exactly balanced by their reciprocal results, that the species, with respect to the sum of good and evil, knowledge and ignorance, happiness and misery, remains exactly and perpetually *in statu quo.*'

'Surely,' said Mr Foster, 'you cannot maintain such a proposition in the face of evidence so luminous. Look at the progress of all the arts and sciences – see chemistry, botany, astronomy —'

'Surely,' said Mr Escot, 'experience deposes against you. Look at the rapid growth of corruption, luxury, selfishness —'

'Really, gentlemen,' said the Reverend Doctor Gaster, after clearing the husk in his throat with two or three hems, 'this is a very sceptical, and, I must say, atheistical conversation, and I should have thought, out of respect to my cloth —'

Here the coach stopped, and the coachman, opening the door, vociferated – 'Breakfast, gentlemen'; a sound which so gladdened the ears of the divine, that the alacrity with which he sprang from the vehicle superinduced a distortion of his ankle, and he was obliged to limp into the inn between Mr Escot and Mr Jenkison; the former observing, that he ought to look for nothing but evil, and, therefore, should not be surprised at this little accident; the latter remarking, that the comfort of a good breakfast, and the pain of a sprained ankle, pretty exactly balanced each other.

CHAPTER II

THE SQUIRE – THE BREAKFAST

SQUIRE HEADLONG, in the meanwhile, was quadripartite in his locality; that is to say, he was superintending the operations in four scenes of action – namely, the cellar, the library, the picture-gallery, and the dining-room – preparing for the reception of his philosophical and dilettanti visitors. His myrmidon on this occasion was a little red-nosed butler, whom nature seemed to have cast in the genuine mould of an antique Silenus,[1] and who waddled about the house after his master, wiping his forehead and panting for breath, while the latter bounced from room to room like a cracker, and was indefatigable in his requisitions for the proximity of his vinous Achates,[2] whose advice and co-operation he deemed no less necessary in the library than in the cellar. Multitudes of packages had arrived, by land and water, from London, and Liverpool, and Chester, and Manchester, and Birmingham, and various parts of the mountains: books, wine, cheese, globes, mathematical instruments, turkeys, telescopes, hams, tongues, microscopes, quadrants, sextants, fiddles, flutes, tea, sugar, electrical machines, figs, spices, air-pumps, soda-water, chemical apparatus, eggs, French-horns, drawing books, palettes, oils and colours, bottled ale and porter, scenery for a private theatre, pickles and fish-sauce, patent lamps and chandeliers, barrels of oysters, sofas, chairs, tables, carpets, beds, looking-glasses, pictures, fruits and confections, nuts, oranges, lemons, packages of salt salmon, and jars of Portugal grapes. These, arriving with infinite rapidity, and in inexhaustible succession, had been deposited at random, as the convenience of the moment dictated – sofas in the cellar, chandeliers in the kitchen, hampers of ale in the drawing-room, and fiddles and fish-sauce in the library. The servants, unpacking all these in furious haste, and flying with them from place to place, according to the tumultuous directions of Squire Headlong and the little fat butler who fumed at his heels, chafed, and crossed, and clashed, and tumbled over one another up stairs and down. All was bustle, uproar, and confusion; yet nothing seemed to advance: while the rate and impetuosity of the Squire continued fermenting to the highest degree of exasperation, which he signified, from time to time, by converting some newly unpacked article, such as a book, a bottle, a ham, or a fiddle, into a missile against the head of some unfortunate servant who did not seem to move in a ratio of velocity corresponding to the intensity of his master's desires.

In this state of eager preparation we shall leave the happy inhabitants of Headlong Hall, and return to the three philosophers and the unfortunate divine, whom we left limping with a sprained ankle into the breakfast-room of the inn; where his two supporters deposited him safely in a large arm-chair, with his wounded leg comfortably stretched out on another. The morning being extremely cold, he contrived to be seated as near the fire as was consistent with his other object of having a perfect command of the table and its apparatus; which consisted not only of the ordinary comforts of tea and toast, but of a delicious supply of new-laid eggs, and a magnificent round of beef; against which Mr Escot immediately pointed all the artillery of his eloquence, declaring the use of animal food, conjointly with that of fire, to be one of the principal causes of the present degeneracy of mankind. 'The natural and original man,' said he, 'lived in the woods: the roots and fruits of the earth supplied his simple nutriment: he had few desires, and no diseases. But, when he began to sacrifice victims on the altar of superstition, to pursue the goat and the deer, and, by the pernicious invention of fire, to pervert their flesh into food, luxury, disease, and premature death, were let loose upon the world. Such is clearly the correct interpretation of the fable of Prometheus,[3] which is a symbolical portraiture of that disastrous epoch, when man first applied fire to culinary purposes, and thereby surrendered his liver to the vulture of disease. From that period the stature of mankind has been in a state of gradual diminution, and I have not the least doubt that it will continue to grow *small by degrees, and lamentably less*, till the whole race will vanish imperceptibly from the face of the earth.'

'I cannot agree,' said Mr Foster, 'in the consequences being so very disastrous. I admit, that in some respects the use of animal food retards, though it cannot materially inhibit, the perfectibility of the species. But the use of fire was indispensably necessary, as Aeschylus and Virgil expressly assert, to give being to the various arts of life, which, in their rapid

and interminable progress, will finally conduct every individual of the race to the philosophic pinnacle of pure and
perfect felicity.'

'In the controversy concerning animal and vegetable food,'
said Mr Jenkison, 'there is much to be said on both sides;
and, the question being in equipoise, I content myself with a
mixed diet, and make a point of eating whatever is placed
before me, provided it be good in its kind.'

In this opinion his two brother philosophers practically
coincided, though they both ran down the theory as highly
detrimental to the best interests of man.

'I am really astonished,' said the Reverend Doctor Gaster,
gracefully picking off the supernal fragments of an egg he had
just cracked, and clearing away a space at the top for the reception of a small piece of butter – 'I am really astonished,
gentlemen, at the very heterodox opinions I have heard you
deliver: since nothing can be more obvious than that all animals were created solely and exclusively for the use of man.'

'Even the tiger that devours him?' said Mr Escot.

'Certainly,' said Doctor Gaster.

'How do you prove it?' said Mr Escot.

'It requires no proof,' said Doctor Gaster: 'it is a point of
doctrine. It is written, therefore it is so.'

'Nothing can be more logical,' said Mr Jenkison. 'It has
been said,' continued he, 'that the ox was expressly made to be
eaten by man: it may be said, by a parity of reasoning, that
man was expressly made to be eaten by the tiger: but as wild
oxen exist where there are no men, and men where there are no
tigers, it would seem that in these instances they do not properly answer the ends of their creation.'

'It is a mystery,' said Doctor Gaster.

'Not to launch into the question of final causes,' said Mr
Escot, helping himself at the same time to a slice of beef, 'concerning which I will candidly acknowledge I am as profoundly ignorant as the most dogmatical theologian possibly
can be, I just wish to observe, that the pure and peaceful
manners which Homer ascribes to the Lotophagi, and which
at this day characterize many nations (the Hindoos, for example, who subsist exclusively on the fruits of the earth),
depose very strongly in favour of a vegetable regimen.'

'It may be said, on the contrary,' said Mr Foster, 'that animal food acts on the mind as manure does on flowers, forcing

them into a degree of expansion they would not otherwise have attained. If we can imagine a philosophical auricula falling into a train of theoretical meditation on its original and natural nutriment, till it should work itself up into a profound abomination of bullock's blood, sugar-baker's scum, and other *unnatural* ingredients of that rich composition of soil which had brought it to perfection,* and insist on being planted in common earth, it would have all the advantage of natural theory on its side that the most strenuous advocate of the vegetable system could desire; but it would soon discover the practical error of its retrograde experiment by its lamentable inferiority in strength and beauty to all the auriculas around it. I am afraid, in some instances at least, this analogy holds true with respect to mind. No one will make a comparison, in point of mental power, between the Hindoos and the ancient Greeks.'

'The anatomy of the human stomach,' said Mr Escot, 'and the formation of the teeth, clearly place man in the class of frugivorous animals.'

'Many anatomists,' said Mr Foster, 'are of a different opinion, and agree in discerning the characteristics of the carnivorous classes.'

'I am no anatomist,' said Mr Jenkison, 'and cannot decide where doctors disagree; in the meantime, I conclude that man is omnivorous, and on that conclusion I act.'

'Your conclusion is truly orthodox,' said the Reverend Doctor Gaster: 'indeed, the loaves and fishes are typical of a mixed diet; and the practice of the Church in all ages shows —'

'That it never loses sight of the loaves and fishes,' said Mr Escot.

'It never loses sight of any point of sound doctrine,' said the reverend doctor.

The coachman now informed them their time was elapsed; nor could all the pathetic remonstrances of the reverend divine, who declared he had not half breakfasted, succeed in gaining one minute from the inexorable Jehu.[4]

'You will allow,' said Mr Foster, as soon as they were again in motion, 'that the wild man of the woods could not transport himself over two hundred miles of forest, with as much facility as one of these vehicles transports you and me through the heart of this cultivated country.'

* See *Emmerton on the Auricula.* [P.]

'I am certain,' said Mr Escot, 'that a wild man can travel an immense distance without fatigue; but what is the advantage of locomotion? The wild man is happy in one spot, and there he remains: the civilized man is wretched in every place he happens to be in, and then congratulates himself on being accommodated with a machine, that will whirl him to another, where he will be just as miserable as ever.'

We shall now leave the mail-coach to find its way to Capel Cerig, the nearest point of the Holyhead road to the dwelling of Squire Headlong.

CHAPTER III

THE ARRIVALS

IN THE MIDST of that scene of confusion thrice confounded, in which we left the inhabitants of Headlong Hall, arrived the lovely Caprioletta Headlong, the Squire's sister (whom he had sent for, from the residence of her maiden aunt at Caernarvon, to do the honours of his house), beaming like light on chaos, to arrange disorder and harmonize discord. The tempestuous spirit of her brother became instantaneously as smooth as the surface of the lake of Llanberris; and the little fat butler 'plessed Cot, and St Tafit, and the peautiful tamsel', for being permitted to move about the house in his natural pace. In less than twenty-four hours after her arrival, everything was disposed in its proper station, and the Squire began to be all impatience for the appearance of his promised guests.

The first visitor with whom he had the felicity of shaking hands was Marmaduke Milestone, Esquire, who arrived with a portfolio under his arm. Mr Milestone* was a picturesque

* Mr Knight, in a note to the Landscape, having taken the liberty of laughing at a notable device of a celebrated *improver*, for giving greatness of character to a place, and showing an undivided extent of property, by placing the family arms on the neighbouring *milestones*, the improver retorted on him with a charge of misquotation, misrepresentation, and malice prepense. Mr Knight, in the preface to the second edition of his poem, quotes the improver's words: 'The market-house, or other public edifice, or even a *mere stone with distances*, may bear the arms of the family': and adds: 'By a *mere stone with distances*, the author of the Landscape certainly thought he meant a *milestone*; but, if he did not, any other interpretation which he may think more advantageous to himself shall readily be adopted, as it will equally answer the purpose of the quotation.' The

landscape gardener of the first celebrity,[1] who was not without hopes of persuading Squire Headlong to put his romantic pleasure-grounds under a process of improvement, promising himself a signal triumph for his incomparable art in the difficult, and, therefore, glorious achievement of polishing and trimming the rocks of Llanberris.

Next arrived a post-chaise from the inn at Capel Cerig, containing the Reverend Doctor Gaster. It appeared, that, when the mail-coach deposited its valuable cargo, early on the second morning, at the inn at Capel Cerig, there was only one post-chaise to be had; it was therefore determined that the reverend doctor and the luggage should proceed in the chaise and that the three philosophers should walk. When the reverend gentleman first seated himself in the chaise, the windows were down all round; but he allowed it to drive off under the idea that he could easily pull them up. This task, however, he had considerable difficulty in accomplishing, and when he had succeeded, it availed him little; for the frames and glasses had long since discontinued their ancient familiarity. He had, however, no alternative but to proceed, and to comfort himself, as he went, with some choice quotations from the book of Job. The road led along the edges of tremendous chasms, with torrents dashing in the bottom; so that, if his teeth had not chattered with cold, they would have done so with fear. The Squire shook him heartily by the hand, and congratulated him on his safe arrival at Headlong Hall. The Doctor returned the squeeze, and assured him that the congratulation was by no means misapplied.

Next came the three philosophers, highly delighted with their walk, and full of rapturous exclamations on the sublime beauties of the scenery.

The Doctor shrugged up his shoulders, and confessed he preferred the scenery of Putney and Kew, where a man could go comfortably to sleep in his chaise, without being in momentary terror of being hurled headlong down a precipice.

Mr Milestone observed, that there were great capabilities in the scenery, but it wanted shaving and polishing. If he could

---

improver, however, did not condescend to explain what he really meant by a *mere stone with distances*, though he strenuously maintained that he did *not* mean a *milestone*. His idea, therefore, stands on record, invested with all the sublimity that obscurity can confer. [P.]

but have it under his care for a single twelvemonth, he assured them no one would be able to know it again.

Mr Jenkison thought the scenery was just what it ought to be, and required no alteration.

Mr Foster thought it could be improved, but doubted if that effect would be produced by the system of Mr Milestone.

Mr Escot did not think that any human being could improve it, but had no doubt of its having changed very considerably for the worse, since the days when the now barren rocks were covered with the immense forest of Snowdon, which must have contained a very fine race of wild men, not less than ten feet high.

The next arrival was that of Mr Cranium, and his lovely daughter Miss Cephalis Cranium, who flew to the arms of her dear friend Caprioletta, with all that warmth of friendship which young ladies usually assume towards each other in the presence of young gentlemen.*

Miss Cephalis blushed like a carnation at the sight of Mr Escot, and Mr Escot glowed like a corn-poppy at the sight of Miss Cephalis. It was at least obvious to all observers, that he could imagine the possibility of one change for the better, even in this terrestrial theatre of universal deterioration.

Mr Cranium's eyes wandered from Mr Escot to his daughter, and from his daughter to Mr Escot; and his complexion, in the course of the scrutiny, underwent several variations, from the dark red of the piony to the deep blue of the convolvulus.

Mr Escot had formerly been the received lover of Miss Cephalis, till he incurred the indignation of her father by laughing at a very profound craniological dissertation which the old gentleman delivered; nor had Mr Escot yet discovered the means of mollifying his wrath.

Mr Cranium carried in his own hands a bag, the contents of which were too precious to be entrusted to anyone but himself; and earnestly entreated to be shown to the chamber appropriated for his reception, that he might deposit his treasure in safety. The little butler was accordingly summoned to conduct him to his *cubiculum.*

* 'Il est constant qu'elles se baisent de meilleur cœur, et se caressent avec plus de grâce devant les hommes, fieres d'aiguiser impunément leur convoitise par l'image des faveurs qu'elles savent leur faire envier.' – Rousseau, *Emile*, liv. 5. [P.]

Next arrived a post-chaise, carrying four insides, whose extreme thinness enabled them to travel thus economically without experiencing the slightest inconvenience. These four personages were, two very profound critics, Mr Gall and Mr Treacle, who followed the trade of reviewers, but occasionally indulged themselves in the composition of bad poetry; and two very multitudinous versifiers, Mr Nightshade and Mr Mac Laurel,[2] who followed the trade of poetry, but occasionally indulged themselves in the composition of bad criticism. Mr Nightshade and Mr Mac Laurel were the two senior lieutenants of a very formidable corps of critics, of whom Timothy Treacle, Esquire, was captain, and Geoffrey Gall, Esquire, generalissimo.

The last arrivals were Mr Cornelius Chromatic, the most profound and scientific of all amateurs of the fiddle, with his two blooming daughters, Miss Tenorina and Miss Graziosa; Sir Patrick O'Prism,[3] a dilettante painter of high renown, and his maiden aunt, Miss Philomela Poppyseed,[4] an indefatigable compounder of novels, written for the express purpose of supporting every species of superstition and prejudice; and Mr Panscope,[5] the chemical, botanical, geological, astronomical, mathematical, metaphysical, meteorological, anatomical, physiological, galvanistical, musical, pictorial, bibliographical, critical philosopher, who had run through the whole circle of the sciences, and understood them all equally well.

Mr Milestone was impatient to take a walk round the grounds, that he might examine how far the system of clumping and levelling could be carried advantageously into effect. The ladies retired to enjoy each other's society in the first happy moments of meeting: the Reverend Doctor Gaster sat by the library fire, in profound meditation over a volume of the *Almanach des Gourmands*: Mr Panscope sat in the opposite corner with a volume of Rees's *Cyclopaedia*: Mr Cranium was busy up stairs: Mr Chromatic retreated to the music-room, where he fiddled through a book of solos before the ringing of the first dinner-bell. The remainder of the party supported Mr Milestone's proposition; and, accordingly, Squire Headlong and Mr Milestone leading the van, they commenced their perambulation.

CHAPTER IV

THE GROUNDS

'I PERCEIVE,' said Mr Milestone, after they had walked a few paces, 'these grounds have never been touched by the finger of taste.'

'The place is quite a wilderness,' said Squire Headlong: 'for during the latter part of my father's life, while I was *finishing* my *education*, he troubled himself about nothing but the cellar, and suffered everything else to go to rack and ruin. A mere wilderness, as you see, even now in December; but in summer a complete nursery of briers, a forest of thistles, a plantation of nettles, without any live stock but goats, that have eaten up all the bark of the trees. Here you see is the pedestal of a statue, with only half a leg and four toes remaining: there were many here once. When I was a boy, I used to sit every day on the shoulders of Hercules: what became of *him* I have never been able to ascertain. Neptune has been lying these seven years in the dust-hole; Atlas had his head knocked off to fit him for propping a shed; and only the day before yesterday we fished Bacchus out of the horse-pond.'

'My dear sir,' said Mr Milestone, 'accord me your permission to wave the wand of enchantment over your grounds. The rocks shall be blown up, the trees shall be cut down, the wilderness and all its goats shall vanish like mist. Pagodas and Chinese bridges, gravel walks and shrubberies, bowling-greens, canals, and clumps of larch, shall rise upon its ruins. One age, sir, has brought to light the treasures of ancient learning; a second has penetrated into the depths of metaphysics; a third has brought to perfection the science of astronomy; but it was reserved for the exclusive genius of the present times, to invent the noble art of picturesque gardening, which has given, as it were, a new tint to the complexion of nature, and a new outline to the physiognomy of the universe!'

'Give me leave,' said Sir Patrick O'Prism, 'to take an exception to that same. Your system of levelling, and trimming, and clipping, and docking, and clumping, and polishing, and cropping, and shaving, destroys all the beautiful intricacies of natural luxuriance, and all the graduated harmonies of light and shade, melting into one another, as you see them on that rock over yonder. I never saw one of your improved places, as you call them, and which are nothing but big bowling-greens, like sheets of green paper, with a parcel of round clumps scattered over them, like so many spots of ink, flicked at random out of a pen,* and a solitary animal here and there looking as if it were lost, that I did not think it was for all the world like Hounslow Heath, thinly sprinkled over with bushes and highwaymen.'

'Sir,' said Mr Milestone, 'you will have the goodness to make a distinction between the picturesque and the beautiful.'

'Will I?' said Sir Patrick, 'och! but I won't. For what is beautiful? That which pleases the eye. And what pleases the eye? Tints variously broken and blended. Now, tints variously broken and blended constitute the picturesque.'

'Allow me,' said Mr Gall. 'I distinguish the picturesque and the beautiful, and I add to them, in the laying out of grounds, a third and distinct character, which I call *unexpectedness*.'

'Pray, sir,' said Mr Milestone, 'by what name do you distinguish this character, when a person walks round the grounds for the second time?'†

Mr Gall bit his lips, and inwardly vowed to revenge himself on Milestone, by cutting up his next publication.

A long controversy now ensued concerning the picturesque and the beautiful, highly edifying to Squire Headlong.

The three philosophers stopped, as they wound round a projecting point of rock, to contemplate a little boat which was gliding over the tranquil surface of the lake below.

'The blessings of civilization,' said Mr Foster, 'extend themselves to the meanest individuals of the community. That boatman, singing as he sails along, is, I have no doubt, a very happy, and, comparatively to the men of his class some centuries back, a very enlightened and intelligent man.'

'As a partisan of the system of the moral perfectibility of the human race,' said Mr Escot – who was always for considering things on a large scale, and whose thoughts immediately wandered from the lake to the ocean, from the little boat to a ship of the line – 'you will probably be able to point out to me the degree of improvement that you suppose to have taken place in the character of a sailor, from the days when Jason

* See *Price on the Picturesque*. [P.]
† See *Knight on Taste*, and the *Edinburgh Review*, No. XIV. [P.]

sailed through the Cyanean Symplegades,[1] or Noah moored his ark on the summit of Ararat.'

'If you talk to me,' said Mr Foster, 'of mythological personages, of course I cannot meet you on fair grounds.'

'We will begin, if you please, then,' said Mr Escot, 'no further back than the battle of Salamis;[2] and I will ask you if you think the mariners of England are, in any one respect, morally or intellectually, superior to those who then preserved the liberties of Greece, under the direction of Themistocles?'

'I will venture to assert,' said Mr Foster, 'that, considered merely as sailors, which is the only fair mode of judging them, they are as far superior to the Athenians, as the structure of our ships is superior to that of theirs. Would not one English seventy-four, think you, have been sufficient to have sunk, burned, and put to flight, all the Persian and Grecian vessels in that memorable bay? Contemplate the progress of naval architecture, and the slow, but immense, succession of concatenated intelligence, by which it has gradually attained its present stage of perfectibility. In this, as in all other branches of art and science, every generation possesses all the knowledge of the preceding, and adds to it its own discoveries in a progression to which there seems no limit. The skill requisite to direct these immense machines is proportionate to their magnitude and complicated mechanism; and, therefore, the English sailor, considered merely as a sailor, is vastly superior to the ancient Greek.'

'You make a distinction, of course,' said Mr Escot, 'between scientific and moral perfectibility?'

'I conceive,' said Mr Foster, 'that men are virtuous in proportion as they are enlightened; and that, as every generation increases in knowledge, it also increases in virtue.'

'I wish it were so,' said Mr Escot; 'but to me the very reverse appears to be the fact. The progress of knowledge is not general: it is confined to a chosen few of every age. How far these are better than their neighbours, we may examine by and by. The mass of mankind is composed of beasts of burden, mere clods, and tools of their superiors. By enlarging and complicating your machines, you degrade, not exalt, the human animals you employ to direct them. When the boatswain of a seventy-four pipes all hands to the main tack, and flourishes his rope's end over the shoulders of the poor fellows who are tugging at the ropes, do you perceive so dignified, so gratifying a picture, as Ulysses exhorting his dear friends, his ΕΡΙΗΡΕΣ ΄ΕΤΑΙΡΟΙ[3], to ply their oars with energy? You will say, Ulysses was a fabulous character. But the economy of his vessel is drawn from nature. Every man on board has a character and a will of his own. He talks to them, argues with them, convinces them; and they obey him, because they love him, and know the reason of his orders. Now, as I have said before, all singleness of character is lost. We divide men into herds like cattle: an individual man, if you strip him of all that is extraneous to himself, is the most wretched and contemptible creature on the face of the earth. The sciences advance. True. A few years of study puts a modern mathematician in possession of more than Newton knew, and leaves him at leisure to add new discoveries of his own. Agreed. But does this make him a Newton? Does it put him in possession of that range of intellect, that grasp of mind, from which the discoveries of Newton sprang? It is mental power that I look for: if you can demonstrate the increase of that, I will give up the field. Energy – independence – individuality –disinterested virtue – active benevolence – self-oblivion – universal philanthropy – these are the qualities I desire to find, and of which I contend that every succeeding age produces fewer examples. I repeat it; there is scarcely such a thing to be found as a single individual man: a few classes compose the whole frame of society, and when you know one of a class you know the whole of it. Give me the wild man of the woods; the original, unthinking, unscientific, unlogical savage: in him there is at least some good; but, in a civilized, sophisticated, cold-blooded, mechanical, calculating slave of Mammon and the world, there is none – absolutely none. Sir, if I fall into a river, an unsophisticated man will jump in and bring me out; but a philosopher will look on with the utmost calmness, and consider me in the light of a projectile, and, making a calculation of the degree of force with which I have impinged the surface, the resistance of the fluid, the velocity of the current, and the depth of the water in that particular place, he will ascertain with the greatest nicety in what part of the mud at the bottom I may probably be found, at any given distance of time from the moment of my first immersion.'

Mr Foster was preparing to reply, when the first dinner-bell rang, and he immediately commenced a precipitate return towards the house; followed by his two companions, who both admitted that he was now leading the way to at least a temporary period of physical amelioration: 'but, alas!' added Mr Escot, after a moment's reflection, 'Epulae NOCUERE repostae!'*

CHAPTER V

THE DINNER

THE SUN WAS now terminating his diurnal course, and the lights were glittering on the festal board. When the ladies had retired, and the Burgundy had taken two or three tours of the table, the following conversation took place:

SQUIRE HEADLONG. Push about the bottle: Mr Escot, it stands with you. No heeltaps.[1] As to skylight, liberty-hall.[2]

MR MAC LAUREL. Really, Squire Headlong, this is the vara nactar itsel. Ye hae saretainly descovered the tarrestrial paradise, but it flows wi' a better leecor than milk an' honey.

THE REVEREND DOCTOR GASTER. Hem! Mr Mac Laurel! there is a degree of profaneness in that observation, which I should not have looked for in so staunch a supporter of church and state. Milk and honey was the pure food of the antediluvian patriarchs, who knew not the use of the grape, happily for them – (*Tossing off a bumper of Burgundy.*)

MR ESCOT. Happily, indeed! The first inhabitants of the world knew not the use either of wine or animal food; it is, therefore, by no means incredible that they lived to the age of several centuries, free from war, and commerce, and arbitrary government, and every other species of desolating wickedness. But man was then a very different animal to what he now is: he had not the faculty of speech; he was not encumbered with clothes; he lived in the open air; his first step out of which, as Hamlet truly observes, is *into his grave.*† His first dwellings, of course, were the hollows of trees and rocks. In process of time he began to build: thence grew villages; thence grew cities. Luxury, oppression, poverty, misery, and disease kept pace with the progress of his pretended improvements, till, from a free, strong, healthy, peaceful animal, he has become a weak, distempered, cruel, carnivorous slave.

* Protracted banquets have been copious sources of evil [P.]
† See Lord Monboddo's *Ancient Metaphysics.* [P.]

THE REVEREND DOCTOR GASTER. Your doctrine is orthodox, in so far as you assert that the original man was not encumbered with clothes, and that he lived in the open air; but, as to the faculty of speech, that, it is certain, he had, for the authority of Moses —

MR ESCOT. Of course, sir, I do not presume to dissent from the very exalted authority of that most enlightened astronomer and profound cosmogonist, who had, moreover, the advantage of being inspired; but when I indulge myself with a ramble in the fields of speculation, and attempt to deduce what is probable and rational from the sources of analysis, experience, and comparison, I confess I am too often apt to lose sight of the doctrines of that great fountain of theological and geological philosophy.

SQUIRE HEADLONG. Push about the bottle.

MR FOSTER. Do you suppose the mere animal life of a wild man, living on acorns, and sleeping on the ground, comparable in felicity to that of a Newton, ranging through unlimited space, and penetrating into the arcana of universal motion – to that of a Locke, unravelling the labyrinth of mind – to that of a Lavoisier, detecting the minutest combinations of matter, and reducing all nature to its elements – to that of a Shakespeare, piercing and developing the springs of passion – or of a Milton, identifying himself, as it were, with the beings of an invisible world?

MR ESCOT. You suppose extreme cases: but, on the score of happiness, what comparison can you make between the tranquil being of the wild man of the woods and the wretched and turbulent existence of Milton, the victim of persecution, poverty, blindness, and neglect? The records of literature demonstrate that Happiness and Intelligence are seldom sisters. Even if it were otherwise, it would prove nothing. The many are always sacrificed to the few. Where one man advances, hundreds retrograde; and the balance is always in favour of universal deterioration.

MR FOSTER. Virtue is independent of external circumstances. The exalted understanding looks into the truth of things, and, in its own peaceful contemplations, rises superior to the world. No philosopher would resign his mental acquisitions for the purchase of any terrestrial good.

MR ESCOT. In other words, no man whatever would resign his identity, which is nothing more than the consciousness of his perceptions, as the price of any acquisition. But every man, without exception, would willingly effect a very material change in his relative situation to other individuals. Unluckily for the rest of your argument, the understanding of literary people is for the most part *exalted*, as you express it, not so much by the love of truth and virtue, as by arrogance and self-sufficiency; and there is, perhaps, less disinterestedness, less liberality, less general benevolence, and more envy, hatred, and uncharitableness among them, than among any other description of men.

(*The eye of Mr Escot, as he pronounced these words, rested very innocently and unintentionally on Mr Gall.*)

MR GALL. You allude, sir, I presume, to my review.

MR ESCOT. Pardon me, sir. You will be convinced it is impossible I can allude to your review, when I assure you that I have never read a single page of it.

MR GALL, MR TREACLE, MR NIGHTSHADE, AND MR MAC LAUREL. Never read our review ! ! ! !

MR ESCOT. Never. I look on periodical criticism in general to be a species of shop, where panegyric and defamation are sold, wholesale, retail, and for exportation. I am not inclined to be a purchaser of these commodities, or to encourage a trade which I consider pregnant with mischief.

MR MAC LAUREL. I can readily conceive, sir, ye wou'd na wullinly encoorage ony dealer in panegeeric: but, frae the manner in which ye speak o' the first creetics an' scholars o' the age, I shou'd think ye wou'd hae a leetle mair predilaction for deefamation.

MR ESCOT. I have no predilection, sir, for defamation. I make a point of speaking the truth on all occasions; and it seldom happens that the truth can be spoken without some stricken deer pronouncing it a libel.

MR NIGHTSHADE. You are perhaps, sir, an enemy to literature in general?

MR ESCOT. If I were, sir, I should be a better friend to periodical critics.

SQUIRE HEADLONG. Buz!

MR TREACLE. May I simply take the liberty to inquire into the basis of your objection?

MR ESCOT. I conceive that periodical criticism disseminates superficial knowledge, and its perpetual adjunct, vanity; that it checks in the youthful mind the habit of thinking for itself;

that it delivers partial opinions, and thereby misleads the judgement; that it is never conducted with a view to the general interests of literature, but to serve the interested ends of individuals, and the miserable purposes of party.

MR MAC LAUREL. Ye ken, sir, a mon mun leeve.

MR ESCOT. While he can live honourably, naturally, justly, certainly: no longer.

MR MAC LAUREL. Every mon, sir, leeves according to his ain notions of honour an' justice: there is a wee defference amang the learned wi' respact to the defineetion o' the terms.

MR ESCOT. I believe it is generally admitted, that one of the ingredients of justice is disinterestedness.

MR MAC LAUREL. It is na admetted, sir, amang the phee-losophers of Edinbroo', that there is ony sic thing as desen-terestedness in the warld, or that a mon can care for onything sae much as his ain sel: for ye mun observe, sir, every mon has his ain parteecular feelings of what is gude, an' beautifu', an' consentaneous to his ain indiveedual nature, an' desires to see everything aboot him in that parteecular state which is maist conformable to his ain notions o' the moral an' poleetical fetness o' things. Twa men, sir, shall purchase a piece o' grund atween 'em, and ae mon shall cover his half wi' a park —

MR MILESTONE. Beautifully laid out in lawns and clumps, with a belt of trees at the circumference, and an artificial lake in the centre.

MR MAC LAUREL. Exactly, sir: an' shall keep it a' for his ain sel: an' the other mon shall divide his half into leetle farms of two or three acres —

MR ESCOT. Like those of the Roman republic, and build a cottage on each of them, and cover his land with a simple, in-nocent, and smiling population, who shall owe, not only their happiness, but their existence, to his benevolence.

MR MAC LAUREL. Exactly, sir: an' ye will ca' the first mon selfish, an' the second desenterested; but the pheelosophical truth is semply this, that the ane is pleased wi' looking at trees, an' the other wi' seeing people happy an' comfortable. It is aunly a matter of indiveedual feeling. A paisant saves a mon's life for the same reason that a hero or a footpad cuts his thrapple: an' a pheelosopher delevers a mon frae a preson, for the same reason that a tailor or a prime menester puts him into it: because it is conformable to his ain parteecular feelings o' the moral an' poleetical fetness o' things.

SQUIRE HEADLONG. Wake the Reverend Doctor. Doctor, the bottle stands with you.

THE REVEREND DOCTOR GASTER. It is an error of which I am seldom guilty.

MR MAC LAUREL. Noo, ye ken, sir, every mon is the centre of his ain system, an' endaivours as much as possible to adapt everything aroond him to his ain parteecular views.

MR ESCOT. Thus, sir, I presume, it suits the particular views of a poet, at one time to take the part of the people against their oppressors, and at another, to take the part of the oppressors, against the people.

MR MAC LAUREL. Ye mun alloo, sir, that poetry is a sort of ware or commodity, that is brought into the public market wi' a' other descreptions of merchandise, an' that a mon is pairfectly justified in getting the best price he can for his article. Noo, there are three reasons for taking the part o' the people: the first is, when general leeberty an' public happiness are conformable to your ain parteecular feelings o' the moral an' poleetical fetness o' things: the second is, when they happen to be, as it were, in a state of exceetabeelity, an' ye think ye can get a gude price for your commodity, by flingin' in a leetle seasoning o' pheelanthropy an' republican speerit: the third is, when ye think ye can bully the menestry into gieing ye a place or a pansion to hau'd your din, an' in that case, ye point an attack against them within the pale o' the law; an' if they tak nae heed o' ye, ye open a stronger fire; an' the less heed they tak, the mair ye bawl; an' the mair factious ye grow, always within the pale o' the law, till they send a plenipotentiary to treat wi' ye for yoursel, an' then the mair popular ye happen to be, the better price ye fetch.

SQUIRE HEADLONG. Off with your heeltaps.

MR CRANIUM. I perfectly agree with Mr Mac Laurel in his definition of self-love and disinterestedness: every man's actions are determined by his peculiar views, and those views are determined by the organization of his skull. A man in whom the organ of benevolence is not developed, cannot be benevolent: he, in whom it is so, cannot be otherwise. The organ of self-love is prodigiously developed in the greater number of subjects that have fallen under my observation.

MR ESCOT. Much less, I presume, among savage than civilized men, who, *constant only to the love of self, and consistent* *only in their aim to deceive, are always actuated by the hope of personal advantage, or by the dread of personal punishment.**

MR CRANIUM. Very probably.

MR ESCOT. You have, of course, found very copious specimens of the organs of hypocrisy, destruction, and avarice.

MR CRANIUM. Secretiveness, destructiveness, and covetiveness. You may add, if you please, that of constructiveness.

MR ESCOT. Meaning, I presume, the organ of building; which I contend to be not a natural organ of the *featherless biped*.[3]

MR CRANIUM. Pardon me: it is here. – (*As he said these words, he produced a skull from his pocket, and placed it on the table, to the great surprise of the company.*) – This was the skull of Sir Christopher Wren. You observe this protuberance. – (*The skull was handed round the table.*)

MR ESCOT. I contend that the original unsophisticated man was by no means constructive. He lived in the open air, under a tree.

THE REVEREND DOCTOR GASTER. The tree of life. Unquestionably. Till he had tasted the forbidden fruit.

MR JENKISON. At which period, probably, the organ of constructiveness was added to his anatomy, as a punishment for his transgression.

MR ESCOT. There could not have been a more severe one, since the propensity which has led him to building cities has proved the greatest curse of his existence.

SQUIRE HEADLONG (*taking the skull*). *Memento mori*.[4] Come, a bumper of Burgundy.

MR NIGHTSHADE. A very classical application, Squire Headlong. The Romans were in the practice of adhibiting skulls at their banquets, and sometimes little skeletons of silver, as a silent admonition to the guests to enjoy life while it lasted.

THE REVEREND DOCTOR GASTER. Sound doctrine, Mr Nightshade.

MR ESCOT. I question its soundness. The use of vinous spirit has a tremendous influence in the deterioration of the human race.

MR FOSTER. I fear, indeed, it operates as a considerable check to the progress of the species towards moral and intellectual perfection. Yet many great men have been of opinion

* Drummond's *Academical Questions*. [P.]

that it exalts the imagination, fires the genius, accelerates the
flow of ideas, and imparts to dispositions naturally cold and
deliberative that enthusiastic sublimation which is the source
of greatness and energy.

MR NIGHTSHADE. *Laudibus arguitur vini vinosus Homerus.**

MR JENKISON. I conceive the use of wine to be always
pernicious in excess, but often useful in moderation: it certainly kills some, but it saves the lives of others: I find that an
occasional glass, taken with judgement and caution, has a very
salutary effect in maintaining that equilibrium of the system,
which it is always my aim to preserve; and this calm and
temperate use of wine was, no doubt, what Homer meant to
inculcate, when he said:

Παρ δε δεπας οινοιο, πιειν ότε θυμος ανωγοι.†

SQUIRE HEADLONG. Good. Pass the bottle.
(*Un morne silence.*)

Sir Christopher does not seem to have raised our spirits. Chromatic, favour us with a specimen of your vocal powers. Something in point.

Mr Chromatic, without further preface, immediately struck
up the following

SONG

In his last binn SIR PETER lies,
  Who knew not what it was to frown:
Death took him mellow, by surprise,
  And in his cellar stopped him down.
Through all our land we could not boast
  A knight more gay, more prompt than he,
To rise and fill a bumper toast,
  And pass it round with THREE TIMES THREE.

None better knew the feast to sway,
  Or keep Mirth's boat in better trim;
For Nature had but little clay
  Like that of which she moulded him.
The meanest guest that graced his board
  Was there the freest of the free,
His bumper toast when PETER poured,
  And passed it round with THREE TIMES THREE.

* Homer is proved to have been a lover of wine by the praises he bestows
upon it. [P.]
† A cup of wine at hand, to drink as inclination prompts. [P.]

> He kept at true good humour's mark
>   The social flow of pleasure's tide:
> He never made a brow look dark,
>   Nor caused a tear, but when he died.
> No sorrow round his tomb should dwell:
>   More pleased his gay old ghost would be,
> For funeral song, and passing bell,
>   To hear no sound but THREE TIMES THREE.

(Hammering of knuckles and glasses, and shouts of Bravo!)

MR PANSCOPE. (*suddenly emerging from a deep reverie.*) I have heard, with the most profound attention, everything which the gentleman on the other side of the table has thought proper to advance on the subject of human deterioration; and I must take the liberty to remark, that it augurs a very considerable degree of presumption in any individual, to set himself up against the *authority* of so many great men, as may be marshalled in metaphysical phalanx under the opposite banners of the controversy; such as Aristotle, Plato, the scholiast on Aristophanes, St Chrysostom, St Jerome, St Athanasius, Orpheus, Pindar, Simonides, Gronovius, Hemsterhusius, Longinus, Sir Isaac Newton, Thomas Paine, Doctor Paley, the King of Prussia, the King of Poland, Cicero, Monsieur Gautier, Hippocrates, Machiavelli, Milton, Colley Cibber, Bojardo, Gregory, Nazianzenus, Locke, D'Alembert, Boccaccio, Daniel Defoe, Erasmus, Doctor Smollett, Zimmermann, Solomon, Confucius, Zoroaster, and Thomas-a-Kempis.

MR ESCOT. I presume, sir, you are one of those who value an *authority* more than a reason.

MR PANSCOPE. The *authority*, sir, of all these great men, whose works, as well as the whole of the *Encyclopaedia Britannica*, the entire series of the *Monthly Review*, the complete set of the *Variorum Classics*, and the *Memoirs of the Academy of Inscriptions*, I have read through from beginning to end, deposes, with irrefragable refutation, against your ratiocinative speculations, wherein you seem desirous, by the futile process of analytical dialectics, to subvert the pyramidal structure of synthetically deduced opinions, which have withstood the secular revolutions of physiological disquisition, and which I maintain to be transcendentally self-evident, categorically certain, and syllogistically demonstrable.

SQUIRE HEADLONG. Bravo! Pass the bottle. The very best speech that ever was made.

MR ESCOT. It has only the slight disadvantage of being un-intelligible.

MR PANSCOPE. I am not obliged, sir, as Dr Johnson observed on a similar occasion, to furnish you with an understanding.

MR ESCOT. I fear, sir, you would have some difficulty in furnishing me with such an article from your own stock.

MR PANSCOPE. 'Sdeath, sir, do you question my understanding?

MR ESCOT. I only question, sir, where I expect a reply; which, from things that have no existence, I am not visionary enough to anticipate.

MR PANSCOPE. I beg leave to observe, sir, that my language was perfectly perspicuous, and etymologically correct; and, I conceive, I have demonstrated what I shall now take the liberty to say in plain terms, that all your opinions are extremely absurd.

MR ESCOT. I should be sorry, sir, to advance any opinion that you would not think absurd.

MR PANSCOPE. Death and fury, sir —

MR ESCOT. Say no more, sir. That apology is quite sufficient.

MR PANSCOPE. Apology, sir?

MR ESCOT. Even so, sir. You have lost your temper, which I consider equivalent to a confession that you have the worst of the argument.

MR PANSCOPE. Lightning and devils! sir —

SQUIRE HEADLONG. No civil war! – Temperance, in the name of Bacchus! – A glee! a glee! *Music has charms to bend the knotted oak*. Sir Patrick, you'll join?

SIR PATRICK O'PRISM. Troth, with all my heart: for, by my soul, I'm bothered completely.

SQUIRE HEADLONG. Agreed, then: you, and I, and Chromatic. Bumpers! – bumpers! Come, strike up.

Squire Headlong, Mr Chromatic, and Sir Patrick O'Prism, each holding a bumper, immediately vociferated the following

GLEE

A heeltap! a heeltap! I never could bear it!
So fill me a bumper, a bumper of claret!
Let the bottle pass freely, don't shirk it nor spare it,
For a heeltap! a heeltap! I never could bear it!

No skylight! no twilight! while Bacchus rules o'er us:
No thinking! no shrinking! all drinking in chorus:
Let us moisten our clay, since 'tis thirsty and porous:
No thinking! no shrinking! all drinking in chorus!

GRAND CHORUS

*By Squire Headlong, Mr Chromatic, Sir Patrick O'Prism, Mr
Panscope, Mr Jenkison, Mr Gall, Mr Treacle, Mr Nightshade,
Mr Mac Laurel, Mr Cranium, Mr Milestone, and the Reverend
Doctor Gaster.*

A heeltap! a heeltap! I never could bear it!
So fill me a bumper, a bumper of claret!
Let the bottle pass freely, don't shirk it nor spare it,
For a heeltap! a heeltap! I never could bear it!

'ΟΜΑΔΟΣ ΚΑΙ ΔΟΥΠΟΣ ΟΡΩΡΕΙ!'[5]

The little butler now waddles in with a summons from the
ladies to tea and coffee. The squire was unwilling to leave his
Burgundy. Mr Escot strenuously urged the necessity of immediate adjournment, observing, that the longer they continued drinking the worse they should be. Mr Foster seconded
the motion, declaring the transition from the bottle to female
society to be an indisputable amelioration of the state of the
sensitive man. Mr Jenkison allowed the squire and his two
brother philosophers to settle the point between them, concluding that he was just as well in one place as another. The
question of adjournment was then put, and carried by a large
majority.

CHAPTER VI

THE EVENING

MR PANSCOPE, highly irritated by the cool contempt with
which Mr Escot had treated him, sate sipping his coffee and
meditating revenge. He was not long in discovering the passion of his antagonist for the beautiful Cephalis, for whom he
had himself a species of predilection; and it was also obvious
to him, that there was some lurking anger in the mind of her

father, unfavourable to the hopes of his rival. The stimulus of revenge, superadded to that of preconceived inclination, determined him, after due deliberation, to *cut out* Mr Escot in the young lady's favour. The practicability of this design he did not trouble himself to investigate; for the havoc he had made in the hearts of some silly girls, who were extremely vulnerable to flattery, and who, not understanding a word he said, considered him a *prodigious clever man*, had impressed him with an unhesitating idea of his own irresistibility. He had not only the requisites already specified for fascinating female vanity, he could likewise fiddle with tolerable dexterity, though by no means so *quick* as Mr Chromatic (for our readers are of course aware that rapidity of execution, not delicacy of expression, constitutes the scientific perfection of modern music), and could warble a fashionable love-ditty with considerable affectation of feeling: besides this, he was always extremely well dressed, and was heir-apparent to an estate of ten thousand a-year. The influence which the latter consideration might have on the minds of the majority of his female acquaintance, whose morals had been formed by the novels of such writers as Miss Philomela Poppyseed, did not once enter into his calculation of his own personal attractions. Relying, therefore, on past success, he determined *to appeal to his fortune*, and already, in imagination, considered himself sole lord and master of the affections of the beautiful Cephalis.

Mr Escot and Mr Foster were the only two of the party who had entered the library (to which the ladies had retired, and which was interior to the music-room) in a state of perfect sobriety. Mr Escot had placed himself next to the beautiful Cephalis: Mr Cranium had laid aside much of the terror of his frown; the short craniological conversation, which had passed between him and Mr Escot, had softened his heart in his favour; and the copious libations of Burgundy in which he had indulged had smoothed his brow into unusual serenity.

Mr Foster placed himself near the lovely Caprioletta, whose artless and innocent conversation had already made an impression on his susceptible spirit.

The Reverend Doctor Gaster seated himself in the corner of a sofa near Miss Philomela Poppyseed. Miss Philomela detailed to him the plan of a very moral and aristocratical novel she was preparing for the press, and continued holding forth, with her eyes half shut, till a long-drawn nasal tone from the

reverend divine compelled her suddenly to open them in all
the indignation of surprise. The cessation of the hum of her
voice awakened the reverend gentleman, who, lifting up first
one eyelid, then the other, articulated, or rather murmured,
'Admirably planned, indeed!'

'I have not quite finished, sir,' said Miss Philomela, bridling.
'Will you have the goodness to inform me where I left off?'

The doctor hummed a while, and at length answered: 'I
think you had just laid it down as a position, that a thousand
a-year is an indispensable ingredient in the passion of love,
and that no man, who is not so far gifted by *nature*, can reasonably presume to feel that passion himself, or be correctly the
object of it with a well-educated female.'

'That, sir,' said Miss Philomela, highly incensed, 'is the
fundamental principle which I lay down in the first chapter,
and which the whole four volumes, of which I detailed to you
the outline, are intended to set in a strong practical light.'

'Bless me!' said the doctor, 'what a nap I must have had!'

Miss Philomela flung away to the side of her dear friends
Gall and Treacle, under whose fostering patronage she had
been puffed into an extensive reputation, much to the advantage of the young ladies of the age, whom she taught to
consider themselves as a sort of commodity, to be put up at
public auction, and knocked down to the highest bidder. Mr
Nightshade and Mr Mac Laurel joined the trio; and it was
secretly resolved, that Miss Philomela should furnish them
with a portion of her manuscripts, and that Messieurs Gall and
Co. should devote the following morning to cutting and dry-
ing a critique on a work calculated to prove so extensively
beneficial, that Mr Gall protested he really *envied* the writer.

While this amiable and enlightened quintetto were busily
employed in flattering one another, Mr Cranium retired to
complete the preparations he had begun in the morning for a
lecture, with which he intended, on some future evening, to
favour the company: Sir Patrick O'Prism walked out into the
grounds to study the effect of moonlight on the snow-clad
mountains: Mr Foster and Mr Escot continued to make love,
and Mr Panscope to digest his plan of attack on the heart of
Miss Cephalis: Mr Jenkison sate by the fire, reading *Much Ado
about Nothing*: the Reverend Doctor Gaster was still enjoying
the benefit of Miss Philomela's opiate, and serenading the
company from his solitary corner: Mr Chromatic was reading

music, and occasionally humming a note: and Mr Milestone
had produced his portfolio for the edification and amusement
of Miss Tenorina, Miss Graziosa, and Squire Headlong, to
whom he was pointing out the various beauties of his plan for
Lord Littlebrain's park.

MR MILESTONE. This, you perceive, is the natural state of
one part of the grounds. Here is a wood, never yet touched by
the finger of taste; thick, intricate, and gloomy. Here is a little
stream, dashing from stone to stone, and overshadowed with
these untrimmed boughs.

MISS TENORINA. The sweet romantic spot! How beautifully the birds must sing there on a summer evening!

MISS GRAZIOSA. Dear sister! how can you endure the
horrid thicket?

MR MILESTONE. You are right, Miss Graziosa: your taste is
correct – perfectly *en règle*. Now, here is the same place cor-
rected – trimmed – polished – decorated – adorned. Here
sweeps a plantation, in that beautiful regular curve: there winds
a gravel walk: here are parts of the old wood, left in these
majestic circular clumps, disposed at equal distances with
wonderful symmetry: there are some single shrubs scattered
in elegant profusion: here a Portugal laurel, there a juniper;
here a lauristinus, there a spruce fir; here a larch, there a lilac;
here a rhododendron, there an arbutus. The stream, you see,
is become a canal: the banks are perfectly smooth and green,
sloping to the water's edge: and there is Lord Littlebrain,
rowing in an elegant boat.

SQUIRE HEADLONG. Magical, faith!

MR MILESTONE. Here is another part of the grounds in its
natural state. Here is a large rock, with the mountain-ash
rooted in its fissures, overgrown, as you see, with ivy and
moss; and from this part of it bursts a little fountain, that runs
bubbling down its rugged sides.

MISS TENORINA. O how beautiful! How I should love the
melody of that miniature cascade!

MR MILESTONE. Beautiful, Miss Tenorina! Hideous. Base,
common, and popular. Such a thing as you may see anywhere,
in wild and mountainous districts. Now, observe the metamorphosis. Here is the same rock, cut into the shape of a giant.
In one hand he holds a horn, through which that little fountain is thrown to a prodigious elevation. In the other is a
ponderous stone, so exactly balanced as to be apparently ready

to fall on the head of any person who may happen to be beneath:* and there is Lord Littlebrain walking under it.

SQUIRE HEADLONG. Miraculous, by Mahomet!

MR MILESTONE. This is the summit of a hill, covered, as you perceive, with wood, and with those mossy stones scattered at random under the trees.

MISS TENORINA. What a delightful spot to read in, on a summer's day! The air must be so pure, and the wind must sound so divinely in the tops of those old pines!

MR MILESTONE. Bad taste, Miss Tenorina. Bad taste, I assure you. Here is the spot improved. The trees are cut down: the stones are cleared away: this is an octagonal pavilion, exactly on the centre of the summit: and there you see Lord Littlebrain, on the top of the pavilion, enjoying the prospect with a telescope.

SQUIRE HEADLONG. Glorious, egad!

MR MILESTONE. Here is a rugged mountainous road, leading through impervious shades: the ass and the four goats characterize a wild uncultured scene. Here, as you perceive, it is totally changed into a beautiful gravel-road, gracefully curving through a belt of limes: and there is Lord Littlebrain driving four-in-hand.

SQUIRE HEADLONG. Egregious, by Jupiter!

MR MILESTONE. Here is Littlebrain Castle, a Gothic, moss-grown structure, half-bosomed in trees. Near the casement of that turret is an owl peeping from the ivy.

SQUIRE HEADLONG. And devilish wise he looks.

MR MILESTONE. Here is the new house, without a tree near it, standing in the midst of an undulating lawn: a white, polished, angular building, reflected to a nicety in this waveless lake: and there you see Lord Littlebrain looking out of the window.

SQUIRE HEADLONG. And devilish wise he looks too. You shall cut me a giant before you go.

MR MILESTONE. Good. I'll order down my little corps of pioneers.

During this conversation, a hot dispute had arisen between Messieurs Gall and Nightshade; the latter pertinaciously insisting on having his new poem reviewed by Treacle, who he knew would extol it most loftily, and not by Gall, whose sarcastic commendation he held in superlative horror. The

* See *Knight on Taste.*[P.]

remonstrances of Squire Headlong silenced the disputants, but did not mollify the inflexible Gall, nor appease the irritated Nightshade, who secretly resolved that, on his return to London, he would beat his drum in Grub Street, form a masti-gophoric[1] corps of his own, and hoist the standard of deter-mined opposition against this critical Napoleon.

Sir Patrick O'Prism now entered, and, after some rapturous exclamations on the effect of the mountain-moonlight, en-treated that one of the young ladies would favour him with a song. Miss Tenorina and Miss Graziosa now enchanted the company with some very scientific compositions, which, as usual, excited admiration and astonishment in every one, without a single particle of genuine pleasure. The beautiful Cephalis being then summoned to take her station at the harp, sang with feeling and simplicity the following air:

LOVE AND OPPORTUNITY

Oh! who art thou, so swiftly flying?
   My name is Love, the child replied:
Swifter I pass than south-winds sighing,
   Or streams, through summer vales that glide.
And who art thou, his flight pursuing?
   'Tis cold Neglect whom now you see:
The little god you there are viewing,
   Will die, if once he's touched by me.

Oh! who art thou so fast proceeding,
   Ne'er glancing back thine eyes of flame?
Marked but by few, through earth I'm speeding,
   And Opportunity's my name.
What form is that, which scowls beside thee?
   Repentance is the form you see:
Learn then, the fate may yet betide thee:
   She seizes them who seize not me.*

The little butler now appeared with a summons to supper, shortly after which the party dispersed for the night.

* This stanza is imitated from Machiavelli's *Capitolo dell' Occasione*. [P.

CHAPTER VII

THE WALK

IT WAS AN OLD custom in Headlong Hall to have breakfast ready at eight, and continue it till two; that the various guests might rise at their own hour, breakfast when they came down, and employ the morning as they thought proper; the squire only expecting that they should punctually assemble at dinner. During the whole of this period, the little butler stood sentinel at a side-table near the fire, copiously furnished with all the apparatus of tea, coffee, chocolate, milk, cream, eggs, rolls, toast, muffins, bread, butter, potted beef, cold fowl and part-ridge, ham, tongue, and anchovy. The Reverend Doctor Gaster found himself rather *queasy* in the morning, therefore preferred breakfasting in bed, on a mug of buttered ale and an anchovy toast. The three philosophers made their appearance at eight, and enjoyed *les prémices des dépouilles*.[1] Mr Foster pro-posed that, as it was a fine frosty morning, and they were all good pedestrians, they should take a walk to Tremadoc, to see the improvements carrying on in that vicinity. This being readily acceded to, they began their walk.

After their departure, appeared Squire Headlong and Mr Milestone, who agreed, over their muffin and partridge, to walk together to a ruined tower, within the precincts of the squire's grounds, which Mr Milestone thought he could im-prove.

The other guests dropped in by one's and two's, and made their respective arrangements for the morning. Mr Panscope took a little ramble with Mr Cranium, in the course of which, the former professed a great enthusiasm for the science of craniology, and a great deal of love for the beautiful Cephalis, adding a few words about his expectations: the old gentleman was unable to withstand this triple battery, and it was accord-ingly determined – after the manner of the heroic age, in which it was deemed superfluous to consult the opinions and feelings of the lady, as to the manner in which she should be disposed of – that the lovely Miss Cranium should be made the happy bride of the accomplished Mr Panscope. We shall leave them for the present to settle preliminaries, while we accompany the three philosophers in their walk to Tremadoc.

The vale contracted as they advanced, and, when they had passed the termination of the lake, their road wound along a narrow and romantic pass, through the middle of which an impetuous torrent dashed over vast fragments of stone. The pass was bordered on both sides by perpendicular rocks, broken into the wildest forms of fantastic magnificence.

'These are, indeed,' said Mr Escot, '*confracti mundi rudera*:* yet they must be feeble images of the valleys of the Andes, where the philosophic eye may contemplate, in their utmost extent, the effects of that tremendous convulsion which destroyed the perpendicularity of the poles, and inundated this globe with that torrent of physical evil, from which the greater torrent of moral evil has issued, that will continue to roll on, with an expansive power and an accelerated impetus, till the whole human race shall be swept away in its vortex.'

'The precession of the equinoxes,' said Mr Foster, 'will gradually ameliorate the physical state of our planet, till the ecliptic shall again coincide with the equator, and the equal diffusion of light and heat over the whole surface of the earth typify the equal and happy existence of man, who will then have attained the final step of pure and perfect intelligence.'

'It is by no means clear,' said Mr Jenkison, 'that the axis of the earth was ever perpendicular to the plane of its orbit, or that it ever will be so. Explosion and convulsion are necessary to the maintenance of either hypothesis: for La Place has demonstrated, that the precession of the equinoxes is only a secular equation of a very long period, which, of course, proves nothing either on one side or the other.'

They now emerged, by a winding ascent, from the vale of Llanberris, and after some little time arrived at Bedd Gelert. Proceeding through the sublimely romantic pass of Aberglaslynn, their road led along the edge of Traeth Mawr, a vast arm of the sea, which they then beheld in all the magnificence of the flowing tide. Another five miles brought them to the embankment, which has since been completed, and which, by connecting the two counties of Meirionnydd and Caernarvon, excludes the sea from an extensive tract.[2] The embankment, which was carried on at the same time from both the opposite coasts, was then very nearly meeting in the centre. They walked to the extremity of that part of it which was thrown out from the Caernarvonshire shore. The tide was now

* Fragments of a demolished world. [P.]

ebbing: it had filled the vast basin within, forming a lake about five miles in length and more than one in breadth. As they looked upwards with their backs to the open sea, they beheld a scene which no other in this country can parallel, and which the admirers of the magnificence of nature will ever remember with regret, whatever consolation may be derived from the probable utility of the works which have excluded the waters from their ancient receptacle. Vast rocks and precipices, intersected with little torrents, formed the barrier on the left: on the right, the triple summit of Moëlwyn reared its majestic boundary: in the depth was that sea of mountains, the wild and stormy outline of the Snowdonian chain, with the giant Wyddfa towering in the midst. The mountain-frame remains unchanged, unchangeable; but the liquid mirror it enclosed is gone.

The tide ebbed with rapidity: the waters within, retained by the embankment, poured through its two points an impetuous cataract, curling and boiling in innumerable eddies, and making a tumultuous melody admirably in unison with the surrounding scene. The three philosophers looked on in silence; and at length unwillingly turned away, and proceeded to the little town of Tremadoc, which is built on land recovered in a similar manner from the sea. After inspecting the manufactories, and refreshing themselves at the inn on a cold saddle of mutton and a bottle of sherry, they retraced their steps towards Headlong Hall, commenting as they went on the various objects they had seen.

MR ESCOT. I regret that time did not allow us to see the caves on the sea-shore. There is one of which the depth is said to be unknown. There is a tradition in the country, that an adventurous fiddler once resolved to explore it; that he entered, and never returned; but that the subterranean sound of a fiddle was heard at a farm-house seven miles inland. It is, therefore, concluded that he lost his way in the labyrinth of caverns, supposed to exist under the rocky soil of this part of the country.

MR JENKISON. A supposition that must always remain in force, unless a second fiddler, equally adventurous and more successful, should return with an accurate report of the true state of the fact.

MR FOSTER. What think you of the little colony we have just been inspecting; a city, as it were, in its cradle?

MR ESCOT. With all the weakness of infancy, and all the vices of maturer age. I confess, the sight of those manufactories, which have suddenly sprung up, like fungous excrescences, in the bosom of these wild and desolate scenes, impressed me with as much horror and amazement as the sudden appearance of the stocking manufactory struck into the mind of Rousseau, when, in a lonely valley of the Alps, he had just congratulated himself on finding a spot where man had never been.

MR FOSTER. The manufacturing system is not yet purified from some evils which necessarily attend it, but which I conceive are greatly overbalanced by their concomitant advantages. Contemplate the vast sum of human industry to which this system so essentially contributes: seas covered with vessels, ports resounding with life, profound researches, scientific inventions, complicated mechanism, canals carried over deep valleys and through the bosoms of hills: employment and existence thus given to innumerable families, and the multiplied comforts and conveniences of life diffused over the whole community.

MR ESCOT. You present to me a complicated picture of artificial life, and require me to admire it. Seas covered with vessels: every one of which contains two or three tyrants, and from fifty to a thousand slaves, ignorant, gross, perverted, and active only in mischief. Ports resounding with life: in other words, with noise and drunkenness, the mingled din of avarice, intemperance, and prostitution. Profound researches, scientific inventions: to what end? To contract the sum of human wants? to teach the art of living on a little? to disseminate independence, liberty, and health? No; to multiply factitious desires, to stimulate depraved appetites, to invent unnatural wants, to heap up incense on the shrine of luxury, and accumulate expedients of selfish and ruinous profusion. Complicated machinery: behold its blessings. Twenty years ago, at the door of every cottage sate the good woman with her spinning-wheel: the children, if not more profitably employed than in gathering heath and sticks, at least laid in a stock of health and strength to sustain the labours of maturer years. Where is the spinning-wheel now, and every simple and insulated occupation of the industrious cottager? Wherever this boasted machinery is established, the children of the poor are death-doomed from their cradles. Look for one moment

at midnight into a cotton-mill, amidst the smell of oil, the
smoke of lamps, the rattling of wheels, the dizzy and complicated motions of diabolical mechanism: contemplate the
little human machines that keep play with the revolutions of
the iron work, robbed at that hour of their natural rest, as of
air and exercise by day: observe their pale and ghastly features,
more ghastly in that baleful and malignant light, and tell me if
you do not fancy yourself on the threshold of Virgil's hell,
where

> Continuò auditae voces, vagitus et ingens,
> *Infantumque animae flentes,* in limine primo,
> Quos *dulcis vitae exsortes,* et ab ubere raptos,
> *Abstulit atra dies,* et FUNERE MERSIT ACERBO![3]

As Mr Escot said this, a little rosy-cheeked girl, with a
basket of heath on her head, came tripping down the side of
one of the rocks on the left. The force of contrast struck even
on the phlegmatic spirit of Mr Jenkison, and he almost inclined for a moment to the doctrine of deterioration. Mr Escot
continued:

'Nor is the lot of the parents more enviable. Sedentary
victims of unhealthy toil, they have neither the corporeal
energy of the savage, nor the mental acquisitions of the civilized man. Mind, indeed, they have none, and scarcely animal
life. They are mere automata, component parts of the enormous machines which administer to the pampered appetites of
the few, who consider themselves the most valuable portion
of a state, because they consume in indolence the fruits of the
earth, and contribute nothing to the benefit of the community.'

MR JENKISON. That these are evils cannot be denied; but
they have their counterbalancing advantages. That a man
should pass the day in a furnace and the night in a cellar, is bad
for the individual, but good for others who enjoy the benefit
of his labour.

MR ESCOT. By what right do they so?

MR JENKISON. By the right of all property and all possession: *le droit du plus fort.*[4]

MR ESCOT. Do you justify that principle?

MR JENKISON. I neither justify nor condemn it. It is practically recognized in all societies; and, though it is certainly the
source of enormous evil, I conceive it is also the source of
abundant good, or it would not have so many supporters.

MR ESCOT. That is by no means a consequence. Do we not every day see men supporting the most enormous evils, which they know to be so with respect to others, and which in reality are so with respect to themselves, though an erroneous view of their own miserable self-interest induces them to think otherwise?

MR JENKISON. Good and evil exist only as they are perceived. I cannot therefore understand, how that which a man perceives to be good can be in reality an evil to him: indeed, the word *reality* only signifies *strong belief*.

MR ESCOT. The views of such a man I contend are false. If he could be made to see the truth —

MR JENKISON. He sees his own truth. Truth is that which a man *troweth*. Where there is no man there is no truth. Thus the truth of one is not the truth of another.*

MR ESCOT. I am aware of the etymology; but I contend that there is an universal and immutable truth, deducible from the nature of things.

MR JENKISON. By whom deducible? Philosophers have investigated the nature of things for centuries, yet no two of them will agree in *trowing* the same conclusion.

MR FOSTER. The progress of philosophical investigation, and the rapidly increasing accuracy of human knowledge, approximate by degrees the diversities of opinion; so that, in process of time, moral science will be susceptible of mathematical demonstration; and, clear and indisputable principles being universally recognized, the coincidence of deduction will necessarily follow.

MR ESCOT. Possibly, when the inroads of luxury and disease shall have exterminated nine hundred and ninety-nine thousand nine hundred and ninety-nine of every million of the human race, the remaining fractional units may congregate into one point, and come to something like the same conclusion.

MR JENKISON. I doubt it much. I conceive, if only we three were survivors of the whole system of terrestrial being, we should never agree in our decisions as to the cause of the calamity.

MR ESCOT. Be that as it may, I think you must at least assent to the following positions: that the many are sacrificed to the few; that ninety-nine in a hundred are occupied in a perpetual

* Tooke's *Diversions of Purley*. [P.]

struggle for the preservation of a perilous and precarious existence, while the remaining one wallows in all the redundancies of luxury that can be wrung from their labours and privations; that luxury and liberty are incompatible; and that every new want you invent for civilized man is a new instrument of torture for him who cannot indulge it.

They had now regained the shores of the lake, when the conversation was suddenly interrupted by a tremendous explosion, followed by a violent splashing of water, and various sounds of tumult and confusion, which induced them to quicken their pace towards the spot whence they proceeded.

CHAPTER VIII

THE TOWER

IN ALL THE THOUGHTS, words, and actions of Squire Headlong, there was a remarkable alacrity of progression, which almost annihilated the interval between conception and execution. He was utterly regardless of obstacles, and seemed to have expunged their very name from his vocabulary. His designs were never nipped in their infancy by the contemplation of those trivial difficulties which often turn awry the current of enterprise; and, though the rapidity of his movements was sometimes arrested by a more formidable barrier, either naturally existing in the pursuit he had undertaken, or created by his own impetuosity, he seldom failed to succeed either in knocking it down or cutting his way through it. He had little idea of gradation: he saw no interval between the first step and the last, but pounced upon his object with the impetus of a mountain cataract. This rapidity of movement, indeed, subjected him to some disasters which cooler spirits would have escaped. He was an excellent sportsman, and almost always killed his game; but now and then he killed his dog.* Rocks,

---

* Some readers will, perhaps, recollect the Archbishop of Prague, who also was an excellent sportsman, and who,

> Com' era scritto in certi suoi giornali,
> Ucciso avea con le sue proprie mani
> Un numero infinito d'animali:
> Cinquemila con quindici fagiani,
> Seimila lepri, ottantatr; cignali,
> E per disgrazia, ancor *tredici cani*, &c. [P.][1]

streams, hedges, gates, and ditches, were objects of no account in his estimation; though a dislocated shoulder, several severe bruises, and two or three narrow escapes for his neck, might have been expected to teach him a certain degree of caution in effecting his transitions. He was so singularly alert in climbing precipices and traversing torrents, that, when he went out on a shooting party, he was very soon left to continue his sport alone, for he was sure to dash up or down some nearly perpendicular path, where no one else had either ability or inclination to follow. He had a pleasure boat on the lake, which he steered with amazing dexterity; but as he always indulged himself in the utmost possible latitude of sail, he was occasionally upset by a sudden gust, and was indebted to his skill in the art of swimming for the opportunity of tempering with a copious libation of wine the unnatural frigidity introduced into his stomach by the extraordinary intrusion of water, an element which he had religiously determined should never pass his lips, but of which, on these occasions, he was sometimes compelled to swallow no inconsiderable quantity. This circumstance alone, of the various disasters that befell him, occasioned him any permanent affliction, and he accordingly noted the day in his pocket-book as a *dies nefastus*, with this simple abstract, and brief chronicle of the calamity: *Mem. Swallowed two or three pints of water*: without any notice whatever of the concomitant circumstances. These days, of which there were several, were set apart in Headlong Hall for the purpose of anniversary expiation; and, as often as the day returned on which the squire had swallowed water, he not only made a point of swallowing a treble allowance of wine himself, but imposed a heavy mulct on every one of his servants who should be detected in a state of sobriety after sunset: but their conduct on these occasions was so uniformly exemplary, that no instance of the infliction of the penalty appears on record.

The squire and Mr Milestone, as we have already said, had set out immediately after breakfast to examine the capabilities of the scenery. The object that most attracted Mr Milestone's admiration was a ruined tower on a projecting point of rock almost totally overgrown with ivy. This ivy, Mr Milestone observed, required trimming and clearing in various parts: a little pointing and polishing was also necessary for the dilapidated walls: and the whole effect would be materially increased by a plantation of spruce fir, interspersed with cypress and juniper, the present rugged and broken ascent from the land side being first converted into a beautiful slope, which might be easily effected by blowing up a part of the rock with gunpowder, laying on a quantity of fine mold, and covering the whole with an elegant stratum of turf.

Squire Headlong caught with avidity at this suggestion; and, as he had always a store of gunpowder in the house, for the accommodation of himself and his shooting visitors, and for the supply of a small battery of cannon, which he kept for his private amusement, he insisted on commencing operations immediately. Accordingly, he bounded back to the house, and very speedily returned, accompanied by the little butler, and half a dozen servants and labourers, with pickaxes and gunpowder, a hanging stove and a poker, together with a basket of cold meat and two or three bottles of Madeira: for the Squire thought, with many others, that a copious supply of provision is a very necessary ingredient in all rural amusements.

Mr Milestone superintended the proceedings. The rock was excavated, the powder introduced, the apertures strongly blockaded with fragments of stone: a long train was laid to a spot which Mr Milestone fixed on as sufficiently remote from the possibility of harm: the Squire seized the poker, and, after flourishing it in the air with a degree of dexterity which induced the rest of the party to leave him in solitary possession of an extensive circumference, applied the end of it to the train; and the rapidly communicated ignition ran hissing along the surface of the soil.

At this critical moment, Mr Cranium and Mr Panscope appeared at the top of the tower, which, unseeing and unseen, they had ascended on the opposite side to that where the Squire and Mr Milestone were conducting their operations. Their sudden appearance a little dismayed the Squire, who, however, comforted himself with the reflection, that the tower was perfectly safe, or at least was intended to be so, and that his friends were in no probable danger but of a knock on the head from a flying fragment of stone.

The succession of these thoughts in the mind of the Squire was commensurate in rapidity to the progress of the ignition, which having reached its extremity, the explosion took place, and the shattered rock was hurled into the air in the midst of fire and smoke.

Mr Milestone had properly calculated the force of the explosion; for the tower remained untouched: but the Squire, in his consolatory reflections, had omitted the consideration of the influence of sudden fear, which had so violent an effect on Mr Cranium, who was just commencing a speech concerning the very fine prospect from the top of the tower, that, cutting short the thread of his observations, he bounded, under the elastic influence of terror, several feet into the air. His ascent being unluckily a little out of the perpendicular, he descended with a proportionate curve from the apex of his projection, and alighted, not on the wall of the tower, but in an ivy-bush by its side, which, giving way beneath him, transferred him to a tuft of hazel at its base, which, after upholding him an instant, consigned him to the boughs of an ash that had rooted itself in a fissure about half way down the rock, which finally transmitted him to the waters below.

Squire Headlong anxiously watched the tower as the smoke which at first enveloped it rolled away; but when this shadowy curtain was withdrawn, and Mr Panscope was discovered, *solus*, in a tragical attitude, his apprehensions became boundless, and he concluded that the unlucky collision of a flying fragment of rock had indeed emancipated the spirit of the craniologist from its terrestrial bondage.

Mr Escot had considerably outstripped his companions, and arrived at the scene of the disaster just as Mr Cranium, being utterly destitute of natatorial skill, was in imminent danger of final submersion. The deteriorationist, who had cultivated this valuable art with great success, immediately plunged in to his assistance, and brought him alive and in safety to a shelving part of the shore. Their landing was hailed with a view-holla from the delighted Squire, who, shaking them both heartily by the hand, and making ten thousand lame apologies to Mr Cranium, concluded by asking, in a pathetic tone, *How much water he had swallowed?* and without waiting for his answer, filled a large tumbler with Madeira, and insisted on his tossing it off, which was no sooner said than done. Mr Jenkison and Mr Foster now made their appearance. Mr Panscope descended the tower, which he vowed never again to approach within a quarter of a mile. The tumbler of Madeira was replenished, and handed round to recruit the spirits of the party, which now began to move towards Headlong Hall, the Squire capering for joy in the van, and the little fat butler waddling in the rear.

The Squire took care that Mr Cranium should be seated next to him at dinner, and plied him so hard with Madeira to prevent him, as he said, from taking cold, that long before the ladies sent in their summons to coffee, every organ in his brain was in a complete state of revolution, and the Squire was under the necessity of ringing for three or four servants to carry him to bed, observing, with a smile of great satisfaction, that he was in a very excellent way for escaping any ill consequences that might have resulted from his accident.

The beautiful Cephalis, being thus freed from his *surveillance*, was enabled, during the course of the evening, to develop to his preserver the full extent of her gratitude.

CHAPTER IX

THE SEXTON

MR ESCOT PASSED a sleepless night, the ordinary effect of love, according to some amatory poets, who seem to have composed their whining ditties for the benevolent purpose of bestowing on others that gentle slumber of which they so pathetically lament the privation. The deteriorationist entered into a profound moral soliloquy, in which he first examined *whether a philosopher ought to be in love?* Having decided this point affirmatively against Plato and Lucretius, he next examined, *whether that passion ought to have the effect of keeping a philosopher awake?* Having decided this negatively, he resolved to go to sleep immediately: not being able to accomplish this to his satisfaction, he tossed and tumbled, like Achilles or Orlando, first on one side, then on the other; repeated to himself several hundred lines of poetry; counted a thousand; began again, and counted another thousand: in vain: the beautiful Cephalis was the predominant image in all his soliloquies, in all his repetitions: even in the numerical process from which he sought relief, he did but associate the idea of number with that of his dear tormentor, till she appeared to his mind's eye in a thousand similitudes, distinct, not different. These thousand images, indeed, were but one; and yet the one was a thousand, a sort of uni-multiplex phantasma, which will be very intelligible to some understandings.

He arose with the first peep of day, and sallied forth to enjoy the balmy breeze of morning, which any but a lover might have thought too cool; for it was an intense frost, the sun had not risen, and the wind was rather fresh from north-east and by north. But a lover, who, like Ladurlad in the Curse of Kehama,[1] always has, or at least is supposed to have, 'a fire in his heart and a fire in his brain', feels a wintry breeze from N.E. and by N. steal over his cheek like the south over a bank of violets: therefore, on walked the philosopher, with his coat unbuttoned and his hat in his hand, careless of whither he went, till he found himself near the enclosure of a little mountain-chapel. Passing through the wicket, and stepping over two or three graves, he stood on a rustic tombstone, and peeped through the chapel window, examining the interior with as much curiosity as if he had 'forgotten what the inside of a church was made of ',[2] which, it is rather to be feared, was the case. Before him and beneath him were the font, the altar, and the grave; which gave rise to a train of moral reflections on the three great epochs in the course of the *featherless biped* – birth, marriage, and death. The middle stage of the process arrested his attention; and his imagination placed before him several figures, which he thought, with the addition of his own, would make a very picturesque group; the beautiful Cephalis, 'arrayed in her bridal apparel of white'; her friend Caprioletta officiating as bridesmaid; Mr Cranium giving her away; and, last not least, the Reverend Doctor Gaster, intoning the marriage ceremony with the regular orthodox allowance of nasal recitative. Whilst he was feasting his eyes on this imaginary picture, the demon of mistrust insinuated himself into the storehouse of his conceptions, and, removing his figure from the group, substituted that of Mr Panscope, which gave such a violent shock to his feelings, that he suddenly exclaimed, with an extraordinary elevation of voice, Οἰμοι κακοδαιμων, και τρις κακοδαιμων, και τετρακις, και πεντακις, και δωδεκακις, και μυριακις* to the great terror of the sexton, who was just entering the churchyard, and, not knowing from whence the voice proceeded, *pensa que fut un diableteau.*[3] The sight of the philosopher dispelled his apprehensions, when, growing suddenly valiant, he immediately addressed him:

'Cot pless your honour, I shouldn't have thought of meeting

* Me miserable! and thrice miserable! and four times, and five times, and twelve times, and ten thousand times miserable! [P.]

any pody here at this time of the morning, except, look
you, it was the tevil – who, to pe sure, toes not often come
upon consecrated cround – put for all that, I think I have seen
him now and then, in former tays, when old Nanny Llwyd of
Llyn-isa was living – Cot teliver us! a terriple old witch to pe
sure she was – I tidn't much like tigging her crave – put I
prought two cocks with me – the tevil hates cocks – and tied
them py the leg on two tombstones – and I tug, and the cocks
crowed, and the tevil kept at a tistance. To pe sure now, if I
hadn't peen very prave py nature – as I ought to pe truly – for
my father was Owen Ap-Llwyd Ap-Gryffydd Ap-Shenkin Ap-
Williams Ap-Thomas Ap-Morgan Ap-Parry Ap-Evan Ap-
Rhys, a coot preacher and a lover of *cwrw** – I should have
thought just now pefore I saw your honour, that the foice I
heard was the tevil's calling Nanny Llwyd – Cot pless us! to pe
sure she should have been puried in the middle of the river,
where the tevil can't come, as your honour fery well knows.'

'I am perfectly aware of it,' said Mr Escot.

'True, true,' continued the sexton; 'put to pe sure, Owen
Thomas of Morfa-Bach will have it that one summer evening –
when he went over to Cwm Cynfael in Meirionnydd, apout
some cattles he wanted to puy – he saw a strange figure – pless
us! – with five horns! – Cot save us! sitting on Hugh Llwyd's
pulpit, which, your honour fery well knows, is a pig rock in
the middle of the river —'

'Of course he was mistaken,' said Mr Escot.

'To pe sure he was,' said the sexton. 'For there is no toubt
put the tevil, when Owen Thomas saw him, must have peen
sitting on a piece of rock in a straight line from him on the
other side of the river, where he used to sit, look you, for a
whole summer's tay, while Hugh Llwyd was on his pulpit, and
there they used to talk across the water! for Hugh Llwyd,
please your honour, never raised the tevil except when he was
safe in the middle of the river, which proves that Owen
Thomas, in his fright, didn't pay proper attention to the exact
spot where the tevil was.'

The sexton concluded his speech with an approving smile at
his own sagacity, in so luminously expounding the nature of
Owen Thomas's mistake.

'I perceive,' said Mr Escot, 'you have a very deep insight
into things, and can, therefore, perhaps, facilitate the

* Pronounced *cooroo* – the Welsh word for *ale*. [P.]

resolution of a question, concerning which, though I have little doubt on the subject, I am desirous of obtaining the most extensive and accurate information.'

The sexton scratched his head, the language of Mr Escot not being to his apprehension quite so luminous as his own.

'You have been sexton here,' continued Mr Escot, in the language of Hamlet, 'man and boy, forty years.'

The sexton turned pale. The period Mr Escot named was so nearly the true one, that he began to suspect the personage before him of being rather too familiar with Hugh Llwyd's sable visitor. Recovering himself a little, he said, 'Why, there-apouts, sure enough.'

'During this period, you have of course dug up many bones of the people of ancient times.'

'Pones! Cot pless you, yes! pones as old as the 'orlt.'[4]

'Perhaps you can show me a few.'

The sexton grinned horribly a ghastly smile. 'Will you take your Pible oath you ton't want them to raise the tevil with?'

'Willingly,' said Mr Escot, smiling; 'I have an abstruse reason for the inquiry.'

'Why, if you have an *obtuse* reason,' said the sexton, who thought this a good opportunity to show that he could pro-nounce hard words as well as other people; 'if you have an *obtuse* reason, that alters the case.'

So saying he led the way to the bone-house, from which he began to throw out various bones and skulls of more than common dimensions, and amongst them a skull of very extra-ordinary magnitude, which he swore by St David was the skull of Cadwallader.

'How do you know this to be his skull?' said Mr Escot,

'He was the piggest man that ever lived, and he was puried here; and this is the piggest skull I ever found: you see now—'

'Nothing can be more logical,' said Mr Escot. 'My good friend, will you allow me to take this skull away with me?'

'St Winifred pless us!' exclaimed the sexton: 'would you have me haunted py his chost for taking his plessed pones out of consecrated cround? Would you have him come in the tead of the night, and fly away with the roof of my house? Would you have all the crop of my carden come to nothing? for, look you, his epitaph says,

> ' He that my pones shall ill pestow,
>   Leek in his cround shall never crow.'

'You will ill bestow them,' said Mr Escot, 'in confounding them with those of the sons of little men, the degenerate dwarfs of later generations: you will well bestow them in giving them to me; for I will have this illustrious skull bound with a silver rim, and filled with mantling wine, with this inscription, NUNC TANDEM[5]: signifying that that pernicious liquor has at length found its proper receptacle; for, when the wine is in, the brain is out.'

Saying these words, he put a dollar into the hands of the sexton, who instantly stood spell-bound by the talismanic influence of the coin, while Mr Escot walked off in triumph with the skull of Cadwallader.

CHAPTER X

THE SKULL

WHEN MR ESCOT entered the breakfast-room he found the majority of the party assembled, and the little butler very active at his station. Several of the ladies shrieked at the sight of the skull; and Miss Tenorina, starting up in great haste and terror, caused the subversion of a cup of chocolate, which a servant was handing to the Reverend Doctor Gaster, into the nape of the neck of Sir Patrick O'Prism. Sir Patrick, rising impetuously, *to clap an extinguisher*, as he expressed himself, *on the farthing rushlight of the rascal's life*, pushed over the chair of Marmaduke Milestone, Esquire, who, catching for support at the first thing that came in his way, which happened unluckily to be the corner of the table-cloth, drew it instantaneously with him to the floor, involving plates, cups, and saucers, in one promiscuous ruin. But, as the principal *matériel* of the breakfast apparatus was on the little butler's side-table, the confusion occasioned by this accident was happily greater than the damage. Miss Tenorina was so agitated that she was obliged to retire: Miss Graziosa accompanied her through pure sisterly affection and sympathy, not without a lingering look at Sir Patrick, who likewise retired to change his coat, but was very expeditious in returning to resume his attack on the cold partridge. The broken cups were cleared away, the cloth relaid, and the array of the table restored with wonderful celerity.

Mr Escot was a little surprised at the scene of confusion

which signalized his entrance; but, perfectly unconscious that it originated with the skull of Cadwallader, he advanced to seat himself at the table by the side of the beautiful Cephalis, first placing the skull in a corner, out of the reach of Mr Cranium, who sate eyeing it with lively curiosity, and after several efforts to restrain his impatience, exclaimed, 'You seem to have found a rarity.'

'A rarity indeed,' said Mr Escot, cracking an egg as he spoke; 'no less than the genuine and indubitable skull of Cadwallader.'

'The skull of Cadwallader!' vociferated Mr Cranium: 'O treasure of treasures!'

Mr Escot then detailed by what means he had become possessed of it, which gave birth to various remarks from the other individuals of the party: after which, rising from table, and taking the skull again in his hand,

'This skull,' said he, 'is the skull of a hero, παλαι κατατεθ-νειωτος, and sufficiently demonstrates a point, concerning which I never myself entertained a doubt, that the human race is undergoing a gradual process of diminution in length, breadth, and thickness. Observe this skull. Even the skull of our reverend friend, which is the largest and thickest in the company, is not more than half its size. The frame this skull belonged to could scarcely have been less than nine feet high. Such is the lamentable progress of degeneracy and decay. In the course of ages, a boot of the present generation would form an ample chateau for a large family of our remote posterity. The mind, too, participates in the contraction of the body. Poets and philosophers of all ages and nations have lamented this too visible process of physical and moral deterioration. "The sons of little men," says Ossian. Οιοι νυν βροτοι εισιν, says Homer: "such men as live in these degenerate days". "All things," says Virgil,* "have a retrocessive tendency, and grow worse and worse by the inevitable doom of fate." "We live in the ninth age," says Juvenal,† "an age worse than the age of iron; nature has no metal sufficiently pernicious to give a denomination to its wickedness." "Our fathers," says Horace,‡ "worse than our grandfathers, have given birth to us, their more vicious progeny, who, in our turn, shall become the parents of a still viler generation." You all know the fable of the buried Pict, who bit off the end of a

* *Georg.* I. 199. [P.]   † *Sat.* XIII. 28· [P.]   ‡ *Carm.* III. 6. 46. [P.]

pickaxe, with which sacrilegious hands were breaking open his grave, and called out with a voice like subterranean thunder, *I perceive the degeneracy of your race by the smallness of your little finger!* videlicet, the pickaxe. This, to be sure, is a fiction; but it shows the prevalent opinion, the feeling, the conviction, of absolute, universal, irremediable deterioration.'

'I should be sorry,' said Mr Foster, 'that such an opinion should become universal, independently of my conviction of its fallacy. Its general admission would tend, in a great measure, to produce the very evils it appears to lament. What could be its effect, but to check the ardour of investigation, to extinguish the zeal of philanthropy, to freeze the current of enterprising hope, to bury in the torpor of scepticism and in the stagnation of despair, every better faculty of the human mind, which will necessarily become retrograde in ceasing to be progressive?'

'I am inclined to think, on the contrary,' said Mr Escot, 'that the deterioration of man is accelerated by his blindness – in many respects wilful blindness – to the truth of the fact itself, and to the causes which produce it; that there is no hope whatever of ameliorating his condition but in a total and radical change of the whole scheme of human life, and that the advocates of his indefinite perfectibility are in reality the greatest enemies to the practical possibility of their own system, by so strenuously labouring to impress on his attention that he is going on in a good way, while he is really in a deplorably bad one.'

'I admit,' said Mr Foster, 'there are many things that may, and therefore will, be changed for the better.'

'Not on the present system,' said Mr Escot, 'in which every change is for the worse.'

'In matters of taste I am sure it is,' said Mr Gall: 'there is, in fact, no such thing as good taste left in the world.'

'O, Mr Gall!' said Miss Philomela Poppyseed, 'I thought my novel —'

'My paintings,' said Sir Patrick O'Prism —

'My ode,' said Mr Mac Laurel —

'My ballad,' said Mr Nightshade —

'My plan for Lord Littlebrain's park,' said Marmaduke Milestone, Esquire —

'My essay,' said Mr Treacle —

'My sonata,' said Mr Chromatic —

'My claret,' said Squire Headlong—
'My lectures,' said Mr Cranium —
'Vanity of vanities,' said the Reverend Doctor Gaster, turning down an empty egg-shell; 'all is vanity and vexation of spirit.'

CHAPTER XI

THE ANNIVERSARY

AMONG THE *dies albâ cretâ notandos*,[1] which the beau monde of the Cambrian mountains was in the habit of remembering with the greatest pleasure, and anticipating with the most lively satisfaction, was the Christmas ball which the ancient family of the Headlongs had been accustomed to give from time immemorial. Tradition attributed the honour of its foundation to Headlong Ap-Headlong Ap-Breakneck Ap-Headlong Ap-Cataract Ap-Pistyll* Ap-Rhaidr Ap-Headlong, who lived about the time of the Trojan war. Certain it is, at least, that a grand chorus was always sung after supper in honour of this illustrious ancestor of the squire. This ball was, indeed, an aera in the lives of all the beauty and fashion of Caernarvon, Meirionnydd, and Anglesea, and, like the Greek Olympiads and the Roman consulates, served as the main pillar of memory, round which all the events of the year were suspended and entwined. Thus, in recalling to mind any circumstances imperfectly recollected, the principal point to be ascertained was, whether it had occurred in the year of the first, second, third, or fourth ball of Headlong Ap-Breakneck, or Headlong Ap-Torrent, or Headlong Ap-Hurricane; and, this being satisfactorily established, the remainder followed of course in the natural order of its ancient association.

This eventful anniversary being arrived, every chariot, coach, barouche, and barouchette, landau and landaulet, chaise, curricle, buggy, whiskey, and tilbury, of the three counties, was in motion: not a horse was left idle within five miles of any gentleman's seat, from the high-mettled hunter to the heath-cropping galloway. The ferrymen of the Menai were at their stations before day-break, taking a double allowance of rum and *cwrw* to strengthen them for the fatigues of the day.

* Pistyll, in Welsh, signifies a cataract, and Rhaidr a cascade. [P.]

The ivied towers of Caernarvon, the romantic woods of Tan-y-bwlch, the heathy hills of Kernioggau, the sandy shores of Tremadoc, the mountain recesses of Bedd-Gelert, and the lonely lakes of Capel-Cerig, re-echoed to the voices of the delighted ostlers and postillions, who reaped on this happy day their wintry harvest. Landlords and landladies, waiters, chambermaids, and toll-gate keepers, roused themselves from the torpidity which the last solitary tourist, flying with the yellow leaves on the wings of the autumnal wind, had left them to enjoy till the returning spring: the bustle of August was renewed on all the mountain roads, and, in the meanwhile, Squire Headlong and his little fat butler carried most energetically into effect the lessons of the *savant* in the Court of Quintessence, *qui par engin mirificque jectoit les maisons par les fenestres*.[2]

It was the custom for the guests to assemble at dinner on the day of the ball, and depart on the following morning after breakfast. Sleep during this interval was out of the question: the ancient harp of Cambria suspended the celebration of the noble race of Shenkin, and the songs of Hoel and Cyveilioc,[3] to ring to the profaner but more lively modulation of *Voulez vous danser, Mademoiselle?* in conjunction with the symphonious scraping of fiddles, the tinkling of triangles, and the beating of tambourines. Comus and Momus were the deities of the night; and Bacchus of course was not forgotten by the male part of the assembly (with them, indeed, a ball was invariably a scene of '*tipsy dance and jollity*'): the servants flew about with wine and negus, and the little butler was indefatigable with his corkscrew, which is reported on one occasion to have grown so hot under the influence of perpetual friction that it actually set fire to the cork.

The company assembled. The dinner, which on this occasion was a secondary object, was despatched with uncommon celerity. When the cloth was removed, and the bottle had taken its first round, Mr Cranium stood up and addressed the company.

'Ladies and gentlemen,' said he, 'the golden key of mental phaenomena, which has lain buried for ages in the deepest vein of the mine of physiological research, is now, by a happy combination of practical and speculative investigations, grasped, if I may so express myself, firmly and inexcusibly, in the hands of physiognomical empiricism.' The Cambrian visitors listened with profound attention, not comprehending a single syllable he said, but concluding he would finish his speech by proposing the health of Squire Headlong. The gentlemen accordingly tossed off their heel taps, and Mr Cranium proceeded: 'Ardently desirous, to the extent of my feeble capacity, of disseminating, as much as possible, the inexhaustible treasures to which this golden key admits the humblest votary of philosophical truth, I invite you, when you have sufficiently restored, replenished, refreshed, and exhilarated that osteosarchaematosplanchnochondroneuromuelous, or to employ a more intelligible term, osseocarnisangguineoviscericartilaginonervomedullary,[4] *compages*, or shell, the body, which at once envelops and develops that mysterious and inestimable kernel, the desiderative, determinative, ratiocinative, imaginative, inquisitive, appetitive, comparative, reminiscent, congeries of ideas and notions, simple and compound, comprised in the comprehensive denomination of mind, to take a peep with me into the mechanical arcana of the anatomico-metaphysical universe. Being not in the least dubitative of your spontaneous compliance, I proceed,' added he, suddenly changing his tone, 'to get everything ready in the library.' Saying these words, he vanished.

The Welsh squires now imagined they had caught a glimpse of his meaning, and set him down in their minds for a sort of gentleman conjuror, who intended to amuse them before the ball with some tricks of legerdemain. Under this impression, they became very impatient to follow him, as they had made up their minds not to be drunk before supper. The ladies, too, were extremely curious to witness an exhibition which had been announced in so singular a preamble; and the squire, having previously insisted on every gentleman tossing off a half-pint bumper, adjourned the whole party to the library, where they were not a little surprised to discover Mr Cranium seated, in a pensive attitude, at a large table, decorated with a copious variety of skulls.

Some of the ladies were so much shocked at this extraordinary display, that a scene of great confusion ensued. Fans were very actively exercised, and water was strenuously called for by some of the most officious of the gentlemen; on which the little butler entered with a large allowance of liquid, which bore, indeed, the name of *water*, but was in reality a very powerful spirit. This was the only species of water which the little butler had ever heard called for in Headlong Hall. The mistake was not attended with any evil effects: for the fluid was no sooner applied to the lips of the fainting fair ones, than it resuscitated them with an expedition truly miraculous.

Order was at length restored; the audience took their seats; and the craniological orator held forth in the following terms:

CHAPTER XII

THE LECTURE

'PHYSIOLOGISTS HAVE been much puzzled to account for the varieties of moral character in men, as well as for the remarkable similarity of habit and disposition in all the individual animals of every other respective species. A few brief sentences, perspicuously worded, and scientifically arranged, will enumerate all the characteristics of a lion, or a tiger, or a wolf, or a bear, or a squirrel, or a goat, or a horse, or an ass, or a rat, or a cat, or a hog, or a dog; and whatever is physiologically predicated of any individual lion, tiger, wolf, bear, squirrel, goat, horse, ass, hog, or dog, will be found to hold true of all lions, tigers, wolves, bears, squirrels, goats, horses, asses, hogs, and dogs, whatsoever. Now, in man, the very reverse of this appears to be the case; for he has so few distinct and characteristic marks which hold true of all his species, that philosophers in all ages have found it a task of infinite difficulty to give him a definition. Hence one has defined him to be a *featherless biped*, a definition which is equally applicable to an unfledged fowl: another, to be *an animal which forms opinions*, than which nothing can be more inaccurate, for a very small number of the species form opinions, and the remainder take them upon trust, without investigation or inquiry.

'Again, man has been defined to be *an animal that carries a stick*: an attribute which undoubtedly belongs to man only, but not to all men always; though it uniformly characterizes some of the graver and more imposing varieties, such as physicians, oran-outangs, and lords in waiting.

'We cannot define man to be a reasoning animal, for we do not dispute that idiots are men; to say nothing of that very numerous description of persons who consider themselves reasoning animals, and are so denominated by the ironical courtesy of the world, who labour, nevertheless, under a very gross delusion in that essential particular.

'It appears to me, that man may be correctly defined an animal, which, without any peculiar or distinguishing faculty of its own, is, as it were, a bundle or compound of faculties of other animals, by a distinct enumeration of which any individual of the species may be satisfactorily described. This is manifest, even in the ordinary language of conversation, when, in summing up, for example, the qualities of an accomplished courtier, we say he has the vanity of a peacock, the cunning of a fox, the treachery of an hyaena, the coldheartedness of a cat, and the servility of a jackal. That this is perfectly consentaneous to scientific truth, will appear in the further progress of these observations.

'Every particular faculty of the mind has its corresponding organ in the brain. In proportion as any particular faculty or propensity acquires paramount activity in any individual, these organs develop themselves, and their development becomes externally obvious by corresponding lumps and bumps, exuberances and protuberances, on the osseous compages of the occiput and sinciput. In all animals but man, the same organ is equally developed in every individual of the species: for instance, that of migration in the swallow, that of destruction in the tiger, that of architecture in the beaver, and that of parental affection in the bear. The human brain, however, consists, as I have said, of a bundle or compound of all the faculties of all other animals; and from the greater development of one or more of these, in the infinite varieties of combination, result all the peculiarities of individual character.

'Here is the skull of a beaver, and that of Sir Christopher Wren. You observe, in both these specimens, the prodigious development of the organ of constructiveness.

'Here is the skull of a bullfinch, and that of an eminent fiddler. You may compare the organ of music.

'Here is the skull of a tiger. You observe the organ of carnage. Here is the skull of a fox. You observe the organ of plunder. Here is the skull of a peacock. You observe the organ of vanity. Here is the skull of an illustrious robber, who, after a long and triumphant process of depredation and murder, was suddenly checked in his career by means of a certain quality inherent in preparations of hemp, which, for the sake of perspicuity, I shall call *suspensiveness*. Here is the skull of a

conqueror, who, after over-running several kingdoms, burning
a number of cities, and causing the deaths of two or three
millions of men, women, and children, was entombed with all
the pageantry of public lamentation, and figured as the hero of
several thousand odes and a round dozen of epics; while the
poor highwayman was twice executed —

> " At the gallows first, and after in a ballad,
>   Sung to a villanous tune."[1]

You observe, in both these skulls, the combined development
of the organs of carnage, plunder, and vanity, which I have
separately pointed out in the tiger, the fox, and the peacock.
The greater enlargement of the organ of vanity in the hero is
the only criterion by which I can distinguish them from each
other. Born with the same faculties, and the same propensities,
these two men were formed by nature to run the same career:
the different combinations of external circumstances decided
the differences of their destinies.

'Here is the skull of a Newfoundland dog. You observe the
organ of benevolence, and that of attachment. Here is a human
skull, in which you may observe a very striking negation of
both these organs; and an equally striking development of
those of destruction, cunning, avarice, and self-love. This was
one of the most illustrious statesmen that ever flourished in the
page of history.

'Here is the skull of a turnspit, which, after a wretched life
of *dirty work*, was turned out of doors to die on a dunghill.
I have been induced to preserve it, in consequence of its remarkable similarity to this, which belonged to a courtly poet,
who having grown grey in flattering the great, was cast off in
the same manner to perish by the same catastrophe.'

*After these, and several other illustrations, during which the skulls
were handed round for the inspection of the company, Mr Cranium
proceeded thus:*

'It is obvious, from what I have said, that no man can hope
for worldly honour or advancement, who is not placed in such
a relation to external circumstances as may be consentaneous
to his peculiar cerebral organs; and I would advise every
parent, who has the welfare of his son at heart, to procure as
extensive a collection as possible of the skulls of animals, and,
before determining on the choice of a profession, to compare
with the utmost nicety their bumps and protuberances with

those of the skull of his son. If the development of the organ of
destruction point out a similarity between the youth and the
tiger, let him be brought to some profession (whether that of a
butcher, a soldier, or a physician, may be regulated by circumstances) in which he may be furnished with a licence to kill:
as, without such licence, the indulgence of his natural propensity may lead to the untimely rescission of his vital thread,
"with edge of penny cord and vile reproach." [2] If he show an
analogy with the jackal, let all possible influence be used to
procure him a place at court, where he will infallibly thrive.
If his skull bear a marked resemblance to that of a magpie, it
cannot be doubted that he will prove an admirable lawyer; and
if with this advantageous conformation be combined any
similitude to that of an owl, very confident hopes may be
formed of his becoming a judge.'

A furious flourish of music was now heard from the ball-
room, the squire having secretly despatched the little butler to
order it to strike up, by way of a hint to Mr Cranium to finish
his harangue. The company took the hint and adjourned
tumultuously, having just understood as much of the lecture
as furnished them with amusement for the ensuing twelvemonth, in feeling the skulls of all their acquaintance.

CHAPTER XIII

THE BALL

THE BALL-ROOM was adorned with great taste and elegance,
under the direction of Miss Caprioletta and her friend Miss
Cephalis, who were themselves its most beautiful ornaments;
even though romantic Meirion,[1] the pre-eminent in loveliness,
sent many of its loveliest daughters to grace the festive scene.
Numberless were the solicitations of the dazzled swains of
Cambria for the honour of the two first dances with the one or
the other of these fascinating friends; but little availed, on this
occasion, the pedigree lineally traced from Caractacus[2] or
King Arthur: their two philosophical lovers, neither of whom
could have given the least account of his great-great-grand-
father, had engaged them many days before. Mr Panscope
chafed and fretted like Llugwy[3] in his bed of rocks, when
the object of his adoration stood up with his rival: but he

consoled himself with a lively damsel from the vale of Ed-eirnion, having first compelled Miss Cephalis to promise him her hand for the fourth set.

The ball was accordingly opened by Miss Caprioletta and Mr Foster, which gave rise to much speculation among the Welsh gentry, as to who this Mr Foster could be; some of the more learned among them secretly resolving to investigate most profoundly the antiquity of the name of Foster, and ascertain what right a person so denominated could have to open the most illustrious of all possible balls with the lovely Caprioletta Headlong, the only sister of Harry Headlong, Esquire, of Headlong Hall, in the Vale of Llanberris, the only surviving male representative of the antediluvian family of Headlong Ap-Rhaiader.

When the two first dances were ended, Mr Escot, who did not choose to dance with anyone but his adorable Cephalis, looking round for a convenient seat, discovered Mr Jenkison in a corner by the side of the Reverend Doctor Gaster, who was keeping excellent time with his nose to the lively melody of the harp and fiddle. Mr Escot seated himself by the side of Mr Jenkison, and inquired if he took no part in the amusement of the night?

MR JENKISON. No. The universal cheerfulness of the company induces me to rise; the trouble of such violent exercise induces me to sit still. Did I see a young lady in want of a partner, gallantry would incite me to offer myself as her devoted knight for half an hour: but, as I perceive there are enough without me, that motive is null. I have been weighing these points *pro* and *con*, and remain *in statu quo*.

MR ESCOT. I have danced, contrary to my system, as I have done many other things since I have been here, from a motive that you will easily guess. (*Mr Jenkison smiled.*) I have great objections to dancing. The wild and original man is a calm and contemplative animal. The stings of natural appetite alone rouse him to action. He satisfies his hunger with roots and fruits, unvitiated by the malignant adhibition of fire, and all its diabolical processes of elixion and assation[4]: he slakes his thirst in the mountain-streams, συμμισγεται τη επιτυχουση,[5] and returns to his peaceful state of meditative repose.

MR JENKISON. Like the metaphysical statue of Condillac.[6]

MR ESCOT. With all its senses and purely natural faculties developed, certainly. Imagine this tranquil and passionless being, occupied in his first meditation on the simple question of *Where am I? Whence do I come? And what is the end of my existence?* Then suddenly place before him a chandelier, a fiddler, and a magnificent beau in silk stockings and pumps, bounding, skipping, swinging, capering, and throwing himself into ten thousand attitudes, till his face glows with fever, and distils with perspiration: the first impulse excited in his mind by such an apparition will be that of violent fear, which, by the reiterated perception of its harmlessness, will subside into simple astonishment, Then let any genius, sufficiently powerful to impress on his mind all the terms of the communication, impart to him, that after a long process of ages, when his race shall have attained what some people think proper to denominate a very advanced stage of perfectibility, the most favoured and distinguished of the community shall meet by hundreds, to grin, and labour, and gesticulate, like the phantasma before him, from sunset to sunrise, while all nature is at rest, and that they shall consider this a happy and pleasurable mode of existence, and furnishing the most delightful of all possible contrasts to what they will call his vegetative state: would he not groan from his inmost soul for the lamentable condition of his posterity?

MR JENKISON. I know not what your wild and original man might think of the matter in the abstract; but comparatively, I conceive, he would be better pleased with the vision of such a scene as this, than with that of a party of Indians (who would have all the advantage of being nearly as wild as himself), dancing their infernal war-dance round a midnight fire in a North American forest.

MR ESCOT. Not if you should impart to him the true nature of both, by laying open to his view the springs of action in both parties.

MR JENKISON. To do this with effect, you must make him a profound metaphysician, and thus transfer him at once from his wild and original state to a very advanced stage of intellectual progression; whether that progression be towards good or evil, I leave you and our friend Foster to settle between you.

MR ESCOT. I wish to make no change in his habits and feelings, but to give him, hypothetically, so much mental illumination, as will enable him to take a clear view of two distinct stages of the deterioration of his posterity, that he may be enabled to compare them with each other, and with his own more happy condition. The Indian, dancing round the midnight fire, is very far deteriorated; but the magnificent beau, dancing to the light of chandeliers, is infinitely more so. The Indian is a hunter: he makes great use of fire, and subsists almost entirely on animal food. The malevolent passions that spring from these pernicious habits involve him in perpetual war. He is, therefore, necessitated, for his own preservation, to keep all the energies of his nature in constant activity: to this end his midnight war-dance is very powerfully subservient, and, though in itself a frightful spectacle, is at least justifiable on the iron plea of necessity.

MR JENKISON. On the same iron plea, the modern system of dancing is more justifiable. The Indian dances to prepare himself for killing his enemy: but while the beaux and belles of our assemblies dance, they are in the very act of killing theirs – TIME! – a more inveterate and formidable foe than any the Indian has to contend with; for, however completely and ingeniously killed, he is sure to rise again, 'with twenty mortal murders on his crown',[7] leading his army of blue devils,[8] with ennui in the van, and vapours in the rear.

MR ESCOT. Your observation militates on my side of the question; and it is a strong argument in favour of the Indian, that he has no such enemy to kill.

MR JENKISON. There is certainly a great deal to be said against dancing: there is also a great deal to be said in its favour. The first side of the question I leave for the present to you: on the latter, I may venture to allege that no amusement seems more natural and more congenial to youth than this. It has the advantage of bringing young persons of both sexes together, in a manner which its publicity renders perfectly unexceptionable, enabling them to see and know each other better than, perhaps, any other mode of general association. *Tête-à-têtes* are dangerous things. Small family parties are too much under mutual observation. A ball-room appears to me almost the only scene uniting that degree of rational and innocent liberty of intercourse, which it is desirable to promote as much as possible between young persons, with that scrupulous attention to the delicacy and propriety of female conduct, which I consider the fundamental basis of all our most valuable social relations.

MR ESCOT. There would be some plausibility in your argu-

ment, if it were not the very essence of this species of intercourse to exhibit them to each other under false colours. Here
all is show, and varnish, and hypocrisy, and coquetry; they
dress up their moral character for the evening at the same toilet
where they manufacture their shapes and faces. Ill-temper lies
buried under a studied accumulation of smiles. Envy, hatred,
and malice, retreat from the countenance, to entrench themselves more deeply in the heart. Treachery lurks under the
flowers of courtesy. Ignorance and folly take refuge in that
unmeaning gabble which it would be profanation to call
language, and which even those whom long experience in 'the
dreary intercourse of daily life' has screwed up to such a pitch
of stoical endurance that they can listen to it by the hour, have
branded with the ignominious appellation of '*small talk*'.
Small indeed! – the absolute minimum of the infinitely little.

MR JENKISON. Go on. I have said all I intended to say on
the favourable side. I shall have great pleasure in hearing you
balance the argument.

MR ESCOT. I expect you to confess that I shall have more
than balanced it. A ball-room is an epitome of all that is most
worthless and unamiable in the great sphere of human life.
Every petty and malignant passion is called into play. Coquetry is perpetually on the alert to captivate, caprice to
mortify, and vanity to take offence. One amiable female is
rendered miserable for the evening by seeing another, whom
she intended to outshine, in a more attractive dress than her
own; while the other omits no method of giving stings to her
triumph, which she enjoys with all the secret arrogance of an
oriental sultana. Another is compelled to dance with a *monster*
she abhors. A third has set her heart on dancing with a particular partner, perhaps for the amiable motive of annoying
one of her *dear friends*: not only he does not ask her, but she
sees him dancing with that identical *dear friend*, whom from
that moment she hates more cordially than ever. Perhaps, what
is worse than all, she has set her heart on refusing some impertinent fop, who does not give her the opportunity. – As to
the men, the case is very nearly the same with them. To be
sure, they have the privilege of making the first advances, and
are, therefore, less liable to have an odious partner forced
upon them; though this sometimes happens, as I know by
woful experience: but it is seldom they can procure the very
partner they prefer; and when they do, the absurd necessity of

changing every two dances forces them away, and leaves them only the miserable alternative of taking up with something disagreeable perhaps in itself, and at all events rendered so by contrast, or of retreating into some solitary corner, to vent their spleen on the first idle coxcomb they can find.

MR JENKISON. I hope that is not the motive which brings you to me.

MR ESCOT. Clearly not. But the most afflicting consideration of all is, that these malignant and miserable feelings are masked under that uniform disguise of pretended benevolence, *that fine and delicate irony, called politeness, which gives so much ease and pliability to the mutual intercourse of civilized man, and enables him to assume the appearance of every virtue, without the reality of one.**

The second set of dances was now terminated, and Mr Escot flew off to reclaim the hand of the beautiful Cephalis, with whom he figured away with surprising alacrity, and probably felt at least as happy among the chandeliers and silk stockings, at which he had just been railing, as he would have been in an American forest, making one in an Indian ring, by the light of a blazing fire, even though his hand had been locked in that of the most beautiful *squaw* that ever listened to the roar of Niagara.

Squire Headlong was now beset by his maiden aunt, Miss Brindle-mew Grimalkin Phoebe Tabitha Ap-Headlong, on one side, and Sir Patrick O'Prism on the other; the former insisting that he should immediately procure her a partner; the latter earnestly requesting the same interference in behalf of Miss Philomela Poppyseed. The squire thought to emancipate himself from his two petitioners by making them dance with each other; but Sir Patrick vehemently pleading a prior engagement, the squire threw his eyes around till they alighted on Mr Jenkison and the Reverend Doctor Gaster; both of whom, after waking the latter, he pressed into the service. The doctor, arising with a strange kind of guttural sound, which was half a yawn and half a groan, was handed by the officious squire to Miss Philomela, who received him with sullen dignity: she had not yet forgotten his falling asleep during the first chapter of her novel, while she was condescending to detail to him the outlines of four superlative volumes. The doctor, on his part, had most completely forgotten it; and though he thought

* Rousseau, *Discours sur les Sciences*. [P.]

there was something in her physiognomy rather more forbidding than usual, he gave himself no concern about the cause, and had not the least suspicion that it was at all connected with himself. Miss Brindle-mew was very well contented with Mr Jenkison, and gave him two or three ogles, accompanied by a most risible distortion of the countenance which she intended for a captivating smile. As to Mr Jenkison, it was all one to him with whom he danced, or whether he danced or not: he was therefore just as well pleased as if he had been left alone in his corner; which is probably more than could have been said of any other human being under similar circumstances.

At the end of the third set, supper was announced; and the party, pairing off like turtles, adjourned to the supper-room. The squire was now the happiest of mortal men, and the little butler the most laborious. The centre of the largest table was decorated with a model of Snowdon, surmounted with an enormous artificial leek, the leaves of angelica, and the bulb of blanc-mange. A little way from the summit was a tarn, or mountain-pool, supplied through concealed tubes with an inexhaustible flow of milk-punch, which, dashing in cascades down the miniature rocks, fell into the more capacious lake below, washing the mimic foundations of Headlong Hall. The reverend doctor handed Miss Philomela to the chair most conveniently situated for enjoying this interesting scene, protesting he had never before been sufficiently impressed with the magnificence of that mountain, which he now perceived to be well worthy of all the fame it had obtained.

'Now, when they had eaten and were satisfied,' Squire Headlong called on Mr Chromatic for a song; who, with the assistance of his two accomplished daughters, regaled the ears of the company with the following

TERZETTO*

Grey Twilight, from her shadowy hill,
    Discolours Nature's vernal blood,
And shed on grove, and field, and rill,
    One placid tint of deepening gloom.

* Imitated from a passage in the *Purgatorio* of Dante. [P.]

The sailor sighs 'mid shoreless seas,
    Touched by the thought of friends afar,
As, fanned by ocean's flowing breeze,
    He gazes on the western star.

The wanderer hears, in pensive dream,
    The accents of the last farewell,
As, pausing by the mountain stream,
    He listens to the evening bell.

This terzetto was of course much applauded; Mr Milestone observing, that he thought the figure in the last verse would have been more picturesque, if it had been represented with its arms folded and its back against a tree; or leaning on its staff, with a cockle-shell in its hat, like a pilgrim of ancient times.

Mr Chromatic professed himself astonished that a gentleman of genuine modern taste, like Mr Milestone, should consider the words of a song of any consequence whatever, seeing that they were at the best only a species of pegs, for the more convenient suspension of crochets and quavers. This remark drew on him a very severe reprimand from Mr Mac Laurel, who said to him, 'Dinna ye ken, sir, that soond is a thing utterly worthless in itsel, and only effectual in agreeable excitements, as far as it is an aicho to sense? Is there ony soond mair meeserable an' peetifu' than the scrape o' a feddle, when it does na touch ony chord i' the human sensorium? Is there ony mair divine than the deep note o' a bagpipe, when it breathes the auncient meelodies o' leeberty an' love? It is true, there are peculiar trains o' feeling an' sentiment, which parteecular combinations o' meelody are calculated to excite; an' sae far music can produce its effect without words: but it does na follow, that, when ye put words to it, it becomes a matter of indefference what they are; for a gude strain of impassioned poetry will greatly increase the effect, and a tessue o' nonsensical doggrel will destroy it a' thegither. Noo, as gude poetry can produce its effect without music, sae will gude music without poetry; and as gude music will be mair pooerfu' by itsel' than wi' bad poetry, sae will gude poetry than wi' bad music: but, when ye put gude music an' gude poetry thegither, ye produce the divinest compound o' sentimental harmony that can possibly find its way through the lug to the saul.'

Mr Chromatic admitted that there was much justice in these

observations, but still maintained the subserviency of poetry to music. Mr Mac Laurel as strenuously maintained the contrary; and a furious war of words was proceeding to perilous lengths, when the squire interposed his authority towards the reproduction of peace, which was forthwith concluded, and all animosities drowned in a libation of milk-punch, the Reverend Doctor Gaster officiating as high priest on the occasion.

Mr Chromatic now requested Miss Caprioletta to favour the company with an air. The young lady immediately complied and sung the following simple

BALLAD

'O Mary, my sister, thy sorrow give o'er,
I soon shall return, girl, and leave thee no more:
But with children so fair, and a husband so kind,
I shall feel less regret when I leave thee behind.

'I have made thee a bench for the door of thy cot,
And more would I give thee, but more I have not:
Sit and think of me there, in the warm summer day,
And give me three kisses, my labour to pay.'

She gave him three kisses, and forth did he fare,
And long did he wander, and no one knew where;
And long from her cottage, through sunshine and rain,
She watched his return, but he came not again.

Her children grew up, and her husband grew grey;
She sate on the bench through the long summer day:
One evening, when twilight was deep on the shore,
There came an old soldier, and stood by the door.

In English he spoke, and none knew what he said,
But her oatcake and milk on the table she spread;
Then he sate to his supper, and blithely he sung,
And she knew the dear sounds of her own native tongue:

'O rich are the feasts in the Englishman's hall,
And the wine sparkles bright in the goblets of Gaul:
But their mingled attractions I well could withstand,
For the milk and the oatcake of Meirion's dear land.'

'And art thou a Welshman, old soldier?' she cried.
'Many years have I wandered,' the stranger replied:
''Twixt Danube and Thames many rivers there be,
But the bright waves of Cynfael are fairest to me.

'I felled the grey oak, ere I hastened to roam,
And I fashioned a bench for the door of my home;
And well my dear sister my labour repaid,
Who gave me three kisses when first it was made.

'In the old English soldier thy brother appears:
Here is gold in abundance, the saving of years:
Give me oatcake and milk in return for my store,
And a seat by thy side on the bench at the door.'

Various other songs succeeded, which, as we are not composing a song book, we shall lay aside for the present.

An old squire, who had not missed one of these anniver-
saries, during more than half a century, now stood up, and
filling a half-pint bumper, pronounced, with a stentorian
voice – 'To the immortal memory of Headlong Ap-Rhaiader,
and to the health of his noble descendant and worthy representative!' This example was followed by all the gentlemen
present. The harp struck up a triumphal strain; and, the old
squire already mentioned vociferating the first stave, they
sang, or rather roared, the following

CHORUS

Hail to the Headlong! the Headlong Ap-Headlong!
All hail to the Headlong, the Headlong Ap-Headlong!
    The Headlong Ap-Headlong
    Ap-Breakneck Ap-Headlong
Ap-Cataract Ap-Pistyll Ap-Rhaiader Ap-Headlong!

The bright bowl we steep in the name of the Headlong:
Let the youths pledge it deep to the Headlong Ap-Headlong,
    And the rosy-lipped lasses
    Touch the brim as it passes,
And kiss the red tide for the Headlong Ap-Headlong!

The loud harp resounds in the hall of the Headlong:
The light step rebounds in the hall of the Headlong:
    Where shall music invite us,
    Or beauty delight us,
If not in the hall of the Headlong Ap-Headlong?

Huzza! to the health of the Headlong Ap-Headlong!
Fill the bowl, fill in floods, to the health of the Headlong!
    Till the stream ruby-glowing,
      On all sides o'erflowing,
Shall fall in cascades to the health of the Headlong!
    The Headlong Ap-Headlong
    Ap-Breakneck Ap-Headlong
Ap-Cataract Ap-Pistyll Ap-Rhaiader Ap-Headlong!

Squire Headlong returned thanks with an appropriate libation, and the company re-adjourned to the ball-room, where
they kept it up till sun-rise, when the little butler summoned
them to breakfast.

CHAPTER XIV

THE PROPOSALS

THE CHORUS, which celebrated the antiquity of her lineage,
had been ringing all night in the ears of Miss Brindle-mew
Grimalkin Phoebe Tabitha Ap-Headlong, when, taking the
squire aside, while the visitors were sipping their tea and
coffee, 'Nephew Harry,' said she, 'I have been noting your
behaviour, during the several stages of the ball and supper;
and, though I cannot tax you with any want of gallantry, for
you are a very gallant young man, nephew Harry, very gallant – I wish I could say as much for everyone' (added she,
throwing a spiteful look towards a distant corner, where Mr
Jenkison was sitting with great *nonchalance*, and at the moment
dipping a rusk in a cup of chocolate); 'but I lament to perceive
that you were at least as pleased with your lakes of milk-
punch, and your bottles of Champagne and Burgundy, as with
any of your delightful partners. Now, though I can readily
excuse this degree of incombustibility in the descendant of a
family so remarkable in all ages for personal beauty as ours,
yet I lament it exceedingly, when I consider that, in conjunction with your present predilection for the easy life of a
bachelor, it may possibly prove the means of causing our
ancient genealogical tree, which has its roots, if I may so
speak, in the foundations of the world, to terminate suddenly
in a point: unless you feel yourself moved by my exhortations

to follow the example of all your ancestors, by choosing your-self a fitting and suitable helpmate to immortalise the pedigree of Headlong Ap-Rhaiader.'

'Egad!' said Squire Headlong, 'that is very true. I'll marry directly. A good opportunity to fix on someone, now they are all here; and I'll pop the question without further ceremony.'

'What think you,' said the old lady, 'of Miss Nanny Glyn-Du, the lineal descendant of Llewelyn Ap Yorwerth?'

'She won't do,' said Squire Headlong.

'What say you, then,' said the lady, 'to Miss Williams, of Pontyglasrhydyrallt, the descendant of the ancient family of ——?'

'I don't like her,' said Squire Headlong; 'and as to her ancient family, that is a matter of no consequence. I have anti-quity enough for two. They are all moderns, people of yester-day, in comparison with us. What signify six or seven centuries, which are the most they can make up?'

'Why, to be sure,' said the aunt, 'on that view of the ques-tion, it is of no consequence. What think you, then, of Miss Owen, of Nidd-y-Gygfraen? She will have six thousand a year.'

'I would not have her,' said Squire Headlong, 'if she had fifty. I'll think of somebody presently. I should like to be married on the same day with Caprioletta.'

'Caprioletta!' said Miss Brindle-mew; 'without my being consulted!'

'Consulted!' said the squire: 'I was commissioned to tell you, but somehow or other I let it slip. However, she is going to be married to my friend Mr Foster, the philosopher.'

'Oh!' said the maiden aunt, 'that a daughter of our ancient family should marry a philosopher! It is enough to make the bones of all the Ap-Rhaiaders turn in their graves!'

'I happen to be more enlightened,' said Squire Headlong, 'than any of my ancestors were. Besides, it is Caprioletta's affair, not mine. I tell you, the matter is settled, fixed, deter-mined; and so am I, to be married on the same day. I don't know, now I think of it, whom I can choose than one of the daughters of my friend Chromatic.'

'A Saxon!' said the aunt, turning up her nose, and was commencing a vehement remonstrance; but the squire, ex-claiming 'Music has charms!' flew over to Mr Chromatic, and, with a hearty slap on the shoulder, asked him 'how he should like him for a son-in-law?' Mr Chromatic, rubbing his shoulder, and highly delighted with the proposal, answered, 'Very much indeed': but, proceeding to ascertain which of his daughters had captivated the squire, the squire demurred, and was unable to satisfy his curiosity. 'I hope,' said Mr Chromatic, 'it may be Tenorina; for I imagine Graziosa has conceived a *penchant* for Sir Patrick O'Prism.' — 'Tenorina, exactly,' said Squire Headlong; and became so impatient to bring the matter to a conclusion, that Mr Chromatic undertook to communicate with his daughter immediately. The young lady proved to be as ready as the squire, and the preliminaries were arranged in little more than five minutes.

Mr Chromatic's words, that he imagined his daughter Graziosa had conceived a *penchant* for Sir Patrick O'Prism, were not lost on the squire, who at once determined to have as many companions in the scrape as possible, and who, as soon as he could tear himself from Mrs Headlong elect, took three flying bounds across the room to the baronet, and said, 'So, Sir Patrick, I find you and I are going to be married?'

'Are we?' said Sir Patrick: 'then sure won't I wish you joy, and myself too? for this is the first I have heard of it.'

'Well,' said Squire Headlong, 'I have made up my mind to it, and you must not disappoint me.'

'To be sure I won't, if I can help it,' said Sir Patrick; 'and I am very much obliged to you for taking so much trouble off my hands. And pray, now, who is it that I am to be metamorphosing into Lady O'Prism?'

'Miss Graziosa Chromatic,' said the squire.

'Och violet and vermilion!' said Sir Patrick; 'though I never thought of it before, I dare say she will suit me as well as another: but then you must persuade the ould Orpheus to draw out a few *notes* of rather a more magical description than those he is so fond of scraping on his crazy violin.'

'To be sure he shall,' said the squire; and, immediately returning to Mr Chromatic, concluded the negotiation for Sir Patrick as expeditiously as he had done for himself.

The squire next addressed himself to Mr Escot: 'Here are three couple of us going to throw off together, with the Reverend Doctor Gaster for whipper-in: now, I think you cannot do better than make the fourth with Miss Cephalis; and then, as my father-in-law that is to be would say, we shall compose a very harmonious octave.'

'Indeed,' said Mr Escot, 'nothing would be more agreeable to both of us than such an arrangement: but the old gentleman, since I first knew him, has changed, like the rest of the world, very lamentably for the worse: now, we wish to bring him to reason, if possible, though we mean to dispense with his consent, if he should prove much longer refractory.'

'I'll settle him,' said Squire Headlong; and immediately posted up to Mr Cranium, informing him that four marriages were about to take place by way of a merry winding up of the Christmas festivities.

'Indeed!' said Mr Cranium; 'and who are the parties?'

'In the first place,' said the squire, 'my sister and Mr Foster: in the second, Miss Graziosa Chromatic and Sir Patrick O'Prism: in the third, Miss Tenorina Chromatic and your humble servant: and in the fourth – to which, by the by, your consent is wanted —'

'Oho!' said Mr Cranium.

'Your daughter,' said Squire Headlong.

'And Mr Panscope?' said Mr Cranium.

'And Mr Escot,' said Squire Headlong. 'What would you have better? He has ten thousand virtues.'

'So has Mr Panscope,' said Mr Cranium; 'he has ten thousand a year.'

'Virtues?' said Squire Headlong.

'Pounds,' said Mr Cranium.

'I have set my mind on Mr Escot,' said the squire.

'I am much obliged to you,' said Mr Cranium, 'for dethroning me from my paternal authority.'

'Who fished you out of the water?' said Squire Headlong.

'What is that to the purpose?' said Mr Cranium. 'The whole process of the action was mechanical and necessary. The application of the poker necessitated the ignition of the powder: the ignition necessitated the explosion: the explosion necessitated my sudden fright, which necessitated my sudden jump, which, from a necessity equally powerful, was in a curvilinear ascent: the descent, being in a corresponding curve, and commencing at a point perpendicular to the extreme line of the edge of the tower, I was, by the necessity of gravitation, attracted, first, through the ivy, and secondly through the hazel, and thirdly through the ash, into the water beneath. The motive or impulse thus adhibited in the person of a drowning man, was as powerful on his material compages as the force of gravitation on mine; and he could no more help jumping into the water than I could help falling into it.'

'All perfectly true,' said Squire Headlong; 'and, on the same principle, you make no distinction between the man who knocks you down and him who picks you up.'

'I make this distinction,' said Mr Cranium, 'that I avoid the former as a machine containing a peculiar *cataballitive*[1] quality, which I have found to be not consentaneous to my mode of pleasurable existence; but I attach no moral merit or demerit to either of them, as these terms are usually employed, seeing that they are equally creatures of necessity, and must act as they do from the nature of their organization. I no more blame or praise a man for what is called vice or virtue, than I tax a tuft of hemlock with malevolence, or discover great philanthropy in a field of potatoes, seeing that the men and the plants are equally incapacitated, by their original internal organization, and the combinations and modifications of external circumstances, from being anything but what they are. *Quod victus fateare necesse est.*'[2]

'Yet you destroy the hemlock,' said Squire Headlong, 'and cultivate the potatoe: that is my way, at least.'

'I do,' said Mr Cranium; 'because I know that the farinaceous qualities of the potatoe will tend to preserve the great requisites of unity and coalescence in the various constituent portions of my animal republic; and that the hemlock, if gathered by mistake for parsley, chopped up small with butter, and eaten with a boiled chicken, would necessitate a great derangement, and perhaps a total decomposition, of my corporeal mechanism.'

'Very well,' said the squire; 'then you are necessitated to like Mr Escot better than Mr Panscope?'

'That is a *non sequitur*,' said Mr Cranium.

'Then this is a *sequitur*,' said the squire: 'your daughter and Mr Escot are necessitated to love one another; and, unless you feel necessitated to adhibit your consent, they will feel necessitated to dispense with it; since it does appear to moral and political economists to be essentially inherent in the eternal fitness of things.'

Mr Cranium fell into a profound reverie: emerging from which, he said, looking Squire Headlong full in the face, 'Do you think Mr Escot would give me that skull?'

'Skull!' said Squire Headlong.

'Yes,' said Mr Cranium, 'the skull of Cadwallader.'

'To be sure he will,' said the squire.

'Ascertain the point,' said Mr Cranium.

'How can you doubt it?' said the squire.

'I simply know,' said Mr Cranium, 'that if it were once in my possession, I would not part with it for any acquisition on earth, much less for a wife. I have had one: and, as marriage has been compared to a pill, I can very safely assert that *one is a dose*: and my reason for thinking that he will not part with it is, that its extraordinary magnitude tends to support his system, as much as its very marked protuberances tend to support mine; and you know his own system is of all things the dearest to every man of liberal thinking and a philosophical tendency.'

The squire flew over to Mr Escot. 'I told you,' said he, 'I would settle him: but there is a very hard condition attached to his compliance.'

'I submit to it,' said Mr Escot, 'be it what it may.'

'Nothing less,' said Squire Headlong, 'than the absolute and unconditional surrender of the skull of Cadwallader.'

'I resign it,' said Mr Escot.

'The skull is yours,' said the squire, skipping over to Mr Cranium.

'I am perfectly satisfied,' said Mr Cranium.

'The lady is yours,' said the squire, skipping back to Mr Escot.

'I am the happiest man alive,' said Mr Escot.

'Come,' said the squire, 'then there is an amelioration in the state of the sensitive man.'

'A slight oscillation of good in the instance of a solitary individual,' answered Mr Escot, 'by no means affects the solidity of my opinions concerning the general deterioration of the civilized world; which when I can be induced to contemplate with feelings of satisfaction, I doubt not but that I may be persuaded *to be in love with tortures, and to think charitably of the rack*.'*

Saying these words, he flew off as nimbly as Squire Headlong himself, to impart the happy intelligence to his beautiful Cephalis.

Mr Cranium now walked up to Mr Panscope, to condole with him on the disappointment of their mutual hopes. Mr Panscope begged him not to distress himself on the subject, observing, that the monotonous system of female education

* Jeremy Taylor. [P.]

brought every individual of the sex to so remarkable an approximation of similarity, that no wise man would suffer himself to be annoyed by a loss so easily repaired; and that there was much truth, though not much elegance, in a remark which he had heard made on a similar occasion by a post-captain of his acquaintance, 'that there never was a fish taken out of the sea, but left another as good behind.'

Mr Cranium replied, that no two individuals having all the organs of the skull similarly developed, the universal resemblance of which Mr Panscope had spoken could not possibly exist. Mr Panscope rejoined; and a long discussion ensued, concerning the comparative influence of natural organization and artificial education, in which the beautiful Cephalis was totally lost sight of, and which ended, as most controversies do, by each party continuing firm in his own opinion, and professing his profound astonishment at the blindness and prejudices of the other.

In the meanwhile, a great confusion had arisen at the outer doors, the departure of the ball-visitors being impeded by a circumstance which the experience of ages had discovered no means to obviate. The grooms, coachmen, and postillions, were all drunk. It was proposed that the gentlemen should officiate in their places: but the gentlemen were almost all in the same condition. This was a fearful dilemma: but a very diligent investigation brought to light a few servants and a few gentlemen not above *half-seas-over*; and by an equitable distribution of these rarities, the greater part of the guests were enabled to set forward, with very nearly an even chance of not having their necks broken before they reached home.

CHAPTER XV

THE CONCLUSION

THE SQUIRE AND his select party of philosophers and dilettanti were again left in peaceful possession of Headlong Hall: and, as the former made a point of never losing a moment in the accomplishment of a favourite object, he did not suffer many days to elapse, before the spiritual metamorphosis of eight into four was effected by the clerical dexterity of the Reverend Doctor Gaster.

Immediately after the ceremony, the whole party dispersed, the squire having first extracted from every one of his chosen guests a positive promise to re-assemble in August, when they would be better enabled, in its most appropriate season, to form a correct judgement of Cambrian hospitality.

Mr Jenkison shook hands at parting with his two brother philosophers. 'According to your respective systems,' said he, 'I ought to congratulate *you* on a change for the better, which I do most cordially: and to condole with *you* on a change for the worse, though, when I consider whom you have chosen, I should violate every principle of probability in doing so.'

'You will do well,' said Mr Foster, 'to follow our example. The extensive circle of general philanthropy, which, in the present advanced stage of human nature, comprehends in its circumference the destinies of the whole species, originated, and still proceeds, from that narrower circle of domestic affection, which first set limits to the empire of selfishness, and, by purifying the passions and enlarging the affections of mankind, has given to the views of benevolence an increasing and illimitable expansion, which will finally diffuse happiness and peace over the whole surface of the world.'

'The affection,' said Mr Escot, 'of two congenial spirits, united not by legal bondage and superstitious imposture, but by mutual confidence and reciprocal virtues, is the only counterbalancing consolation in this scene of mischief and misery. But how rarely is this the case according to the present system of marriage! So far from being a central point of expansion to the great circle of universal benevolence, it serves only to concentrate the feelings of natural sympathy in the reflected selfishness of family interest, and to substitute for the *humani nihil alienum puto*[1] of youthful philanthropy, the *charity begins at home* of maturer years. And what accession of individual happiness is acquired by this oblivion of the general good? Luxury, despotism, and avarice have so seized and entangled nine hundred and ninety-nine out of every thousand of the human race, that the matrimonial compact, which ought to be the most easy, the most free, and the most simple of all engagements, is become the most slavish and complicated – a mere question of finance – a system of bargain, and barter, and commerce, and trick, and chicanery, and dissimulation, and fraud. Is there one instance in ten thousand, in which the buds of first affection are not most cruelly and hopelessly blasted, by avarice, or ambition, or arbitrary power? Females, condemned during the whole flower of their youth to a worse than monastic celibacy, irrevocably debarred from the hope to which their first affections pointed, will, at a certain period of life, as the natural delicacy of taste and feeling is gradually worn away by the attrition of society, become willing to take up with any coxcomb or scoundrel, whom that merciless and mercenary gang of cold-blooded slaves and assassins, called, in the ordinary prostitution of language *friends*, may agree in designating as a *prudent choice*. Young men, on the other hand, are driven by the same vile superstitions from the company of the most amiable and modest of the opposite sex, to that of those miserable victims and outcasts of a world which dares to call itself virtuous, whom that very society whose pernicious institutions first caused their aberrations – consigning them, without one tear of pity or one struggle of remorse, to penury, infamy, and disease – condemns to bear the burden of its own atrocious absurdities! Thus, the youth of one sex is consumed in slavery, disappointment, and spleen: that of the other, in frantic folly and selfish intemperance: till at length, on the necks of a couple so enfeebled, so perverted, so distempered both in body and soul, society throws the yoke of marriage: that yoke which, once rivetted on the necks of its victims, clings to them like the poisoned garments of Nessus or Medea.[2] What can be expected from these ill-assorted yoke-fellows, but that, like two ill-tempered hounds, coupled by a tyrannical sportsman, they should drag on their indissoluble fetter, snarling and growling, and pulling in different directions? What can be expected for their wretched offspring, but sickness and suffering, premature decrepitude, and untimely death? In this, as in every other institution of civilized society, avarice, luxury, and disease constitute the TRIANGULAR HARMONY of the life of man. Avarice conducts him to the abyss of toil and crime; luxury seizes on his ill-gotten spoil; and, while he revels in her enchantments, or groans beneath her tyranny, disease bursts upon him, and sweeps him from the earth.'

'Your theory,' said Mr Jenkison, 'forms an admirable counterpoise to your example. As far as I am attracted by the one, I am repelled by the other. Thus, the scales of my philosophical balance remain eternally equiponderant, and I see no reason to say of either of them, *ΟΙΧΕΤΑΙ ΕΙΣ ΑΪΔΑΟ*.'*

* *It descends to the shades*: or, in other words, *it goes to the devil*. [P.]

NIGHTMARE
ABBEY

There's a dark lantern of the spirit,
Which none see by but those who bear it,
That makes them in the dark see visions
And hag themselves with apparitions,
Find racks for their own minds, and vaunt
Of their own misery and want. BUTLER

Nightmare Abbey was first published in 1818

Matthew. Oh! it's your only fine humour, sir. Your true melancholy breeds your perfect fine wit, sir. I am melancholy myself, divers times, sir; and then do I no more but take pen and paper presently, and overflow you half a score or a dozen of sonnets at a sitting.

Stephen. Truly, sir, and I love such things out of measure.

Matthew. Why, I pray you, sir, make use of my study: it's at your service.

Stephen. I thank you, sir, I shall be bold, I warrant you. Have you a stool there, to be melancholy upon?

Ben Jonson, *Every man in his Humour*,

A. 3, Sc. 1.

Ay esleu gazouiller et siffler oye, comme dit le commun proverbe, entre les cygnes, plutoust que d'estre entre tant de gentils poëtes et faconds orateurs mut du tout estimé. – RABELAIS, *Prol. L.* 5.[1]

CHAPTER I

NIGHTMARE ABBEY, a venerable family-mansion, in a highly picturesque state of semi-dilapidation, pleasantly situated on a strip of dry land between the sea and the fens, at the verge of the county of Lincoln, had the honour to be the seat of Christopher Glowry, Esquire. This gentleman was naturally of an atrabilarious temperament, and much troubled with those phantoms of indigestion which are commonly called *blue devils*.[2] He had been deceived in an early friendship: he had been crossed in love; and had offered his hand, from pique, to a lady, who accepted it from interest, and who, in so doing, violently tore asunder the bonds of a tried and youthful attachment. Her vanity was gratified by being the mistress of a very extensive, if not very lively, establishment; but all the springs of her sympathies were frozen. Riches she possessed, but that which enriches them, the participation of affection, was wanting. All that they could purchase for her became indifferent to her, because that which they could not purchase, and which was more valuable than themselves, she had, for their sake, thrown away. She discovered, when it was too late, that she had mistaken the means for the end – that riches, rightly used, are instruments of happiness, but are not in themselves happiness. In this wilful blight of her affections, she found them valueless as means: they had been the end to which she had immolated all her affections, and were now the only end that remained to her. She did not confess this to herself as a principle of action, but it operated through the medium of unconscious self-deception, and terminated in inveterate avarice. She laid on external things the blame of her mind's internal disorder, and thus became by degrees an accomplished scold. She often went her daily rounds through a series of deserted apartments, every creature in the house vanishing at the creak of her shoe, much more at the sound of her voice, to which the nature of things affords no simile; for, as far as the voice of woman, when attuned by gentleness and love, transcends all other sounds in harmony, so far does it surpass all others in discord, when stretched into unnatural shrillness by anger and impatience.

Mr Glowry used to say that his house was no better than a spacious kennel, for every one in it led the life of a dog. Disappointed both in love and in friendship, and looking upon human learning as vanity, he had come to a conclusion that there was but one good thing in the world, *videlicet*, a good dinner; and this his parsimonious lady seldom suffered him to enjoy: but, one morning, like Sir Leoline in Christabel,[3] 'he woke and found his lady dead', and remained a very consolate widower, with one small child.

This only son and heir Mr Glowry had christened Scythrop,[4] from the name of a maternal ancestor, who had hanged himself one rainy day in a fit of *taedium vitae*, and had been eulogized by a coroner's jury in the comprehensive phrase of *felo de se*; on which account, Mr Glowry held his memory in high honour, and made a punchbowl of his skull.

When Scythrop grew up, he was sent, as usual, to a public school, where a little learning was painfully beaten into him, and from thence to the university, where it was carefully taken out of him; and he was sent home like a well-threshed ear of corn, with nothing in his head: having finished his education to the high satisfaction of the master and fellows of his college, who had, in testimony of their approbation, presented him with a silver fish-slice, on which his name figured at the head of a laudatory inscription in some semi-barbarous dialect of Anglo-Saxonized Latin.

His fellow-students, however, who drove tandem and random[5] in great perfection, and were connoisseurs in good inns, had taught him to drink deep ere he departed. He had passed much of his time with these choice spirits, and had seen the rays of the midnight lamp tremble on many a lengthening file of empty bottles. He passed his vacations sometimes at Nightmare Abbey, sometimes in London, at the house of his uncle, Mr Hilary, a very cheerful and elastic gentleman, who had married the sister of the melancholy Mr Glowry. The company that frequented his house was the gayest of the gay. Scythrop danced with the ladies and drank with the gentlemen, and was pronounced by both a very accomplished charming fellow, and an honour to the university.

At the house of Mr Hilary, Scythrop first saw the beautiful

Miss Emily Girouette. He fell in love; which is nothing new. He was favourably received; which is nothing strange. Mr Glowry and Mr Girouette had a meeting on the occasion, and quarrelled about the terms of the bargain; which is neither new nor strange. The lovers were torn asunder, weeping and vowing everlasting constancy; and, in three weeks after this tragical event, the lady was led a smiling bride to the altar, by the Honourable Mr Lackwit; which is neither strange nor new.

Scythrop received this intelligence at Nightmare Abbey, and was half distracted on the occasion. It was his first disappointment, and preyed deeply on his sensitive spirit. His father, to comfort him, read him a Commentary on Ecclesiastes, which he had himself composed, and which demonstrated incontrovertibly that all is vanity. He insisted particularly on the text, 'One man among a thousand have I found, but a woman amongst all those have I not found.'

'How could he expect it,' said Scythrop, 'when the whole thousand were locked up in his seraglio?[6] His experience is no precedent for a free state of society like that in which we live.'

'Locked up or at large,' said Mr Glowry, 'the result is the same: their minds are always locked up, and vanity and interest keep the key. I speak feelingly, Scythrop.'

'I am sorry for it, sir,' said Scythrop. 'But how is it that their minds are locked up? The fault is in their artificial education, which studiously models them into mere musical dolls, to be set out for sale in the great toy-shop of society.'

'To be sure,' said Mr Glowry, 'their education is not so well finished as yours has been; and your idea of a musical doll is good. I bought one myself, but it was confoundedly out of tune; but, whatever be the cause, Scythrop, the effect is certainly this, that one is pretty nearly as good as another, as far as any judgement can be formed of them before marriage. It is only after marriage that they show their true qualities, as I know by bitter experience. Marriage is, therefore, a lottery, and the less choice and selection a man bestows on his ticket the better; for, if he has incurred considerable pains and expense to obtain a lucky number, and his lucky number proves a blank, he experiences not a simple, but a complicated disappointment; the loss of labour and money being superadded to the disappointment of drawing a blank, which, constituting simply and entirely the grievance of him who has chosen his

ticket at random, is, from its simplicity, the more endurable.'
This very excellent reasoning was thrown away upon Scythrop,
who retired to his tower as dismal and disconsolate as before.

The tower which Scythrop inhabited stood at the south-
eastern angle of the Abbey; and, on the southern side, the foot
of the tower opened on a terrace, which was called the garden,
though nothing grew on it but ivy, and a few amphibious
weeds. The southwestern tower, which was ruinous and full
of owls, might, with equal propriety, have been called the
aviary. This terrace or garden, or terrace-garden, or garden-
terrace (the reader may name it *ad libitum*), took in an oblique
view of the open sea, and fronted a long tract of level sea-
coast, and a fine monotony of fens and windmills.

The reader will judge, from what we have said, that this
building was a sort of castellated abbey; and it will, probably,
occur to him to inquire if it had been one of the strong-holds
of the ancient church militant. Whether this was the case, or
how far it had been indebted to the taste of Mr Glowry's
ancestors for any transmutations from its original state, are,
unfortunately, circumstances not within the pale of our
knowledge.

The northwestern tower contained the apartments of Mr
Glowry. The moat at its base, and the fens beyond, comprised
the whole of his prospect. This moat surrounded the Abbey,
and was in immediate contact with the walls on every side but
the south.

The northeastern tower was appropriated to the domestics,
whom Mr Glowry always chose by one of two criterions – a
long face, or a dismal name. His butler was Raven; his
steward was Crow; his valet was Skellet. Mr Glowry maintained that the valet was of French extraction, and that his
name was Squelette. His grooms were Mattocks and Graves.
On one occasion, being in want of a footman, he received a
letter from a person signing himself Diggory Deathshead, and
lost no time in securing this acquisition; but on Diggory's
arrival, Mr Glowry was horror-struck by the sight of a round
ruddy face, and a pair of laughing eyes. Deathshead was always
grinning – not a ghastly smile, but the grin of a comic mask;
and disturbed the echoes of the hall with so much unhallowed
laughter, that Mr Glowry gave him his discharge. Diggory,
however, had staid long enough to make conquests of all the
old gentleman's maids, and left him a flourishing colony of

young Deathsheads to join chorus with the owls, that had before been the exclusive choristers of Nightmare Abbey.

The main body of the building was divided into rooms of state, spacious apartments for feasting, and numerous bed-rooms for visitors, who, however, were few and far between.

Family interests compelled Mr Glowry to receive occasional visits from Mr and Mrs Hilary, who paid them from the same motive; and, as the lively gentleman on these occasions found few conductors for his exuberant gaiety, he became like a double-charged electric jar, which often exploded in some burst of outrageous merriment to the signal discomposure of Mr Glowry's nerves.

Another occasional visitor, much more to Mr Glowry's taste, was Mr Flosky,* a very lachrymose and morbid gentle-man, of some note in the literary world, but in his own estimation of much more merit than name. The part of his character which recommended him to Mr Glowry, was his very fine sense of the grim and the tearful. No one could relate a dismal story with so many minutiae of supererogatory wretchedness. No one could call up a *raw-head and bloody-bones* with so many adjuncts and circumstances of ghastliness. Mystery was his mental element. He lived in the midst of that visionary world in which nothing is but what is not. He dreamed with his eyes open, and saw ghosts dancing round him at noontide. He had been in his youth an enthusiast for liberty, and had hailed the dawn of the French Revolution as the promise of a day that was to banish war and slavery, and every form of vice and misery, from the face of the earth. Because all this was not done, he deduced that nothing was done; and from this deduction, according to his system of logic, he drew a conclusion that worse than nothing was done; that the overthrow of the feudal fortresses of tyranny and superstition was the greatest calamity that had ever befallen mankind; and that their only hope now was to rake the rub-bish together, and rebuild it without any of those loopholes by which the light had originally crept in. To qualify himself for a coadjutor in this laudable task, he plunged into the central opacity of Kantian metaphysics, and lay *perdu*[8] several years in transcendental darkness, till the common daylight of common sense became intolerable to his eyes. He called the

* A *corruption* of Filosky, quasi Φιλοσκιος, a lover, or sectator, of shadows. [P.][7]

sun an *ignis fatuus*;[9] and exhorted all who would listen to his
friendly voice, which were about as many as called 'God save
King Richard',[10] to shelter themselves from its delusive
radiance in the obscure haunt of Old Philosophy. This word
Old had great charms for him. The good old times were always on his lips; meaning the days when polemic theology[11]
was in its prime, and rival prelates beat the drum ecclesiastic
with Herculean vigour, till the one wound up his series of
syllogisms with the very orthodox conclusion of roasting the
other.

But the dearest friend of Mr Glowry, and his most welcome
guest, was Mr Toobad, the Manichaean Millenarian.[12] The
twelfth verse of the twelfth chapter of Revelations was always
in his mouth: 'Woe to the inhabiters of the earth and of the
sea! for the devil is come among you, having great wrath,
because he knoweth that he hath but a short time.' He maintained that the supreme dominion of the world was, for wise
purposes, given over for a while to the Evil Principle; and
that this precise period of time, commonly called the enlightened age, was the point of his plenitude of power. He
used to add that by and by he would be cast down, and a high
and happy order of things succeed; but he never omitted the
saving clause, 'Not in our time': which last words were
always echoed in doleful response by the sympathetic Mr
Glowry.

Another and very frequent visitor, was the Reverend Mr
Larynx, the vicar of Claydyke, a village about ten miles distant;
a good-natured accommodating divine, who was always most
obligingly ready to take a dinner and a bed at the house of any
country gentleman in distress for a companion. Nothing came
amiss to him – a game at billiards, at chess, at draughts, at
backgammon, at piquet, or at all-fours in a *tête-à-tête* – or any
game on the cards, round, square, or triangular, in a party of
any number exceeding two. He would even dance among
friends, rather than that a lady, even if she were on the wrong
side of thirty, should sit still for want of a partner. For a ride,
a walk, or a sail in the morning – a song after dinner, a ghost
story after supper – a bottle of port with the squire, or a cup
of green tea with his lady – for all or any of these, or for anything else that was agreeable to anyone else, consistently with
the dye of his coat, the Reverend Mr Larynx was at all times
equally ready. When at Nightmare Abbey, he would condole

with Mr Glowry – drink Madeira with Scythrop – crack jokes
with Mr Hilary – hand Mrs Hilary to the piano, take charge
of her fan and gloves, and turn over her music with surprising
dexterity – quote Revelations with Mr Toobad – and lament
the good old times of feudal darkness with the transcendental
Mr Flosky.

CHAPTER II

SHORTLY AFTER THE disastrous termination of Scythrop's
passion for Miss Emily Girouette, Mr Glowry found himself,
much against his will, involved in a lawsuit, which compelled him to dance attendance on the High Court of Chancery.
Scythrop was left alone at Nightmare Abbey. He was a burnt
child, and dreaded the fire of female eyes. He wandered about
the ample pile, or along the garden-terrace, with 'his cogitative faculties immersed in cogibundity of cogitation'.[1] The
terrace terminated at the southwestern tower, which, as we
have said, was ruinous and full of owls. Here would Scythrop
take his evening seat, on a fallen fragment of mossy stone,
with his back resting against the ruined wall – a thick canopy
of ivy, with an owl in it, over his head – and the Sorrows of
Werter in his hand.[2] He had some taste for romance reading
before he went to the university, where, we must confess, in
justice to his college, he was cured of the love of reading in all
its shapes; and the cure would have been radical, if disappointment in love, and total solitude, had not conspired to
bring on a relapse. He began to devour romances and German
tragedies, and, by the recommendation of Mr Flosky, to pore
over ponderous tomes of transcendental philosophy, which
reconciled him to the labour of studying them by their mystical
jargon and necromantic imagery. In the congenial solitude of
Nightmare Abbey, the distempered ideas of metaphysical
romance and romantic metaphysics had ample time and space
to germinate into a fertile crop of chimeras, which rapidly
shot up into vigorous and abundant vegetation.

He now became troubled with the *passion for reforming the
world*.* He built many castles in the air, and peopled them
with secret tribunals, and bands of illuminati,[3] who were always
the imaginary instruments of his projected regeneration

* See Forsyth's *Principles of Moral Science*. [P.]

of the human species. As he intended to institute a perfect republic, he invested himself with absolute sovereignty over these mystical dispensers of liberty. He slept with Horrid Mysteries[4] under his pillow, and dreamed of venerable eleutherarchs[5] and ghastly confederates holding midnight conventions in subterranean caves. He passed whole mornings in his study, immersed in gloomy reverie, stalking about the room in his nightcap, which he pulled over his eyes like a cowl, and folding his striped calico dressing-gown about him like the mantle of a conspirator.

'Action,' thus he soliloquized, 'is the result of opinion, and to new-model opinion would be to new-model society. Knowledge is power; it is in the hands of a few, who employ it to mislead the many, for their own selfish purposes of aggrandizement and appropriation. What if it were in the hands of a few who should employ it to lead the many? What if it were universal, and the multitude were enlightened? No. The many must be always in leading-strings; but let them have wise and honest conductors. A few to think, and many to act; that is the only basis of perfect society. So thought the ancient philosophers: they had their esoterical and exoterical doctrines. So thinks the sublime Kant, who delivers his oracles in language which none but the initiated can comprehend. Such were the views of those secret associations of illuminati, which were the terror of superstition and tyranny, and which, carefully selecting wisdom and genius from the great wilderness of society, as the bee selects honey from the flowers of the thorn and the nettle, bound all human excellence in a chain, which, if it had not been prematurely broken, would have commanded opinion, and regenerated the world.'

Scythrop proceeded to meditate on the practicability of reviving a confederation of regenerators. To get a clear view of his own ideas, and to feel the pulse of the wisdom and genius of the age, he wrote and published a treatise, in which his meanings were carefully wrapt up in the monk's hood of transcendental technology, but filled with hints of matter deep and dangerous, which he thought would set the whole nation in a ferment; and he awaited the result in awful expectation, as a miner who has fired a train awaits the explosion of a rock. However, he listened and heard nothing; for the explosion, if any ensued, was not sufficiently loud to shake a single leaf of the ivy on the towers of Nightmare Abbey; and some months afterwards he received a letter from his book-seller, informing him that only seven copies had been sold, and concluding with a polite request for the balance.

Scythrop did not despair. 'Seven copies,' he thought, 'have been sold. Seven is a mystical number, and the omen is good. Let me find the seven purchasers of my seven copies, and they shall be the seven golden candle-sticks with which I will illuminate the world.'

Scythrop had a certain portion of mechanical genius, which his romantic projects tended to develop. He constructed models of cells and recesses, sliding panels and secret passages, that would have baffled the skill of the Parisian police. He took the opportunity of his father's absence to smuggle a dumb carpenter into the Abbey, and between them they gave reality to one of these models in Scythrop's tower. Scythrop foresaw that a great leader of human regeneration would be involved in fearful dilemmas, and determined, for the benefit of man-kind in general, to adopt all possible precautions for the preservation of himself.

The servants, even the women, had been tutored into silence. Profound stillness reigned throughout and around the Abbey, except when the occasional shutting of a door would peal in long reverberations through the galleries, or the heavy tread of the pensive butler would wake the hollow echoes of the hall. Scythrop stalked about like the grand inquisitor, and the servants flitted past him like familiars. In his evening meditations on the terrace, under the ivy of the ruined tower, the only sound that came to his ear were the rustling of the wind in the ivy, the plaintive voices of the feathered choristers, the owls, the occasional striking of the Abbey clock, and the monotonous dash of the sea on its low and level shore. In the meantime, he drank Madeira, and laid deep schemes for a thorough repair of the crazy fabric of human nature.

CHAPTER III

MR GLOWRY returned from London with the loss of his law-suit. Justice was with him, but the law was against him. He found Scythrop in a mood most sympathetically tragic; and they vied with each other in enlivening their cups by lamenting the depravity of this degenerate age, and occasionally, interspersing divers grim jokes about graves, worms, and epitaphs. Mr Glowry's friends, whom we have mentioned in the first chapter, availed themselves of his return to pay him a simultaneous visit. At the same time arrived Scythrop's friend and fellow-collegian, the Honourable Mr Listless.[1] Mr Glowry had discovered this fashionable young gentleman in London, 'stretched on the rack of a too easy chair', and devoured with a gloomy and misanthropical *nil curo*, and had pressed him so earnestly to take the benefit of the pure country air, at Nightmare Abbey, that Mr Listless, finding it would give him more trouble to refuse than to comply, summoned his French valet, Fatout, and told him he was going to Lincolnshire. On this simple hint, Fatout went to work, and the imperials were packed, and the post-chariot was at the door, without the Honourable Mr Listless having said or thought another syllable on the subject.

Mr and Mrs Hilary brought with them an orphan niece, a daughter of Mr Glowry's youngest sister, who had made a runaway love-match with an Irish officer. The lady's fortune disappeared in the first year: love, by a natural consequence, disappeared in the second: the Irishman himself, by a still more natural consequence, disappeared in the third. Mr Glowry had allowed his sister an annuity, and she had lived in retirement with her only daughter, whom, at her death, which had recently happened, she commended to the care of Mrs Hilary.

Miss Marionetta Celestina O'Carroll was a very blooming and accomplished young lady.[2] Being a compound of the *Allegro Vivace* of the O'Carrolls, and of the *Andante Doloroso* of the Glowries, she exhibited in her own character all the diversities of an April sky. Her hair was light-brown; her eyes hazel, and sparkling with a mild but fluctuating light; her features regular; her lips full, and of equal size; and her person surpassingly graceful. She was a proficient in music. Her conversation was sprightly, but always on subjects light in their nature and limited in their interest: for moral sympathies, in any general sense, had no place in her mind. She had some coquetry, and more caprice, liking and disliking almost in the same moment; pursuing an object with earnestness while it seemed unattainable, and rejecting it when in her power as not worth the trouble of possession.

Whether she was touched with a *penchant* for her cousin Scythrop, or was merely curious to see what effect the tender passion would have on so *outré* a person, she had not been three days in the Abbey before she threw out all the lures of her beauty and accomplishments to make a prize of his heart. Scythrop proved an easy conquest. The image of Miss Emily Girouette was already sufficiently dimmed by the power of philosophy and the exercise of reason: for to these influences, or to any influence but the true one, are usually ascribed the mental cures performed by the great physician Time. Scythrop's romantic dreams had indeed given him many *pure anticipated cognitions* of combinations of beauty and intelligence, which, he had some misgivings, were not exactly realized in his cousin Marionetta; but, in spite of these misgivings, he soon became distractedly in love; which, when the young lady clearly perceived, she altered her tactics, and assumed as much coldness and reserve as she had before shown ardent and ingenuous attachment. Scythrop was confounded at the sudden change; but, instead of falling at her feet and requesting an explanation, he retreated to his tower, muffled himself in his nightcap, seated himself in the president's chair of his imaginary secret tribunal, summoned Marionetta with all terrible formalities, frightened her out of her wits, disclosed himself, and clasped the beautiful penitent to his bosom.

While he was acting this reverie – in the moment in which the awful president of the secret tribunal was throwing back his cowl and his mantle, and discovering himself to the lovely culprit as her adoring and magnanimous lover, the door of the study opened, and the real Marionetta appeared.

The motives which had led her to the tower were a little penitence, a little concern, a little affection, and a little fear as to what the sudden secession of Scythrop, occasioned by her sudden change of manner, might portend. She had tapped several times unheard, and of course unanswered; and at length, timidly and cautiously opening the door, she discovered him standing up before a black velvet chair, which was mounted on an old oak table, in the act of throwing open his striped calico dressing-gown, and flinging away his nightcap – which is what the French call an imposing attitude.

Each stood a few moments fixed in their respective places – the lady in astonishment, and the gentleman in confusion.

Marionetta was the first to break silence. 'For heaven's sake,' said she, 'my dear Scythrop, what is the matter?'

'For heaven's sake, indeed!' said Scythrop, springing from the table; 'for your sake, Marionetta, and you are my heaven – distraction is the matter. I adore you, Marionetta, and your cruelty drives me mad.' He threw himself at her knees, devoured her hand with kisses, and breathed a thousand vows in the most passionate language of romance.

Marionetta listened a long time in silence, till her lover had exhausted his eloquence and paused for a reply. She then said, with a very arch look, 'I prithee deliver thyself like a man of this world.'[3] The levity of this quotation, and of the manner in which it was delivered, jarred so discordantly on the high-wrought enthusiasm of the romantic inamorato, that he sprang upon his feet, and beat his forehead with his clenched fists. The young lady was terrified; and, deeming it expedient to soothe him, took one of his hands in hers, placed the other hand on his shoulder, looked up in his face with a winning seriousness, and said, in the tenderest possible tone, 'What would you have, Scythrop?'

Scythrop was in heaven again. 'What would I have? What but you, Marionetta? You, for the companion of my studies, the partner of my thoughts, the auxiliary of my great designs for the emancipation of mankind.'

'I am afraid I should be but a poor auxiliary, Scythrop. What would you have me do?'

'Do as Rosalia does with Carlos, divine Marionetta.[4] Let us each open a vein in the other's arm, mix our blood in a bowl, and drink it as a sacrament of love. Then we shall see visions of transcendental illumination, and soar on the wings of ideas into the space of pure intelligence.'

Marionetta could not reply; she had not so strong a stomach as Rosalia, and turned sick at the proposition. She disengaged herself suddenly from Scythrop, sprang through the door of the tower, and fled with precipitation along the corridors. Scythrop pursued her, crying, 'Stop, stop, Marionetta – my life, my love!' and was gaining rapidly on her flight, when, at an ill-omened corner, where two corridors ended in an angle, at the head of a staircase, he came into sudden and violent contact with Mr Toobad, and they both plunged together to the foot of the stairs, like two billiard-balls into one pocket. This gave the young lady time to escape, and enclose herself in her chamber; while Mr Toobad, rising slowly, and rubbing his knees and shoulders, said, 'You see, my dear Scythrop, in this little incident, one of the innumerable proofs of the temporary supremacy of the devil; for what but a systematic design and concurrent contrivance of evil could have made the angles of time and place coincide in our unfortunate persons at the head of this accursed staircase?'

'Nothing else, certainly,' said Scythrop: 'you are perfectly in the right, Mr Toobad. Evil, and mischief, and misery, and confusion, and vanity, and vexation of spirit, and death, and disease, and assassination, and war, and poverty, and pestilence, and famine, and avarice, and selfishness, and rancour, and jealousy, and spleen, and malevolence, and the disappointments of philanthropy, and the faithlessness of friendship, and the crosses of love – all prove the accuracy of your views, and the truth of your system; and it is not impossible that the infernal interruption of this fall downstairs may throw a colour of evil on the whole of my future existence.'

'My dear boy,' said Mr Toobad, 'you have a fine eye for consequences.'

So saying, he embraced Scythrop, who retired, with a disconsolate step, to dress for dinner; while Mr Toobad stalked across the hall, repeating, 'Woe to the inhabiters of the earth, and of the sea, for the devil is come among you, having great wrath.'

CHAPTER IV

THE FLIGHT OF Marionetta, and the pursuit of Scythrop had been witnessed by Mr Glowry, who, in consequence, narrowly observed his son and his niece in the evening; and, concluding from their manner, that there was a better understanding between them than he wished to see, he determined on obtaining the next morning from Scythrop a full and satisfactory explanation. He, therefore, shortly after breakfast, entered Scythrop's tower, with a very grave face, and said, without ceremony or preface, 'So, sir, you are in love with your cousin.'

Scythrop, with as little hesitation, answered, 'Yes, sir.'

'That is candid, at least; and she is in love with you.'

'I wish she were, sir.'

'You know she is, sir.'

'Indeed, sir, I do not.'

'But you hope she is.'

'I do, from my soul.'

'Now that is very provoking, Scythrop, and very disappointing: I could not have supposed that you, Scythrop Glowry, of Nightmare Abbey, would have been infatuated with such a dancing, laughing, singing, thoughtless, careless, merry-hearted thing, as Marionetta – in all respects the reverse of you and me. It is very disappointing, Scythrop. And do you know, sir, that Marionetta has no fortune?'

'It is the more reason, sir, that her husband should have one.'

'The more reason for her; but not for you. My wife had no fortune, and I had no consolation in my calamity. And do you reflect, sir, what an enormous slice this lawsuit has cut out of our family estate? we who used to be the greatest landed proprietors in Lincolnshire.'

'To be sure, sir, we had more acres of fen than any man on this coast: but what are fens to love? What are dykes and windmills to Marionetta?'

'And what, sir, is love to a windmill? Not grist, I am certain: besides, sir, I have made a choice for you. I have made a choice for you, Scythrop. Beauty, genius, accomplishments, and a great fortune into the bargain. Such a lovely, serious creature, in a fine state of high dissatisfaction with the world, and everything in it. Such a delightful surprise I had prepared for you. Sir, I have pledged my honour to the contract – the honour of the Glowries of Nightmare Abbey: and now, sir, what is to be done?'

'Indeed, sir, I cannot say. I claim, on this occasion, that liberty of action which is the co-natal prerogative of every rational being.'

'Liberty of action, sir? there is no such thing as liberty of action. We are all slaves and puppets of a blind and unpathetic necessity.'

'Very true, sir; but liberty of action, between individuals, consists of their being differently influenced, or modified, by the same universal necessity; so that the results are unconsentaneous, and their respective necessitated volitions clash and fly off in a tangent.'

'Your logic is good, sir: but you are aware, too, that one individual may be a medium of adhibiting to another a mode or form of necessity, which may have more or less influence in the production of consentaneity; and, therefore, sir, if you do not comply with my wishes in this instance (you have had your own way in everything else), I shall be under the necessity of disinheriting you, though I shall do it with tears in my eyes.' Having said these words, he vanished suddenly, in the dread of Scythrop's logic.

Mr Glowry immediately sought Mrs Hilary, and communicated to her his views of the case in point. Mrs Hilary, as the phrase is, was as fond of Marionetta as if she had been her own child: but – there is always a *but* on these occasions – she could do nothing for her in the way of fortune, as she had two hopeful sons, who were finishing their education at Brazennose, and who would not like to encounter any diminution of their prospects, when they should be brought out of the house of mental bondage – i.e. the university – to the land flowing with milk and honey – i.e. the west end of London.

Mrs Hilary hinted to Marionetta, that propriety, and delicacy, and decorum, and dignity, etc., etc., etc.,* would require them to leave the Abbey immediately. Marionetta listened in silent submission, for she knew that her inheritance was passive obedience; but, when Scythrop, who had watched the opportunity of Mrs Hilary's departure, entered, and, without speaking a word, threw himself at her feet in a paroxysm of grief, the young lady, in equal silence and sorrow, threw her arms round his neck and burst into tears. A very tender scene ensued, which the sympathetic susceptibilities of the soft-hearted reader can more accurately imagine than we can delineate. But when Marionetta hinted that she was to leave the Abbey immediately, Scythrop snatched from its repository his ancestor's skull,[1] filled it with Madeira, and presenting himself before Mr Glowry, threatened to drink off the contents if Mr Glowry did not immediately promise that Marionetta should not be taken from the Abbey without her own consent. Mr Glowry, who took the Madeira to be some deadly brewage, gave the required promise in dismal panic. Scythrop returned to Marionetta with a joyful heart, and drank the Madeira by the way.

Mr Glowry, during his residence in London, had come to an agreement with his friend Mr Toobad, that a match between

* We are not masters of the whole vocabulary. See any novel by any literary lady. [P.]

Scythrop and Mr Toobad's daughter would be a very desirable occurrence. She was finishing her education in a German
convent, but Mr Toobad described her as being fully impressed with the truth of his Ahrimanic* philosophy, and
being altogether as gloomy and antithalian[2] a young lady as
Mr Glowry himself could desire for the future mistress of
Nightmare Abbey. She had a great fortune in her own right,
which was not, as we have seen, without its weight in inducing
Mr Glowry to set his heart upon her as his daughter-in-law
that was to be; he was therefore very much disturbed by
Scythrop's untoward attachment to Marionetta. He condoled
on the occasion with Mr Toobad; who said, that he had been
too long accustomed to the intermeddling of the devil in all
his affairs, to be astonished at this new trace of his cloven claw;
but that he hoped to outwit him yet, for he was sure there
could be no comparison between his daughter and Marionetta
in the mind of anyone who had a proper perception of the
fact, that, the world being a great theatre of evil, seriousness
and solemnity are the characteristics of wisdom, and laughter
and merriment make a human being no better than a baboon.
Mr Glowry comforted himself with this view of the subject,
and urged Mr Toobad to expedite his daughter's return from
Germany. Mr Toobad said he was in daily expectation of her
arrival in London, and would set off immediately to meet her,
that he might lose no time in bringing her to Nightmare
Abbey. 'Then,' he added, 'we shall see whether Thalia or
Melpomene[3] – whether the Allegra or the Penserosa – will
carry off the symbol of victory.' – 'There can be no doubt,'
said Mr Glowry, 'which way the scale will incline, or Scythrop is no true scion of the venerable stem of the Glowrys.'

* Ahrimanes, in the Persian mythology, is the evil power, the prince of
the kingdom of darkness. He is the rival of Oromazes, the prince of the
kingdom of light. These two powers have divided and equal dominion.
Sometimes one of the two has a temporary supremacy. – According to Mr
Toobad, the present period would be the reign of Ahrimanes. Lord Byron
seems to be of the same opinion, by the use he has made of Ahrimanes in
Manfred; where the great Alastor, or Κακος Δαιμων, of Persia, is hailed
king of the world by the Nemesis of Greece, in concert with three of the
Scandinavian Valkyrae, under the name of the Destinies; the astrological
spirits of the alchemists of the middle ages; an elemental witch, trans-
planted from Denmark to the Alps; and a chorus of Dr Faustus's devils,
who come in the last act for a soul. It is difficult to conceive where this
mythological company could have originally met, except at a *table d'hôte*,
like the six kings in *Candide*. [P.]

CHAPTER V

MARIONETTA FELT secure of Scythrop's heart; and not-withstanding the difficulties that surrounded her, she could not debar herself from the pleasure of tormenting her lover, whom she kept in a perpetual fever. Sometimes she would meet him with the most unqualified affection; sometimes with the most chilling indifference; rousing him to anger by artificial coldness – softening him to love by eloquent tender-ness – or inflaming him to jealousy by coquetting with the Honourable Mr Listless, who seemed, under her magical influence, to burst into sudden life, like the bud of the evening primrose. Sometimes she would sit by the piano, and listen with becoming attention to Scythrop's pathetic remonstrances; but, in the most impassioned part of his oratory, she would convert all his ideas into a chaos, by striking up some Rondo Allegro, and saying, 'Is it not pretty?' Scythrop would begin to storm; and she would answer him with,

> 'Zitti, zitti, piano, piano,
> Non facciamo confusione',[1]

or some other similar *facezia*, till he would start away from her, and enclose himself in his tower, in an agony of agitation, vowing to renounce her, and her whole sex, for ever; and returning to her presence at the summons of the billet, which she never failed to send with many expressions of penitence and promises of amendment. Scythrop's schemes for regen-erating the world, and detecting his seven golden candlesticks, went on very slowly in this fever of his spirit.

Things proceeded in this train for several days; and Mr Glowry began to be uneasy at receiving no intelligence from Mr Toobad; when one evening the latter rushed into the library, where the family and the visitors were assembled, vociferating, 'The devil is come among you, having great wrath!' He then drew Mr Glowry aside into another apart-ment, and after remaining some time together, they re-entered the library with faces of great dismay, but did not condescend to explain to anyone the cause of their discom-fiture.

The next morning, early, Mr Toobad departed. Mr Glowry sighed and groaned all day, and said not a word to anyone.

Scythrop had quarrelled, as usual, with Marionetta, and was enclosed in his tower, in a fit of morbid sensibility. Marionetta was comforting herself at the piano, with singing the airs of *Nina pazza per amore*;[2] and the Honourable Mr Listless was listening to the harmony, as he lay supine on the sofa, with a book in his hand, into which he peeped at intervals. The Reverend Mr Larynx approached the sofa, and proposed a game of billiards.

THE HONOURABLE MR LISTLESS. Billiards! Really I should be very happy; but, in my present exhausted state, the exertion is too much for me. I do not know when I have been equal to such an effort. (*He rang the bell for his valet. Fatout entered.*) Fatout! when did I play at billiards last?

FATOUT. De fourteen December de last year, Monsieur. (*Fatout bowed and retired.*)

THE HONOURABLE MR LISTLESS. So it was. Seven months ago. You see, Mr Larynx; you see, sir. My nerves, Miss O'Carroll, my nerves are shattered. I have been advised to try Bath. Some of the faculty recommend Cheltenham.[3] I think of trying both, as the seasons don't clash. The season, you know, Mr Larynx – the season, Miss O'Carroll – the season is everything.

MARIONETTA. And health is something. *N'est-ce pas*, Mr Larynx?

THE REVEREND MR LARYNX. Most assuredly, Miss O'Carroll. For, however reasoners may dispute about the *summum bonum*, none of them will deny that a very good dinner is a very good thing: and what is a good dinner without a good appetite? and whence is a good appetite but from good health? Now, Cheltenham, Mr Listless, is famous for good appetites.

THE HONOURABLE MR LISTLESS. The best piece of logic I ever heard, Mr Larynx; the very best, I assure you. I have thought very seriously of Cheltenham: very seriously and profoundly. I thought of it – let me see – when did I think of it? (*He rang again, and Fatout reappeared.*) Fatout! when did I think of going to Cheltenham, and did not go?

FATOUT. De Juillet twenty-von, de last summer, Monsieur. (*Fatout retired.*)

THE HONOURABLE MR LISTLESS. So it was. An invaluable fellow that, Mr Larynx – invaluable, Miss O'Carroll.

MARIONETTA. So I should judge, indeed. He seems to

serve you as a walking memory, and to be a living chronicle, not of your actions only, but of your thoughts.

THE HONOURABLE MR LISTLESS. An excellent definition of the fellow, Miss O'Carroll – excellent, upon my honour. Ha! ha! ha! Heigho? Laughter is pleasant, but the exertion is too much for me.

A parcel was brought in for Mr Listless; it had been sent express. Fatout was summoned to unpack it; and it proved to contain a new novel, and a new poem, both of which had long been anxiously expected by the whole host of fashionable readers; and the last number of a popular Review, of which the editor and his coadjutors were in high favour at court, and enjoyed ample pensions* for their services to church and state. As Fatout left the room, Mr Flosky entered, and curiously inspected the literary arrivals.

MR FLOSKY (*turning over the leaves*). 'Devilman, a novel.'[4] Hm. Hatred – revenge – misanthropy – and quotations from the Bible. Hm. This is the morbid anatomy of black bile – 'Paul Jones, a poem.'[5] Hm. I see how it is. Paul Jones, an amiable enthusiast – disappointed in his affections – turns pirate from ennui and magnanimity – cuts various masculine throats, wins various feminine hearts – is hanged at the yard-arm! The catastrophe is very awkward, and very unpoetical – *The Downing Street Review*. Hm. First article – An Ode to the Red Book,[6] by Roderick Sackbut, Esquire.[7] Hm. His own poem reviewed by himself. Hm-m-m.

(*Mr Flosky proceeded in silence to look over the other articles of the* Review; *Marionetta inspected the novel, and Mr Listless the poem.*)

THE REVEREND MR LARYNX. For a young man of fashion and family, Mr Listless, you seem to be of a very studious turn.

THE HONOURABLE MR LISTLESS. Studious! You are pleased to be facetious, Mr Larynx. I hope you do not suspect me of being studious. I have finished my education. But there are some fashionable books that one must read, because they are ingredients of the talk of the day; otherwise, I am no fonder of books than I dare say you yourself are, Mr Larynx.

THE REVEREND MR LARYNX. Why, sir, I cannot say that

* 'PENSION. Pay given to a slave of state for treason to his country.' – Johnson's *Dictionary*. [P.]

I am indeed particularly fond of books; yet neither can I say that I never do read. A tale or a poem, now and then, to a circle of ladies over their work, is no very heterodox employment of the vocal energy. And I must say, for myself, that few men have a more Job-like endurance of the eternally recurring questions and answers that interweave themselves, on these occasions, with the crisis of an adventure, and heighten the distress of a tragedy.

THE HONOURABLE MR LISTLESS. And very often make the distress when the author has omitted it.

MARIONETTA. I shall try your patience some rainy morning, Mr Larynx; and Mr Listless shall recommend us the very newest new book, that everybody reads.

THE HONOURABLE MR LISTLESS. You shall receive it, Miss O'Carroll, with all the gloss of novelty; fresh as a ripe green-gage in all the downiness of its bloom. A mail-coach copy from Edinburgh, forwarded express from London.

MR FLOSKY. This rage for novelty is the bane of literature. Except my works and those of my particular friends, nothing is good that is not as old as Jeremy Taylor: and, *entre nous*, the best parts of my friends' books were either written or suggested by myself.

THE HONOURABLE MR LISTLESS. Sir, I reverence you. But I must say, modern books are very consolatory and congenial to my feelings. There is, as it were, a delightful north-east wind, an intellectual blight breathing through them; a delicious misanthropy and discontent, that demonstrates the nullity of virtue and energy, and puts me in good humour with myself and my sofa.

MR FLOSKY. Very true, sir. Modern literature is a north-east wind – a blight of the human soil. I take credit to myself for having helped to make it so. The way to produce fine fruit is to blight the flower. You call this a paradox. Marry, so be it. Ponder thereon.

The conversation was interrupted by the reappearance of Mr Toobad, covered with mud. He just showed himself at the door, muttered 'The devil is come among you!' and vanished. The road which connected Nightmare Abbey with the civilized world, was artificially raised above the level of the fens, and ran through them in a straight line as far as the eye could reach, with a ditch on each side, of which the water was rendered invisible by the aquatic vegetation that covered the surface. Into one of these ditches the sudden action of a shy horse, which took fright at a windmill, had precipitated the travelling chariot of Mr Toobad, who had been reduced to the necessity of scrambling in dismal plight through the window. One of the wheels was found to be broken; and Mr Toobad, leaving the postillion to get the chariot as well as he could to Claydyke for the purposes of cleaning and repairing, had walked back to Nightmare Abbey, followed by his servant with the imperial, and repeating all the way his favourite quotation from the Revelations.

CHAPTER VI

MR TOOBAD HAD found his daughter Celinda in London, and after the first joy of meeting was over, told her he had a husband ready for her. The young lady replied, very gravely, that she should take the liberty to choose for herself. Mr Toobad said he saw the devil was determined to interfere with all his projects, but he was resolved on his own part, not to have on his conscience the crime of passive obedience and non-resistance to Lucifer, and therefore she should marry the person he had chosen for her. Miss Toobad replied, *très posément*, she assuredly would not. 'Celinda, Celinda,' said Mr Toobad, 'you most assuredly shall.' – 'Have I not a fortune in my own right, sir?' said Celinda. 'The more is the pity,' said Mr Toobad: 'but I can find means, miss; I can find means. There are more ways than one of breaking in obstinate girls.' They parted for the night with the expression of opposite resolutions, and in the morning the young lady's chamber was found empty, and what was become of her Mr Toobad had no clue to conjecture. He continued to investigate town and country in search of her; visiting and revisiting Nightmare Abbey at intervals, to consult with his friend, Mr Glowry. Mr Glowry agreed with Mr Toobad that this was a very flagrant instance of filial disobedience and rebellion; and Mr Toobad declared, that when he discovered the fugitive, she should find that 'the devil was come unto her, having great wrath.'

In the evening, the whole party met, as usual, in the library. Marionetta sat at the harp; the Honourable Mr Listless sat by her and turned over her music, though the exertion was almost too much for him. The Reverend Mr Larynx relieved him occasionally in this delightful labour. Scythrop, tormented by the demon Jealousy, sat in the corner biting his lips and fingers. Marionetta looking at him every now and then with a smile of most provoking good humour, which he pretended not to see, and which only the more exasperated his troubled spirit. He took down a volume of Dante, and pretended to be deeply interested in the Purgatorio, though he knew not a word he was reading, as Marionetta was well aware; who, tripping across the room, peeped into his book, and said to him, 'I see you are in the middle of Purgatory.' – 'I am in the middle of hell,' said Scythrop furiously. 'Are you?' said she; 'then come across the room, and I will sing you the finale of Don Giovanni.'

'Let me alone,' said Scythrop. Marionetta looked at him with a deprecating smile, and said, 'You unjust, cross creature, you.' – 'Let me alone,' said Scythrop, but much less emphatically than at first, and by no means wishing to be taken at his word. Marionetta left him immediately, and returning to the harp, said, just loud enough for Scythrop to hear – 'Did you ever read Dante, Mr Listless? Scythrop is reading Dante, and is just now in Purgatory.' – 'And I,' said the Honourable Mr Listless, 'am not reading Dante, and am just now in Paradise,' bowing to Marionetta.

MARIONETTA. You are very gallant, Mr Listless; and I dare say you are very fond of reading Dante.

THE HONOURABLE MR LISTLESS. I don't know how it is, but Dante never came in my way till lately. I never had him in my collection, and if I had had him I should not have read him. But I find he is growing fashionable, and I am afraid I must read him some wet morning.

MARIONETTA. No, read him some evening, by all means. Were you ever in love, Mr Listless?

THE HONOURABLE MR LISTLESS. I assure you, Miss O'Carroll, never – till I came to Nightmare Abbey. I dare say it is very pleasant; but it seems to give so much trouble that I fear the exertion would be too much for me.

MARIONETTA. Shall I teach you a compendious method of courtship, that will give you no trouble whatever?

THE HONOURABLE MR LISTLESS. You will confer on me an inexpressible obligation. I am all impatience to learn it.

MARIONETTA. Sit with your back to the lady and read Dante; only be sure to begin in the middle, and turn over three or four pages at once – backwards as well as forwards, and she will immediately perceive that you are desperately in love with her – desperately.

(*The Honourable Mr Listless sitting between Scythrop and Marionetta, and fixing all his attention on the beautiful speaker, did not observe Scythrop, who was doing as she described.*)

THE HONOURABLE MR LISTLESS. You are pleased to be facetious, Miss O'Carroll. The lady would infallibly conclude that I was the greatest brute in town.

MARIONETTA. Far from it. She would say, perhaps, some people have odd methods of showing their affection.

THE HONOURABLE MR LISTLESS. But I should think, with submission —

MR FLOSKY (*joining them from another part of the room*). Did I not hear Mr Listless observe that Dante is becoming fashionable?

THE HONOURABLE MR LISTLESS. I did hazard a remark to that effect, Mr Flosky, though I speak on such subjects with a consciousness of my own nothingness, in the presence of so great a man as Mr Flosky. I know not what is the colour of Dante's devils, but as he is certainly becoming fashionable I conclude they are blue; for the blue devils, as it seems to me, Mr Flosky, constitute the fundamental feature of fashionable literature.

MR FLOSKY. The blue are, indeed, the staple commodity; but as they will not always be commanded, the black, red, and grey may be admitted as substitutes. Tea, late dinners, and the French Revolution, have played the devil, Mr Listless, and brought the devil into play.

MR TOOBAD (*starting up*). Having great wrath.

MR FLOSKY. This is no play upon words, but the sober sadness of veritable fact.

THE HONOURABLE MR LISTLESS. Tea, late dinner, and the French Revolution. I cannot exactly see the connection of ideas.

MR FLOSKY. I should be sorry if you could; I pity the man who can see the connection of his own ideas. Still more do I pity him, the connection of whose ideas any other person can see. Sir, the great evil is, that there is too much commonplace light in our moral and political literature; and light is a great enemy to mystery, and mystery is a great friend to enthusiasm. Now the enthusiasm for abstract truth is an exceedingly fine thing, as long as the truth, which is the object of the enthusiasm, is so completely abstract as to be altogether out of the reach of the human faculties; and, in that sense, I have myself an enthusiasm for truth, but in no other, for the pleasure of metaphysical investigation lies in the means, not in the end; and if the end could be found, the pleasure of the means would cease. The mind, to be kept in health, must be kept in exercise. The proper exercise of the mind is elaborate reasoning. Analytical reasoning is a base and mechanical process, which takes to pieces and examines, bit by bit, the rude material of knowledge, and extracts therefrom a few hard and obstinate things called facts, everything in the shape of which I cordially hate. But synthetical reasoning, setting up as its goal some unattainable abstraction, like an imaginary quantity in algebra, and commencing its course with taking for granted some two assertions which cannot be proved, from the union of these two assumed truths produces a third assumption, and so on in infinite series, to the unspeakable benefit of the human intellect. The beauty of this process is, that at every step it strikes out into two branches, in a compound ratio of ramification; so that you are perfectly sure of losing your way, and keeping your mind in perfect health, by the perpetual exercise of an interminable quest; and for these reasons I have christened my eldest son Emanuel Kant Flosky.

THE REVEREND MR LARYNX. Nothing can be more luminous.

THE HONOURABLE MR LISTLESS. And what has all that to do with Dante, and the blue devils?

MR HILARY. Not much, I should think, with Dante, but a great deal with the blue devils.

MR FLOSKY. It is very certain, and much to be rejoiced at, that our literature is hag-ridden. Tea has shattered our nerves; late dinners make us slaves of indigestion; the French Revolution has made us shrink from the name of philosophy, and has destroyed, in the more refined part of the community (of which number I am one), all enthusiasm for political liberty. That part of the *reading public* which shuns the solid food of reason for the light diet of fiction, requires a perpetual adhibition of *sauce piquante* to the palate of its depraved imagina-

tion. It lived upon ghosts, goblins, and skeletons (I and my
friend Mr Sackbut served up a few of the best), till even the
devil himself, though magnified to the size of Mount Athos,
became too base, common, and popular, for its surfeited
appetite. The ghosts have therefore been laid, and the devil
has been cast into outer darkness, and now the delight of our
spirits is to dwell on all the vices and blackest passions of our
nature, tricked out in a masquerade dress of heroism and
disappointed benevolence; the whole secret of which lies in
forming combinations that contradict all our experience, and
affixing the purple shred of some particular virtue to that
precise character, in which we should be most certain not to
find it in the living world; and making this single virtue not
only redeem all the real and manifest vices of the character, but
make them actually pass for necessary adjuncts, and indispensable accompaniments and characteristics of the said
virtue.

MR TOOBAD. That is, because the devil is come among us,
and finds it for his interest to destroy all our perceptions of the
distinctions of right and wrong.

MARIONETTA. I do not precisely enter into your meaning,
Mr Flosky, and should be glad if you would make it a little
more plain to me.

MR FLOSKY. One or two examples will do it, Miss O'Carroll.
If I were to take all the mean and sordid qualities of a money-
dealing Jew, and tack on to them, as with a nail, the quality of
extreme benevolence, I should have a very decent hero for a
modern novel; and should contribute my quota to the fashionable method of administering a mass of vice, under a thin and
unnatural covering of virtue, like a spider wrapt in a bit of
gold leaf, and administered as a wholesome pill. On the same
principle, if a man knocks me down, and takes my purse and
watch by main force, I turn him to account, and set him forth
in a tragedy as a dashing young fellow, disinherited for his
romantic generosity, and full of a most amiable hatred of the
world in general, and his own country in particular, and of a
most enlightened and chivalrous affection for himself: then,
with the addition of a wild girl to fall in love with him, and a
series of adventures in which they break all the Ten Com-
mandments in succession (always, you will observe, for some
sublime motive, which must be carefully analysed in its
progress), I have as amiable a pair of tragic characters as ever

issued from that new region of the belles lettres, which I have called the Morbid Anatomy of Black Bile, and which is greatly to be admired and rejoiced at, as affording a fine scope for the exhibition of mental power.

MR HILARY. Which is about as well employed as the power of a hot-house would be in forcing up a nettle to the size of an elm. If we go on in this way, we shall have a new art of poetry, of which one of the first rules will be: To remember to forget that there are any such things as sunshine and music in the world.

THE HONOURABLE MR LISTLESS. It seems to be the case with us at present, or we should not have interrupted Miss O'Carroll's music with this exceedingly dry conversation.

MR FLOSKY. I should be most happy if Miss O'Carroll would remind us that there are yet both music and sunshine —

THE HONOURABLE MR LISTLESS. In the voice and the smile of beauty. May I entreat the favour of – (*turning over the pages of music*).

All were silent, and Marionetta sung:

> Why are thy looks so blank, grey friar?
>   Why are thy looks so blue?
> Thou seem'st more pale and lank, grey friar,
>   Than thou wast used to do:
>   Say, what has made thee rue?
>
> Thy form was plump, and a light did shine
>   In thy round and ruby face,
> Which showed an outward visible sign
>   Of an inward spiritual grace:
>   Say, what has changed thy case?
>
> Yet will I tell thee true, grey friar,
>   I very well can see,
> That, if thy looks are blue, grey friar,
>   'Tis all for love of me –
>   'Tis all for love of me.
>
> But breathe not thy vows to me, grey friar,
>   Oh, breathe them not, I pray;
> For ill beseems in a reverend friar,
>   The love of a mortal may;
>   And I needs must say thee nay.

But, could'st thou think my heart to move
  With that pale and silent scowl?
Know, he who would win a maiden's love,
  Whether clad in cap or cowl,
  Must be more of a lark than an owl.

Scythrop immediately replaced Dante on the shelf, and joined the circle round the beautiful singer. Marionetta gave him a smile of approbation that fully restored his complacency, and they continued on the best possible terms during the remainder of the evening. The Honourable Mr Listless turned over the leaves with double alacrity, saying, 'You are severe upon invalids, Miss O'Carroll: to escape your satire, I must try to be sprightly, though the exertion is too much for me.'

CHAPTER VII

A NEW VISITOR arrived at the Abbey, in the person of Mr Asterias, the ichthyologist. This gentleman had passed his life in seeking the living wonders of the deep through the four quarters of the world; he had a cabinet of stuffed and dried fishes, of shells, sea-weeds, corals, and madrepores, that was the admiration and envy of the Royal Society. He had penetrated into the watery den of the Sepia Octopus, disturbed the conjugal happiness of that turtle-dove of the ocean, and come off victorious in a sanguinary conflict. He had been becalmed in the tropical seas, and had watched, in eager expectation, though unhappily always in vain, to see the colossal polypus rise from the water, and entwine its enormous arms round the masts and the rigging. He maintained the origin of all things from water, and insisted that the polypodes were the first of animated things, and that, from their round bodies and many-shooting arms, the Hindoos had taken their gods, the most ancient of deities. But the chief object of his ambition, the end and aim of his researches, was to discover a triton and a mermaid, the existence of which he most potently and implicitly believed, and was prepared to demonstrate, *à priori, à posteriori, à fortiori*,[1] synthetically and analytically, syllogistically and inductively, by arguments deduced both from acknowledged facts and plausible hypotheses. A report that a mermaid had been seen 'sleeking her soft alluring locks'² on the sea-coast of Lincolnshire, had brought him in great haste from London, to pay a long-promised and often-postponed visit to his old acquaintance, Mr Glowry.

Mr Asterias was accompanied by his son, to whom he had given the name of Aquarius – flattering himself that he would, in the process of time, become a constellation among the stars of ichthyological science. What charitable female had lent him the mould in which this son was cast, no one pretended to know; and, as he never dropped the most distant allusion to Aquarius's mother, some of the wags of London maintained that he had received the favours of a mermaid, and that the scientific perquisitions which kept him always prowling about the sea-shore, were directed by the less philosophical motive of regaining his lost love.

Mr Asterias perlustrated the sea-coast for several days, and reaped disappointment, but not despair. One night, shortly after his arrival, he was sitting in one of the windows of the library, looking towards the sea, when his attention was attracted by a figure which was moving near the edge of the surf, and which was dimly visible through the moonless summer night. Its motions were irregular, like those of a person in a state of indecision. It had extremely long hair, which floated in the wind. Whatever else it might be, it certainly was not a fisherman. It might be a lady; but it was neither Mrs Hilary nor Miss O'Carroll, for they were both in the library. It might be one of the female servants; but it had too much grace, and too striking an air of habitual liberty, to render it probable. Besides, what should one of the female servants be doing there at this hour, moving to and fro, as it seemed, without any visible purpose? It could scarcely be a stranger; for Claydyke, the nearest village, was ten miles distant; and what female would come ten miles across the fens, for no purpose but to hover over the surf under the walls of Nightmare Abbey? Might it not be a mermaid? It was possibly a mermaid. It was probably a mermaid. It was very probably a mermaid. Nay, what else could it be but a mermaid? It certainly was a mermaid. Mr Asterias stole out of the library on tiptoe, with his finger on his lips, having beckoned Aquarius to follow him.

The rest of the party was in great surprise at Mr Asterias's movement, and some of them approached the window to see if the locality would tend to elucidate the mystery. Presently they saw him and Aquarius cautiously stealing along on the other side of the moat, but they saw nothing more; and Mr Asterias returning, told them, with accents of great disappointment, that he had had a glimpse of a mermaid, but she had eluded him in the darkness, and was gone, he presumed, to sup with some enamoured triton, in a submarine grotto.

'But, seriously, Mr Asterias,' said the Honourable Mr Listless, 'do you positively believe there are such things as mermaids?'

MR ASTERIAS. Most assuredly; and tritons too.

THE HONOURABLE MR LISTLESS. What! things that are half human and half fish?

MR ASTERIAS. Precisely. They are the oran-outangs of the sea. But I am persuaded that there are also complete sea men, differing in no respect from us, but that they are stupid, and covered with scales; for, though our organization seems to exclude us essentially from the class of amphibious animals, yet anatomists well know that the *foramen ovale* may remain open in an adult, and that respiration is, in that case, not necessary to life: and how can it be otherwise explained that the Indian divers, employed in the pearl fishery, pass whole hours under the water; and that the famous Swedish gardener of Troningholm lived a day and a half under the ice without being drowned? A nereid, or mermaid, was taken in the year 1403 in a Dutch lake, and was in every respect like a French woman, except that she did not speak. Towards the end of the seventeenth century, an English ship, a hundred and fifty leagues from land, in the Greenland seas, discovered a flotilla of sixty or seventy little skiffs, in each of which was a triton, or sea man: at the approach of the English vessel the whole of them, seized with simultaneous fear, disappeared, skiffs and all, under the water, as if they had been a human variety of the nautilus. The illustrious Don Feijoo[3] has preserved an authentic and well-attested story of a young Spaniard, named Francis de la Vega, who, bathing with some of his friends in June, 1674, suddenly dived under the sea and rose no more. His friends thought him drowned; they were plebeians and pious Catholics; but a philosopher might very legitimately have drawn the same conclusion.

THE REVEREND MR LARYNX. Nothing could be more logical.

MR ASTERIAS. Five years afterwards, some fishermen near Cadiz found in their nets a triton, or sea man; they spoke to him in several languages –

THE REVEREND MR LARYNX. They were very learned fishermen.

MR HILARY. They had the gift of tongues by especial favour of their brother fisherman, Saint Peter.

THE HONOURABLE MR LISTLESS. Is Saint Peter the tutelar saint of Cadiz?

(*None of the company could answer this question, and* MR ASTERIA *proceeded.*)

They spoke to him in several languages, but he was as mute as a fish. They handed him over to some holy friars, who exorcized him; but the devil was mute too. After some days he pronounced the name Lierganes. A monk took him to that village. His mother and brothers recognized and embraced him; but he was as insensible to their caresses as any other fish would have been. He had some scales on his body, which dropped off by degrees; but his skin was as hard and rough as shagreen. He stayed at home nine years, without recovering his speech or his reason: he then disappeared again; and one of his old acquaintance, some years after, saw him pop his head out of the water near the coast of the Asturias. These facts were certified by his brothers, and by Don Gaspardo de la Riba Aguero, Knight of Saint James, who lived near Lierganes, and often had the pleasure of our triton's company to dinner – Pliny mentions an embassy of the Olyssiponians to Tiberius, to give him intelligence of a triton which had been heard playing on its shell in a certain cave; with several other authenticated facts on the subject of tritons and nereids.

THE HONOURABLE MR LISTLESS. You astonish me. I have been much on the sea-shore, in the season, but I do not think I ever saw a mermaid. (*He rang, and summoned Fatout, who made his appearance half-seas-over.*) Fatout! did I ever see a mermaid?

FATOUT. Mermaid! mer-r-m-m-aid! Ah! merry maid! Oui, monsieur! Yes, sir, very many. I vish dere vas von or two here in de kitchen – ma foi! Dey be all as melancholic as so many tombstone.

THE HONOURABLE MR LISTLESS. I mean, Fatout, an odd kind of human fish.

FATOUT. De odd fish! Ah, oui! I understand de phrase: ve have seen nothing else since ve left town – ma foi!

THE HONOURABLE MR LISTLESS. You seem to have a cup too much, sir.

FATOUT. Non, monsieur: de cup too little. De fen be very unwholesome, and I drink-a-de ponch vid Raven de butler, to keep out de bad air.

THE HONOURABLE MR LISTLESS. Fatout! I insist on your being sober.

FATOUT. Oui, monsieur; I vil be as sober as de révéren-dissime père Jean.[4] I should be ver glad of de merry maid; but de butler be de odd fish, and he swim in de bowl de ponch. Ah! ah! I do recollect de leetle-a song: 'About fair maids, and about fair maids, and about my merry maids all.' (*Fatout reeled out, singing.*)

THE HONOURABLE MR LISTLESS. I am overwhelmed: I never saw the rascal in such a condition before. But will you allow me, Mr Asterias, to inquire into the *cui bono* of all the pains and expense you have incurred in search of a mermaid? The *cui bono*, sir, is the question I always take the liberty to ask when I see anyone taking much trouble for any object. I am myself a sort of Signor Pococurante, and should like to know if there be anything better or pleasanter, than the state of existing and doing nothing?

MR ASTERIAS. I have made many voyages, Mr Listless, to remote and barren shores: I have travelled over desert and inhospitable lands: I have defied danger – I have endured fatigue – I have submitted to privation. In the midst of these I have experienced pleasures which I would not at any time have exchanged for that of existing and doing nothing. I have known many evils, but I have never known the worst of all which, as it seems to me, are those which are comprehended in the inexhaustible varieties of *ennui*: spleen, chagrin, vapours, blue devils, time-killing, discontent, misanthropy, and all their interminable train of fretfulness, querulousness, suspicions, jealousies, and fears, which have alike infected society, and the literature of society; and which would make an arctic ocean of the human mind, if the more humane pursuits of philosophy and science did not keep alive the better feelings and more valuable energies of our nature.

THE HONOURABLE MR LISTLESS. You are pleased to be severe upon our fashionable belles lettres.

MR ASTERIAS. Surely not without reason, when pirates, highwaymen, and other varieties of the extensive genus Marauder,[5] are the only *beau idéal* of the active, as splenetic and railing misanthropy is of the speculative energy. A gloomy brow and a tragical voice seem to have been of late the characteristics of fashionable manners: and a morbid, withering, deadly, antisocial sirocco, loaded with moral and political despair, breathes through all the groves and valleys of the modern Parnassus; while science moves on in the calm dignity of its course, affording to youth delights equally pure and vivid – to maturity, calm and grateful occupation – to old age, the most pleasing recollections and inexhaustible materials of agreeable and salutary reflection; and, while its votary enjoys the disinterested pleasure of enlarging the intellect and increasing the comforts of society, he is himself independent of the caprices of human intercourse and the accidents of human fortune. Nature is his great and inexhaustible treasure. His days are always too short for his enjoyment: *ennui* is a stranger to his door. At peace with the world and with his own mind, he suffices to himself, makes all around him happy, and the close of his pleasing and beneficial existence is the evening of a beautiful day.*

THE HONOURABLE MR LISTLESS. Really I should like very well to lead such a life myself, but the exertion would be too much for me. Besides, I have been at college. I contrive to get through my day by sinking the morning in bed, and killing the evening in company; dressing and dining in the intermediate space, and stopping the chinks and crevices of the few vacant moments that remain with a little easy reading. And that amiable discontent and antisociality which you reprobate in our present drawing-room-table literature, I find, I do assure you, a very fine mental tonic, which reconciles me to my favourite pursuit of doing nothing, by showing me that nobody is worth doing anything for.

MARIONETTA. But is there not in such compositions a kind of unconscious self-detection, which seems to carry their own antidote with them? For surely no one who cordially and truly either hates or despises the world will publish a volume every three months to say so.

MR FLOSKY. There is a secret in all this, which I will

* See Denys Montfort: *Histoire Naturelle des Mollusques; Vues Générales,* pp. 37, 38. [P.]

elucidate with a dusky remark. According to Berkeley,[6] the *esse* of things is *percipi*. They exist as they are perceived. But, leaving for the present, as far as relates to the material world, the materialists, hyloists, and antihyloists, to settle this point among them, which is indeed

> A subtle question, raised among
> Those out o' their wits, and those i' the wrong:[7]

for only we transcendentalists are in the right: we may very safely assert that the *esse* of happiness is *percipi*. It exists as it is perceived. 'It is the mind that maketh well or ill.' The elements of pleasure and pain are everywhere. The degree of happiness that any circumstances or objects can confer on us depends on the mental disposition with which we approach them. If you consider what is meant by the common phrases, a happy disposition and a discontented temper, you will perceive that the truth for which I am contending is universally admitted.

(Mr Flosky suddenly stopped: he found himself unintentionally trespassing within the limits of common sense.)

MR HILARY. It is very true; a happy disposition finds materials of enjoyment everywhere. In the city, or the country – in society, or in solitude – in the theatre, or the forest – in the hum of the multitude, or in the silence of the mountains, are alike materials of reflection and elements of pleasure. It is one mode of pleasure to listen to the music of *Don Giovanni*, in a theatre glittering with light, and crowded with elegance and beauty: it is another to glide at sunset over the bosom of a lonely lake, where no sound disturbs the silence but the motion of the boat through the waters. A happy disposition derives pleasure from both, a discontented temper from neither, but is always busy in detecting deficiencies, and feeding dissatisfaction with comparisons. The one gathers all the flowers, the other all the nettles, in its path. The one has the faculty of enjoying everything, the other of enjoying nothing. The one realizes all the pleasure of the present good; the other converts it into pain, by pining after something better, which is only better because it is not present, and which, if it were present, would not be enjoyed. These morbid spirits are in life what professed critics are in literature; they see nothing but faults, because they are predetermined to shut their eyes to beauties. The critic does his utmost to blight genius in its infancy; that which rises in spite of him he will not see; and then he complains of the decline of literature. In like manner, these cankers of society complain of human nature and society, when they have wilfully debarred themselves from all the good they contain, and done their utmost to blight their own happiness and that of all around them. Misanthropy is sometimes the product of disappointed benevolence; but it is more frequently the offspring of overweening and mortified vanity, quarrelling with the world for not being better treated than it deserves.

SCYTHROP (*to Marionetta*). These remarks are rather uncharitable. There is great good in human nature, but it is at present ill-conditioned. Ardent spirits cannot but be dissatisfied with things as they are; and according to their views of the probabilities of amelioration, they will rush into the extremes of either hope or despair – of which the first is enthusiasm, and the second misanthropy; but their sources in this case are the same, as the Severn and the Wye run in different directions, and both rise in Plinlimmon.

MARIONETTA. 'And there is salmon in both;' for the resemblance is about as close as that between Macedon and Monmouth.[8]

CHAPTER VIII

MARIONETTA OBSERVED the next day a remarkable perturbation in Scythrop, for which she could not imagine any probable cause. She was willing to believe at first that it had some transient and trifling source, and would pass off in a day or two; but, contrary to this expectation, it daily increased. She was well aware that Scythrop had a strong tendency to the love of mystery, for its own sake; that is to say, he would employ mystery to serve a purpose, but would first choose his purpose by its capability of mystery. He seemed now to have more mystery on his hands than the laws of the system allowed, and to wear his coat of darkness with an air of great discomfort. All her little playful arts lost by degrees much of their power either to irritate or to soothe; and the first perception of her diminished influence produced in her an immediate depression of spirits, and a consequent sadness of demeanour, that rendered her very interesting to Mr Glowry; who, duly considering the improbability of accomplishing his wishes with respect to Miss Toobad (which improbability naturally increased in the diurnal ratio of that young lady's absence), began to reconcile himself by degrees to the idea of Marionetta being his daughter.

Marionetta made many ineffectual attempts to extract from Scythrop the secret of his mystery; and, in despair of drawing it from himself, began to form hopes that she might find a clue to it from Mr Flosky, who was Scythrop's dearest friend, and was more frequently than any other person admitted to his solitary tower. Mr Flosky, however, had ceased to be visible in a morning. He was engaged in the composition of a dismal ballad; and, Marionetta's uneasiness overcoming her scruples of decorum, she determined to seek him in the apartment which he had chosen for his study. She tapped at the door, and at the sound 'Come in', entered the apartment. It was noon, and the sun was shining in full splendour, much to the annoyance of Mr Flosky, who had obviated the inconvenience by closing the shutters, and drawing the window-curtains. He was sitting at his table by the light of a solitary candle, with a pen in one hand, and a muffineer in the other, with which he occasionally sprinkled salt on the wick to make it burn blue. He sate with 'his eye in a fine frenzy rolling',[1] and turned his inspired gaze on Marionetta as if she had been the ghastly ladie of a magical vision; then placed his hand before his eyes, with an appearance of manifest pain – shook his head – withdrew his hand – rubbed his eyes, like a waking man – and said, in a tone of ruefulness most jeremitaylorically pathetic, 'To what am I to attribute this very unexpected pleasure, my dear Miss O'Carroll?'

MARIONETTA. I must apologize for intruding on you, Mr Flosky; but the interest which I – you – take in my cousin Scythrop —

MR FLOSKY. Pardon me, Miss O'Carroll; I do not take any interest in any person or thing on the face of the earth; which sentiment, if you analyse it, you will find to be the quintessence of the most refined philanthropy.

MARIONETTA. I will take it for granted that it is so, Mr Flosky; I am not conversant with metaphysical subtleties, but —

MR FLOSKY. Subtleties! my dear Miss O'Carroll. I am

sorry to find you participating in the vulgar error of the *reading public*, to whom an unusual collocation of words, involving a juxtaposition of antiperistatical ideas, immediately suggests the notion of hyperoxysophistical paradoxology.[2]

MARIONETTA. Indeed, Mr Flosky, it suggests no such notion to me. I have sought you for the purpose of obtaining information.

MR FLOSKY (*shaking his head*). No one ever sought me for such a purpose before.

MARIONETTA. I think, Mr Flosky – that is, I believe – that is, I fancy – that is, I imagine —

MR FLOSKY. The τουτεστι, the *id est*, the *cioè*, the *c'est à dire*, the *that is*, my dear Miss O'Carroll, is not applicable in this case – if you will permit me to take the liberty of saying so. Think is not synonymous with believe – for belief, in many most important particulars, results from the total absence, the absolute negation of thought, and is thereby the sane and orthodox condition of mind; and thought and belief are both essentially different from fancy, and fancy, again, is distinct from imagination. This distinction between fancy and imagination is one of the most abstruse and important points of metaphysics. I have written seven hundred pages of promise to elucidate it, which promise I shall keep as faithfully as the bank will its promise to pay.

MARIONETTA. I assure you, Mr Flosky, I care no more about metaphysics than I do about the bank; and, if you will condescend to talk to a simple girl in intelligible terms —

MR FLOSKY. Say not condescend! Know you not that you talk to the most humble of men, to one who has buckled on the armour of sanctity, and clothed himself with humility as with a garment?

MARIONETTA. My cousin Scythrop has of late had an air of mystery about him, which gives me great uneasiness.

MR FLOSKY. That is strange: nothing is so becoming to a man as an air of mystery. Mystery is the very key-stone of all that is beautiful in poetry, all that is sacred in faith, and all that is recondite in transcendental psychology. I am writing a ballad which is all mystery; it is 'such stuff as dreams are made of',[3] and is, indeed, stuff made of a dream; for, last night I fell asleep as usual over my book, and had a vision of pure reason. I composed five hundred lines in my sleep;[4] so that, having had a dream of a ballad, I am now officiating as my own Peter Quince, and making a ballad of my dream, and it shall be called Bottom's Dream, because it has no bottom.

MARIONETTA. I see, Mr Flosky, you think my intrusion unseasonable, and are inclined to punish it, by talking nonsense to me. (*Mr Flosky gave a start at the word nonsense, which almost overturned the table.*) I assure you, I would not have intruded if I had not been very much interested in the question I wish to ask you. (*Mr Flosky listened in sullen dignity.*) My cousin Scythrop seems to have some secret preying on his mind. (*Mr Flosky was silent.*) He seems very unhappy – Mr Flosky. Perhaps you are acquainted with the cause. (*Mr Flosky was still silent.*) I only wish to know – Mr Flosky – if it is anything – that could be remedied by anything – that anyone – of whom I know anything – could do.

MR FLOSKY (*after a pause*). There are various ways of getting at secrets. The most approved methods, as recommended both theoretically and practically in philosophical novels, are eavesdropping at key-holes, picking the locks of chests and desks, peeping into letters, steaming wafers, and insinuating hot wire under sealing wax; none of which methods I hold it lawful to practise.

MARIONETTA. Surely, Mr Flosky, you cannot suspect me of wishing to adopt or encourage such base and contemptible arts.

MR FLOSKY. Yet are they recommended, and with well-strung reasons, by writers of gravity and note, as simple and easy methods of studying character, and gratifying that laudable curiosity which aims at the knowledge of man.

MARIONETTA. I am as ignorant of this morality which you do not approve, as of the metaphysics which you do: I should be glad to know by your means, what is the matter with my cousin; I do not like to see him unhappy, and I suppose there is some reason for it.

MR FLOSKY. Now I should rather suppose there is no reason for it: it is the fashion to be unhappy. To have a reason for being so would be exceedingly common-place: to be so without any is the province of genius: the art of being miserable for misery's sake, has been brought to great perfection in our days; and the ancient Odyssey, which held forth a shining example of the endurance of real misfortune, will give place to a modern one, setting out a more instructive picture of querulous impatience under imaginary evils.

MARIONETTA. Will you oblige me, Mr Flosky, by giving me a plain answer to a plain question?

MR FLOSKY. It is impossible, my dear Miss O'Carroll. I never gave a plain answer to a question in my life.

MARIONETTA. Do you, or do you not, know what is the matter with my cousin?

MR FLOSKY. To say that I do not know, would be to say that I am ignorant of something; and God forbid, that a transcendental metaphysician, who has pure anticipated cognitions of everything, and carries the whole science of geometry in his head without ever having looked into Euclid, should fall into so empirical an error as to declare himself ignorant of anything: to say that I do know, would be to pretend to positive and circumstantial knowledge touching present matter of fact, which, when you consider the nature of evidence, and the various lights in which the same thing may be seen —

MARIONETTA. I see, Mr Flosky, that either you have no information, or are determined not to impart it; and I beg your pardon for having given you this unnecessary trouble.

MR FLOSKY. My dear Miss O'Carroll, it would have given me great pleasure to have said anything that would have given you pleasure; but if any person living could make report of having obtained any information on any subject from Ferdinando Flosky, my transcendental reputation would be ruined for ever.

CHAPTER IX

SCYTHROP GREW every day more reserved, mysterious, and *distrait*; and gradually lengthened the duration of his diurnal seclusions in his tower. Marionetta thought she perceived in all this very manifest symptoms of a warm love cooling.

It was seldom that she found herself alone with him in the morning, and, on these occasions, if she was silent in the hope of his speaking first, not a syllable would he utter; if she spoke to him indirectly, he assented monosyllabically; if she questioned him, his answers were brief, constrained, and evasive. Still, though her spirits were depressed, her playfulness had not so totally forsaken her, but that it illuminated at intervals the gloom of Nightmare Abbey; and if, on any occasion, she observed in Scythrop tokens of unextinguished or returning passion, her love of tormenting her lover immediately got the better both of her grief and her sympathy, though not of her curiosity, which Scythrop seemed determined not to satisfy. This playfulness, however, was in a great measure artificial, and usually vanished with the irritable Strephon, to whose annoyance it had been exerted. The Genius Loci, the *tutela* of Nightmare Abbey, the spirit of black melancholy, began to set his seal on her pallescent countenance. Scythrop perceived the change, found his tender sympathies awakened, and did his utmost to comfort the afflicted damsel, assuring her that his seeming inattention had only proceeded from his being involved in a profound meditation on a very hopeful scheme for the regeneration of human society. Marionetta called him ungrateful, cruel, cold-hearted, and accompanied her reproaches with many sobs and tears: poor Scythrop growing every moment more soft and submissive – till, at length, he threw himself at her feet, and declared that no competition of beauty, however dazzling, genius, however transcendent, talents, however cultivated, or philosophy, however enlightened, should ever make him renounce his divine Marionetta.

'Competition!' thought Marionetta, and suddenly, with an air of the most freezing indifference, she said, 'You are perfectly at liberty, sir, to do as you please; I beg you will follow your own plans, without any reference to me.'

Scythrop was confounded. What was become of all her passion and her tears? Still kneeling, he kissed her hand with rueful timidity, and said, in most pathetic accents, 'Do you not love me, Marionetta?'

'No,' said Marionetta, with a look of cold composure: 'No.' Scythrop still looked up incredulously. 'No, I tell you.'

'Oh! very well, madam,' said Scythrop, rising, 'if that is the case, there are those in the world —'

'To be sure there are, sir; and do you suppose I do not see through your designs, you ungenerous monster?'

'My designs? Marionetta!'

'Yes, your designs, Scythrop. You have come here to cast me off, and artfully contrive that it should appear to be my doing, and not yours, thinking to quiet your tender conscience with this pitiful stratagem. But do not suppose that you are of so much consequence to me: do not suppose it: you are of no consequence to me at all – none at all: therefore, leave me: I renounce you: leave me; why do you not leave me?'

Scythrop endeavoured to remonstrate, but without success. She reiterated her injunctions to him to leave her, till, in the simplicity of his spirit, he was preparing to comply. When he had nearly reached the door, Marionetta said, 'Farewell.' Scythrop looked back. 'Farewell, Scythrop,' she repeated, 'you will never see me again.'

'Never see you again, Marionetta?'

'I shall go from hence tomorrow, perhaps today; and before we meet again, one of us will be married, and we might as well be dead, you know, Scythrop.'

The sudden change of her voice in the last few words, and the burst of tears that accompanied them, acted like electricity on the tender-hearted youth; and, in another instant, a complete reconciliation was accomplished without the intervention of words.

There are, indeed, some learned casuists, who maintain that love has no language, and that all the misunderstandings and dissensions of lovers arise from the fatal habit of employing words on a subject to which words are inapplicable; that love, beginning with looks, that is to say, with the physiognomical expression of congenial mental dispositions, tends through a regular gradation of signs and symbols of affection, to that consummation which is most devoutly to be wished; and that it neither is necessary that there should be, nor probable that there would be, a single word spoken from first to last between two sympathetic spirits, were it not that the arbitrary institutions of society have raised, at every step of this very simple process, so many complicated impediments and barriers in the shape of settlements and ceremonies, parents and guardians, lawyers, Jew-brokers, and parsons, that many an adventurous knight (who, in order to obtain the conquest of the Hesperian fruit, is obliged to fight his way through all these monsters), is either repulsed at the onset, or vanquished before the achievement of his enterprise: and such a quantity of unnatural talking is rendered inevitably necessary through all the stages of the progression, that the tender and volatile spirit of love often takes flight on the pinions of some of the επεα πτεροεντα, or *winged words*, which are pressed into his service in despite of himself.

At this conjuncture, Mr Glowry entered, and sitting down near them, said, 'I see how it is; and, as we are all sure to be miserable do what we may, there is no need of taking pains to make one another more so; therefore, with God's blessing and mine, there' – joining their hands as he spoke.

Scythrop was not exactly prepared for this decisive step; but he could only stammer out, 'Really, sir, you are too good;' and Mr Glowry departed to bring Mr Hilary to ratify the act.

Now, whatever truth there may be in the theory of love and language, of which we have so recently spoken, certain it is, that during Mr Glowry's absence, which lasted half an hour, not a single word was spoken by either Scythrop or Marionetta.

Mr Glowry returned with Mr Hilary, who was delighted at the prospect of so advantageous an establishment for his orphan niece, of whom he considered himself in some manner the guardian, and nothing remained, as Mr Glowry observed, but to fix the day.

Marionetta blushed, and was silent. Scythrop was also silent for a time, and at length hesitatingly said, 'My dear sir, your goodness overpowers me; but really you are so precipitate.'

Now, this remark, if the young lady had made it, would, whether she thought it or not – for sincerity is a thing of no account on these occasions, nor indeed on any other, according to Mr Flosky – this remark, if the young lady had made it, would have been perfectly *comme il faut*;[1] but, being made by the young gentleman, it was *toute autre chose*,[2] and was, indeed, in the eyes of his mistress, a most heinous and irremissible offence. Marionetta was angry, very angry, but she concealed her anger, and said, calmly and coldly, 'Certainly, you are much too precipitate, Mr Glowry. I assure you, sir, I have by no means made up my mind; and, indeed, as far as I know it, it inclines the other way; but it will be quite time enough to think of these matters seven years hence.' Before surprise permitted reply, the young lady had locked herself up in her own apartment.

'Why, Scythrop,' said Mr Glowry, elongating his face exceedingly, 'the devil is come among us sure enough, as Mr Toobad observes: I thought you and Marionetta were both of a mind.'

'So we are, I believe, sir,' said Scythrop, gloomily, and stalked away to his tower.

'Mr Glowry,' said Mr Hilary, 'I do not very well under-stand all this.'

'Whims, brother Hilary,' said Mr Glowry; 'some little foolish love quarrel, nothing more. Whims, freaks, April showers. They will be blown over by tomorrow.'

'If not,' said Mr Hilary, 'these April showers have made us April fools.'

'Ah!' said Mr Glowry, 'you are a happy man, and in all your afflictions you can console yourself with a joke, let it be ever so bad, provided you crack it yourself. I should be very happy to laugh with you, if it would give you any satisfaction; but, really, at present, my heart is so sad, that I find it impossible to levy a contribution on my muscles.'

CHAPTER X

ON THE EVENING on which Mr Asterias had caught a glimpse of a female figure on the sea-shore, which he had translated into the visual sign of his interior cognition of a mermaid, Scythrop, retiring to his tower, found his study pre-occupied. A stranger, muffled in a cloak,[1] was sitting at his table. Scythrop paused in surprise. The stranger rose at his entrance, and looked at him intently a few minutes, in silence. The eyes of the stranger alone were visible. All the rest of the figure was muffled and mantled in the folds of a black cloak, which was raised, by the right hand, to the level of the eyes. This scrutiny being completed, the stranger, dropping the cloak, said, 'I see, by your physiognomy, that you may be trusted;' and revealed to the astonished Scythrop a female form and countenance of dazzling grace and beauty, with long flowing hair of raven blackness, and large black eyes of al-most oppressive brilliancy, which strikingly contrasted with a complexion of snowy whiteness. Her dress was extremely elegant, but had an appearance of foreign fashion, as if both the lady and her mantua-maker were of 'a far countree'.

> 'I guess 'twas frightful there to see
> A lady so richly clad as she,
> Beautiful exceedingly.'[2]

For, if it be terrible to one young lady to find another under a tree at midnight, it must, *a fortiori*, be much more terrible to a young gentleman to find a young lady in his study at that hour. If the logical consecutiveness of this conclusion be not manifest to my readers, I am sorry for their dulness, and must refer them, for more ample elucidation, to a treatise which Mr Flosky intends to write, on the Categories of Relation, which comprehend Substance and Accident, Cause and Effect, Action and Reaction.

Scythrop, therefore, either was or ought to have been frightened; at all events, he was astonished; and astonishment, though not in itself fear, is nevertheless a good stage towards it, and is, indeed, as it were, the halfway house between respect and terror, according to Mr Burke's graduated scale of the sublime.*

'You are surprised,' said the lady; 'yet why should you be surprised? If you had met me in a drawing-room, and I had been introduced to you by an old woman, it would have been a matter of course: can the division of two or three walls, and the absence of an unimportant personage, make the same object essentially different in the perception of a philosopher?'

'Certainly not,' said Scythrop; 'but when any class of objects has habitually presented itself to our perceptions in invariable conjunction with particular relations, then, on the sudden appearance of one object of the class divested of those accompaniments, the essential difference of the relation is, by an involuntary process, transferred to the object itself, which thus offers itself to our perceptions with all the strangeness of novelty.'

* There must be some mistake in this, for the whole honourable band of gentlemen-pensioners has resolved unanimously, that Mr Burke was a very sublime person, particularly after he had prostituted his own soul, and betrayed his country and mankind, for £1,200 a year: yet he does not appear to have been a very terrible personage, and certainly went off with a very small portion of human respect, though he contrived to excite, in a great degree, the astonishment of all honest men. Our immaculate laureate[3] (who gives us to understand that, if he had not been purified by holy matrimony into a mystical type, he would have died a virgin), is another sublime gentleman of the same genus: he very much astonished some persons when he sold his birthright for a pot of sack; but not even his *Sosia* has a grain of respect for him, though, doubtless, he thinks his name very terrible to the enemy, when he flourishes his criticopoetico-political tomahawk, and sets up his Indian yell for the blood of his old friends: but, at best, he is a mere political scarecrow, a man of straw, ridiculous to all who know of what material he is made; and to none more so, than to those who have stuffed him, and set him up, as the Priapus of the garden of the golden apples of corruption. [P.][4]

'You are a philosopher,' said the lady, 'and a lover of liberty. You are the author of a treatise called "Philosophical Gas; or, a Project for a General Illumination of the Human Mind".'

'I am,' said Scythrop, delighted at this first blossom of his renown.

'I am a stranger in this country,' said the lady; 'I have been but a few days in it, yet I find myself immediately under the necessity of seeking refuge from an atrocious persecution. I had no friend to whom I could apply; and, in the midst of my difficulties, accident threw your pamphlet in my way. I saw that I had, at least, one kindred mind in this nation, and determined to apply to you.'

'And what would you have me do?' said Scythrop, more and more amazed, and not a little perplexed.

'I would have you,' said the young lady, 'assist me in finding some place of retreat, where I can remain concealed from the indefatigable search that is being made for me. I have been so nearly caught once or twice already, that I cannot confide any longer in my own ingenuity.'

Doubtless, thought Scythrop, this is one of my golden candlesticks. 'I have constructed,' said he, 'in this tower, an entrance to a small suite of unknown apartments in the main building, which I defy any creature living to detect. If you would like to remain there a day or two, till I can find you a more suitable concealment, you may rely on the honour of a transcendental eleutherarch.'

'I rely on myself,' said the lady. 'I act as I please, go where I please, and let the world say what it will. I am rich enough to set it at defiance. It is the tyrant of the poor and the feeble, but the slave of those who are above the reach of its injury.'

Scythrop ventured to inquire the name of his fair *protégée*. 'What is a name?' said the lady: 'any name will serve the purpose of distinction. Call me Stella.[5] I see by your looks,' she added, 'that you think all this very strange. When you know me better, your surprise will cease. I submit not to be an accomplice in my sex's slavery. I am, like yourself, a lover of freedom, and I carry my theory into practice. *They alone are subject to blind authority who have no reliance on their own strength.*'[6]

Stella took possession of the recondite apartments. Scythrop intended to find her another asylum; but from day to day he postponed his intention, and by degrees forgot it. The young

lady reminded him of it from day to day, till she also forgot it.
Scythrop was anxious to learn her history; but she would add
nothing to what she had already communicated, that she was
shunning an atrocious persecution. Scythrop thought of Lord
C. and the Alien Act, and said, 'As you will not tell your name,
I suppose it is in the green bag.' Stella, not understanding
what he meant, was silent; and Scythrop, translating silence
into acquiescence, concluded that he was sheltering an
illuminée whom Lord S.[7] suspected of an intention to take the
Tower, and set fire to the Bank: exploits, at least, as likely to
be accomplished by the hands and eyes of a young beauty, as
by a drunken cobbler and doctor, armed with a pamphlet and
an old stocking.

Stella, in her conversations with Scythrop, displayed a
highly cultivated and energetic mind, full of impassioned
schemes of liberty, and impatience of masculine usurpation.
She had a lively sense of all the oppressions that are done under
the sun; and the vivid pictures which her imagination
presented to her of the numberless scenes of injustice and
misery which are being acted at every moment in every part of
the inhabited world, gave an habitual seriousness to her
physiognomy, that made it seem as if a smile had never once
hovered on her lips. She was intimately conversant with the
German language and literature; and Scythrop listened with
delight to her repetitions of her favourite passages from
Schiller and Goethe, and to her encomiums on the sublime
Spartacus Weishaupt, the immortal founder of the sect of the
Illuminati.[8] Scythrop found that his soul had a greater capacity
of love than the image of Marionetta had filled. The form of
Stella took possession of every vacant corner of the cavity, and
by degrees displaced that of Marionetta from many of the
outworks of the citadel; though the latter still held possession
of the *keep*. He judged, from his new friend calling herself
Stella, that, if it were not her real name, she was an admirer of
the principles of the German play from which she had taken
it, and took an opportunity of leading the conversation to that
subject; but to his great surprise, the lady spoke very ardently
of the singleness and exclusiveness of love, and declared that
the reign of affection was one and indivisible; that it might be
transferred, but could not be participated. 'If I ever love,' said
she, 'I shall do so without limit or restriction. I shall hold all
difficulties light, all sacrifices cheap, all obstacles gossamer.

But for love so total, I shall claim a return as absolute. I will have no rival: whether more or less favoured will be of little moment. I will be neither first nor second – I will be alone. The heart which I shall possess I will possess entirely, or entirely renounce.'

Scythrop did not dare to mention the name of Marionetta; he trembled lest some unlucky accident should reveal it to Stella, though he scarcely knew what result to wish or anticipate, and lived in the double fever of a perpetual dilemma. He could not dissemble to himself that he was in love, at the same time, with two damsels of minds and habits as remote as the antipodes. The scale of predilection always inclined to the fair one who happened to be present; but the absent was never effectually outweighed, though the degrees of exaltation and depression varied according to accidental variations in the outward and visible signs of the inward and spiritual graces of his respective charmers. Passing and repassing several times a day from the company of the one to that of the other, he was like a shuttle-cock between two battle-dores, changing its direction as rapidly as the oscillations of a pendulum, receiving many a hard knock on the cork of a sensitive heart, and flying from point to point on the feathers of a super-sublimated head. This was an awful state of things. He had now as much mystery about him as any romantic transcendentalist or transcendental romancer could desire. He had his esoterical and his exoterical love. He could not endure the thought of losing either of them, but he trembled when he imagined the possibility that some fatal discovery might deprive him of both. The old proverb concerning two strings to a bow gave him some gleams of comfort; but that concerning two stools occurred to him more frequently, and covered his forehead with a cold perspiration. With Stella, he could indulge freely in all his romantic and philosophical visions. He could build castles in the air, and she would pile towers and turrets on the imaginary edifices. With Marionetta it was otherwise: she knew nothing of the world and society beyond the sphere of her own experience. Her life was all music and sunshine, and she wondered what anyone could see to complain of in such a pleasant state of things. She loved Scythrop, she hardly knew why; indeed she was not always sure that she loved him at all: she felt her fondness increase or diminish in an inverse ratio to his. When she had manoeuvred him into a fever of passionate love, she often felt and always assumed indifference: if she found that her coldness was contagious, and that Scythrop either was, or pretended to be, as indifferent as herself, she would become doubly kind, and raise him again to that elevation from which she had previously thrown him down. Thus, when his love was flowing, hers was ebbing: when his was ebbing, hers was flowing. Now and then there were moments of level tide, when reciprocal affection seemed to promise imperturbable harmony; but Scythrop could scarcely resign his spirit to the pleasing illusion, before the pinnace of the lover's affections was caught in some eddy of the lady's caprice, and he was whirled away from the shore of his hopes, without rudder or compass, into an ocean of mists and storms. It resulted, from this system of conduct, that all that passed between Scythrop and Marionetta consisted in making and unmaking love. He had no opportunity to take measure of her understanding by conversations on general subjects, and on his favourite designs; and, being left in this respect to the exercise of indefinite conjecture, he took it for granted, as most lovers would do in similar circumstances, that she had great natural talents, which she wasted at present on trifles: but coquetry would end with marriage, and leave room for philosophy to exert its influence on her mind. Stella had no coquetry, no disguise: she was an enthusiast in subjects of general interest; and her conduct to Scythrop was always uniform, or rather showed a regular progression of partiality which seemed fast ripening into love.

CHAPTER XI

SCYTHROP, ATTENDING one day the summons to dinner, found in the drawing-room his friend Mr Cypress the poet,[1] whom he had known at college, and who was a great favourite of Mr Glowry. Mr Cypress said, he was on the point of leaving England, but could not think of doing so without a farewell-look at Nightmare Abbey and his respected friends, the moody Mr Glowry and the mysterious Mr Scythrop, the sublime Mr Flosky and the pathetic Mr Listless; to all of whom, and the morbid hospitality of the melancholy dwelling in which they were then assembled, he assured them he should always look back with as much affection as his lacerated spirit could feel for anything. The sympathetic condolence of their respective replies was cut short by Raven's announcement of 'dinner on table.'

The conversation that took place when the wine was in circulation, and the ladies were withdrawn, we shall report with our usual scrupulous fidelity.

MR GLOWRY. You are leaving England, Mr Cypress. There is a delightful melancholy in saying farewell to an old acquaintance, when the chances are twenty to one against ever meeting again. A smiling bumper to a sad parting, and let us all be unhappy together.

MR CYPRESS (*filling a bumper*). This is the only social habit that the disappointed spirit never unlearns.

THE REVEREND MR LARYNX (*filling*). It is the only piece of academical learning that the finished educatee retains.

MR FLOSKY (*filling*). It is the only objective fact which the sceptic can realize.

SCYTHROP (*filling*). It is the only styptic for a bleeding heart.

THE HONOURABLE MR LISTLESS (*filling*). It is the only trouble that is very well worth taking.

MR ASTERIAS (*filling*). It is the only key of conversational truth.

MR TOOBAD (*filling*). It is the only antidote to the great wrath of the devil.

MR HILARY (*filling*). It is the only symbol of perfect life. The inscription 'HIC NON BIBITUR' will suit nothing but a tombstone.[2]

MR GLOWRY. You will see many fine old ruins, Mr Cypress; crumbling pillars, and mossy walls – many a one-legged Venus and headless Minerva – many a Neptune buried in sand – many a Jupiter turned topsy-turvy – many a perforated Bacchus doing duty as a water-pipe – many reminiscences of the ancient world, which I hope was better worth living in than the modern; though, for myself, I care not a straw more for one than the other, and would not go twenty miles to see anything that either could show.

MR CYPRESS. It is something to seek, Mr Glowry. The mind is restless, and must persist in seeking, though to find is to be disappointed. Do you feel no aspirations towards the countries of Socrates and Cicero? No wish to wander among the venerable remains of the greatness that has passed for ever?

MR GLOWRY. Not a grain.

SCYTHROP. It is, indeed, much the same as if a lover should dig up the buried form of his mistress, and gaze upon relics which are anything but herself, to wander among a few mouldy ruins, that are only imperfect indexes to lost volumes of glory, and meet at every step the more melancholy ruins of human nature – a degenerate race of stupid and shrivelled slaves, grovelling in the lowest depths of servility and superstition.

THE HONOURABLE MR LISTLESS. It is the fashion to go abroad. I have thought of it myself, but am hardly equal to the exertion. To be sure, a little eccentricity and originality are allowable in some cases; and the most eccentric and original of all characters is an Englishman who stays at home.

SCYTHROP. I should have no pleasure in visiting countries that are past all hope of regeneration. There is great hope of our own; and it seems to me that an Englishman, who, either by his station in society, or by his genius, or (as in your instance, Mr Cypress,) by both, has the power of essentially serving his country in its arduous struggle with its domestic enemies, yet forsakes his country, which is still so rich in hope, to dwell in others which are only fertile in the ruins of memory, does what none of those ancients, whose fragmentary memorials you venerate, would have done in similar circumstances.

MR CYPRESS. Sir, I have quarrelled with my wife; and a man who has quarrelled with his wife is absolved from all duty to his country. I have written an ode to tell the people as much, and they may take it as they list.

SCYTHROP. Do you suppose, if Brutus had quarrelled with his wife, he would have given it as a reason to Cassius for having nothing to do with his enterprise? Or would Cassius have been satisfied with such an excuse?

MR FLOSKY. Brutus was a senator; so is our dear friend: but the cases are different. Brutus had some hope of political good: Mr Cypress has none. How should he, after what we have seen in France?

SCYTHROP. A Frenchman is born in harness, ready saddled, bitted, and bridled, for any tyrant to ride. He will fawn under his rider one moment, and throw him and kick him to death the next; but another adventurer springs on his back, and by dint of whip and spur on he goes as before. We may, without much vanity, hope better of ourselves.

MR CYPRESS. I have no hope for myself or for others. Our life is a false nature; it is not in the harmony of things; it is an all-blasting upas, whose root is earth, and whose leaves are the skies which rain their poison-dews upon mankind. We wither from our youth; we gasp with unslaked thirst for unattainable good; lured from the first to the last by phantoms – love, fame, ambition, avarice – all idle, and all ill – one meteor of many names, that vanishes in the smoke of death.*

MR FLOSKY. A most delightful speech, Mr Cypress. A most amiable and instructive philosophy. You have only to impress its truth on the minds of all living men, and life will then, indeed, be the desert and the solitude; and I must do you, myself, and our mutual friends, the justice to observe, that let society only give fair play at one and the same time, as I flatter myself it is inclined to do, to your system of morals, and my system of metaphysics, and Scythrop's system of politics, and Mr Listless's system of manners, and Mr Toobad's system of religion, and the result will be as fine a mental chaos as even the immortal Kant himself could ever have hoped to see; in the prospect of which I rejoice.

MR HILARY. 'Certainly, ancient, it is not a thing to rejoice at:'[3] I am one of those who cannot see the good that is to result from all this mystifying and blue-devilling of society. The contrast it presents to the cheerful and solid wisdom of antiquity is too forcible not to strike anyone who has the least knowledge of classical literature. To represent vice and misery as the necessary accompaniments of genius, is as mischievous as it is false, and the feeling is as unclassical as the language in which it is usually expressed.

MR TOOBAD. It is our calamity. The devil has come among us, and has begun by taking possession of all the cleverest fellows. Yet, forsooth, this is the enlightened age. Marry, how? Did our ancestors go peeping about with dark lanterns, and do we walk at our ease in broad sunshine? Where is the manifestation of our light? By what symptoms do you recognize it? What are its signs, its tokens, its symptoms, its symbols, its categories, its conditions? What is it, and why? How, where, when is it to be seen, felt, and understood? What do

* *Childe Harold*, canto 4. cxxiv. cxxvi. [P.]

we see by it which our ancestors saw not, and which at the same time is worth seeing? We see a hundred men hanged, where they saw one. We see five hundred transported, where they saw one. We see five thousand in the workhouse, where they saw one. We see scores of Bible Societies, where they saw none. We see paper, where they saw gold. We see men in stays, where they saw men in armour. We see painted faces, where they saw healthy ones. We see children perishing in manufactories, where they saw them flourishing in the fields. We see prisons, where they saw castles. We see masters, where they saw representatives. In short, they saw true men, where we see false knaves. They saw Milton, and we see Mr Sackbut.

MR FLOSKY. 'The false knave, sir, is my honest friend; therefore, I beseech you, let him be countenanced. God forbid but a knave should have some countenance at his friend's request.'[4]

MR TOOBAD. 'Good men and true' was their common term, like the καλος καγαθος[5] of the Athenians. It is so long since men have been either good or true, that it is to be questioned which is most obsolete, the fact or the phraseology.

MR CYPRESS. There is no worth nor beauty but in the mind's idea. Love sows the wind and reaps the whirlwind.* Confusion, thrice confounded, is the portion of him who rests even for an instant on that most brittle of reeds – the affection of a human being. The sum of our social destiny is to inflict or to endure.†

MR HILARY. Rather to bear and forbear, Mr Cypress – a maxim which you perhaps despise. Ideal beauty is not the mind's creation: it is real beauty, refined and purified in the mind's alembic,[6] from the alloy which always more or less accompanies it in our mixed and imperfect nature. But still the gold exists in a very ample degree. To expect too much is a disease in the expectant, for which human nature is not responsible; and, in the common name of humanity, I protest against these false and mischievous ravings. To rail against humanity for not being abstract perfection, and against human love for not realizing all the splendid visions of the poets of chivalry, is to rail at the summer for not being all sunshine, and at the rose for not being always in bloom.

MR CYPRESS. Human love! Love is not an inhabitant of the earth. We worship him as the Athenians did their unknown

* *Childe Harold*, canto 4. cxxiii. [P.]   † Ibid:, canto 3. lxxi. [P.]

God: but broken hearts are the martyrs of his faith, and the eye shall never see the form which phantasy paints, and which passion pursues through paths of delusive beauty, among flowers whose odours are agonies, and trees whose gums are poison.*

MR HILARY. You talk like a Rosicrucian, who will love nothing but a sylph, who does not believe in the existence of a sylph, and who yet quarrels with the whole universe for not containing a sylph.

MR CYPRESS. The mind is diseased of its own beauty, and fevers into false creation. The forms which the sculptor's soul has seized exist only in himself.†

MR FLOSKY. Permit me to discept. They are the mediums of common forms combined and arranged into a common standard. The ideal beauty of the Helen of Zeuxis was the combined medium of the real beauty of the virgins of Crotona.[7]

MR HILARY. But to make ideal beauty the shadow in the water, and, like the dog in the fable, to throw away the substance in catching at the shadow, is scarcely the characteristic of wisdom, whatever it may be of genius. To reconcile man as he is to the world as it is, to preserve and improve all that is good, and destroy or alleviate all that is evil, in physical and moral nature – have been the hope and aim of the greatest teachers and ornaments of our species. I will say, too, that the highest wisdom and the highest genius have been invariably accompanied with cheerfulness. We have sufficient proofs on record that Shakespeare and Socrates were the most festive of companions. But now the little wisdom and genius we have seem to be entering into a conspiracy against cheerfulness.

MR TOOBAD. How can we be cheerful with the devil among us?

THE HONOURABLE MR LISTLESS. How can we be cheerful when our nerves are shattered?

MR FLOSKY. How can we be cheerful when we are surrounded by a *reading public*, that is growing too wise for its betters?

SCYTHROP. How can we be cheerful when our great general designs are crossed every moment by our little particular passions?

* *Childe Harold*, canto 4. cxxi. cxxxvi. [P].
† Ibid., canto 4. cxxii. [P.]

MR CYPRESS. How can we be cheerful in the midst of disappointment and despair?

MR GLOWRY. Let as all be unhappy together.

MR HILARY. Let us sing a catch.

MR GLOWRY. No: a nice tragical ballad. The Norfolk Tragedy[8] to the tune of the Hundredth Psalm.

MR HILARY. I say a catch.

MR GLOWRY. I say no. A song from Mr Cypress.

ALL. A song from Mr Cypress.

MR CYPRESS *sung* —

> There is a fever of the spirit,
>   The brand of Cain's unresting doom,
> Which in the lone dark souls that bear it
>   Glows like the lamp in Tullia's tomb:
> Unlike that lamp, its subtle fire
>   Burns, blasts, consumes its cell, the heart,
> Till, one by one, hope, joy, desire,
>   Like dreams of shadowy smoke depart.
>
> When hope, love, life itself, are only
>   Dust — spectral memories — dead and cold —
> The unfed fire burns bright and lonely,
>   Like that undying lamp of old:
> And by that drear illumination,
>   Till time its clay-built home has rent,
> Though broods on feeling's desolation —
>   The soul is its own monument.

MR GLOWRY. Admirable. Let us all be unhappy together.

MR HILARY. Now, I say again, a catch.

THE REVEREND MR LARYNX. I am for you.

MR HILARY. 'Seamen three.'

THE REVEREND MR LARYNX. Agreed. I'll be Harry Gill, with the voice of three.[9] Begin.

MR HILARY AND THE REVEREND MR LARYNX.

> Seamen three! What men be ye?
> Gotham's three wise men we be.
> Whither in your bowl so free?
> To rake the moon from out the sea.
> The bowl goes trim. The moon doth shine.
> And our ballast is old wine;
> And your ballast is old wine.

> Who art thou, so fast adrift?
> I am he they call Old Care.
> Here on board we will thee lift.
> No: I may not enter there.
> Wherefore so? 'Tis Jove's decree,
> In a bowl Care may not be;
> In a bowl Care may not be.
>
> Fear ye not the waves that roll?
> No: in charmed bowl we swim.
> What the charm that floats the bowl?
> Water may not pass the brim.
> The bowl goes trim. The moon doth shine.
> And our ballast is old wine;
> And your ballast is old wine.

This catch was so well executed by the spirit and science of Mr Hilary, and the deep tri-une voice of the reverend gentleman, that the whole party, in spite of themselves, caught the contagion, and joined in chorus at the conclusion, each raising a bumper to his lips:

> The bowl goes trim: the moon doth shine:
> And our ballast is old wine.

Mr Cypress, having his ballast on board, stepped, the same evening, into his bowl, or travelling chariot, and departed to rake seas and rivers, lakes and canals, for the moon of ideal beauty.

CHAPTER XII

IT WAS THE custom of the Honourable Mr Listless, on adjourning from the bottle to the ladies, to retire for a few moments to make a second toilette, that he might present himself in becoming taste. Fatout, attending as usual, appeared with a countenance of great dismay, and informed his master that he had just ascertained that the abbey was haunted. Mrs Hilary's *gentlewoman*, for whom Fatout had lately conceived a *tendresse*, had been, as she expressed it, 'fritted out of her seventeen senses' the preceding night, as she was retiring to her bedchamber, by a ghastly figure which she had met stalking along one of the galleries, wrapped in a white shroud, with a bloody turban on its head. She had fainted away with fear; and, when she recovered, she found herself in the dark, and the figure was gone. '*Sacre – cochon – bleu!*'[1] exclaimed Fatout, giving very deliberate emphasis to every portion of his terrible oath – 'I vould not meet de *revenant*, de ghost – *non* – not for all de *bowl-de-ponch* in de vorld.'

'Fatout,' said the Honourable Mr Listless, 'did I ever see a ghost?'

'*Jamais*, monsieur, never.'

'Then I hope I never shall, for, in the present shattered state of my nerves, I am afraid it would be too much for me. There – loosen the lace of my stays a little, for really this plebeian practice of eating – not too loose – consider my shape. That will do. And I desire that you bring me no more stories of ghosts; for, though I do not believe in such things, yet, when one is awake in the night, one is apt, if one thinks of them, to have fancies that give one a kind of a chill, particularly if one opens one's eyes suddenly on one's dressing-gown, hanging in the moonlight, between the bed and the window.'

The Honourable Mr Listless, though he had prohibited Fatout from bringing him any more stories of ghosts, could not help thinking of that which Fatout had already brought; and, as it was uppermost in his mind, when he descended to the tea and coffee cups, and the rest of the company in the library, he almost involuntarily asked Mr Flosky, whom he looked up to as a most oraculous personage, whether any story of any ghost that had ever appeared to anyone, was entitled to any degree of belief?

MR FLOSKY. By far the greater number, to a very great degree.

THE HONOURABLE MR LISTLESS. Really, that is very alarming!

MR FLOSKY. *Sunt geminae somni portae.*[2] There are two gates through which ghosts find their way to the upper air: fraud and self-delusion. In the latter case, a ghost is a *deceptio visûs*, an ocular spectrum, an idea with the force of a sensation. I have seen many ghosts myself. I dare say there are few in this company who have not seen a ghost.

THE HONOURABLE MR LISTLESS. I am happy to say, I never have, for one.

THE REVEREND MR LARYNX. We have such high authority for ghosts, that it is rank scepticism to disbelieve them. Job saw a ghost, which came for the express purpose of asking a question, and did not wait for an answer.

THE HONOURABLE MR LISTLESS. Because Job was too frightened to give one.

THE REVEREND MR LARYNX. Spectres appeared to the Egyptians during the darkness with which Moses covered Egypt. The witch of Endor raised the ghost of Samuel. Moses and Elias appeared on Mount Tabor. An evil spirit was sent into the army of Sennacherib, and exterminated it in a single night.

MR TOOBAD. Saying, The devil is come among you, having great wrath.

MR FLOSKY. Saint Macarius interrogated a skull, which was found in the desert, and made it relate, in presence of several witnesses, what was going forward in hell. Saint Martin of Tours, being jealous of a pretended martyr, who was the rival saint of his neighbourhood, called up his ghost, and made him confess that he was damned. Saint Germain, being on his travels, turned out of an inn a large party of ghosts, who had every night taken possession of the *table d'hôte*, and consumed a copious supper.

MR HILARY. Jolly ghosts, and no doubt all friars. A similar party took possession of the cellar of M. Swebach, the painter, in Paris, drank his wine, and threw the empty bottles at his head.[3]

THE REVEREND MR LARYNX. An atrocious act.

MR FLOSKY. Pausanias relates, that the neighing of horses and the tumult of combatants were heard every night on the field of Marathon: that those who went purposely to hear these sounds suffered severely for their curiosity; but those who heard them by accident passed with impunity.

THE REVEREND MR LARYNX. I once saw a ghost myself, in my study, which is the last place where anyone but a ghost would look for me. I had not been into it for three months, and was going to consult Tillotson,[4] when, on opening the door, I saw a venerable figure in a flannel dressing-gown, sitting in my armchair, and reading my Jeremy Taylor. It vanished in a moment, and so did I; and what it was or what it wanted I have never been able to ascertain.

MR FLOSKY. It was an idea with the force of a sensation. It is seldom that ghosts appeal to two senses at once; but, when I was in Devonshire, the following story was well attested to me.

A young woman, whose lover was at sea, returning one evening over some solitary fields, saw her lover sitting on a stile over which she was to pass. Her first emotions were surprise and joy, but there was a paleness and seriousness in his face that made them give place to alarm. She advanced towards him, and he said to her, in a solemn voice, 'The eye that hath seen me shall see me no more. Thine eye is upon me, but I am not.' And with these words he vanished; and on that very day and hour, as it afterwards appeared, he had perished by ship-wreck.

The whole party now drew round in a circle, and each related some ghostly anecdote, heedless of the flight of time, till, in a pause of the conversation, they heard the hollow tongue of midnight sounding twelve.

MR HILARY. All these anecdotes admit of solution on psychological principles. It is more easy for a soldier, a philosopher, or even a saint, to be frightened at his own shadow, than for a dead man to come out of his grave. Medical writers cite a thousand singular examples of the force of imagination. Persons of feeble, nervous, melancholy temperament, exhausted by fever, by labour, or by spare diet, will readily conjure up, in the magic ring of their own phantasy, spectres, gorgons, chimaeras, and all the objects of their hatred and their love. We are most of us like Don Quixote, to whom a windmill was a giant, and Dulcinea a magnificent princess: all more or less the dupes of our own imagination, though we do not all go so far as to see ghosts, or to fancy ourselves pipkins and teapots.

MR FLOSKY. I can safely say I have seen too many ghosts myself to believe in their external existence. I have seen all kinds of ghosts: black spirits and white, red spirits and grey. Some in the shapes of venerable old men, who have met me in my rambles at noon; some of beautiful young women, who have peeped through my curtains at midnight.

THE HONOURABLE MR LISTLESS. And have proved, I doubt not, 'palpable to feeling as to sight'.[5]

MR FLOSKY. By no means, sir. You reflect upon my purity. Myself and my friends, particularly my friend Mr Sackbut, are famous for our purity. No, sir, genuine untangible ghosts. I live in a world of ghosts. I see a ghost at this moment.

Mr Flosky fixed his eyes on a door at the farther end of the library. The company looked in the same direction. The door

silently opened, and a ghastly figure, shrouded in white
drapery, with the semblance of a bloody turban on its head,
entered and stalked slowly up the apartment. Mr Flosky,
familiar as he was with ghosts, was not prepared for this
apparition, and made the best of his way out at the opposite
door. Mrs Hilary and Marionetta followed, screaming. The
Honourable Mr Listless, by two turns of his body, rolled first
off the sofa and then under it. The Reverend Mr Larynx
leaped up and fled with so much precipitation, that he overturned the table on the foot of Mr Glowry. Mr Glowry roared
with pain in the ear of Mr Toobad. Mr Toobad's alarm so
bewildered his senses, that, missing the door, he threw up one
of the windows, jumped out in his panic, and plunged over
head and ears in the moat. Mr Asterias and his son, who were
on the watch for their mermaid, were attracted by the splashing, threw a net over him, and dragged him to land.

Scythrop and Mr Hilary meanwhile had hastened to his
assistance, and, on arriving at the edge of the moat, followed
by several servants with ropes and torches, found Mr Asterias
and Aquarius busy in endeavouring to extricate Mr Toobad
from the net, who was entangled in the meshes, and floundering with rage. Scythrop was lost in amazement; but Mr Hilary
saw, at one view, all the circumstances of the adventure, and
burst into an immoderate fit of laughter; on recovering from
which, he said to Mr Asterias, 'You have caught an odd fish,
indeed.' Mr Toobad was highly exasperated at this unseasonable pleasantry; but Mr Hilary softened his anger, by producing a knife, and cutting the Gordian knot of his reticular
envelopement. 'You see,' said Mr Toobad, 'you see, gentlemen, in my unfortunate person proof upon proof of the present
dominion of the devil in the affairs of this world; and I have
no doubt but that the apparition of this night was Apollyon
himself in disguise, sent for the express purpose of terrifying
me into this complication of misadventures. The devil is come
among you, having great wrath, because he knoweth that he
hath but a short time.'

CHAPTER XIII

MR GLOWRY was much surprised, on occasionally visiting Scythrop's tower, to find the door always locked, and to be kept sometimes waiting many minutes for admission: during which he invariably heard a heavy rolling sound like that of a ponderous mangle, or of a waggon on a weighing-bridge, or of theatrical thunder.

He took little notice of this for some time; at length his curiosity was excited, and, one day, instead of knocking at the door, as usual, the instant he reached it, he applied his ear to the key-hole, and like Bottom, in the Midsummer Night's Dream, 'spied a voice', which he guessed to be of the feminine gender, and knew to be not Scythrop's, whose deeper tones he distinguished at intervals. Having attempted in vain to catch a syllable of the discourse, he knocked violently at the door, and roared for immediate admission. The voices ceased, the accustomed rolling sound was heard, the door opened, and Scythrop was discovered alone. Mr Glowry looked round to every corner of the apartment, and then said, 'Where is the lady?'

'The lady, sir?' said Scythrop.

'Yes, sir, the lady.'

'Sir, I do not understand you.'

'You don't, sir?'

'No, indeed, sir. There is no lady here.'

'But, sir, this is not the only apartment in the tower, and I make no doubt there is a lady up stairs.'

'You are welcome to search, sir.'

'Yes, and while I am searching, she will slip out from some lurking place, and make her escape.'

'You may lock this door, sir, and take the key with you.'

'But there is the terrace door: she has escaped by the terrace.'

'The terrace, sir, has no other outlet, and the walls are too high for a lady to jump down.'

'Well, sir, give me the key.'

Mr Glowry took the key, searched every nook of the tower, and returned.

'You are a fox, Scythrop; you are an exceedingly cunning

fox, with that demure visage of yours. What was that lumbering sound I heard before you opened the door?'

'Sound, sir?'

'Yes, sir, sound.'

'My dear sir, I am not aware of any sound, except my great table, which I moved on rising to let you in.'

'The table! – let me see that. No, sir; not a tenth part heavy enough, not a tenth part.'

'But, sir, you do not consider the laws of acoustics: a whisper becomes a peal of thunder in the focus of reverberation. Allow me to explain this: sounds striking on concave surfaces are reflected from them, and, after reflection, converge to points which are the foci of these surfaces. It follows, therefore, that the ear may be so placed in one, as that it shall hear a sound better than when situated nearer to the point of the first impulse: again, in the case of two concave surfaces placed opposite to each other —'

'Nonsense, sir. Don't tell me of foci. Pray, sir, will concave surfaces produce two voices when nobody speaks? I heard two voices, and one was feminine; feminine, sir: what say you to that?'

'Oh, sir, I perceive your mistake: I am writing a tragedy, and was acting over a scene to myself. To convince you, I will give you a specimen; but you must first understand the plot. It is a tragedy on the German model. The Great Mogul is in exile, and has taken lodgings at Kensington, with his only daughter, the Princess Rantrorina, who takes in needlework, and keeps a day school. *The princess is discovered hemming a set of shirts for the parson of the parish: they are to be marked with a large R. Enter to her the Great Mogul. A pause, during which they look at each other expressively. The princess changes colour several times. The Mogul takes snuff in great agitation. Several grains are heard to fall on the stage. His heart is seen to beat through his upper benjamin.* – THE MOGUL (*with a mournful look at his left shoe*). 'My shoe-string is broken.' – THE PRINCESS (*after an interval of melancholy reflection*). 'I know it.' – THE MOGUL. 'My second shoe-string! The first broke when I lost my empire: the second has broken today. When will my poor heart break?' – THE PRINCESS. 'Shoe-strings, hearts, and empires! Mysterious sympathy!'

'Nonsense, sir,' interrupted Mr. Glowry. 'That is not at all like the voice I heard.'

'But, sir,' said Scythrop, 'a key-hole may be so constructed as to act like an acoustic tube, and an acoustic tube, sir, will modify sound in a very remarkable manner. Consider the construction of the ear, and the nature and causes of sound. The external part of the ear is a cartilaginous funnel.'

'It won't do, Scythrop. There is a girl concealed in this tower, and find her I will. There are such things as sliding panels and secret closets.' – He sounded round the room with his cane, but detected no hollowness. – 'I have heard, sir,' he continued, 'that during my absence, two years ago, you had a dumb carpenter closeted with you day after day. I did not dream that you were laying contrivances for carrying on secret intrigues. Young men will have their way: I had my way when I was a young man: but, sir, when your cousin Marionetta —'

Scythrop now saw that the affair was growing serious. To have clapped his hand upon his father's mouth, to have entreated him to be silent, would, in the first place, not have made him so; and, in the second, would have shown a dread of being overheard by somebody. His only resource, therefore, was to try to drown Mr Glowry's voice; and, having no other subject, he continued his description of the ear, raising his voice continually as Mr Glowry raised his.

'When your cousin Marionetta,' said Mr Glowry, 'whom you profess to love – whom you profess to love, sir —'

'The internal canal of the ear,' said Scythrop, 'is partly bony and partly cartilaginous. This internal canal is —'

'Is actually in the house, sir; and, when you are so shortly to be – as I expect —'

'Closed at the further end by the *membrana tympani* —'

'Joined together in holy matrimony —'

'Under which is carried a branch of the fifth pair of nerves —'

'I say, sir, when you are so shortly to be married to your cousin Marionetta —'

'The *cavitas tympani* —'

A loud noise was heard behind the book-case, which, to the astonishment of Mr Glowry, opened in the middle, and the massy compartments, with all their weight of books, receding from each other in the manner of a theatrical scene, with a heavy rolling sound (which Mr Glowry immediately recognized to be the same which had excited his curiosity), disclosed an interior apartment, in the entrance of which stood the beautiful Stella, who, stepping forward, exclaimed, 'Married! Is he going to be married? The profligate!'

'Really, madam,' said Mr Glowry, 'I do not know what he is going to do, or what I am going to do, or what anyone is going to do; for all this is incomprehensible.'

'I can explain it all,' said Scythrop, 'in a most satisfactory manner, if you will but have the goodness to leave us alone.'

'Pray, sir, to which act of the tragedy of the Great Mogul does this incident belong?'

'I entreat you, my dear sir, leave us alone.'

Stella threw herself into a chair, and burst into a tempest of tears. Scythrop sat down by her, and took her hand. She snatched her hand away, and turned her back upon him. He rose, sat down on the other side, and took her other hand. She snatched it away, and turned from him again. Scythrop continued entreating Mr Glowry to leave them alone; but the old gentleman was obstinate, and would not go.

'I suppose, after all,' said Mr Glowry maliciously, 'it is only a phaenomenon in acoustics, and this young lady is a reflection of sound from concave surfaces.'

Someone tapped at the door: Mr Glowry opened it, and Mr Hilary entered. He had been seeking Mr Glowry, and had traced him to Scythrop's tower. He stood a few moments in silent surprise, and then addressed himself to Mr Glowry for an explanation.

'The explanation,' said Mr Glowry, 'is very satisfactory. The Great Mogul has taken lodgings at Kensington, and the external part of the ear is a cartilaginous funnel.'

'Mr Glowry, that is no explanation.'

'Mr Hilary, it is all I know about the matter.'

'Sir, this pleasantry is very unseasonable. I perceive that my niece is sported with in a most unjustifiable manner, and I shall see if she will be more successful in obtaining an intelligible answer.' And he departed in search of Marionetta.

Scythrop was now in a hopeless predicament. Mr Hilary made a hue and cry in the abbey, and summoned his wife and Marionetta to Scythrop's apartment. The ladies, not knowing what was the matter, hastened in great consternation. Mr Toobad saw them sweeping along the corridor, and judging from their manner that the devil had manifested his wrath in some new shape, followed from pure curiosity.

Scythrop meanwhile vainly endeavoured to get rid of Mr Glowry and to pacify Stella. The latter attempted to escape from the tower, declaring she would leave the abbey immediately, and he should never see her or hear of her more. Scythrop held her hand and detained her by force, till Mr Hilary reappeared with Mrs Hilary and Marionetta. Marionetta, seeing Scythrop grasping the hand of a strange beauty, fainted away in the arms of her aunt. Scythrop flew to her assistance; and Stella with redoubled anger sprang towards the door, but was intercepted in her intended flight by being caught in the arms of Mr Toobad, who exclaimed – 'Celinda!'

'Papa!' said the young lady disconsolately.

'The devil is come among you,' said Mr Toobad, 'how came my daughter here?'

'Your daughter!' exclaimed Mr Glowry.

'Your daughter!' exclaimed Scythrop, and Mr and Mrs Hilary.

'Yes,' said Mr Toobad, 'my daughter Celinda.'

Marionetta opened her eyes and fixed them on Celinda; Celinda in return fixed hers on Marionetta. They were at remote points of the apartment. Scythrop was equidistant from both of them, central and motionless, like Mahomet's coffin.

'Mr Glowry,' said Mr Toobad, 'can you tell by what means my daughter came here?'

'I know no more,' said Mr Glowry, 'than the Great Mogul.'

'Mr Scythrop,' said Mr Toobad, 'how came my daughter here?'

'I did not know, sir, that the lady was your daughter.'

'But how came she here?'

'By spontaneous locomotion,' said Scythrop, sullenly.

'Celinda,' said Mr Toobad, 'what does all this mean?'

'I really do not know, sir.'

'This is most unaccountable. When I told you in London that I had chosen a husband for you, you thought proper to run away from him; and now, to all appearance, you have run away to him.'

'How, sir! was that your choice?'

'Precisely; and if he is yours too we shall be both of a mind, for the first time in our lives.'

'He is not my choice, sir. This lady has a prior claim: I renounce him.'

'And I renounce him,' said Marionetta.

Scythrop knew not what to do. He could not attempt to conciliate the one without irreparably offending the other; and he was so fond of both, that the idea of depriving himself for ever of the society of either was intolerable to him: he therefore retreated into his strong-hold, mystery; maintained an impenetrable silence; and contented himself with stealing occasionally a deprecating glance at each of the objects of his idolatry. Mr Toobad and Mr Hilary, in the meantime, were each insisting on an explanation from Mr Glowry, who they thought had been playing a double game on this occasion. Mr Glowry was vainly endeavouring to persuade them of his innocence in the whole transaction. Mrs Hilary was endeavouring to mediate between her husband and brother. The Honourable Mr Listless, the Reverend Mr Larynx, Mr Flosky, Mr Asterias, and Aquarius, were attracted by the tumult to the scene of action, and were appealed to severally and conjointly by the respective disputants. Multitudinous questions, and answers *en masse*, composed a *charivari*, to which the genius of Rossini alone could have given a suitable accompaniment, and which was only terminated by Mrs Hilary and Mr Toobad retreating with the captive damsels. The whole party followed, with the exception of Scythrop, who threw himself into his armchair, crossed his left foot over his right knee, placed the hollow of his left hand on the interior ancle of his left leg, rested his right elbow on the elbow of the chair, placed the ball of his right thumb against his right temple, curved the forefinger along the upper part of his forehead, rested the point of the middle finger on the bridge of his nose, and the points of the two others on the lower part of the palm, fixed his eyes intently on the veins in the back of his left hand, and sat in this position like the immoveable Theseus, who, as is well known to many who have not been at college, and to some few who have, *sedet, aeternumque sedebit*.* We hope the admirers of the *minutiae* in poetry and romance will appreciate this accurate description of a pensive attitude.

* Sits, and will sit for ever. [P.]

CHAPTER XIV

SCYTHROP WAS STILL in this position when Raven entered to announce that dinner was on table.

'I cannot come,' said Scythrop.

Raven sighed. 'Something is the matter,' said Raven: 'but man is born to trouble.'

'Leave me,' said Scythrop: 'go, and croak elsewhere.'

'Thus it is,' said Raven. 'Five-and-twenty years have I lived in Nightmare Abbey, and now all the reward of my affection is – Go, and croak elsewhere. I have danced you on my knee, and fed you with marrow.'

'Good Raven,' said Scythrop, 'I entreat you to leave me.'

'Shall I bring your dinner here?' said Raven. 'A boiled fowl and a glass of Madeira are prescribed by the faculty in cases of low spirits. But you had better join the party: it is very much reduced already.'

'Reduced! how?'

'The Honourable Mr Listless is gone. He declared that, what with family quarrels in the morning, and ghosts at night, he could get neither sleep nor peace; and that the agitation was too much for his nerves: though Mr Glowry assured him that the ghost was only poor Crow walking in his sleep, and that the shroud and bloody turban were a sheet and a red nightcap.'

'Well, sir?'

'The Reverend Mr Larnyx has been called off on duty, to marry or bury (I don't know which) some unfortunate person or persons, at Claydyke: but man is born to trouble!'

'Is that all?'

'No. Mr Toobad is gone too, and a strange lady with him.'

'Gone!'

'Gone. And Mr and Mrs Hilary, and Miss O'Carroll: they are all gone. There is nobody left but Mr Asterias and his son, and they are going tonight.'

'Then I have lost them both.'

'Won't you come to dinner?'

'No.'

'Shall I bring your dinner here?'

'Yes.'

'What will you have?'

'A pint of port and a pistol.'*

'A pistol!'

'And a pint of port. I will make my exit like Werter. Go. Stay. Did Miss O'Carroll say anything?'

'No.'

'Did Miss Toobad say anything?'

'The strange lady? No.'

'Did either of them cry?'

'No.'

'What did they do?'

'Nothing.'

'What did Mr Toobad say?'

'He said, fifty times over, the devil was come among us.'

'And they are gone?'

'Yes; and the dinner is getting cold. There is a time for everything under the sun. You may as well dine first, and be miserable afterwards.'

'True, Raven. There is something in that. I will take your advice: therefore, bring me —'

'The port and the pistol?'

'No; the boiled fowl and Madeira.'

Scythrop had dined, and was sipping his Madeira alone, immersed in melancholy musing, when Mr Glowry entered, followed by Raven, who, having placed an additional glass and set a chair for Mr Glowry, withdrew. Mr Glowry sat down opposite Scythrop. After a pause, during which each filled and drank in silence, Mr Glowry said, 'So, sir, you have played your cards well. I proposed Miss Toobad to you: you refused her. Mr Toobad proposed you to her: she refused you. You fell in love with Marionetta, and were going to poison yourself, because, from pure fatherly regard to your temporal interests, I withheld my consent. When, at length, I offered you my consent, you told me I was too precipitate. And, after all, I find you and Miss Toobad living together in the same tower, and behaving in every respect like two plighted lovers. Now, sir, if there be any rational solution of all this absurdity, I shall be very much obliged to you for a small glimmering of information.'

'The solution, sir, is of little moment; but I will leave it in writing for your satisfaction. The crisis of my fate is come: the world is a stage, and my direction is *exit*.'

* See *The Sorrows of Werter*, Letter 93. [P.]

'Do not talk so, sir; do not talk so, Scythrop. What would you have?'

'I would have my love.'

'And pray, sir, who is your love?'

'Celinda – Marionetta – either – both.'

'Both! That may do very well in a German tragedy; and the Great Mogul might have found it very feasible in his lodgings at Kensington; but it will not do in Lincolnshire. Will you have Miss Toobad?'

'Yes.'

'And renounce Marionetta?'

'No.'

'But you must renounce one.'

'I cannot.'

'And you cannot have both. What is to be done?'

'I must shoot myself.'

'Don't talk so, Scythrop. Be rational, my dear Scythrop. Consider, and make a cool, calm choice, and I will exert myself in your behalf.'

'Why should I choose, sir? Both have renounced *me*: I have no hope of either.'

'Tell me which you will have, and I will plead your cause irresistibly.'

'Well, sir – I will have – no, sir, I cannot renounce either. I cannot choose either. I am doomed to be the victim of eternal disappointments; and I have no resource but a pistol.'

'Scythrop – Scythrop; if one of them should come to you – what then?'

'That, sir, might alter the case: but that cannot be.'

'It can be, Scythrop; it will be: I promise you it will be. Have but a little patience – but a week's patience; and it shall be.'

'A week, sir, is an age: but, to oblige you, as a last act of filial duty, I will live another week. It is now Thursday evening, twenty-five minutes past seven. At this hour and minute, on Thursday next, love and fate shall smile on me, or I will drink my last pint of port in this world.'

Mr Glowry ordered his travelling chariot, and departed from the abbey.

CHAPTER XV

THE DAY AFTER Mr Glowry's departure was one of incessant
rain, and Scythrop repented of the promise he had given. The
next day was one of bright sunshine: he sat on the terrace, read
a tragedy of Sophocles, and was not sorry, when Raven
announced dinner, to find himself alive. On the third evening,
the wind blew, and the rain beat, and the owl flapped against
his windows; and he put a new flint in his pistol. On the
fourth day, the sun shone again; and he locked the pistol up
in a drawer, where he left it undisturbed, till the morning of
the eventful Thursday, when he ascended the turret with a
telescope, and spied anxiously along the road that crossed the
fens from Claydyke: but nothing appeared on it. He watched
in this manner from ten am till Raven summoned him to
dinner at five; when he stationed Crow at the telescope, and
descended to his own funeral-feast. He left open the communications between the tower and turret, and called aloud at
intervals to Crow – 'Crow, Crow, is anything coming?'
Crow answered, 'The wind blows, and the windmills turn, but
I see nothing coming'; and, at every answer, Scythrop found
the necessity of raising his spirits with a bumper. After dinner,
he gave Raven his watch to set by the abbey clock. Raven
brought it, Scythrop placed it on the table, and Raven departed. Scythrop called again to Crow; and Crow, who had
fallen asleep, answered mechanically, 'I see nothing coming.'
Scythrop laid his pistol between his watch and his bottle.
The hour-hand passed the VII – the minute-hand moved on;
it was within three minutes of the appointed time. Scythrop
called again to Crow: Crow answered as before. Scythrop
rang the bell: Raven appeared.

'Raven,' said Scythrop, 'the clock is too fast.'

'No, indeed,' said Raven, who knew nothing of Scythrop's
intentions: 'if anything, it is too slow.'

'Villain!' said Scythrop, pointing the pistol at him; 'it is
too fast.'

'Yes – yes – too fast, I meant,' said Raven, in manifest fear.

'How much too fast?' said Scythrop.

'As much as you please,' said Raven.

'How much, I say?' said Scythrop, pointing the pistol
again.

'An hour, a full hour, sir,' said the terrified butler.

'Put back my watch,' said Scythrop.

Raven, with trembling hand, was putting back the watch, when the rattle of wheels was heard in the court; and Scythrop, springing down the stairs by three steps together, was at the door in sufficient time to have handed either of the young ladies from the carriage, if she had happened to be in it; but Mr Glowry was alone.

'I rejoice to see you,' said Mr Glowry; 'I was fearful of being too late, for I waited till the last moment in the hope of accomplishing my promise; but all my endeavours have been vain, as these letters will show.'

Scythrop impatiently broke the seals. The contents were these:

'Almost a stranger in England, I fled from parental tyranny, and the dread of an arbitrary marriage, to the protection of a stranger and a philosopher, whom I expected to find something better than, or at least something different from, the rest of his worthless species. Could I, after what has occurred, have expected nothing more from you than the commonplace impertinence of sending your father to treat with me, and with mine, for me? I should be a little moved in your favour, if I could believe you capable of carrying into effect the resolutions which your father says you have taken, in the event of my proving inflexible; though I doubt not you will execute them, as far as relates to the pint of wine, twice over, at least. I wish you much happiness with Miss O'Carroll. I shall always cherish a grateful recollection of Nightmare Abbey, for having been the means of introducing me to a true transcendentalist; and, though he is a little older than myself, which is all one in Germany, I shall very soon have the pleasure of subscribing myself

                              CELINDA FLOSKY.'

'I hope, my dear cousin, that you will not be angry with me, but that you will always think of me as a sincere friend, who will always feel interested in your welfare; I am sure you love Miss Toobad much better than me, and I wish you much happiness with her. Mr Listless assures me that people do not kill themselves for love nowadays, though it is still the fashion to talk about it. I shall, in a very short time, change my name and situation, and shall always be happy to see you in Berkeley Square, when, to the unalterable designation of your affectionate cousin, I shall subjoin the signature of

MARIONETTA LISTLESS.'

Scythrop tore both the letters to atoms, and railed in good set terms against the fickleness of women.

'Calm yourself, my dear Scythrop,' said Mr Glowry; 'there are yet maidens in England.'

'Very true, sir,' said Scythrop.

'And the next time,' said Mr Glowry, 'have but one string to your bow.'

'Very good advice, sir,' said Scythrop.

'And, besides,' said Mr. Glowry, 'the fatal time is past, for it is now almost eight.'

'Then that villain, Raven,' said Scythrop, 'deceived me when he said that the clock was too fast; but, as you observe very justly, the time has gone by, and I have just reflected that these repeated crosses in love qualify me to take a very advanced degree in misanthropy; and there is, therefore, good hope that I may make a figure in the world. But I shall ring for the rascal Raven, and admonish him.'

Raven appeared. Scythrop looked at him very fiercely two or three minutes; and Raven, still remembering the pistol, stood quaking in mute apprehension, till Scythrop, pointing significantly towards the dining-room, said, 'Bring some Madeira.'

THE
MISFORTUNES
OF ELPHIN

Unlooked-for good betides us still,
And unanticipated ill:
Blind Fortune rules the hours that roll:
Then fill with good old wine the bowl.[1]

Quod non exspectes ex transverso fit,
Et suprà nos Fortuna negotia curat:
Quare da nobis vina Falerna, puer.

PETRONIUS ARBITER

The Misfortunes of Elphin
was first published in 1829

Contents of
The Misfortunes of Elphin

Index to the Poetry

THE PROSPERITY OF GWAELOD

Regardless of the sweeping whirlwind's sway,
That, hush'd in grim repose, expects his evening prey.
                                                GRAY.

IN THE BEGINNING of the sixth century, when Uther Pendragon held the nominal sovereignty of Britain over a number
of petty kings,[1] Gwythno Garanhir was king of Caredigion.[2]
The most valuable portion of his dominions was the Great
Plain of Gwaelod, an extensive tract of level land, stretching
along that part of the sea-coast which now belongs to the
counties of Merioneth and Cardigan. This district was populous and highly cultivated. It contained sixteen fortified towns,
superior to all the towns and cities of the Cymry,[3] excepting
Caer Lleon upon Usk;[4] and, like Caer Lleon, they bore in their
architecture, their language, and their manners, vestiges of
past intercourse with the Roman lords of the world. It contained also one of the three privileged ports of the isle of
Britain, which was called the Port of Gwythno. This port, we
may believe if we please, had not been unknown to the Phoe-
nicians and Carthaginians, when they visited the island for
metal, accommodating the inhabitants, in return, with luxuries
which they would not otherwise have dreamed of, and which
they could very well have done without; of course, in arrang-
ing the exchange of what they denominated equivalents, imposing on their simplicity, and taking advantage of their
ignorance, according to the approved practice of civilized
nations; which they called imparting the blessings of Phoe-
nician and Carthaginian light.

An embankment of massy stone protected this lowland
country from the sea, which was said, in traditions older than
the embankment, to have, in occasional spring-tides, paid
short but unwelcome visits to the interior inhabitants, and to
have, by slow aggressions, encroached considerably on the
land. To prevent the repetition of the first of these incon-
veniences, and to check the progress of the second, the people
of Gwaelod had built the stony rampart, which had withstood

the shock of the waves for centuries, when Gwythno began his reign.

Gwythno, like other kings, found the business of governing too light a matter to fill up the vacancy of either his time or his head, and took to the more solid pursuits of harping and singing; not forgetting feasting, in which he was glorious; nor hunting, wherein he was mighty. His several pursuits composed a very harmonious triad. The chace conduced to the good cheer of the feast, and to the good appetite which consumed it; the feast inspired the song; and the song gladdened the feast, and celebrated the chace.

Gwythno and his subjects went on together very happily. They had little to do with him but to pay him revenue, and he had little to do with them but to receive it. Now and then they were called on to fight for the protection of his sacred person, and for the privilege of paying revenue to him rather than to any of the kings in his vicinity, a privilege of which they were particularly tenacious. His lands being far more fertile, and his people, consequently, far more numerous, than those of the rocky dwellers on his borders, he was always victorious in the defensive warfare to which he restricted his military achievements; and, after the invaders of his dominions had received two or three inflictions of signal chastisement, they limited their aggressions to coming quietly in the night, and vanishing, before morning, with cattle: an heroic operation, in which the pre-eminent glory of Scotland renders the similar exploits of other nations not worth recording.

Gwythno was not fond of the sea: a moonstruck bard had warned him to beware of the oppression of Gwenhidwy;* and he thought he could best do so by keeping as far as possible out of her way. He had a palace built of choice slate stone on the rocky banks of the Mawddach, just above the point where it quitted its native mountains, and entered the plain of Gwaelod. Here, among green woods and sparkling waters, he lived in festal munificence, and expended his revenue in encouraging agriculture, by consuming a large quantity of produce.

Watchtowers were erected along the embankment, and watchmen were appointed to guard against the first approaches of damage or decay. The whole of these towers, and their companies of guards, were subordinate to a central

* *Gwen-hudiw*, 'the white alluring one': the name of a mermaid. Used figuratiforvely the elemental power of the sea. [P.]

castle, which commanded the sea-port already mentioned, and wherein dwelt Prince Seithenyn ap Seithyn Saidi,[5] who held the office of Arglwyd Gorwarcheidwad yr Argae Breninawl, which signifies, in English, Lord High Commissioner of Royal Embankment; and he executed it as a personage so denominated might be expected to do: he drank the profits, and left the embankment to his deputies, who left it to their assistants, who left it to itself.

The condition of the head, in a composite as in a simple body, affects the entire organization to the extremity of the tail, excepting that, as the tail in the figurative body usually receives the largest share in the distribution of punishment, and the smallest in the distribution of reward, it has the stronger stimulus to ward off evil, and the smaller supply of means to indulge in diversion; and it sometimes happens that one of the least regarded of the component parts of the said tail will, from a pure sense of duty, or an inveterate love of business, or an oppressive sense of ennui, or a development of the organ of order, or some other equally cogent reason, cheerfully undergo all the care and labour, of which the honour and profit will redound to higher quarters.

Such a component portion of the Gwaelod High Commission of Royal Embankment was Teithrin ap Tathral, who had the charge of a watchtower where the embankment terminated at the point of Mochres,[6] in the high land of Ardudwy. Teithrin kept his portion of the embankment in exemplary condition, and paced with daily care the limits of his charge; but one day, by some accident, he strayed beyond them, and observed symptoms of neglect that filled him with dismay. This circumstance induced him to proceed till his wanderings brought him round to the embankment's southern termination in the high land of Caredigion.[7] He met with abundant hospitality at the towers of his colleagues, and at the castle of Seithenyn: he was supposed to be walking for his amusement; he was asked no questions, and he carefully abstained from asking any. He examined and observed in silence; and, when he had completed his observations, he hastened to the palace of Gwythno.

Preparations were making for a high festival, and Gwythno was composing an ode. Teithrin knew better than to interrupt him in his *awen.**

Gwythno had a son named Elphin,[8] who is celebrated in

* The rapturous and abstracted state of poetical inspiration. [P.]

history as the most expert of fishers. Teithrin, finding the king impracticable, went in search of the young prince.

Elphin had been all the morning fishing in the Mawddach, in a spot where the river, having quitted the mountains and not yet entered the plain, ran in alternate streams and pools, sparkling through a pastoral valley. Elphin sat under an ancient ash, enjoying the calm brightness of an autumnal noon, and the melody and beauty of the flying stream, on which the shifting sunbeams fell chequering through the leaves. The monotonous music of the river, and the profound stillness of the air, had contributed to the deep abstraction of a meditation into which Elphin had fallen. He was startled into attention by a sudden rush of the wind through the trees, and during the brief interval of transition from the state of reverie to that of perfect consciousness, he heard, or seemed to hear, in the gust that hurried by him, the repetition of the words, 'Beware of the oppression of Gwenhidwy.' The gust was momentary: the leaves ceased to rustle, and the deep silence of nature returned.

The prophecy, which had long haunted the memory and imagination of his father, had been often repeated to Elphin, and had sometimes occupied his thoughts, but it had formed no part of his recent meditation, and he could not persuade himself that the words had not been actually spoken near him. He emerged from the shade of the trees that fringed the river, and looked round him from the rocky bank.

At this moment Teithrin ap Tathral discovered and approached him.

Elphin knew him not, and inquired his name. He answered, 'Teithrin ap Tathral.'

'And what seek you here?' said Elphin.

'I seek,' answered Teithrin, 'the Prince of Gwaelod, Elphin ap Gwythno Garanhir.'

'You spoke,' said Elphin, 'as you approached.' Teithrin answered in the negative.

'Assuredly you did,' said Elphin. 'You repeated the words, "Beware of the oppression of Gwenhidwy."'

Teithrin denied having spoken the words; but their mysterious impression made Elphin listen readily to his information and advice; and the result of their conference was a determination, on the part of the Prince, to accompany Teithrin ap Tathral on a visit of remonstrance to the Lord High Commissioner.

They crossed the centre of the enclosed country to the privileged port of Gwythno, near which stood the castle of Seithenyn. They walked towards the castle along a portion of the embankment, and Teithrin pointed out to the Prince its dilapidated condition. The sea shone with the glory of the setting sun; the air was calm; and the white surf, tinged with the crimson of sunset, broke lightly on the sands below. Elphin turned his eyes from the dazzling splendour of ocean to the green meadows of the Plain of Gwaelod; the trees, that in the distance thickened into woods; the wreaths of smoke rising from among them, marking the solitary cottages, or the populous towns; the massy barrier of mountains beyond, with the forest rising from their base; the precipices frowning over the forest; and the clouds resting on their summits, reddened with the reflection of the west. Elphin gazed earnestly on the peopled plain, reposing in the calm of evening between the mountains and the sea, and thought, with deep feelings of secret pain, how much of life and human happiness was intrusted to the ruinous mound on which he stood.

CHAPTER II

THE DRUNKENNESS OF SEITHENYN

The three immortal drunkards of the isle of Britain: Ceraint of Essyllwg; Gwrtheyrn Gwrthenau; and Seithenyn ap Seithyn Saidi
TRIADS OF THE ISLE OF BRITAIN.[1]

THE SUN HAD sunk beneath the waves when they reached the castle of Seithenyn. The sound of the harp and the song saluted them as they approached it. As they entered the great hall, which was already blazing with torchlight, they found his highness, and his highness's household, convincing themselves and each other with wine and wassail, of the excellence of their system of virtual superintendence; and the following jovial chorus broke on the ears of the visitors:

THE CIRCLING OF THE MEAD HORNS[2]

Fill the blue horn, the blue buffalo horn:
Natural is mead in the buffalo horn:
As the cuckoo in spring, as the lark in the morn,
So natural is mead in the buffalo horn.

As the cup of the flower to the bee when he sips,
Is the full cup of mead to the true Briton's lips:
From the flower-cups of summer, on field and on tree,
Our mead cups are filled by the vintager bee.

Seithenyn * ap Seithyn, the generous, the bold,
Drinks the wine of the stranger from vessel of gold; †
But we from the horn, the blue silver-rimmed horn,
Drink the ale and the mead in our fields that were born.

The ale-froth is white, and the mead sparkles bright;
They both smile apart, and with smiles they unite: ‡
The mead from the flower, and the ale from the corn,
Smile, sparkle, and sing in the buffalo horn.

The horn, the blue horn, cannot stand on its tip;
Its path is right on from the hand to the lip:
Though the bowl and the wine-cup our tables adorn,
More natural the draught from the buffalo horn.

But Seithenyn ap Seithyn, the generous, the bold,
Drinks the bright-flowing wine from the far-gleaming gold:
The wine, in the bowl by his lip that is worn,
Shall be glorious as mead in the buffalo horn.

The horns circle fast, but their fountains will last,
As the stream passes ever, and never is past:
Exhausted so quickly, replenished so soon,
They wax and they wane like the horns of the moon.

Fill high the blue horn, the blue buffalo horn;
Fill high the long silver-rimmed buffalo horn:
While the roof of the hall by our chorus is torn,
Fill, fill to the brim, the deep silver-rimmed horn.

Elphin and Teithrin stood some time on the floor of the hall
before they attracted the attention of Seithenyn, who, during
the chorus, was tossing and flourishing his golden goblet.
The chorus had scarcely ended when he noticed them, and
immediately roared aloud, 'You are welcome all four.'

* The accent is on the second syllable: Seithényn. [P.]
† Gwin ... o eur ... ANEURIN. [P.]
‡ The mixture of ale and mead made *bradawd*, a favourite drink of the
Ancient Britons. [P.]

Elphin answered, 'We thank you: we are but two.'

'Two or four,' said Seithenyn, 'all is one. You are welcome all. When a stranger enters, the custom in other places is to begin by washing his feet. My custom is, to begin by washing his throat. Seithenyn ap Seithyn Saidi bids you welcome.'

Elphin, taking the wine-cup, answered, 'Elphin ap Gwythno Garanhir thanks you.'

Seithenyn started up. He endeavoured to straighten himself into perpendicularity, and to stand steadily on his legs. He accomplished half his object by stiffening all his joints but those of his ancles, and from these the rest of his body vibrated upwards with the inflexibility of a bar. After thus oscillating for a time, like an inverted pendulum, finding that the attention requisite to preserve his rigidity absorbed all he could collect of his dissipated energies, and that he required a portion of them for the management of his voice, which he felt a dizzy desire to wield with peculiar steadiness in the presence of the son of the king, he suddenly relaxed the muscles that perform the operation of sitting, and dropped into his chair like a plummet. He then, with a gracious gesticulation, invited Prince Elphin to take his seat on his right hand, and proceeded to compose himself into a dignified attitude, throwing his body back into the left corner of his chair, resting his left elbow on its arm and his left cheekbone on the middle of the back of his left hand, placing his left foot on a footstool, and stretching out his right leg as straight and as far as his position allowed. He had thus his right hand at liberty, for the ornament of his eloquence and the conduct of his liquor.

Elphin seated himself at the right hand of Seithenyn. Teithrin remained at the end of the hall: on which Seithenyn exclaimed, 'Come on, man, come on. What, if you be not the son of a king, you are the guest of Seithenyn ap Seithyn Saidi. The most honourable place to the most honourable guest, and the next most honourable place to the next most honourable guest; the least honourable guest above the most honourable inmate; and, where there are but two guests, be the most honourable who he may, the least honourable of the two is next in honour to the most honourable of the two, because they are no more but two; and, where there are only two, there can be nothing between. Therefore sit, and drink. Gwin o eur: wine from gold.'

Elphin motioned Teithrin to approach, and sit next to him.

Prince Seithenyn, whose liquor was 'his eating and his drinking solely', seemed to measure the gastronomy of his guests by his own; but his groom of the pantry thought the strangers might be disposed to eat, and placed before them a choice of provision, on which Teithrin ap Tathral did vigorous execution.

'I pray your excuses,' said Seithenyn, 'my stomach is weak, and I am subject to dizziness in the head, and my memory is not so good as it was, and my faculties of attention are some-what impaired, and I would dilate more upon the topic, whereby you should hold me excused, but I am troubled with a feverishness and parching of the mouth, that very much injures my speech, and impedes my saying all I would say, and will say before I have done, in token of my loyalty and fealty to your highness and your highness's house. I must just moisten my lips, and I will then proceed with my observations. Cupbearer, fill.'

'Prince Seithenyn,' said Elphin, 'I have visited you on a subject of deep moment. Reports have been brought to me, that the embankment, which has been so long intrusted to your care, is in a state of dangerous decay.'

'Decay,' said Seithenyn, 'is one thing, and danger is an-other.[3] Everything that is old must decay. That the embank-ment is old, I am free to confess; that it is somewhat rotten in parts, I will not altogether deny; that it is any worse for that, I do most sturdily gainsay. It does its business well: it works well: it keeps out the water from the land, and it lets in the wine upon the High Commission of Embankment. Cup-bearer, fill. Our ancestors were wiser than we: they built it in their wisdom; and, if we should be so rash as to try to mend it, we should only mar it.'

'The stonework,' said Teithrin, 'is sapped and mined: the piles are rotten, broken, and dislocated: the floodgates and sluices are leaky and creaky.'

'That is the beauty of it,' said Seithenyn. 'Some parts of it are rotten, and some parts of it are sound.'

'It is well,' said Elphin, 'that some parts are sound: it were better that all were so.'

'So I have heard some people say before,' said Seithenyn; 'perverse people, blind to venerable antiquity: that very unamiable sort of people, who are in the habit of indulging their reason. But I say, the parts that are rotten give elasticity to those that are sound: they give them elasticity, elasticity, elasticity. If it were all sound, it would break by its own obstinate stiffness: the soundness is checked by the rottenness, and the stiffness is balanced by the elasticity. There is nothing so dangerous as innovation. See the waves in the equinoctial storms, dashing and clashing, roaring and pouring, spattering and battering, rattling and battling against it. I would not be so presumptuous as to say, I could build anything that would stand against them half an hour; and here this immortal old work, which God forbid the finger of modern mason should bring into jeopardy, this immortal work has stood for centuries, and will stand for centuries more, if we let it alone. It is well: it works well: let well alone. Cupbearer, fill. It was half rotten when I was born, and that is a conclusive reason why it should be three parts rotten when I die.'

The whole body of the High Commission roared approbation.

'And after all,' said Seithenyn, 'the worst that could happen would be the overflow of a spring tide, for that was the worst that happened before the embankment was thought of; and, if the high water should come in, as it did before, the low water would go out again, as it did before. We should be no deeper in it than our ancestors were, and we could mend as easily as they could make.'

'The level of the sea,' said Teithrin, 'is materially altered.'

'The level of the sea!' exclaimed Seithenyn. 'Who ever heard of such a thing as altering the level of the sea? Alter the level of that bowl of wine before you, in which, as I sit here, I see a very ugly reflection of your very goodlooking face. Alter the level of that: drink up the reflection: let me see the face without the reflection, and leave the sea to level itself.'

'Not to level the embankment,' said Teithrin.

'Good, very good,' said Seithenyn. 'I love a smart saying, though it hits at me. But, whether yours is a smart saying or no, I do not very clearly see; and, whether it hits at me or no, I do not very sensibly feel. But all is one. Cupbearer, fill.'

'I think,' pursued Seithenyn, looking as intently as he could at Teithrin ap Tathral, 'I have seen something very like you before. There was a fellow here the other day very like you: he stayed here some time: he would not talk: he did nothing but drink: he used to drink till he could not stand, and then he went walking about the embankment. I suppose he thought it wanted mending; but he did not say anything. If he had, I should have told him to embank his own throat, to keep the liquor out of that. That would have posed him: he could not have answered that: he would not have had a word to say for himself after that.'

'He must have been a miraculous person,' said Teithrin, 'to walk when he could not stand.'

'All is one for that,' said Seithenyn. 'Cupbearer, fill.'

'Prince Seithenyn,' said Elphin, 'if I were not aware that wine speaks in the silence of reason, I should be astonished at your strange vindication of your neglect of duty, which I take shame to myself for not having sooner known and remedied. The wise bard has well observed, "Nothing is done without the eye of the king."'

'I am very sorry,' said Seithenyn, 'that you see things in a wrong light: but we will not quarrel for three reasons: first, because you are the son of the king, and may do and say what you please, without anyone having a right to be displeased: second, because I never quarrel with a guest, even if he grows riotous in his cups: third, because there is nothing to quarrel about; and perhaps that is the best reason of the three; or rather the first is the best, because you are the son of the king; and the third is the second, that is, the second best, because there is nothing to quarrel about; and the second is nothing to the purpose, because, though guests will grow riotous in their cups, in spite of my good orderly example, God forbid I should say, that is the case with you. And I completely agree in the truth of your remark, that reason speaks in the silence of wine.'

Seithenyn accompanied his speech with a vehement swinging of his right hand: in so doing, at this point, he dropped his cup: a sudden impulse of rash volition, to pick it dexterously up before he resumed his discourse, ruined all his devices for maintaining dignity; in stooping forward from his chair, he lost his balance, and fell prostrate on the floor.

The whole body of the High Commission arose in simultaneous confusion, each zealous to be the foremost in uplifting his fallen chief. In the vehemence of their uprise, they hurled the benches backward and the tables forward; the crash of cups and bowls accompanied their overthrow; and rivulets of liquor ran gurgling through the hall. The household wished to redeem the credit of their leader in the eyes of the Prince; but the only service they could render him was to participate in his discomfiture; for Seithenyn, as he was first in dignity, was also, as was fitting, hardest in skull; and that which had impaired his equilibrium had utterly destroyed theirs. Some fell, in the first impulse, with the tables and benches; others were tripped up by the rolling bowls; and the remainder fell at different points of progression, by jostling against each other, or stumbling over those who had fallen before them.

CHAPTER III

THE OPPRESSION OF GWENHIDWY

Nid meddw y dyn a allo
Cwnu ei hun a rhodio,
Ac yved rhagor ddiawd:
Nid yw hyny yn veddwdawd.

Not drunk is he, who from the floor
Can rise alone, and still drink more;
But drunk is he, who prostrate lies,
Without the power to drink or rise.

A SIDE DOOR, at the upper end of the hall, to the left of Seithenyn's chair, opened, and a beautiful young girl entered the hall, with her domestic bard, and her attendant maidens.

It was Angharad, the daughter of Seithenyn. The tumult had drawn her from the solitude of her chamber, apprehensive that some evil might befall her father in that incapability of self-protection to which he made a point of bringing himself by set of sun. She gracefully saluted Prince Elphin, and directed the cupbearers, (who were bound, by their office, to remain half sober till the rest of the company were finished off, after which they indemnified themselves at leisure,) she directed the cupbearers to lift up Prince Seithenyn, and bear him from the hall. The cupbearers reeled off with their lord, who had already fallen asleep, and who now began to play them a pleasant march with his nose, to inspirit their progression.

Elphin gazed with delight on the beautiful apparition, whose gentle and serious loveliness contrasted so strikingly with the broken trophies and fallen heroes of revelry that lay scattered at her feet.

'Stranger,' she said, 'this seems an unfitting place for you: let me conduct you where you will be more agreeably lodged.'

'Still less should I deem it fitting for you, fair maiden,' said Elphin.

She answered, 'The pleasure of her father is the duty of Angharad.'

Elphin was desirous to protract the conversation, and this very desire took from him the power of speaking to the purpose. He paused for a moment to collect his ideas, and Angharad stood still, in apparent expectation that he would show symptoms of following, in compliance with her invitation.

In this interval of silence, he heard the loud dashing of the sea, and the blustering of the wind through the apertures of the walls.

This supplied him with what has been, since Britain was Britain, the alpha and omega of British conversation. He said, 'It seems a stormy night.'

She answered, 'We are used to storms: we are far from the mountains, between the lowlands and the sea, and the winds blow round us from all quarters.'

There was another pause of deep silence. The noise of the sea was louder, and the gusts pealed like thunder through the apertures. Amidst the fallen and sleeping revellers, and confused and littered hall, the low and wavering torches, Angharad, lovely always, shone with single and surpassing loveliness. The gust died away in murmurs, and swelled again into thunder, and died away in murmurs again; and, as it died away, mixed with the murmurs of ocean, a voice, that seemed one of the many voices of the wind, pronounced the ominous words, 'Beware of the oppression of Gwenhidwy.'

They looked at each other, as if questioning whether all had heard alike.

'Did you not hear a voice?' said Angharad, after a pause.

'The same,' said Elphin, 'which has once before seemed to say to me, "Beware of the oppression of Gwenhidwy."'

Teithrin hurried forth on the rampart: Angharad turned pale, and leaned against a pillar of the hall. Elphin was amazed and awed, absorbed as his feelings were in her. The sleepers on the floor made an uneasy movement, and uttered an inarticulate cry.

Teithrin returned. 'What say you?' said Elphin.

Teithrin answered, 'A tempest is coming from the west. The moon has waned three days, and is half hidden in clouds, just visible above the mountains: the bank of clouds is black in the west; the scud is flying before them; and the white waves are rolling to the shore.'

'This is the highest of the springtides,' said Angharad, 'and they are very terrible in the storms from the west, when the spray flies over the embankment, and the breakers shake the tower which has its foot in the surf.'

'Whence was the voice,' said Elphin, 'which we heard erewhile? Was it the cry of a sleeper in his drink, or an error of the fancy, or a warning voice from the elements?'

'It was surely nothing earthly,' said Angharad, 'nor was it an error of the fancy, for we all heard the words, "Beware of the oppression of Gwenhidwy." Often and often, in the storms of the springtides, have I feared to see her roll her power over the fields of Gwaelod.'

'Pray heaven she do not tonight,' said Teithrin.

'Can there be such a danger?' said Elphin.

'I think,' said Teithrin, 'of the decay I have seen, and I fear the voice I have heard.'

A long pause of deep silence ensued, during which they heard the intermitting peals of the wind, and the increasing sound of the rising sea, swelling progressively into wilder and more menacing tumult, till, with one terrific impulse, the whole violence of the equinoctial tempest seemed to burst upon the shore. It was one of those tempests which occur once in several centuries, and which, by their extensive devastations, are chronicled to eternity; for a storm that signalizes its course with extraordinary destruction, becomes as worthy of celebration as a hero for the same reason. The old bard seemed to be of this opinion; for the turmoil which appalled Elphin, and terrified Angharad, fell upon his ears as the sound of inspiration: the *awen* came upon him; and, seizing his harp, he mingled his voice and his music with the uproar of the elements:

THE SONG OF THE FOUR WINDS*

Wind from the north: the young spring day
Is pleasant on the sunny mead;
The merry harps at evening play;
The dance gay youths and maidens lead:
The thrush makes chorus from the thorn:
The mighty drinker fills his horn.

Wind from the east: the shore is still;
The mountain-clouds fly tow'rds the sea;
The ice is on the winter-rill;
The great hall fire is blazing free:
The prince's circling feast is spread:
Drink fills with fumes the brainless head.

Wind from the south: in summer shade
'Tis sweet to hear the loud harp ring;
Sweet is the step of comely maid,
Who to the bard a cup doth bring:
The black crow flies where carrion lies:
Where pignuts lurk, the swine will work.

Wind from the west: the autumnal deep
Rolls on the shore its billowy pride:
He, who the rampart's watch must keep,
Will mark with awe the rising tide:
The high springtide, that bursts its mound,
May roll o'er miles of level ground.

Wind from the west: the mighty wave
Of ocean bounds o'er rock and sand;
The foaming surges roar and rave
Against the bulwarks of the land:
When waves are rough, and winds are high,
Good is the land that's high and dry.

Wind from the west: the storm-clouds rise;
The breakers rave; the whirlblasts roar;
The mingled rage of seas and skies
Bursts on the low and lonely shore:
When safety's far, and danger nigh,
Swift feet the readiest aid supply.

Wind from the west —

* This poem is a specimen of a numerous class of ancient Welsh poems,
in which each stanza begins with a repetition of the predominant idea, and
terminates with a proverb, more or less applicable to the subject. In some
poems, the sequency of the main images is regular and connected, and the

His song was cut short by a tremendous crash.[2] The tower, which had its foot in the sea, had long been sapped by the waves; the storm had prematurely perfected the operation, and the tower fell into the surf, carrying with it a portion of the wall of the main building, and revealing, through the chasm, the white raging of the breakers beneath the blackness of the midnight storm. The wind rushed into the hall, extinguishing the torches within the line of its course, tossing the grey locks and loose mantle of the bard, and the light white drapery and long black tresses of Angharad. With the crash of the falling tower, and the simultaneous shriek of the women, the sleepers started from the floor, staring with drunken amazement; and, shortly after, reeling like an Indian from the wine-rolling Hydaspes,* in staggered Seithenyn ap Seithyn.

Seithenyn leaned against a pillar, and stared at the sea through the rifted wall, with wild and vacant surprise. He perceived that there was an innovation, and he felt that he was injured: how, or by whom, he did not quite so clearly discern. He looked at Elphin and Teithrin, at his daughter, and at the members of his household, with a long and dismal aspect of blank and mute interrogation, modified by the struggling consciousness of puzzled self-importance, which seemed to require from his chiefship some word of command in this incomprehensible emergency. But the longer he looked, the less clearly he saw; and the longer he pondered, the less he understood. He felt the rush of the wind; he saw the white foam of the sea; his ears were dizzy with their mingled roar. He remained at length motionless, leaning against the pillar, and gazing on the breakers with fixed and glaring vacancy.

'The sleepers of Gwaelod,' said Elphin, 'they who sleep in peace and security, trusting to the vigilance of Seithenyn, what will become of them?'

---

proverbial terminations strictly appropriate: in others, the sequency of the main images is loose and incoherent, and the proverbial termination has little or nothing to do with the subject of the stanza. The basis of the poem in the text is in the *Englynion* of Llwyarch Hên.[1] [P.]

* In the fourteenth and fifteenth books of the *Dionysiaca* of Nonnus, Bacchus changes the river Astacis into wine; and the multitudinous army of water-drinking Indians, proceeding to quench their thirst in the stream, become franticly drunk, and fall an easy prey to the Bacchic invaders. In the thirty-fifth book, the experiment is repeated on the Hydaspes. '*Ainsi conquesta Bacchus l'Inde,*' as Rabelais has it. [P.]

'Warn them with the beacon fire,' said Teithrin, 'if there be
uel on the summit of the landward tower.'

'That of course has been neglected too,' said Elphin.

'Not so,' said Angharad, 'that has been my charge.'

Teithrin seized a torch, and ascended the eastern tower, and
in a few minutes, the party in the hall beheld the breakers
reddening with the reflected fire, and deeper and yet deeper
crimson tinging the whirling foam, and sheeting the massy
darkness of the bursting waves.

Seithenyn turned his eyes on Elphin. His recollection of
him was extremely faint, and the longer he looked on him he
remembered him the less. He was conscious of the presence of
strangers, and of the occurrence of some signal mischief, and
associated the two circumstances in his dizzy perceptions with
a confused but close connection. He said at length, looking
sternly at Elphin, 'I do not know what right the wind has to
blow upon me here; nor what business the sea has to show
itself here; nor what business you have here: but one thing is
very evident, that either my castle or the sea is on fire; and I
shall be glad to know who has done it, for terrible shall be the
vengeance of Seithenyn ap Seithyn. Show me the enemy,' he
pursued, drawing his sword furiously, and flourishing it over
his head. 'Show me the enemy; show me the enemy.'

An unusual tumult mingled with the roar of the waves; a
sound, the same in kind, but greater in degree, with that produced by the loose stones of the beach, which are rolled to and
fro by the surf.

Teithrin rushed into the hall, exclaiming, 'All is over! the
mound is broken; and the springtide is rolling through the
breach.'

Another portion of the castle wall fell into the mining
waves, and, by the dim and thickly clouded moonlight, and
the red blaze of the beacon fire, they beheld a torrent pouring
in from the sea upon the plain, and rushing immediately beneath the castle walls, which, as well as the points of the embankment that formed the sides of the breach, continued to
crumble away into the waters.

'Who has done this?' vociferated Seithenyn. 'Show me the
enemy.'

'There is no enemy but the sea,' said Elphin, 'to which you,
in your drunken madness, have abandoned the land. Think, if
you can think, of what is passing in the plain. The storm

drowns the cries of your victims; but the curses of the perishing are upon you.'

'Show me the enemy,' vociferated Seithenyn, flourishing his sword more furiously.

Angharad looked deprecatingly at Elphin, who abstained from further reply.

'There is no enemy but the sea,' said Teithrin, 'against which your sword avails not.'

'Who dares to say so?' said Seithenyn. 'Who dares to say that there is an enemy on earth against whom the sword of Seithenyn ap Seithyn is unavailing? Thus, thus I prove the falsehood.'

And, springing suddenly forward, he leaped into the torrent, flourishing his sword as he descended.

'Oh, my unhappy father!' sobbed Angharad, veiling her face with her arm on the shoulder of one of her female attendants, whom Elphin dexterously put aside, and substituted himself as the supporter of the desolate beauty.

'We must quit the castle,' said Teithrin, 'or we shall be buried in its ruins. We have but one path of safety, along the summit of the embankment, if there be not another breach between us and the high land, and if we can keep our footing in this hurricane. But there is no alternative. The walls are melting away like snow.'

The bard, who was now recovered from his *awen*, and beginning to be perfectly alive to his own personal safety, conscious at the same time that the first duty of his privileged order was to animate the less-gifted multitude by examples of right conduct in trying emergencies, was the first to profit by Teithrin's admonition, and to make the best of his way through the door that opened to the embankment, on which he had no sooner set his foot than he was blown down by the wind, his harp-strings ringing as he fell. He was indebted to the impediment of his harp, for not being rolled down the mound into the waters which were rising within.

Teithrin picked him up, and admonished him to abandon his harp to its fate, and fortify his steps with a spear. The bard murmured objections: and even the reflection that he could more easily get another harp than another life, did not reconcile him to parting with his beloved companion. He got over the difficulty by slinging his harp, cumbrous as it was, to his left side, and taking a spear in his right hand.

Angharad, recovering from the first shock of Seithenyn's catastrophe, became awake to the imminent danger. The spirit of the Cymric female, vigilant and energetic in peril, disposed her and her attendant maidens to use their best exertions for their own preservation. Following the advice and example of Elphin and Teithrin, they armed themselves with spears, which they took down from the walls.

Teithrin led the way, striking the point of his spear firmly into the earth, and leaning from it on the wind: Angharad followed in the same manner: Elphin followed Angharad, looking as earnestly to her safety as was compatible with moderate care of his own: the attendant maidens followed Elphin; and the bard, whom the result of his first experiment had rendered unambitious of the van, followed the female train. Behind them went the cupbearers, whom the accident of sobriety had qualified to march: and behind them reeled and roared those of the bacchanal rout who were able and willing to move; those more especially who had wives or daughters to support their tottering steps. Some were incapable of loco-motion, and others, in the heroic madness of liquor, sat down to await their destiny, as they finished the half-drained vessels.

The bard, who had somewhat of a picturesque eye, could not help sparing a little leisure from the care of his body, to observe the effects before him: the volumed blackness of the storm; the white bursting of the breakers in the faint and scarcely-perceptible moonlight; the rushing and rising of the waters within the mound; the long floating hair and waving drapery of the young women; the red light of the beacon fire falling on them from behind; the surf rolling up the side of the embankment, and breaking almost at their feet; the spray flying above their heads; and the resolution with which they impinged the stony ground with their spears, and bore themselves up against the wind.

Thus they began their march. They had not proceeded far, when the tide began to recede, the wind to abate somewhat of its violence, and the moon to look on them at intervals through the rifted clouds, disclosing the desolation of the in-undated plain, silvering the tumultuous surf, gleaming on the distant mountains, and revealing a lengthened prospect of their solitary path, that lay in its irregular line like a ribbon on the deep.

CHAPTER IV

THE LAMENTATIONS OF GWYTHNO

Οὐ παύσομαι τὰς Χάριτας
Μούσαις συγκαταμιγνύς,
Ἡδίσταν ουζυγίαν.

EURIPIDES.

·Not, though grief my age defaces,
Will I cease, in concert dear,
Blending still the gentle graces
With the muses more severe.

KING GWYTHNO had feasted joyously, and had sung his new
ode to a chosen party of his admiring subjects, amidst their, of
course, enthusiastic applause. He heard the storm raging
without, as he laid himself down to rest: he thought it a very
hard case for those who were out in it, especially on the sea;
congratulated himself on his own much more comfortable
condition; and went to sleep with a pious reflection on the
goodness of Providence to himself.

He was roused from a pleasant dream by a confused and
tumultuous dissonance, that mingled with the roar of the
tempest. Rising with much reluctance, and looking forth from
his window, he beheld in the moonlight a half-naked multitude, larger than his palace thrice multiplied could have
contained, pressing round the gates, and clamouring for admission and shelter; while beyond them his eye fell on the
phaenomenon of stormy waters, rolling in the place of the
fertile fields from which he derived his revenue.

Gwythno, though a king and his own laureate, was not
without sympathy for the people who had the honour and
happiness of victualling his royal house, and he issued forth on
his balcony full of perplexities and alarms, stunned by the
sudden sense of the half-understood calamity, and his head
still dizzy from the effects of abruptly-broken sleep, and the
vapours of the overnight's glorious festival.

Gwythno was altogether a reasonably good sort of person,
and a poet of some note. His people were somewhat proud of
him on the latter score, and very fond of him on the former;
for even the tenth part of those homely virtues, that decorate
the memories of 'husbands kind and fathers dear' in every

churchyard, are matters of plebeian admiration in the persons of royalty; and every tangible point in every such virtue so located, becomes a convenient peg for the suspension of love and loyalty. While, therefore, they were unanimous in consigning the soul of Seithenyn to a place that no well-bred divine will name to a polite congregation, they overflowed, in the abundance of their own griefs, with a portion of sympathy for Gwythno, and saluted him, as he issued forth on his balcony, with a hearty *Duw cadw y Brenin*, or God save the King, which he returned with a benevolent wave of the hand; but they followed it up by an intense vociferation for food and lodging, which he received with a pitiful shake of the head.

Meanwhile the morning dawned: the green spots, that peered with the ebbing tide above the waste of waters, only served to indicate the irremediableness of the general desolation.

Gwythno proceeded to hold a conference with his people, as deliberately as the stormy state of the weather and their minds, and the confusion of his own, would permit. The result of the conference was, that they should use their best exertions to catch some stray beeves, which had escaped the inundation, and were lowing about the rocks in search of new pastures. This measure was carried into immediate effect: the victims were killed and roasted, carved, distributed, and eaten, in a very Homeric fashion, and washed down with a large portion of the contents of the royal cellars; after which, having more leisure to dwell on their losses, the fugitives of Gwaelod proceeded to make loud lamentation, all collectively for home and for country, and severally for wife or husband, parent or child, whom the flood had made its victims.

In the midst of these lamentations arrived Elphin and Angharad, with her bard and attendant maidens, and Teithrin ap Tathral. Gwythno, after a consultation, dispatched Teithrin and Angharad's domestic bard on an embassy to the court of Uther Pendragon, and to such of the smaller kings as lay in the way, to solicit such relief as their several majesties might be able and willing to afford to a king in distress. It is said, that the bard, finding a royal bardship vacant in a more prosperous court, made the most of himself in the market, and stayed where he was better fed and lodged than he could expect to be in Caredigion; but that Teithrin returned, with many valuable gifts, and most especially one from Merlin, being a hamper, which multiplied an hundredfold by morning whatever was put into it overnight, so that, for a ham and a flask put by in the evening, an hundred hams and an hundred flasks were taken out in the morning. It is at least certain that such a hamper is enumerated among the thirteen wonders of Merlin's art, and, in the authentic catalogue thereof, is called the Hamper of Gwythno.

Be this as it may, Gwythno, though shorn of the beams of his revenue, kept possession of his palace. Elphin married Angharad, and built a salmon-weir on the Mawddach, the produce of which, with that of a series of beehives, of which his princess and her maidens made mead, constituted for some time the principal wealth and subsistence of the royal family of Caredigion.

King Gwythno, while his son was delving or fishing, and his daughter spinning or making mead, sat all day on the rocks, with his harp between his knees, watching the rolling of ocean over the locality of his past dominion, and pouring forth his soul in pathetic song on the change of his own condition, and the mutability of human things. Two of his songs of lamentation have been preserved by tradition: they are the only relics of his muse which time has spared.

GWYDDNAU EI CANT,

PAN DDOAI Y MOR DROS CANTREV Y GWAELAWD

A SONG OF GWYTHNO GARANHIR,

ON THE INUNDATION OF THE SEA OVER THE PLAIN OF GWAELOD.

Stand forth, Seithenyn: winds are high:
Look down beneath the lowering sky;
Look from the rock: what meets thy sight?
Nought but the breakers rolling white.

Stand forth, Seithenyn: winds are still:
Look from the rock and heathy hill
For Gwythno's realm: what meets thy view?
Nought but the ocean's desert blue.

Curst be the treacherous mound, that gave
A passage to the mining wave:
Curst be the cup, with mead-froth crowned,
That charmed from thought the trusted mound.

A tumult, and a cry to heaven!
The white surf breaks; the mound is riven:
Through the wide rift the ocean-spring
Bursts with tumultuous ravaging.

The western ocean's stormy might
Is curling o'er the rampart's height:
Destruction strikes with want and scorn
Presumption, from abundance born.

The tumult of the western deep
Is on the winds, affrighting sleep:
It thunders at my chamber-door;
It bids me wake, to sleep no more.

The tumult of the midnight sea
Swells inland, wildly, fearfully:
The mountain-caves respond its shocks
Among the unaccustomed rocks.

The tumult of the vext sea-coast
Rolls inland like an armed host:
It leaves, for flocks and fertile land,
But foaming waves and treacherous sand.

The wild sea rolls where long have been
Glad homes of men, and pastures green:
To arrogance and wealth succeed
Wide ruin and avenging need.

Seithenyn, come: I call in vain:
The high of birth and weak of brain
Sleeps under ocean's lonely roar
Between the rampart and the shore.

The eternal waste of waters, spread
Above his unrespected head,
The blue expanse, with foam besprent,
Is his too glorious monument.

ANOTHER SONG OF GWYTHNO

I love the green and tranquil shore;
I hate the ocean's dizzy roar,
Whose devastating spray has flown
High o'er the monarch's barrier-stone.

Sad was the feast, which he who spread
Is numbered with the inglorious dead;
The feast within the torch-lit hall,
While stormy breakers mined the wall.

To him repentance came too late:
In cups the chatterer met his fate:
Sudden and sad the doom that burst
On him and me, but mine the worst.

I love the shore, and hate the deep:
The wave has robbed my nights of sleep:
The heart of man is cheered by wine;
But now the wine-cup cheers not mine.

The feast, which bounteous hands dispense,
Makes glad the soul, and charms the sense:
But in the circling feast I know
The coming of my deadliest foe.

Blest be the rock, whose foot supplied
A step to them that fled the tide;
The rock of bards, on whose rude steep
I bless the shore, and hate the deep.

'The sigh of Gwythno Garanhir when the breakers
ploughed up his land'* is the substance of a proverbial distich,
which may still be heard on the coast of Merioneth and
Cardigan, to express the sense of an overwhelming calamity.
The curious investigator may still land on a portion of the
ancient stony rampart; which stretches, off the point of
Mochres, far out into Cardigan Bay, nine miles of the summit
being left dry, in calm weather, by the low water of the springtides; and which is now called Sarn Badrig, or St Patrick's
Causeway.

Thus the kingdom of Caredigion fell into ruin: its people
were destroyed, or turned out of house and home; and its
royal family were brought to a condition in which they found
it difficult to get loaves to their fishes. We, who live in more
enlightened times, amidst the 'gigantic strides of intellect',
when offices of public trust are so conscientiously and zea-
lously discharged, and so vigilantly checked and superintended, may wonder at the wicked negligence of Seithenyn;

* Ochenaid Gwyddnau Garanhir
  Pan droes y don dros ei dir. [P.]

at the sophisms with which, in his liquor, he vindicated his system, and pronounced the eulogium of his old dilapidations, and at the blind confidence of Gwythno and his people in this virtual guardian of their lives and property: happy that our own public guardians are too virtuous to act or talk like Seithenyn, and that we ourselves are too wise not to perceive, and too free not to prevent it, if they should be so disposed.

CHAPTER V

THE PRIZE OF THE WEIR

> Weave a circle round him thrice,
> And close your eyes with holy dread;
> For he on honey-dew hath fed,
> And drank the milk of paradise.
>   COLERIDGE.[1]

PRINCE ELPHIN constructed his salmon-weir on the Mawddach at the point where the fresh water met the top of the springtides. He built near it a dwelling for himself and Angharad, for which the old king Gwythno gradually deserted his palace. An amphitheatre of rocky mountains enclosed a pastoral valley. The meadows gave pasture to a few cows; and the flowers of the mountain-heath yielded store of honey to the bees of many hives, which were tended by Angharad and her handmaids. Elphin had also some sheep, which wandered on the mountains. The worst was, they often wandered out of reach; but, when he could not find his sheep, he brought down a wild goat, the venison of Gwyneth. The woods and turbaries supplied unlimited fuel. The straggling cultivators, who had escaped from the desolation of Gwaelod, and settled themselves above the level of the sea, on a few spots propitious to the plough, still acknowledged their royalty, and paid them tribute in corn. But their principal wealth was fish. Elphin was the first Briton who caught fish on a large scale, and salted them for other purposes than home consumption.

The weir was thus constructed: a range of piles crossed the river from shore to shore, slanting upwards from both shores, and meeting at an angle in the middle of the river. A little down the stream a second range of piles crossed the river in the same manner, having towards the middle several wide intervals with light wicker gates, which, meeting at an angle, were held together by the current, but were so constructed as to yield easily to a very light pressure from below. These gates gave all fish of a certain magnitude admission to a chamber, from which they could neither advance nor retreat, and from which, standing on a narrow bridge attached to the lower piles, Elphin bailed them up at leisure. The smaller fish passed freely up and down the river through the interstices of the piles. This weir was put together in the early summer, and taken to pieces and laid by in the autumn.

Prince Elphin, one fine July night, was sleepless and troubled in spirit. His fishery had been beyond all precedent unproductive, and the obstacle which this circumstance opposed to his arrangements for victualling his little garrison kept him for the better half of the night vigilant in unprofitable cogitation. Soon after the turn of midnight, when dreams are true, he was startled from an incipient doze by a sudden cry of Angharad, who had been favoured with a vision of a miraculous draught of fish. Elphin, as a drowning man catches at a straw, caught at the shadowy promise of Angharad's dream, and at once, beneath the clear light of the just-waning moon, he sallied forth with his princess to examine his weir.

The weir was built across the stream of the river, just above the flow of the ordinary tides; but the springtide had opened the wicker gates, and had floated up a coracle* between a pair of them, which closing, as the tide turned, on the coracle's nose, retained it within the chamber of the weir, at the same time that it kept the gates sufficiently open to permit the escape of any fish that might have entered the chamber. The great prize, which undoubtedly might have been there when Angharad dreamed of it, was gone to a fish.

Elphin, little pleased, stepped on the narrow bridge, and opened the gates with a pole that terminated piscatorially in a hook. The coracle began dropping down the stream. Elphin arrested its course, and guided it to land.

In the coracle lay a sleeping child, clothed in splendid apparel. Angharad took it in her arms. The child opened its eyes, and stretched its little arms towards her with a smile; and she uttered, in delight and wonder at its surpassing beauty, the exclamation of 'Taliesin!' 'Radiant brow!'

* A small boat of basketwork, sheathed with leather. [P.]

Elphin, nevertheless, looked very dismal on finding no food, and an additional mouth; so dismal, that his physiognomy on that occasion passed into a proverb: 'As rueful as Elphin when he found Taliesin.'*

In after years, Taliesin, being on the safe side of prophecy, and writing after the event, addressed a poem to Elphin, in the character of the foundling of the coracle, in which he supposes himself, at the moment of his discovery, to have addressed Elphin as follows:

DYHUDDIANT ELFFIN.
THE CONSOLATION OF ELPHIN.

> Lament not, Elphin: do no measure
> By one brief hour thy loss or gain:
> Thy weir tonight has borne a treasure,
> Will more than pay thee years of pain.
> St Cynllo's aid will not be vain:
> Smooth thy bent brow, and cease to mourn:
> Thy weir will never bear again
> Such wealth as it tonight has borne.

> The stormy seas, the silent rivers,
> The torrents down the steeps that spring,
> Alike of weal or woe are givers,
> As pleases heaven's immortal king.
> Though frail I seem, rich gifts I bring,
> Which in Time's fulness shall appear,
> Greater than if the stream should fling
> Three hundred salmon in thy weir.

> Cast off this fruitless sorrow, loading
> With heaviness the unmanly mind:
> Despond not; mourn not; evil boding
> Creates the ill it fears to find.
> When fates are dark, and most unkind
> Are they who most should do thee right,
> Then wilt thou know thine eyes were blind
> To thy good fortune of tonight.

* Mor drist ac Elffin pan gavod Taliesin. [P.]²

Though, small and feeble, from my coracle
To thee my helpless hands I spread,
Yet in me breathes a holy oracle
To bid thee lift thy drooping head.
When hostile steps around thee tread,
A spell of power my voice shall wield,
That, more than arms with slaughter red,
Shall be thy refuge and thy shield.

Two years after this event, Angharad presented Elphin with
a daughter, whom they named Melanghel. The fishery prospered; and the progress of cultivation and population among
the more fertile parts of the mountain districts brought in a
little revenue to the old king.

CHAPTER VI

THE EDUCATION OF TALIESIN

The three objects of intellect: the true, the beautiful, and the
beneficial.
The three foundations of wisdom: youth, to acquire learning;
memory, to retain learning; and genius, to illustrate learning.

TRIADS OF WISDOM.[1]

The three primary requisites of poetical genius: an eye, that can
see nature; a heart, that can feel nature; and a resolution, that dares
follow nature.

TRIADS OF POETRY.

As TALIESIN GREW UP, Gwythno instructed him in all the
knowledge of the age, which was of course not much, in comparison with ours. The science of political economy was
sleeping in the womb of time. The advantage of growing rich
by getting into debt and paying interest was altogether unknown: the safe and economical currency, which is produced
by a man writing his name on a bit of paper, for which other
men give him their property, and which he is always ready to
exchange for another bit of paper, of an equally safe and
economical manufacture, being also equally ready to render
his own person, at a moment's notice, as impalpable as the
metal which he promises to pay, is a stretch of wisdom to
which the people of those days had nothing to compare. They

had no steam-engines, with fires as eternal as those of the nether world, wherein the squalid many, from infancy to age, might be turned into component portions of machinery for the benefit of the purple-faced few. They could neither poison the air with gas, nor the waters with its dregs: in short, they made their money of metal, and breathed pure air, and drank pure water, like unscientific barbarians.

Of moral science they had little; but morals, without science, they had about the same as we have. They had a number of fine precepts, partly from their religion, partly from their bards, which they remembered in their liquor, and forgot in their business.

Political science they had none. The blessings of virtual representation were not even dreamed of; so that, when any of their barbarous metallic currency got into their pockets or coffers, it had a chance to remain there, subjecting them to the inconvenience of unemployed capital. Still they went to work politically much as we do. The powerful took all they could get from their subjects and neighbours; and called something or other sacred and glorious, when they wanted the people to fight for them. They repressed disaffection by force, when it showed itself in an overt act; but they encouraged freedom of speech, when it was, like Hamlet's reading, 'words, words, words.'

There was no liberty of the press, because there was no press; but there was liberty of speech to the bards, whose persons were inviolable, and the general motto of their order was y GWIR YN ERBYN y BYD: the Truth against the World. If many of them, instead of acting up to this splendid profession, chose to advance their personal fortunes by appealing to the selfishness, the passions, and the prejudices, of kings, factions, and the rabble, our free press gentry may afford them a little charity out of the excess of their own virtue.

In physical science, they supplied the place of knowledge by converting conjectures into dogmas; an art which is not yet lost. They held that the earth was the centre of the universe; that an immense ocean surrounded the earth; that the sky was a vast frame resting on the ocean; that the circle of their contact was a mystery of infinite mist; with a great deal more of cosmogony and astronomy, equally correct and profound, which answered the same purpose as our more correct and profound astronomy answers now, that of elevating the mind,

as the eidouranion[2] lecturers have it, to sublime contemplations.

Medicine was cultivated by the Druids, and it was just as
much a science with them as with us; but they had not the wit
or the means to make it a flourishing trade; the principal means
to that end being women with nothing to do, articles which
especially belong to a high state of civilization.

The laws lay in a small compass: every bard had those of his
own community by heart. The king, or chief, was the judge;
the plaintiff and defendant told their own story; and the cause
was disposed of in one hearing. We may well boast of the progress of light, when we turn from this picture to the statutes at
large, and the Court of Chancery; and we may indulge in a
pathetic reflection on our sweet-faced myriads of 'learned
friends', who would be under the unpleasant necessity of
suspending themselves by the neck, if this barbaric 'practice
of the courts' were suddenly revived.

The religion of the time was Christianity grafted on Druid-
ism. The Christian faith had been very early preached in
Britain. Some of the Welsh historians are of opinion that it
was first preached by some of the apostles: most probably by
St John. They think the evidence inconclusive with respect to
St Paul. But, at any rate, the faith had made considerable
progress among the Britons at the period of the arrival of
Hengist; for many goodly churches, and, what was still better,
richly-endowed abbeys, were flourishing in many places. The
British clergy were, however, very contumacious towards the
see of Rome, and would only acknowledge the spiritual
authority of the archbishopric of Caer Lleon, which was,
during many centuries, the primacy of Britain. St Augustin,
when he came over, at a period not long subsequent to that of
the present authentic history, to preach Christianity to the
Saxons, who had for the most part held fast to their Odinism,[3]
had also the secondary purpose of making them instruments
for teaching the British clergy submission to Rome: as a
means to which end, the newly converted Saxons set upon the
monastery of Bangor Iscoed, and put its twelve hundred
monks to the sword. This was the first overt act in which the
Saxons set forth their new sense of a religion of peace. It is
alleged, indeed, that these twelve hundred monks supported
themselves by the labour of their own hands. If they did so, it
was, no doubt, a gross heresy; but whether it deserved the

castigation it received from St Augustin's proselytes, may be a question in polemics.

As the people did not read the Bible, and had no religious tracts, their religion, it may be assumed, was not very pure. The rabble of Britons must have seen little more than the superficial facts, that the lands, revenues, privileges, and so forth, which once belonged to Druids and so forth, now belonged to abbots, bishops, and so forth; who, like their extruded precursors, walked occasionally in a row, chanting unintelligible words, and never speaking in common language but to exhort the people to fight; having, indeed, better notions than their predecessors of building, apparel, and cookery; and a better knowledge of the means of obtaining good wine, and of the final purpose for which it was made.

They were observant of all matters of outward form, and tradition even places among them personages who were worthy to have founded a society for the suppression of vice. It is recorded, in the Triads, that 'Cwrgi Garwlwyd killed a male and female of the Cymry daily, and devoured them; and, on the Saturday, he killed two of each, that he might not kill on the Sunday.' This can only be a type of some sanctimonious hero, who made a cloak of piety for oppressing the poor.

But, even among the Britons, in many of the least populous and most mountainous districts, Druidism was still struggling with Christianity. The lamb had driven the wolf from the rich pastures of the vallies to the high places of the wilderness, where the rites and mysteries of the old religion flourished in secrecy, and where a stray proselyte of the new light was occasionally caught and roasted for the glory of Andraste.

Taliesin, worshipping Nature in her wildest solitudes, often strayed away for days from the dwelling of Elphin, and penetrated the recesses of Eryri,* where one especial spot on the banks of Lake Ceirionydd became the favourite haunt of his youth. In these lonely recesses, he became familiar with Druids, who initiated him in their mysteries, which, like all other mysteries, consisted of a quantity of allegorical mummery, pretending to be symbolical of the immortality of the soul, and of its progress through various stages of being; interspersed with a little, too literal, ducking and singeing of the aspirant, by way of trying his mettle, just enough to put him in fear, but not in risk, of his life.

* Snowdon. [P.]

That Taliesin was thoroughly initiated in these mysteries is evident from several of his poems, which have neither head nor tail, and which, having no sense in any other point of view, must necessarily, as a learned mythologist has demonstrated, be assigned to the class of theology, in which an occult sense can be found or made for them, according to the views of the expounder. One of them, a shade less obscure than its companions, unquestionably adumbrates the Druidical doctrine of transmigration. According to this poem, Taliesin had been with the cherubim at the fall of Lucifer, in Paradise at the fall of man, and with Alexander at the fall of Babylon; in the ark with Noah, and in the milky-way with Tetragrammaton; and in many other equally marvellous or memorable conditions: showing that, though the names and histories of the new religion were adopted, its doctrines had still to be learned; and, indeed, in all cases of this description, names are changed more readily than doctrines, and doctrines more readily than ceremonies.

When any of the Romans or Saxons, who invaded the island, fell into the hands of the Britons, before the introduction of Christianity, they were handed over to the Druids, who sacrificed them, with pious ceremonies, to their goddess Andraste. These human sacrifices have done much injury to the Druidical character, amongst us, who never practise them in the same way. They lacked, it must be confessed, some of our light, and also some of our prisons. They lacked some of our light, to enable them to perceive that the act of coming, in great multitudes, with fire and sword, to the remote dwellings of peaceable men, with the premeditated design of cutting their throats, ravishing their wives and daughters, killing their children, and appropriating their worldly goods, belongs, not to the department of murder and robbery, but to that of legitimate war, of which all the practitioners are gentlemen, and entitled to be treated like gentlemen. They lacked some of our prisons, in which our philanthropy had provided accommodation for so large a portion of our own people, wherein, if they had left their prisoners alive, they could have kept them from returning to their countrymen, and being at their old tricks again immediately. They would also, perhaps, have found some difficulty in feeding them, from the lack of the county rates, by which the most sensible and amiable part of our nation, the country squires, contrive to coop up, and feed, at the public charge, all who meddle with the wild animals of which they have given themselves the monopoly. But as the Druids could neither lock up their captives, nor trust them at large, the darkness of their intellect could suggest no alternative to the process they adopted, of putting them out of the way, which they did with all the sanctions of religion and law. If one of these old Druids could have slept, like the seven sleepers of Ephesus,[4] and awaked, in the nineteenth century, some fine morning near Newgate, the exhibition of some half-dozen funipendulous forgers[5] might have shocked the tender bowels of his humanity, as much as one of his wicker baskets of captives in the flames shocked those of Caesar; and it would, perhaps, have been difficult to convince him that paper credit was not an idol, and one of a more sanguinary character than his Andraste. The Druids had their view of these matters, and we have ours; and it does not comport with the steam-engine speed of our march of mind to look at more than one side of a question.

The people lived in darkness and vassalage. They were lost in the grossness of beef and ale. They had no pamphleteering societies to demonstrate that reading and writing are better than meat and drink; and they were utterly destitute of the blessings of those 'schools for all', the house of correction, and the treadmill, wherein the autochthonal[6] justice of our agrestic kakistocracy[7] now castigates the heinous sins which were then committed with impunity, of treading on old foot-paths, picking up dead wood, and moving on the face of the earth within sound of the whir of a partridge.

The learning of the time was confined to the bards. It consisted in a somewhat complicated art of versification; in a great number of pithy apophthegms, many of which have been handed down to posterity under the title of the Wisdom of Catog; in an interminable accumulation of Triads, in which form they bound up all their knowledge, physical, traditional, and mythological; and in a mighty condensation of mysticism, being the still-cherished relics of the Druidical rites and doctrines.

The Druids were the sacred class of the bardic order. Before the change of religion, it was by far the most numerous class; for the very simple reason, that there was most to be got by it: all ages and nations having been sufficiently enlightened to make the trade of priest more profitable than that of poet.

During this period, therefore, it was the only class that much attracted the notice of foreigners. After the change of religion, the denomination was retained as that of the second class of the order. The Bardd Braint,[8] or Bard of Presidency, was of the ruling order, and wore a robe of sky-blue. The Derwydd, or Druid, wore a robe of white. The Ovydd, or Ovate, was of the class of initiation, and wore a robe of green. The Awenyddion, or disciples, the candidates for admission into the Bardic order, wore a variegated dress of the three colours, and were passed through a very severe moral and intellectual probation.

Gwythno was a Bardd Braint, or Bard of Presidency, and as such he had full power in his own person, without the intervention of a Bardic Congress, to make his Awenydd or disciple, Taliesin, an Ovydd or Ovate, which he did accordingly. Angharad, under the old king's instructions, prepared the green robe of the young aspirant's investiture. He afterwards acquired the white robe amongst the Druids of Eryri.

In all Bardic learning, Gwythno was profound. All that he knew he taught to Taliesin. The youth drew in the draughts of inspiration among the mountain forests and the mountain streams, and grew up under the roof of Elphin, in the perfection of genius and beauty.

CHAPTER VII

THE HUNTINGS OF MAELGON

Ἀεὶ τὸ μὲν ζῇ, τὸ δὲ μεθίσταται κακὸν,
Τὸ δ' ἐκπέφηνεν αὐτίκ' ἐξ ἀρχῆς νέον.
EURIPIDES.

One ill is ever clinging;
One treads upon its heels;
A third, in distance springing,
Its fearful front reveals.

GWYTHNO SLEPT, not with his fathers, for they were under the sea, but as near to them as was found convenient, within the sound of the breakers that rolled over their ancient dwellings. Elphin was now king of Caredigion, and was lord of a large but thinly peopled tract of rock, mountain, forest, and bog. He held his sovereignty, however, not, as Gwythno had done during the days of the glory of Gwaelod, by that most indisputable sort of right which consists in might, but by the more precarious tenure of the absence of inclination in any of his brother kings to take away anything he had.

Uther Pendragon, like Gwythno, went the way of all flesh, and Arthur reigned in Caer Lleon, as king of the kings of Britain. Maelgon Gwyneth was then king of that part of North Wales which bordered on the kingdom of Caredigion.[1]

Maelgon was a mighty hunter, and roused the echoes of the mountains with horn and with hound. He went forth to the chace as to war, provisioned for days and weeks, supported by bard and butler, and all the apparel of princely festivity. He pitched his tents in the forest of Snowdon, by the shore of lake or torrent; and, after hunting all the day, he feasted half the night. The light of his torches gleamed on the foam of the cataracts, and the sound of harp and song was mingled with their midnight roar.

When not thus employed, he was either feasting in his Castle of Diganwy,[2] on the Conwy, or fighting with any of the neighbouring kings, who had anything which he wanted, and which he thought himself strong enough to take from them.

Once, towards the close of autumn, he carried the tumult of the chace into the recesses of Meirion. The consonance, or dissonance, of men and dogs, outpealed the noise of the torrents among the rocks and woods of the Mawddach. Elphin and Teithrin were gone after the sheep or goats in the mountains; Taliesin was absent on the borders of his favourite lake; Angharad and Melanghel were alone. The careful mother, alarmed at the unusual din, and knowing, by rumour, of what materials the Nimrods of Britain were made, fled, with her daughter and handmaids, to the refuge of a deeply secluded cavern, which they had long before noted as a safe retreat from peril. As they ascended the hills that led to the cavern, they looked back, at intervals, through the openings of the woods, to the growing tumult on the opposite side of the valley. The wild goats were first seen, flying in all directions, taking prodigious leaps from crag to crag, now and then facing about, and rearing themselves on their hind legs, as if in act to butt, and immediately thinking better of it, and springing away on all fours among the trees. Next, the more rare spectacle of a noble stag presented itself on the summit of a projecting rock, pausing a moment to snuff the air, then bounding down the most practicable slope to the valley. Next, on the summit which the stag had just deserted, appeared a solitary huntsman, sitting on a prancing horse, and waking a hundred echoes with the blast of his horn. Next rushed into view the main body of the royal company, and the two-legged and four-legged avalanche came thundering down on the track of the flying prey: not without imminent hazard of broken necks; though the mountain-bred horses, which possessed by nature almost the surefootedness of mules, had finished their education under the first professors of the age.

The stag swam the river, and stood at bay before the dwelling of Elphin, where he was in due time dispatched by the conjoint valour of dog and man. The royal train burst into the solitary dwelling, where, finding nothing worthy of much note, excepting a large store of salt salmon and mead, they proceeded to broil and tap, and made fearful havoc among the family's winter provision. Elphin and Teithrin, returning to their expected dinner, stood aghast on the threshold of their plundered sanctuary. Maelgon condescended to ask them who they were; and, learning Elphin's name and quality, felt himself bound to return his involuntary hospitality by inviting him to Diganwy. So strong was his sense of justice on this head, that, on Elphin's declining the invitation, which Maelgon ascribed to modesty, he desired two of his grooms to take him up and carry him off.

So Elphin was impressed into royal favour, and was feasted munificently in the castle of Diganwy. Teithrin brought home the ladies from the cavern, and, during the absence of Elphin, looked after the sheep and goats, and did his master's business as well as his own.

One evening, when the royal 'nowle' was 'tottie of the must,'[3] while the bards of Maelgon were singing the praises of their master, and of all and everything that belonged to him, as the most eximious and transcendent persons and things of the superficial garniture of the earth, Maelgon said to Elphin, 'My bards say that I am the best and bravest of kings, that my queen is the most beautiful and chaste of women, and that they themselves, by virtue of belonging to me, are the best and wisest of bards. Now what say you, on these heads?'

This was a perplexing question to Elphin, who, nevertheless, answered: 'That you are the best and bravest of kings I do not in the least doubt; yet I cannot think that any woman surpasses my own wife in beauty and chastity; or that any bard equals my bard in genius and wisdom.'

'Hear you him, Rhûn?' said Maelgon.

'I hear,' said Rhûn, 'and mark.'

Rhûn was the son of Maelgon, and a worthy heir-apparent of his illustrious sire. Rhûn set out the next morning on an embassy very similar to Tarquin's,[4] accompanied by only one attendant. They lost their way and each other, among the forests of Meirion.[5] The attendant, after riding about some time in great trepidation, thought he heard the sound of a harp, mixed with the roar of the torrents, and following its indications, came at length within sight of an oak-fringed precipice, on the summit of which stood Taliesin, playing and singing to the winds and waters. The attendant could not approach him without dismounting; therefore, tying his horse to a branch, he ascended the rock, and, addressing the young bard, inquired his way to the dwelling of Elphin. Taliesin, in return, inquired his business there; and, partly by examination, partly by divination, ascertained his master's name, and the purport of his visit.

Taliesin deposited his harp in a dry cavern of the rock, and undertook to be the stranger's guide. The attendant remounted his horse, and Taliesin preceded him on foot. But the way by which he led him grew more and more rugged, till the stranger called out, 'Whither lead you, my friend? My horse can no longer keep his footing.' 'There is no other way,' said Taliesin. 'But give him to my management, and do you follow on foot.' The attendant consented. Taliesin mounted the horse, and presently struck into a more practicable track; and immediately giving the horse the reins, he disappeared among the woods, leaving the unfortunate equerry to follow as he might, with no better guide than the uncertain recollection of the sound of his horse's heels.

Taliesin reached home before the arrival of Rhûn, and warned Angharad of the mischief that was designed her.

Rhûn, arriving at his destination, found only a handmaid dressed as Angharad, and another officiating as her attendant. The fictitious princess gave him a supper, and everything else he asked for; and, at parting in the morning, a lock of her hair, and a ring, which Angharad had placed on her finger.

After riding a short distance on his return, Rhûn met his unlucky attendant, torn, tired, and half-starved, and cursing

some villain who had stolen his horse. Rhûn was too happy
in his own success to have a grain of sympathy for his miserable follower, whom he left to find his horse and his way, or
either, or neither, as he might, and returned alone to Diganwy.

Maelgon exultingly laid before Elphin the proofs of his
wife's infidelity. Elphin examined the lock of hair, and listened
to the narration of Rhûn. He divined at once the trick that
had been put upon the prince; but he contented himself with
saying, 'I do not believe that Rhûn has received the favours
of Angharad; and I still think that no wife in Britain, not even
the queen of Maelgon Gwyneth, is more chaste or more beautiful than mine.'

Hereupon Maelgon waxed wroth. Elphin, in a point which
much concerned him, held a belief of his own, different from
that which his superiors in worldly power required him to
hold. Therefore Maelgon acted as the possessors of worldly
power usually act in similar cases: he locked Elphin up within
four stone walls, with an intimation that he should keep him
there till he pronounced a more orthodox opinion on the
question in dispute.

CHAPTER VIII

THE LOVE OF MELANGHEL

Ἀλλὰ τεαῖς παλάμῃσι μαχήμονα θύρσον ἀείρων,
Αἰθέρος ἄξια ῥέξον· ἐπεὶ Διὸς ἄμβροτος αὐλὴ
Οὔ σε πόνων ἀπάνευθε δεδέξεται· οὐδέ σοι Ὧραι
Μήπω ἀεθλεύσαντι πύλας πετάσωσιν Ὀλύμπου.

Grasp the bold thyrsus; seek the field's array;
And do things worthy of ethereal day:
Not without toil to earthborn man befalls
To tread the floors of Jove's immortal halls:
Never to him, who not by deeds has striven,
Will the bright Hours roll back the gates of heaven.

IRIS TO BACCHUS, *in the 13th Book of the
Dionysiaca of* NONNUS.

THE HOUSEHOLD OF Elphin was sufficiently improsperous
during the absence of its chief. The havoc which Maelgon's
visitation had made in their winter provision, it required the

utmost exertions of their collective energies to repair. Even the young princess Melanghel sallied forth, in the garb of a huntress, to strike the deer or the wild goat among the wintry forest, on the summits of the bleak crags, or in the vallies of the flooded streams.

Taliesin, on these occasions, laid aside his harp, and the robe of his order, and accompanied the princess with his hunting spear, and more succinctly apparelled.

Their retinue, it may be supposed, was neither very numerous nor royal, nor their dogs very thoroughbred. It sometimes happened that the deer went one way, the dogs another; the attendants, losing sight of both, went a third, leaving Taliesin, who never lost sight of Melanghel, alone with her among the hills.

One day, the ardour of the chace having carried them far beyond their ordinary bounds, they stood alone together on Craig Aderyn, the Rock of Birds, which overlooks the river Dysyni. This rock takes its name from the flocks of birds which have made it their dwelling, and which make the air resonant with their multitudinous notes. Around, before, and above them, rose mountain beyond mountain, soaring above the leafless forests, to lose their heads in mist; beneath them lay the silent river; and along the opening of its narrow valley, they looked to the not-distant sea.

'Prince Llywarch,' said Taliesin, 'is a bard and a warrior: he is the son of an illustrious line. Taliesin is neither prince nor warrior: he is the unknown child of the waters.'

'Why think you of Llywarch?' said Melanghel, to whom the name of the prince was known only from Taliesin, who knew it only from fame.

'Because,' said Taliesin, 'there is that in my soul which tells me that I shall have no rival among the bards of Britain: but, if its princes and warriors seek the love of Melanghel, I shall know that I am but a bard, and not as Llywarch.'

'You would be Prince Taliesin,' said Melanghel, smiling, 'to make me your princess. Am I not a princess already? and such an one as is not on earth, for the land of my inheritance is under the sea, under those very waves that now roll within our view; and, in truth, you are as well qualified for a prince as I am for a princess, and have about as valuable a dominion in the mists and the clouds as I have under the waters.'

Her eyes sparkled with affectionate playfulness, while her long black hair floated loosely in the breeze that pressed the folds of her drapery against the matchless symmetry of her form.

'Oh, maid!' said Taliesin, 'what shall I do to win your love?'

'Restore me my father,' said Melanghel, with a seriousness as winning as her playfulness had been fascinating.

'That will I do,' said Taliesin, 'for his own sake. What shall I do for yours?'

'Nothing more,' said Melanghel, and she held out her hand to the youthful bard. Taliesin seized it with rapture, and pressed it to his lips; then, still grasping her hand, and throwing his left arm round her, he pressed his lips to hers.

Melanghel started from him, blushing, and looked at him a moment with something like severity; but he blushed as much as she did, and seemed even more alarmed at her displeasure than she was at his momentary audacity. She reassured him with a smile; and, pointing her spear in the direction of her distant home, she bounded before him down the rock.

This was the kiss of Taliesin to the daughter of Elphin, which is celebrated in an inedited triad, as one of 'the Three Chaste Kisses of the island of Britain'.[1]

CHAPTER IX

THE SONGS OF DIGANWY

Three things that will always swallow, and never be satisfied: the sea; a burial ground; and a king.

TRIADS OF WISDOM[1]

THE HALL OF Maelgon Gwyneth was ringing with music and revelry, when Taliesin stood on the floor, with his harp, in the midst of the assembly, and, without introduction or preface, struck a few chords, that, as if by magic, suspended all other sounds, and fixed the attention of all in silent expectation. He then sang as follows:

CANU Y MEDD
THE MEAD SONG OF TALIESIN

The King of kings upholds the heaven,
And parts from earth the billowy sea:
By Him all earthly joys are given;
He loves the just, and guards the free.
Round the wide hall, for thine and thee,
With purest draughts the mead-horns foam,
Maelgon of Gwyneth! Can it be
That here a prince bewails his home?

The bee tastes not the sparkling draught
Which mortals from his toils obtain;
That sends, in festal circles quaffed,
Sweet tumult through the heart and brain.
The timid, while the horn they drain,
Grow bold; the happy more rejoice;
The mourner ceases to complain;
The gifted bard exalts his voice.

To royal Elphin life I owe,
Nurture and name, the harp, and mead:
Full, pure, and sparkling be their flow,
The horns to Maelgon's lips decreed:
For him may horn to horn succeed,
Till, glowing with their generous fire,
He bid the captive chief be freed,
Whom at his hands my songs require.

Elphin has given me store of mead,
Mead, ale, and wine, and fish, and corn;
A happy home; a splendid steed,
Which stately trappings well adorn.
Tomorrow be the auspicious morn
That home the expected chief shall lead;
So may King Maelgon drain the horn
In thrice three million feasts of mead.

'I give you,' said Maelgon, 'all the rights of hospitality, and
as many horns as you please of the mead you so well and justly
extol. If you be Elphin's bard, it must be confessed he spoke
truth with respect to you, for you are a much better bard than
any of mine, as they are all free to confess: I give them that
liberty.'

The bards availed themselves of the royal indulgence, and
confessed their own inferiority to Taliesin, as the king had

commanded them to do. Whether they were all as well convinced of it as they professed to be, may be left to the decision
of that very large class of literary gentlemen who are in the
habit of favouring the reading public with their undisguised
opinions.

'But,' said Maelgon, 'your hero of Caredigion indulged
himself in a very unjustifiable bravado with respect to his
queen; for he said she was as beautiful and as chaste as mine.
Now Rhûn has proved the contrary, with small trouble, and
brought away trophies of his triumph; yet still Elphin persists
in his first assertion, wherein he grossly disparages the queen
of Gwyneth; and for this I hold him in bondage, and will do,
till he make recantation.'

'That he will never do,' said Taliesin. 'Your son received
only the favours of a handmaid, who was willing, by stratagem, to preserve her lady from violence. The real Angharad
was concealed in a cavern.'

Taliesin explained the adventure of Rhûn, and pronounced
an eulogium on Angharad, which put the king and prince into
a towering passion.

Rhûn secretly determined to set forth on a second quest;
and Maelgon swore by his mead-horn he would keep Elphin
till doomsday. Taliesin struck his harp again, and, in a tone of
deep but subdued feeling, he poured forth the

SONG OF THE WIND*

> The winds that wander far and free,
> Bring whispers from the shores they sweep;
> Voices of feast and revelry;
> Murmurs of forests and the deep;
>
> Low sounds of torrents from the steep
> Descending on the flooded vale;
> And tumults from the leaguered keep,
> Where foes the dizzy rampart scale.

* This poem has little or nothing of Taliesin's *Canu y Gwynt*, with the
exception of the title. That poem is apparently a fragment; and, as it
now stands, is an incoherent and scarcely intelligible rhapsody. It contains
no distinct or explicit idea, except the proposition that it is an unsafe
booty to carry off fat kine, which may be easily conceded in a case where
nimbleness of heel, both in man and beast, must have been of great importance. The idea from which, if from anything in the existing portion
of the poem, it takes its name, that the whispers of the wind bring rumours
of war from Deheubarth, is rather implied than expressed. [P.]

The whispers of the wandering wind
Are borne to gifted ears alone;
For them it ranges unconfined,
And speaks in accents of its own.

It tells me of Deheubarth's throne;
The spider weaves not in its shield:*
Already from its towers is blown
The blast that bids the spoiler yield.

Ill with his prey the fox may wend,
When the young lion quits his lair:
Sharp sword, strong shield, stout arm, should tend
On spirits that unjustly dare.

To me the wandering breezes bear
The war-blast from Caer Lleon's brow;
The avenging storm is brooding there
To which Diganwy's towers shall bow.

'If the wind talks to you,' said Maelgon, 'I may say, with the proverb, you talk to the wind; for I am not to be sung, or cajoled, or vapoured, or bullied out of my prisoner. And as to your war-blasts from Caer Lleon, which I construe into a threat that you will stir up King Arthur against me, I can tell you for your satisfaction, and to spare you the trouble of going

---

* The spider weaving in suspended armour, is an old emblem of peace and inaction. Thus Bacchylides, in his fragment on Peace:

> Ἐν δὲ σιδαροδέτοις πόρπαξιν
> Αἰθᾶν ἀραχνᾶν ἔργα πέλονται.

Euripides, in a fragment of *Erechtheus*:

> Κείσθω δόρυ μοι μίτον ἀμφιπλέκειν
> Ἀράχναις.

And Nonnus, whom no poetical image escaped: (*Dionysiaca*, L. xxxviii.)

> Οὐ φόνος, οὐ τότε δῆρις· ἔκειτο δὲ τηλόθι χάρμης
> Βακχιὰς ἐξαέτηρος ἀραχνιόωσα βοείη.

And Beaumont and Fletcher, in the *Wife for a Month*:

> 'Would'st thou live so long, till thy sword hung by,
> And lazy spiders filled the hilt with cobwebs?'

A Persian poet says, describing ruins:

> 'The spider spreads the veil in the palace of the Caesars.'

And among the most felicitous uses of this emblem, must never be forgotten Hogarth's cobweb over the lid of the charity-box. [P.]

so far, that he has enough to do with seeking his wife, who has been carried off by some unknown marauder, and with fighting the Saxons, to have much leisure or inclination to quarrel with a true Briton, who is one of his best friends, and his heir presumptive; for, though he is a man of great prowess, and moreover, saving his reverence and your presence, a cuckold, he has not yet favoured his kingdom with an heir apparent. And I request you to understand, that when I extolled you above my bards, I did so only in respect of your verse and voice, melody and execution, figure and action, in short, of your manner; for your matter is naught; and I must do my own bards the justice to say, that, however much they may fall short of you in the requisites aforesaid, they know much better than you do, what is fitting for bards to sing, and kings to hear.'

The bards, thus encouraged, recovered from the first shock of Maelgon's ready admission of Taliesin's manifest superiority, and struck up a sort of consecutive chorus, in a series of pennillion, or stanzas, in praise of Maelgon and his heirship presumptive, giving him credit for all the virtues of which the reputation was then in fashion; and, amongst the rest, they very loftily celebrated his justice and magnanimity.

Taliesin could not reconcile his notions of these qualities with Maelgon's treatment of Elphin. He changed his measure and his melody, and pronounced, in impassioned numbers, the poem which a learned Welsh historian calls 'The Indignation of the Bards', though, as the indignation was Taliesin's, and not theirs, he seems to have made a small mistake in regard to the preposition.

THE INDIGNATION OF TALIESIN
WITH THE
BARDS OF MAELGON GWYNETH

> False bards the sacred fire pervert,
> Whose songs are won without desert;
> Who falsehoods weave in specious lays,
> To gild the base with virtue's praise.
>
> From court to court, from tower to tower,
> In warrior's tent, in lady's bower,
> For gold, for wine, for food, for fire,
> They tune their throats at all men's hire.

Their harps reecho wide and far
With sensual love, and bloody war,
And drunkenness, and flattering lies:
Truth's light may shine for other eyes.

In palaces they still are found,
At feasts, promoting senseless sound:
He is their demigod at least,
Whose only virtue is his feast.

They love to talk; they hate to think;
All day they sing; all night they drink:
No useful toils their hands employ;
In boisterous throngs is all their joy.

The bird will fly, the fish will swim,
The bee the honied flowers will skim;
Its food by toil each creature brings,
Except false bards and worthless kings.

Learning and wisdom claim to find
Homage and succour from mankind;
But learning's right, and wisdom's due,
Are falsely claimed by slaves like you.

True bards know truth, and truth will show;
Ye know it not, nor care to know:
Your king's weak mind false judgement warps;
Rebuke his wrong, or break your harps.

I know the mountain and the plain;
I know where right and justice reign;
I from the tower will Elphin free;
Your king shall learn his doom from me.

A spectre of the marsh shall rise,
With yellow teeth, and hair, and eyes,
From whom your king in vain aloof
Shall crouch beneath the sacred roof.

He through the half-closed door shall spy
The Yellow Spectre sweeping by;
To whom the punishment belongs
Of Maelgon's crimes and Elphin's wrongs.

By the name of the Yellow Spectre, Taliesin designated a
pestilence, which afterwards carried off great multitudes of the
people, and, amongst them, Maelgon Gwyneth, then sovereign of Britain, who had taken refuge from it in a church.

Maelgon paid little attention to Taliesin's prophecy, but he was much incensed by the general tenor of his song.

'If it were not,' said Maelgon, 'that I do not choose to add to the number of the crimes of which you so readily accuse me, that of disregarding the inviolability of your bardship, I would send you to keep company with your trout-catching king, and you might amuse his salmon-salting majesty with telling him as much truth as he is disposed to listen to; which, to judge by his reception of Rhûn's story of his wife, I take to be exceedingly little. For the present, you are welcome to depart; and, if you are going to Caer Lleon, you may present my respect to King Arthur, and tell him, I hope he will beat the Saxons, and find his wife; but I hope, also, that the cutting me off with an heir apparent will not be the consequence of his finding her, or (which, by the by, is more likely,) of his having lost her.'

Taliesin took his departure from the hall of Diganwy, leaving the bards biting their lips at his rebuke, and Maelgon roaring with laughter at his own very excellent jest.

CHAPTER X

THE DISAPPOINTMENT OF RHÛN

Παρθένε, πῶς μετάμευψας ἐρευθαλέην σέο μορφήν;
Εἰαρινὴν δ' ἀκτῖνα τίς ἔσβεσε σεῖο προσώπου;
Οὐκέτι σῶν μελέων ἀμαρύσσεται ἄργυφος αἴγλη·
Οὐκέτι δ', ὡς τὸ πρόσθε, τεαὶ γελόωσιν ὀπωπαί.

Sweet maid, what grief has changed thy roseate grace,
And quenched the vernal sunshine of thy face?
No more thy light form sparkles as it flies,
Nor laughter flashes from thy radiant eyes.

VENUS TO PASITHEA, *in the 33rd Book of the Dionysiaca of* NONNUS

TALIESIN RETURNED to the dwelling of Elphin, auguring that, in consequence of his information, Rhûn would pay it another visit. In this anticipation he was not mistaken, for Rhûn very soon appeared, with a numerous retinue, determined, apparently, to carry his point by force of arms. He found, however, no inmate in the dwelling but Taliesin and Teithrin ap Tathral.

Rhûn stormed, entreated, promised, and menaced, without success. He perlustrated the vicinity, and found various caverns, but not the one he sought. He passed many days in the search, and, finally, departed; but, at a short distance, he dismissed all his retinue, except his bard of all work, or laureate expectant, and, accompanied by this worthy, returned to the banks of the Mawddach, where they resolved themselves into an ambuscade. It was not long before they saw Taliesin issue from the dwelling, and begin ascending the hill. They followed him, at a cautious distance; first up a steep ascent of the forest-covered rocks; then along a small space of densely wooded tableland, to the edge of a dingle; and, again, by a slight descent, to the bed of a mountain stream, in a spot where the torrent flung itself, in a series of cataracts, down the rift of a precipitous rock, that towered high above their heads. About halfway up the rock, near the base of one of these cataracts, was a projecting ledge, or natural platform of rock, behind which was seen the summit of the opening of a cave. Taliesin paused, and looked around him, as if to ascertain that he was unobserved; and then, standing on a projection of the rock below, he mingled, in spontaneous song, the full power of his voice with the roar of the waters.

TALIESIN

Maid of the rock! though loud the flood,
My voice will pierce thy cell:
No foe is in the mountain wood;
No danger in the dell:
The torrents bound along the glade;
Their path is free and bright;
Be thou as they, Oh mountain maid!
In liberty and light.

Melanghel appeared on the rocky platform, and answered the song of her lover:

MELANGHEL

The cataracts thunder down the steep;
The woods all lonely wave:
Within my heart the voice sinks deep
That calls me from my cave.
The voice is dear, the song is sweet,
And true the words must be:
Well pleased I quit the dark retreat,
To wend away with thee.

TALIESIN

Not yet; not yet: let nightdews fall,
And stars be bright above,
Ere to her long deserted hall
I guide my gentle love.
When torchlight flashes on the roof,
No foe will near thee stray:
Even now his parting courser's hoof
Rings from the rocky way.

MELANGHEL

Yet climb the path, and comfort speak,
To cheer the lonely cave,
Where woods are bare, and rocks are bleak,
And wintry torrents rave.
A dearer home my memory knows,
A home I still deplore;
Where firelight glows, while winds and snows
Assail the guardian door.

Taliesin vanished a moment from the sight of Rhûn, and almost immediately reappeared by the side of Melanghel, who had now been joined by her mother. In a few minutes he returned, and Angharad and Melanghel withdrew.

Rhûn watched him from the dingle, and then proceeded to investigate the path by which he had gained the platform. After some search he discovered it, ascended to the platform, and rushed into the cavern.

They here found a blazing fire, a half-finished dinner, materials of spinning and embroidering, and other signs of female inhabitancy; but they found not the inhabitants. They searched the cavern to its depth, which was not inconsiderable; much marvelling how the ladies had vanished. While thus engaged, they heard a rushing sound, and a crash on the rocks, as of some ponderous body. The mystery of this noise was very soon explained to them, in a manner that gave an unusual length to their faces, and threw a deep tinge of blue into their rosy complexions. A ponderous stone, which had been suspended like a portcullis at the mouth of the cavern, had been dropped by some unseen agency, and made them as close prisoners as Elphin.

They were not long kept in suspense as to how this matter had been managed. The hoarse voice of Teithrin ap Tathral sounded in their ears from without, 'Foxes! you have been seen through, and you are fairly trapped. Eat and drink. You shall want nothing but to get out; which you must want some time; for it is sworn that no hand but Elphin's shall raise the stone of your captivity.'

'Let me out,' vociferated Rhûn, 'and on the word of a prince —' but, before he could finish the sentence, the retreating steps of Teithrin were lost in the roar of the torrent.

CHAPTER XI

THE HEROES OF DINAS VAWR

L'ombra sua torna ch'era dipartita. DANTE.

While there is life there is hope. *English Proverb.*

PRINCE RHÛN being safe in schistous bastile,[1] Taliesin commenced his journey to the court of King Arthur. On his way to Caer Lleon, he was received with all hospitality, entertained with all admiration, and dismissed with all honour, at the castles of several petty kings, and, amongst the rest, at the castle of Dinas Vawr, on the Towy, which was then garrisoned by King Melvas,[2] who had marched with a great force out of his own kingdom, on the eastern shores of the Severn, to levy contributions in the country to the westward, where, as the pleasure of his company had been altogether unlooked for, he had got possession of a good portion of moveable property. The castle of Dinas Vawr presenting itself to him as a convenient hold, he had taken it by storm; and having cut the throats of the former occupants, thrown their bodies into the Towy, and caused a mass to be sung for the good of their souls, he was now sitting over his bowl, with the comfort of a good conscience, enjoying the fruits of the skill and courage with which he had planned and accomplished his scheme of ways and means for the year.

The hall of Melvas was full of magnanimous heroes, who were celebrating their own exploits in sundry chorusses, especially in that which follows, which is here put upon record as being the quintessence of all the war-songs that ever were written, and the sum and substance of all the appetencies, tendencies, and consequences of military glory:

THE WAR-SONG OF DINAS VAWR

The mountain sheep are sweeter,
But the valley sheep are fatter;
We therefore deemed it meeter
To carry off the latter.
We made an expedition;
We met a host, and quelled it;
We forced a strong position,
And killed the men who held it.

On Dyfed's richest valley,
Where herds of kine were brousing,
We made a mighty sally,
To furnish our carousing.
Fierce warriors rushed to meet us;
We met them, and o'erthrew them:
They struggled hard to beat us;
But we conquered them, and slew them.

As we drove our prize at leisure,
The king marched forth to catch us:
His rage surpassed all measure,
But his people could not match us.
He fled to his hall-pillars;
And, ere our force we led off,
Some sacked his house and cellars,
While others cut his head off.

We there, in strife bewild'ring,
Spilt blood enough to swim in:
We orphaned many children,
And widowed many women.
The eagles and the ravens
We glutted with our foemen;
The heroes and the cravens,
The spearmen and the bowmen.

We brought away from battle,
And much their land bemoaned them,
Two thousand head of cattle,
And the head of him who owned them:
Ednyfed, king of Dyfed,
His head was borne before us;
His wine and beasts supplied our feasts,
And his overthrow, our chorus.

As the doughty followers of Melvas, having sung themselves hoarse with their own praises, subsided one by one into drunken sleep, Taliesin, sitting near the great central fire, and throwing around a scrutinizing glance on all the objects in the hall, noticed a portly and somewhat elderly personage, of an aspect that would have been venerable, if it had been less rubicund and Bacchic, who continued plying his potations with undiminished energy, while the heroes of the festival dropped round him, like the leaves of autumn. This figure excited Taliesin's curiosity. The features struck him with a sense of resemblance to objects which had been somewhere familiar to him; but he perplexed himself in vain, with attempts at definite recollections. At length, when these two were almost the sole survivors of the evening, the stranger approached him with a golden goblet, which he had just replenished with the choicest wine of the vaults of Dinas Vawr, and pronounced the oracular monosyllable, 'Drink!' to which he subjoined emphatically 'GWIN O EUR: Wine from gold. That is my taste. Ale is well; mead is better; wine is best. Horn is well; silver is better; gold is best.'

Taliesin, who had been very abstemious during the evening, took the golden goblet, and drank to please the inviter; in the hope that he would become communicative, and satisfy the curiosity his appearance had raised.

The stranger sat down near him, evidently in that amiable state of semi-intoxication which inflates the head, warms the heart, lifts up the veil of the inward man, and sets the tongue flying, or rather tripping, in the double sense of nimbleness and titubancy.

The stranger repeated, taking a copious draught, 'My taste is wine from gold.'

'I have heard those words,' said Taliesin, 'GWIN O EUR, repeated as having been the favourite saying of a person whose memory is fondly cherished by one as dear to me as a mother, though his name, with all others, is the by-word of all that is disreputable.'

'I cannot believe,' said the stranger, 'that a man whose favourite saying was GWIN O EUR, could possibly be a disreputable person, or deserve any other than that honourable remembrance, which, you say, only one person is honest enough to entertain for him.'

'His name,' said Taliesin, 'is too unhappily notorious

throughout Britain, by the terrible catastrophe of which his GWIN O EUR was the cause.'

'And what might that be?' said the stranger.

'The inundation of Gwaelod,' said Taliesin.

'You speak then,' said the stranger, taking an enormous potation, 'of Seithenyn, Prince Seithenyn, Seithenyn ap Seithyn Saidi, Arglwyd Gorwarcheidwad yr Argae Breninawl.'

'I seldom hear his name,' said Taliesin, 'with any of those sounding additions; he is usually called Seithenyn the Drunkard.'

The stranger goggled about his eyes in an attempt to fix them steadily on Taliesin, screwed up the corners of his mouth, stuck out his nether lip, pursed up his chin, thrust forward his right foot, and elevated his golden goblet in his right hand; then, in a tone which he intended to be strongly becoming of his impressive aspect and imposing attitude, he muttered, 'Look at me.'

Taliesin looked at him accordingly, with as much gravity as he could preserve.

After a silence, which he designed to be very dignified and solemn, the stranger spoke again: 'I am the man.'

'What man?' said Taliesin.

'The man,' replied his entertainer, 'of whom you have spoken so disparagingly; Seithenyn ap Seithyn Saidi.'

'Seithenyn,' said Taliesin, 'has slept twenty years under the waters of the western sea, as King Gwythno's Lamentations have made known to all Britain.'

'They have not made it known to me,' said Seithenyn, 'for the best of all reasons, that one can only know the truth; for, if that which we think we know is not truth, it is something which we do not know. A man cannot know his own death; for, while he knows anything, he is alive; at least, I never heard of a dead man who knew anything, or pretended to know anything: if he had so pretended, I should have told him to his face he was no dead man.'

'Your mode of reasoning,' said Taliesin, 'unquestionably corresponds with what I have heard of Seithenyn's: but how is it possible Seithenyn can be living?'

'Everything that is, is possible, says Catog the Wise,' answered Seithenyn, with a look of great sapience. 'I will give you proof that I am not a dead man; for, they say, dead men tell no tales: now I will tell you a tale, and a very interesting one it is. When I saw the sea sapping the tower, I jumped into the water, and just in the nick of time. It was well for me that I had been so provident as to empty so many barrels, and that somebody, I don't know who, but I suppose it was my daughter, had been so provident as to put the bungs into them, to keep them sweet; for the beauty of it was that, when there was so much water in the case, it kept them empty; and when I jumped into the sea, the sea was just making a great hole in the cellar, and they were floating out by dozens. I don't know how I managed it, but I got one arm over one, and the other arm over another: I nipped them pretty tight; and, though my legs were under water, the good liquor I had in me kept me warm. I could not help thinking, as I had nothing else to think of just then that touched me so nearly, that if I had left them full, and myself empty, as a sober man would have done, we should all three, that is, I and the two barrels, have gone to the bottom together, that is to say, separately; for we should never have come together, except at the bottom, perhaps; when no one of us could have done the other any good; whereas they have done me much good, and I have requited it; for, first, I did them the service of emptying them; and then they did me the service of floating me with the tide, whether the ebb, or the flood, or both, is more than I can tell, down to the coast of Dyfed, where I was picked up by fishermen; and such was my sense of gratitude, that, though I had always before detested an empty barrel, except as a trophy, I swore I would not budge from the water unless my two barrels went with me; so we were all marched inland together, and were taken into the service of King Ednyfed, where I stayed till his castle was sacked, and his head cut off, and his beeves marched away with, by the followers of King Melvas, of whom I killed two or three; but they were too many for us: therefore, to make the best of a bad bargain, I followed leisurely in the train of the beeves, and presented myself to King Melvas, with this golden goblet, saying GWIN O EUR. He was struck with my deportment, and made me his chief butler; and now my two barrels are the two pillars of his cellar, where I regularly fill them from affection, and as regularly empty them from gratitude, taking care to put the bungs in them, to keep them sweet.'

'But all this while,' said Taliesin, 'did you never look back to the Plain of Gwaelod, to your old king, and, above all, to your daughter?'

'Why yes,' said Seithenyn, 'I did in a way! But as to the Plain of Gwaelod, that was gone, buried under the sea, along with many good barrels, which I had been improvident enough to leave full: then, as to the old king, though I had a great regard for him, I thought he might be less likely to feast me in his hall, than to set up my head on a spike over his gate: then, as to my daughter —'

Here he shook his head, and looked maudlin; and dashing two or three drops from his eye, he put a great many into his mouth.

'Your daughter,' said Taliesin, 'is the wife of King Elphin, and has a daughter, who is now as beautiful as her mother was.'

'Very likely,' said Seithenyn, 'and I should be very glad to see them all; but I am afraid King Elphin, as you call him, (what he is king of, you shall tell me at leisure,) would do me a mischief. At any rate, he would stint me in liquor. No! If they will visit me, here I am. Fish, and water, will not agree with me. I am growing old, and need cordial nutriment. King Melvas will never want for beeves and wine; nor, indeed, for anything else that is good. I can tell you what,' he added, in a very low voice, cocking his eye, and putting his finger on his lips, 'he has got in this very castle the finest woman in Britain.'

'That I doubt,' said Taliesin.

'She is the greatest, at any rate,' said Seithenyn, 'and ought to be the finest.'

'How the greatest?' said Taliesin.

Seithenyn looked round, to observe if there were any listener near, and fixed a very suspicious gaze on a rotund figure of a fallen hero, who lay coiled up like a maggot in a filbert, and snoring with an energy that, to the muddy apprehensions of Seithenyn, seemed to be counterfeit. He determined, by a gentle experiment, to ascertain if his suspicions were well founded; and proceeded, with what he thought great caution, to apply the point of his foot to the most bulging portion of the fat sleeper's circumference. But he greatly miscalculated his intended impetus, for he impinged his foot with a force that overbalanced himself, and hurled him headlong over his man, who instantly sprang on his legs, shouting 'To arms!' Numbers started up at the cry; the hall rang with the din of arms, and with the vociferation of questions, which there were many to ask, and none to answer. Some stared about for the enemy; some rushed to the gates; others to the walls. Two or three, reeling in the tumult and the darkness, were jostled over the parapet, and went rolling down the precipitous slope of the castle hill, crashing through the bushes, and bellowing for someone to stop them, till their clamours were cut short by a plunge into the Towy, where the conjoint weight of their armour and their liquor carried them at once to the bottom. The rage which would have fallen on the enemy, if there had been one, was turned against the author of the false alarm; but, as none could point him out, the tumult subsided by degrees, through a descending scale of imprecations, into the last murmured malediction of him whom the intensity of his generous anger kept longest awake. By this time, the rotund hero had again coiled himself up into his ring; and Seithenyn was stretched in a right line, as a tangent to the circle, in a state of utter incapacity to elucidate the mystery of King Melvas's possession of the finest woman in Britain.

CHAPTER XII

THE SPLENDOUR OF CAER LLEON

The three principal cities of the isle of Britain: Caer Llion upon Wysg in Cymru; Caer Llundain in Lloegr; and Caer Evrawg in Deifr and Brynaich.*

TRIADS OF THE ISLE OF BRITAIN.[1]

THE SUNSET OF A bright December day was glittering on the waves of the Usk, and on the innumerable roofs, which, being composed chiefly of the glazed tiles of the Romans, reflected the light almost as vividly as the river; when Taliesin descended one of the hills that border the beautiful valley in which then stood Caer Lleon, the metropolis of Britain, and in which now stands, on a small portion of the selfsame space, a little insignificant town, possessing nothing of its ancient glory but the unaltered name of Caer Lleon.

* Caer Lleon upon Usk in Cambria: London in Loegria: and York in Deïra and Bernicia. [P.]

The rapid Usk flowed then, as now, under the walls: the high wooden bridge, with its slender piles, was then much the same as it is at this day: it seems to have been never regularly rebuilt, but to have been repaired, from time to time, on the original Roman model. The same green and fertile meadows, the same gently-sloping wood-covered hills, that now meet the eye of the tourist, then met the eye of Taliesin; except that the woods on one side of the valley, were then only the skirts of an extensive forest, which the nobility and beauty of Caer Lleon made frequently reecho to the clamours of the chace.

The city, which had been so long the centre of the Roman supremacy, which was now the seat of the most illustrious sovereign that had yet held the sceptre of Britain, could not be approached by the youthful bard, whose genius was destined to eclipse that of all his countrymen, without feelings and reflections of deep interest. The sentimental tourist, (who, perching himself on an old wall, works himself up into a soliloquy of philosophical pathos, on the vicissitudes of empire and the mutability of all sublunary things, interrupted only by an occasional peep at his watch, to ensure his not overstaying the minute at which his fowl, comfortably roasting at the nearest inn, has been promised to be ready,) has, no doubt, many fine thoughts well worth recording in a dapper volume; but Taliesin had an interest in the objects before him too deep to have a thought to spare, even for his dinner. The monuments of Roman magnificence, and of Roman domination, still existing in comparative freshness; the arduous struggle, in which his courtrymen were then engaged with the Saxons, and which, notwithstanding the actual triumphs of Arthur, Taliesin's prophetic spirit told him would end in their being dispossessed of all the land of Britain, except the wild region of Wales, (a result which political sagacity might have apprehended from their disunion, but which, as he told it to his countrymen in that memorable prophecy which every child of the Cymry knows, has established for him, among them, the fame of a prophet;) the importance to himself and his benefactors of the objects of his visit to the city, on the result of which depended the liberation of Elphin, and the success of his love for Melanghel; the degree in which these objects might be promoted by the construction he had put on Seithenyn's imperfect communication respecting the lady in Dinas Vawr; furnished, all together, more materials for absorbing thought, than the most zealous peregrinator, even if he be at once poet, antiquary, and philosopher, is likely to have at once in his mind, on the top of the finest old wall on the face of the earth.

Taliesin passed, in deep musing, through the gates of Caer Lleon; but his attention was speedily drawn to the objects around him. From the wild solitudes in which he had passed his earlier years, the transition to the castles and cities he had already visited, furnished much food to curiosity: but the ideas of them sunk into comparative nothingness before the magnificence of Caer Lleon.

He did not stop in the gateway to consider the knotty question, which has since puzzled so many antiquaries, whether the name of Caer Lleon signifies the City of Streams, the City of Legions, or the City of King Lleon? He saw a river filled with ships, flowing through fine meadows, bordered by hills and forests; walls of brick, as well as of stone; a castle, of impregnable strength; stately houses, of the most admirable architecture; palaces, with gilded roofs; Roman temples, and Christian churches; a theatre, and an amphitheatre. The public and private buildings of the departed Romans were in excellent preservation; though the buildings, and especially the temples, were no longer appropriated to their original purposes. The king's butler, Bedwyr, had taken possession of the Temple of Diana, as a cool place of deposit for wine: he had recently effected a stowage of vast quantities therein, and had made a most luminous arrangement of the several kinds; under the judicious and experienced superintendence of Dyvrig, the Ex-Archbishop of Caer Lleon; who had just then nothing else to do, having recently resigned his see in favour of King Arthur's uncle, David, who is, to this day, illustrious as the St David in whose honour the Welshmen annually adorn their hats with a leek. This David was a very respectable character in his way: he was a man of great sanctity and simplicity; and, in order to eschew the vanities of the world, which were continually present to him in Caer Lleon, he removed the metropolitan see, from Caer Lleon, to the rocky, barren, woodless, streamless, meadowless, tempest-beaten point of Mynyw, which was afterwards called St David's. He was the mirror and pattern of a godly life; teaching by example, as by precept; admirable in words, and excellent in deeds; tall in stature, handsome in aspect, noble in deportment, affable in address, eloquent and learned, a model to his followers, the life of the poor, the protector of widows, and the father of orphans. This makes altogether a very respectable saint; and it cannot be said, that the honourable leek is unworthily consecrated. A long series of his Catholic successors maintained, in great magnificence, a cathedral, a college, and a palace; keeping them all in repair, and feeding the poor into the bargain, from the archiepiscopal, or, when the primacy of Caer Lleon had merged in that of Canterbury, from the episcopal, revenues: but these things were reformed altogether by one of the first Protestant bishops, who, having a lady that longed for the gay world, and wanting more than all the revenues for himself and his family, first raised the wind by selling off the lead from the roof of his palace, and then obtained permission to remove from it, on the plea that it was not watertight. The immediate successors of this bishop, whose name was Barlow,[2] were in every way worthy of him: the palace and college have, consequently, fallen into incurable dilapidation, and the cathedral has fallen partially into ruins, and, most impartially, into neglect and defacement.

To return to Taliesin, in the streets of Caer Lleon. Plautus and Terence were not heard in the theatre, nor to be heard of in its neighbourhood;[3] but it was thought an excellent place for an Eisteddfod, or Bardic Congress, and was made the principal place of assembly of the Bards of the island of Britain. This is what Ross of Warwick means,[4] when he says there was a noble university of students in Caer Lleon.

The mild precepts of the new religion had banished the ferocious sports to which the Romans had dedicated the amphitheatre, and, as Taliesin passed, it was pouring forth an improved and humanized multitude, who had been enjoying the pure British pleasure of baiting a bear.

The hot baths and aqueducts, the stoves of 'wonderful artifice,' as Giraldus has it,[5] which diffused hot air through narrow spiracles, and many other wonders of the place, did not all present themselves to a first observation. The streets were thronged with people, especially of the fighting order, of whom a greater number flocked about Arthur, than he always found it convenient to pay. Horsemen, with hawks and hounds, were returning from the neighbouring forest, accompanied by beautiful huntresses, in scarlet and gold.

Taliesin, having perlustrated the city, proceeded to the palace of Arthur. At the gates he was challenged by a formidable guard, but passed by his bardic privilege. It was now very near Christmas, and when Taliesin entered the great hall, it was blazing with artificial light, and glowing with the heat of the Roman stoves.

Arthur had returned victorious from the great battle of Badon hill,[6] in which he had slain with his own hand four hundred and forty Saxons; and was feasting as merrily as an honest man can be supposed to do while his wife is away. Kings, princes, and soldiers of fortune, bards and prelates, ladies superbly apparelled, and many of them surpassingly beautiful; and a most gallant array of handsome young cup-bearers, marshalled and well drilled by the king's butler, Bedwyr, who was himself a petty king, were the chief components of the illustrious assembly.

Amongst the ladies were the beautiful Tegau Eurvron; Dywir the Golden-haired; Enid,[7] the daughter of Yniwl; Garwen, the daughter of Henyn; Gwyl, the daughter of Enddaud; and Indeg, the daughter of Avarwy Hir, of Maelienydd. Of these, Tegau Eurvron, or Tegau of the Golden Bosom, was the wife of Caradoc,[8] and one of the Three Chaste Wives of the island of Britain. She is the heroine, who, as the lady of Sir Cradock, is distinguished above all the ladies of Arthur's court, in the ballad of the Boy and the Mantle.

Amongst the bards were Prince Llywarch, then in his youth, afterwards called Llywarch Hên,[9] or Lywarch the Aged; Aneurin,[10] the British Homer, who sang the fatal battle of the Cattraëth, which laid the foundation of the Saxon ascendency, in heroic numbers, which the gods have preserved to us, and who was called the Monarch of the Bards, before the days of the glory of Taliesin; and Merddin Gwyllt,[11] or Merlin the Wild, who was so deep in the secrets of nature, that he obtained the fame of a magician, to which he had at least as good a title as either Friar Bacon or Cornelius Agrippa.

Amongst the petty kings, princes, and soldiers of fortune, were twenty-four marchawg, or cavaliers, who were the counsellors and champions of Arthur's court. This was the heroic band, illustrious, in the songs of chivalry, as the Knights of the Round Table. Their names and pedigrees would make a very instructive and entertaining chapter; and would include the interesting characters of Gwalchmai ap Gwyar the Courteous, the nephew of Arthur; Caradoc, 'Colofn Cymry,' the Pillar of Cambria, whose lady, as above noticed, was the mirror of chastity; and Trystan ap Tallwch, the lover of the beautiful Essyllt, the daughter, or, according to some, the wife, of his uncle March ap Meirchion; persons known to all the world, as Sir Gawain, Sir Cradock, and Sir Tristram.

On the right hand of King Arthur sate the beautiful Indeg, and on his left the lovely Garwen. Taliesin advanced, along the tesselated floor, towards the upper end of the hall, and, kneeling before King Arthur, said, 'What boon will King Arthur grant to him who brings news of his queen?'

'Any boon,' said Arthur, 'that a king can give.'

'Queen Gwenyvar,' said Taliesin, 'is the prisoner of King Melvas, in the castle of Dinas Vawr.'

The mien and countenance of his informant satisfied the king that he knew what he was saying; therefore, without further parlance, he broke up the banquet, to make preparations for assailing Dinas Vawr.

But, before he began his march, King Melvas had shifted his quarters, and passed beyond the Severn to the isle of Avallon, where the marches and winter-floods assured him some months of tranquillity and impunity.

King Arthur was highly exasperated, on receiving the intelligence of Melvas's movement; but he had no remedy, and was reduced to the alternative of making the best of his Christmas with the ladies, princes, and bards who crowded his court.

The period of the winter solstice had been always a great festival with the northern nations, the commencement of the lengthening of the days being, indeed, of all points in the circle of the year, that in which the inhabitants of cold countries have most cause to rejoice. This great festival was anciently called Yule; whether derived from the Gothic *Iola*, to make merry; or from the Celtic *Hiaul*, the sun; or from the Danish and Swedish *Hiul*, signifying wheel or revolution, December being *Hiul-month*, or the month of return; or from the Cimbric word *Ol*, which has the important signification of ALE, is too knotty a controversy to be settled here: but Yule had been long a great festival, with both Celts and Saxons; and, with the change of religion, became the great festival of Christmas, retaining most of its ancient characteristics while England was Merry England; a phrase which must be a mirifical puzzle to anyone who looks for the first time on its present most lugubrious inhabitants.

The mistletoe of the oak was gathered by the Druids with great ceremonies, as a symbol of the season. The mistletoe continued to be so gathered, and to be suspended in halls and kitchens, if not in temples, implying an unlimited privilege of kissing; which circumstance, probably, led a learned antiquary to opine that it was the forbidden fruit.

The Druids, at this festival, made, in a capacious cauldron, a mystical brewage of carefully-selected ingredients, full of occult virtues, which they kept from the profane, and which was typical of the new year and of the transmigration of the soul. The profane, in humble imitation, brewed a bowl of spiced ale, or wine, throwing therein roasted crabs; the hissing of which, as they plunged, piping hot, into the liquor, was heard with much unction at midwinter, as typical of the conjunct benignant influences of fire and strong drink. The Saxons called this the Wassail-bowl, and the brewage of it is reported to have been one of the charms with which Rowena fascinated Vortigern.

King Arthur kept his Christmas so merrily, that the memory of it passed into a proverb:* 'As merry as Christmas in Caer Lleon.'

Caer Lleon was the merriest of places, and was commonly known by the name of Merry Caer Lleon; which the English ballad-makers, for the sake of the smoother sound, and confounding Cambria with Cumbria, most ignorantly or audaciously turned into Merry Carlisle; thereby emboldening a northern antiquary to set about proving that King Arthur was a Scotchman; according to the old principles of harry and foray, which gave Scotchmen a right to whatever they could find on the English border; though the English never admitted their title to anything there, excepting a halter in Carlisle.

The chace, in the neighbouring forest; tilting in the amphitheatre; trials of skill in archery, in throwing the lance and riding at the quintain, and similar amusements of the morning, created good appetites for the evening feasts; in which Prince Cei, who is well known as Sir Kay, the seneschal, superintended the viands, as King Bedwyr did the liquor[12]; having each a thousand men at command, for their provision, arrange-

* Mor llawen ag Ngdolig yn Nghaerlleon. [P.]

ment, and distribution; and music worthy of the banquet was provided and superintended by the king's chief harper, Geraint, of whom a contemporary poet observes, that when he died, the gates of heaven were thrown wide open, to welcome the ingress of so divine a musician.

CHAPTER XIII

THE GHOSTLINESS OF AVALLON

Poco più poco meno, tutti al mondo vivono d'impostura: e chi è di buon gusto, dissimula quando occorre, gode quando può, crede quel che vuole, ride de' pazzi, e figura un mondo a suo gusto.
                                                  GOLDONI.[1]

'WHERE IS THE young bard,' said King Arthur, after some nights of Christmas had passed by, 'who brought me the news of my queen, and to whom I promised a boon, which he has not yet claimed?'

None could satisfy the king's curiosity. Taliesin had disappeared from Caer Lleon. He knew the power and influence of Maelgon Gwyneth; and he was aware that King Arthur, however favourably he might receive his petition, would not find leisure to compel the liberation of Elphin, till he had enforced from Melvas the surrender of his queen. It occurred to him that her restoration might be effected by peaceable means; and he knew that, if he could be in any degree instrumental to this result, it would greatly strengthen his claims on the king. He engaged a small fishing-vessel, which had just landed a cargo for the Christmas feasts of Caer Lleon, and set sail for the isle of Avallon. At that period, the springtides of the sea rolled round a cluster of islands, of which Avallon was one, over the extensive fens, which wiser generations have embanked and reclaimed.

The abbey of Avallon, afterwards called Glastonbury, was, even then, a comely and commodious pile, though not possessing any of that magnificence which the accumulated wealth of ages subsequently gave to it. A large and strongly fortified castle, almost adjoining the abbey, gave to the entire place the air of a stronghold of the church militant. King Melvas was one of the pillars of the orthodoxy of those days: he was called the Scourge of the Pelagians;[2] and extended the shield of his temporal might over the spiritual brotherhood of Avallon, who, in return, made it a point of conscience not to stint him in absolutions.

Some historians pretend that a comfortable nunnery was erected at a convenient distance from the abbey, that is to say, close to it; but this involves a nice question in monastic antiquity, which the curious may settle for themselves.

It was about midway between nones and vespers when Taliesin sounded, on the gate of the abbey, a notice of his wish for admission. A small trapdoor in the gate was cautiously opened, and a face, as round and as red as the setting sun in November, shone forth in the aperture.

The topographers who have perplexed themselves about the origin of the name of Ynys Avallon, 'the island of apples,' had not the advantage of this piece of meteoroscopy: if they could have looked on this archetype of a Norfolk beefin, with the knowledge that it was only a sample of a numerous fraternity, they would at once have perceived the fitness of the appellation. The brethren of Avallon were the apples of the church. It was the oldest monastic establishment in Britain; and consequently, as of reason, the most plump, succulent, and rosy. It had, even in the sixth century, put forth the fruits of good living, in a manner that would have done honour to a more enlightened age. It went on steadily improving in this line till the days of its last abbot, Richard Whiting,[3] who built the stupendous kitchen, which has withstood the ravages of time and the Reformation; and who, as appears by authentic documents, and, amongst others, by a letter signed with the honoured name of Russell, was found guilty, by a right worshipful jury, of being suspected of great riches, and of an inclination to keep them; and was accordingly sentenced to be hanged forthwith, along with his treasurer and subtreasurer, who were charged with aiding and abetting him in the safe custody of his cash and plate; at the same time that the Abbot of Peterborough was specially reprieved from the gallows, on the ground that he was the said Russell's particular friend. This was a compendium of justice and mercy according to the new light of King Henry the Eighth. The abbot's kitchen is the most interesting and perfect portion of the existing ruins. These ruins were overgrown with the finest ivy in England, till it was, not long since, pulled down by some Vandal, whom the Society of Antiquaries had sent down to make drawings

of the walls, which he executed literally, by stripping them
bare, that he might draw the walls, and nothing else. Its shade
no longer waves over the musing moralist, who, with folded
arms, and his back against a wall, dreams of the days that are
gone; or the sentimental cockney, who, seating himself with
much gravity on a fallen column, produces a flute from his
pocket, and strikes up 'I'd be a butterfly.'⁴

From the phaenomenon of a blushing fruit that was put
forth in the abbey gate of Avallon issued a deep, fat, gurgling
voice, which demanded of Taliesin his name and business.

'I seek the abbot of Avallon,' said Taliesin.

'He is confessing a penitent,' said the ghostly brother, who
was officiating in turn as porter.

'I can await his leisure,' said Taliesin, 'but I must see him.'

'Are you alone?' said the brother.

'I am,' said Taliesin.

The gate unclosed slowly, just wide enough to give him
admittance. It was then again barred and barricaded.

The ghostly brother, of whom Taliesin had now a full view,
had a figure corresponding with his face, and wanted nothing
but a pair of horns and a beard in ringlets, to look like an
avatar of Bacchus. He maintained, however, great gravity of
face, and decorum of gesture, as he said to Taliesin, 'Hospitality is the rule of our house; but we are obliged to be cautious
in these times, though we live under powerful protection.
Those bloody Nimrods, the Saxons, are athirst for the blood
of the righteous. Monsters that are born with tails.'

Taliesin had not before heard this feature of Saxon conformation, and expressed his astonishment accordingly.

'How?' said the monk. 'Did not a rabble of them fasten
goats' tails to the robe of the blessed preacher in Riw, and did
he not, therefore, pray that their posterity might be born with
tails? And it is so. But let that pass. Have they not sacked
monasteries, plundered churches, and put holy brethren to the
sword? The blood of the saints calls for vengeance.'

'And will have it,' said Taliesin, 'from the hand of Arthur.'

The name of Arthur evidently discomposed the monk, who,
desiring Taliesin to follow him, led the way across the hall of
the abbey, and along a short wide passage, at the end of which
was a portly door.

The monk disappeared through this door, and, presently
returning, said, 'The abbot requires your name and quality.'

'Taliesin, the bard of Elphin ap Gwythno Garanhir,' was the reply.

The monk disappeared again, and, returning, after a longer pause than before, said, 'You may enter.'

The abbot was a plump and comely man, of middle age, having three roses in his complexion; one in full blossom on each cheek, and one in bud on the tip of his nose.

He was sitting at a small table, on which stood an enormous vase, and a golden goblet; and opposite to him sat the penitent of whom the round-faced brother had spoken, and in whom Taliesin recognized his acquaintance of Dinas Vawr, who called himself Seithenyn ap Seithyn.

The abbot and Seithenyn sat with their arms folded on the table, leaning forward towards each other, as if in momentous discussion.

The abbot said to Taliesin, 'Sit;' and to his conductor, 'Retire, and be silent.'

'Will it not be better,' said the monk, 'that I cross my lips with the sign of secrecy?'

'It is permitted,' said the abbot.

Seithenyn held forth the goblet to the monk, who swallowed the contents with much devotion. He then withdrew, and closed the door.

'I bid you most heartily welcome,' said Seithenyn to Taliesin. 'Drink off this, and I will tell you more. You are admitted to this special sitting at my special instance. I told the abbot I knew you well. Now I will tell you what I know. You have told King Arthur that King Melvas has possession of Queen Gwenyvar, and, in consequence, King Arthur is coming here, to sack and raze the castle and abbey, and cut every throat in the isle of Avallon. I have just brought the abbot this pleasant intelligence, and, as I knew it would take him down a cup or two, I have also brought what I call my little jug, to have the benefit of his judgement on a piece of rare wine which I have broached this morning: there is no better in Caer Lleon. And now we are holding council on the emergency. But I must say you abuse your bardic privilege, to enjoy people's hospitality, worm out their secrets, and carry the news to the enemy. It was partly to give you this candid opinion, that I have prevailed on the abbot to admit you to this special sitting. Therefore drink. GWIN O EUR: Wine from gold.'

'King Arthur is not a Saxon, at any rate,' sighed the abbot, winding up his fainting spirits with a draught. 'Think not, young stranger, that I am transgressing the laws of temperance: my blood runs so cold when I think of the blood-thirsty Saxons, that I take a little wine medicinally, in the hope of warming it; but it is a slow and tedious remedy.'

'Take a little more,' said Seithenyn. 'That is the true quantity. Wine is my medicine; and my quantity is a little more. A little more.'

'King Arthur,' said Taliesin, 'is not a Saxon; but he does not brook injuries lightly. It were better for your abbey that he came not here in arms. The aiders and abettors of Melvas, even though they be spiritual, may not carry off the matter without some share of his punishment, which is infallible.'

'That is just what I have been thinking,' said Seithenyn.

'God knows,' said the abbot, 'we are not abettors of Melvas, though we need his temporal power to protect us from the Saxons.'

'How can it be otherwise,' said Taliesin, 'than that these Saxon despoilers should be insolent and triumphant, while the princes of Britain are distracted with domestic broils: and for what?'

'Ay,' said Seithenyn, 'that is the point. For what? For a woman, or some such rubbish.'

'Rubbish, most verily,' said the abbot. 'Women are the flesh which we renounce with the devil.'

'Holy father,' said Taliesin, 'have you not spiritual influence with Melvas, to persuade him to surrender the queen without bloodshed, and, renewing his allegiance to Arthur, assist him in his most sacred war against the Saxon invaders?'

'A righteous work' said the abbot; 'but Melvas is headstrong and difficult.'

'Screw yourself up with another goblet,' said Seithenyn; 'you will find the difficulty smooth itself off wonderfully. Wine from gold has a sort of double light, that illuminates a dark path miraculously.'

The abbot sighed deeply, but adopted Seithenyn's method of throwing light on the subject.

'The anger of King Arthur,' said Taliesin, 'is certain, and its consequences infallible. The anger of King Melvas is doubtful, and its consequences to you cannot be formidable.'

'That is nearly true,' said the abbot, beginning to look resolute, as the rosebud at his nose-tip deepened into damask.

'A little more,' said Seithenyn, 'and it will become quite true.'

By degrees the proposition ripened into absolute truth. The abbot suddenly inflated his cheeks, started on his legs, and stalked bolt upright out of the apartment, and forthwith out of the abbey, followed by Seithenyn, tossing his goblet in the air, and catching it in his hand, as he went.

The round-faced brother made his appearance almost immediately. 'The abbot,' he said, 'commends you to the hospitality of the brotherhood. They will presently assemble to supper. In the meanwhile, as I am thirsty, and content with whatever falls in my way, I will take a simple and single draught of what happens to be here.'

His draught was a model of simplicity and singleness; for, having uplifted the ponderous vase, he held it to his lips, till he had drained it of the very copious remnant which the abrupt departure of the abbot had caused Seithenyn to leave in it.

Taliesin proceeded to enjoy the hospitality of the brethren, who set before him a very comfortable hot supper, at which he quickly perceived, that, however dexterous King Elphin might be at catching fish, the monks of Avallon were very far his masters in the three great arts of cooking it, serving it up, and washing it down; but he had not time to profit by their skill and experience in these matters, for he received a pressing invitation to the castle of Melvas, which he obeyed immediately.

CHAPTER XIV

THE RIGHT OF MIGHT

The three triumphs of the bards of the isle of Britain: the triumph of learning over ignorance; the triumph of reason over error; and the triumph of peace over violence.

TRIADS OF BARDISM.[1]

'FRIEND SEITHENYN,' said the abbot, when, having passed the castle gates, and solicited an audience, he was proceeding to the presence of Melvas, 'this task, to which I have accinged[2] myself, is arduous, and in some degree awful; being, in truth, no less than to persuade a king to surrender a possession, which he has inclination to keep for ever, and power to keep, at any rate, for an indefinite time.'

'Not so very indefinite,' said Seithenyn; 'for with the first song of the cuckoo (whom I mention on this occasion as a party concerned,) King Arthur will batter his castle about his ears, and, in all likelihood, the abbey about yours.'

The abbot sighed heavily.

'If your heart fail you,' said Seithenyn, 'another cup of wine will set all to rights.'

'Nay, nay, friend Seithenyn,' said the abbot, 'that which I have already taken has just brought me to the point at which the heart is inspirited, and the wit sharpened, without any infraction of the wisdom and gravity which become my character, and best suit my present business.'

Seithenyn, however, took an opportunity of making signs to some cupbearers, and, when they entered the apartment of Melvas, they were followed by vessels of wine and goblets of gold.

King Melvas was a man of middle age, with a somewhat round, large, regular-featured face, and an habitual smile of extreme self-satisfaction, which he could occasionally convert into a look of terrific ferocity, the more fearful for being rare. His manners were, for the most part, pleasant. He did much mischief, not for mischief's sake, nor yet for the sake of excitement, but for the sake of something tangible. He had a total and most complacent indifference to everything but his own will and pleasure. He took what he wanted wherever he could find it, by the most direct process, and without any false pretence. He would have disdained the trick which the chroniclers ascribe to Hengist, of begging as much land as a bull's hide would surround, and then shaving it into threads, which surrounded a goodly space. If he wanted a piece of land, he encamped upon it, saying, 'This is mine.' If the former possessor could eject him, so; it was not his: if not, so; it remained his. Cattle, wine, furniture, another man's wife, whatever he took a fancy to, he pounced upon and appropriated. He was intolerant of resistance; and, as the shortest way of getting rid of it, and not from any blood-thirstiness of disposition, or, as the phrenologists have it, development of the organ of destructiveness, he always cut through the resisting body, longitudinally, horizontally, or diagonally, as he found most convenient. He was the arch-marauder of West Britain. The abbey of Avallon shared largely in the spoil, and they made up together a most harmonious church and state. He had some respect for King Arthur; wished him success against the Saxons; knew the superiority of his power to his own; but he had heard that Queen Gwenyvar was the most beautiful woman in Britain; was, therefore, satisfied of his own title to her, and, as she was hunting in the forest, while King Arthur was absent from Caer Lleon, he seized her, and carried her off.

'Be seated, holy father,' said Melvas; 'and you, also, Seithenyn, unless the abbot wishes you away.'

But the abbot's heart misgave him, and he assented readily to Seithenyn's stay.

MELVAS. Now, holy father, to your important matter of private conference.

SEITHENYN. He is tongue-tied, and a cup too low.

THE ABBOT. Set the goblet before me, and I will sip in moderation.

MELVAS. Sip, or not sip, tell me your business.

THE ABBOT. My business, of a truth, touches the lady your prisoner, King Arthur's queen.

MELVAS. She is my queen, while I have her, and no prisoner. Drink, man, and be not afraid. Speak your mind: I will listen, and weigh your words.

THE ABBOT. This queen —

SEITHENYN. Obey the king: first drink, then speak.

THE ABBOTT. I drink to please the king.

MELVAS. Proceed.

THE ABBOT. This queen, Gwenyvar, is as beautiful as Helen, who caused the fatal war that expelled our forefathers from Troy: and I fear she will be a second Helen, and expel their posterity from Britain.* The infidel Saxons, to whom the cowardly and perfidious Vortigern gave footing in Britain, have prospered even more by the disunion of her princes than either by his villainy, or their own valour. And now there is no

---

* According to the British Chronicles, Brutus, the great grandson of Æneas, having killed his father, Silvius, to fulfil a prophecy, went to Greece, where he found the posterity of Helenus, the son of Priam; collected all of the Trojan race within the limits of Greece; and, after some adventures by land and sea, settled them in Britain, which was before uninhabited, 'except by a few giants'. [P.]

human hope against them but in the arms of Arthur. And how shall his arms prosper against the common enemy, if he be forced to turn them on the children of his own land for the recovery of his own wife?

MELVAS. What do you mean by his own? That which he has, is his own: but that which I have, is mine. I have the wife in question, and some of the land. Therefore they are mine.

THE ABBOT. Not so. The land is yours under fealty to him.

MELVAS. As much fealty as I please, or he can force me, to give him.

THE ABBOT. His wife, at least, is most lawfully his.

MELVAS. The winner makes the law, and his law is always against the loser. I am so far the winner; and, by my own law, she is lawfully mine.

THE ABBOT. There is a law above all human law, by which she is his.

MELVAS. From that it is for you to absolve me; and I dispense my bounty according to your indulgence.

THE ABBOT. There are limits we must not pass.

MELVAS. You set up your landmark, and I set up mine. They are both moveable.

THE ABBOT. The Church has not been niggardly in its indulgences to King Melvas.

MELVAS. Nor King Melvas in his gifts to the Church.

THE ABBOT. But, setting aside this consideration, I would treat it as a question of policy.

SEITHENYN. Now you talk sense. Right without might is the lees of an old barrel, without a drop of the original liquor.

THE ABBOT. I would appeal to you, King Melvas, by your love to your common country, by your love of the name of Britain, by your hatred of the infidel Saxons, by your respect for the character of Arthur; will you let your passion for a woman, even though she be a second Helen, frustrate, or even impede, the great cause, of driving these spoilers from a land in which they have no right even to breathe?

MELVAS. They have a right to do all they do, and to have all they have. If we can drive them out, they will then have no right here. Have not you and I a right to this good wine, which seems to trip very merrily over your ghostly palate? I got it by seizing a good ship, and throwing the crew overboard, just to remove them out of the way, because they were troublesome. They disputed my right, but I taught them better. I taught them a great moral lesson, though they had not much time to profit by it. If they had had the might to throw me overboard, I should not have troubled myself about their right, any more, or, at any rate, any longer, than they did about mine.

SEITHENYN. The wine was lawful spoil of war.

THE ABBOT. But if King Arthur brings his might to bear upon yours, I fear neither you nor I shall have a right to this wine, nor to anything else that is here.

SEITHENYN. Then make the most of it while you have it.

THE ABBOT. Now, while you have some months of security before you, you may gain great glory by surrendering the lady; and, if you be so disposed, you may no doubt claim, from the gratitude of King Arthur, the fairest princess of his court to wife, and an ample dower withal.

MELVAS. That offers something tangible.

SEITHENYN. Another ray from the golden goblet will set it in a most luminous view.

THE ABBOT. Though I should advise the not making it a condition, but asking it, as a matter of friendship, after the first victory that you have helped him to gain over the Saxons.

MELVAS. The worst of those Saxons is, that they offer nothing tangible, except hard knocks. They bring nothing with them. They come to take; and lately they have not taken much. But I will muse on your advice; and, as it seems, I may get more by following than rejecting it, I shall very probably take it, provided that you now attend me to the banquet in the hall.

SEITHENYN. Now you talk of the hall and the banquet, I will just intimate that the finest of all youths, and the best of all bards, is a guest in the neighbouring abbey.

MELVAS. If so, I have a clear right to him, as a guest for myself.

The abbot was not disposed to gainsay King Melvas's right. Taliesin was invited accordingly, and seated at the left hand of the king, the abbot being on the right. Taliesin summoned all the energies of his genius to turn the passions of Melvas into the channels of Anti-Saxonism, and succeeded so perfectly, that the king and his whole retinue of magnanimous heroes were inflamed with intense ardour to join the standard of

Arthur; and Melvas vowed most solemnly to Taliesin, that another sun should not set, before Queen Gwenyvar should be under the most honourable guidance on her return to Caer Lleon.

CHAPTER XV

THE CIRCLE OF THE BARDS

The three dignities of poetry: the union of the true and the wonderful; the union of the beautiful and the wise; and the union of art and nature.

TRIADS OF POETRY.[1]

AMONGST THE Christmas amusements of Caer Lleon, a grand Bardic Congress was held in the Roman theatre, when the principal bards of Britain contended for the preeminence in the art of poetry, and in its appropriate moral and mystical knowledge. The meeting was held by daylight. King Arthur presided, being himself an irregular bard, and admitted, on this public occasion, to all the efficient honours of a Bard of Presidency.

To preside in the Bardic Congress was long a peculiar privilege of the kings of Britain. It was exercised in the seventh century by King Cadwallader. King Arthur was assisted by twelve umpires, chosen by the bards, and confirmed by the king.

The Court, of course, occupied the stations of honour, and every other part of the theatre was crowded with a candid and liberal audience.

The bards sate in a circle on that part of the theatre corresponding with the portion which we call the stage.

Silence was proclaimed by the herald; and, after a grand symphony, which was led off in fine style by the king's harper, Geraint, Prince Cei[2] came forward, and made a brief oration, to the effect that any of the profane, who should be irregular and tumultuous, would be forcibly removed from the theatre, to be dealt with at the discretion of the officer of the guard. Silence was then a second time proclaimed by the herald.

Each bard, as he stood forward, was subjected to a number of interrogatories, metrical and mystical, which need not be

here reported. Many bards sang many songs. Amongst them,
Prince Llywarch sang

GORWYNION Y GAUAV
THE BRILLIANCIES OF WINTER

Last of flowers, in tufts around
Shines the gorse's golden bloom:
Milkwhite lichens clothe the ground
'Mid the flowerless heath and broom:
Bright are holly-berries, seen
Red, through leaves of glossy green.

Brightly, as on rocks they leap,
Shine the sea-waves, white with spray;
Brightly, in the dingles deep,
Gleams the river's foaming way;
Brightly through the distance show
Mountain-summits clothed in snow.

Brightly, where the torrents bound,
Shines the frozen colonnade,
Which the black rocks, dripping round,
And the flying spray have made:
Bright the icedrops on the ash
Leaning o'er the cataract's dash.

Bright the hearth, where feast and song
Crown the warrior's hour of peace,
While the snow-storm drives along,
Bidding war's worse tempest cease;
Bright the hearthflame, flashing clear
On the up-hung shield and spear.

Bright the torchlight of the hall
When the wintry night-winds blow;
Brightest when its splendours fall
On the mead-cup's sparkling flow:
While the maiden's smile of light
Makes the brightness trebly bright.

Close the portals; pile the hearth;
Strike the harp; the feast pursue;
Brim the horns: fire, music, mirth,
Mead and love, are winter's due.
Spring to purple conflict calls
Swords that shine on winter's walls.

Llywarch's song was applauded, as presenting a series of images with which all present were familiar, and which were all of them agreeable.

Merlin sang some verses of the poem, which is called

AVALLENAU MYRDDIN
MERLIN'S APPLE-TREES

Fair the gift to Merlin given,
Apple-trees seven score and seven;
Equal all in age and size;
On a green hill-slope, that lies
Basking in the southern sun,
Where bright waters murmuring run.

Just beneath the pure stream flows;
High above the forest grows;
Not again on earth is found
Such a slope of orchard ground:
Song of birds, and hum of bees,
Ever haunt the apple-trees.

Lovely green their leaves in spring;
Lovely bright their blossoming:
Sweet the shelter and the shade
By their summer foliage made:
Sweet the fruit their ripe boughs hold,
Fruit delicious, tinged with gold.

Gloyad, nymph with tresses bright,
Teeth of pearl, and eyes of light,
Guards these gifts of Ceidio's son,
Gwendol, the lamented one,
Him, whose keen-edged sword no more
Flashes 'mid the battle's roar.

War has raged on vale and hill:
That fair grove was peaceful still.
There have chiefs and princes sought
Solitude and tranquil thought:
There have kings, from courts and throngs,
Turned to Merlin's wild-wood songs.

Now from echoing woods I hear
Hostile axes sounding near:
On the sunny slope reclined,
Feverish grief disturbs my mind,
Lest the wasting edge consume
My fair spot of fruit and bloom.

Lovely trees, that long alone
In the sylvan vale have grown,
Bare, your sacred plot around,
Grows the once wood-waving ground:
Fervent valour guards ye still;
Yet my soul presages ill.

Well I know, when years have flown,
Briars shall grow where ye have grown:
Them in turn shall power uproot;
Then again shall flowers and fruit
Flourish in the sunny breeze,
On my new-born apple-trees.

This song was heard with much pleasure, especially by those of the audience who could see, in the imagery of the apple-trees, a mystical type of the doctrines and fortunes of Druid-ism, to which Merlin was suspected of being secretly attached, even under the very nose of St David.

Aneurin sang a portion of his poem on the Battle of Cat-traeth; in which he shadowed out the glory of Vortimer, the weakness of Vortigern, the fascinations of Rowena, the treachery of Hengist, and the vengeance of Emrys.

THE MASSACRE OF THE BRITONS

Sad was the day for Britain's land,
A day of ruin to the free,
When Gorthyn * stretched a friendly hand
To the dark dwellers of the sea.†

But not in pride the Saxon trod,
Nor force nor fraud oppressed the brave,
Ere the grey stone and flowery sod
Closed o'er the blessed hero's grave. ‡

The twice-raised monarch § drank the charm,
The love-draught of the ocean-maid:¶
Vain then the Briton's heard and arm,
Keen spear, strong shield, and burnished blade.

* Gwrtheyrn: Vortigern. [P.]
† Hengist and Horsa. [P.]
‡ Gwrthevyr: Vortimer: who drove the Saxons out of Britain. [P.]
§ Vortigern: who was, on the death of his son Vortimer, restored to the throne from which he had been deposed. [P.]
¶ Ronwen: Rowena. [P.]

'Come to the feast of wine and mead,'
Spake the dark dweller of the sea:*
'There shall the hours in mirth proceed;
There neither sword nor shield shall be.'

Hard by the sacred temple's site,
Soon as the shades of evening fall,
Resounds with song and glows with light
The ocean-dweller's rude-built hall.

The sacred ground, where chiefs of yore
The everlasting fire adored,
The solemn pledge of safety bore,
And breathed not of the treacherous sword.

The amber wreath his temples bound;
His vest concealed the murderous blade;
As man to man, the board around,
The guileful chief his host arrayed.

None but the noblest of the land,
The flower of Britain's chiefs, were there:
Unarmed, amid the Saxon band,
They sate, the fatal feast to share.

Three hundred chiefs, three score and three,
Went, where the festal torches burned
Before the dweller of the sea:
They went; and three alone returned.

'Till dawn the pale sweet mead they quaffed:
The ocean-chief unclosed his vest;
His hand was on his dagger's haft,
And daggers glared at every breast.

But him, at Eidiol's† breast who aimed,
The mighty Briton's arm laid low:
His eyes with righteous anger flamed;
He wrenched the dagger from the foe;

And through the throng he cleft his way,
And raised without his battle cry;
And hundreds hurried to the fray,
From towns, and vales, and mountains high.

* Hengist. [P.]
† Eidiol or Emrys: Emrys Wledig: Ambrosius. [P.]

But Britain's best blood dyed the floor
Within the treacherous Saxon's hall;
Of all, the golden chain who wore,
Two only answered Eidiol's call.

Then clashed the sword; then pierced the lance;
Then by the axe the shield was riven;
Then did the steed on Cattraeth prance,
And deep in blood his hoofs were driven.

Even as the flame consumes the wood,
So Eidiol rushed along the field;
As sinks the snow-bank in the flood,
So did the ocean-rovers yield.

The spoilers from the fane he drove
He hurried to the rock-built tower,
Where the base king,* in mirth and love,
Sate with his Saxon paramour.*

The storm of arms was on the gate,
The blaze of torches in the hall,
So swift, that ere they feared their fate,
The flames had scaled their chamber wall.

They died: for them no Briton grieves;
No planted flower above them waves;
No hand removes the withered leaves
That strew their solitary graves.

And time the avenging day brought round
That saw the sea-chief vainly sue:
To make his false host bite the ground
Was all the hope our warrior knew.

And evermore the strife he led,
Disdaining peace, with princely might,
Till, on a spear the spoiler's† head
Was reared on Caer-y-Cynan's height.

The Song of Aneurin touched deeply on the sympathies of
the audience, and was followed by a grand martial symphony,
in the midst of which Taliesin appeared in the Circle of
Bards. King Arthur welcomed him with great joy, and sweet

* Vortigern and Rowena. [P.]   † Hengist. [P.]

smiles were showered upon him from all the beauties of the court.

Taliesin answered the metrical and mystical questions to the astonishment of the most proficient; and, advancing, in his turn, to the front of the circle, he sang a portion of a poem which is now called HANES TALIESIN, The History of Taliesin; but which shall be here entitled

THE CAULDRON OF CERIDWEN

The sage Ceridwen was the wife
Of Tegid Voël, of Pemble Mere:
Two children blest their wedded life,
Morvran and Creirwy, fair and dear:
Morvran, a son of peerless worth,
And Creirwy, loveliest nymph of earth:
But one more son Ceridwen bare,
As foul as they before were fair.

She strove to make Avagddu wise;
She knew he never could be fair:
And, studying magic mysteries,
She gathered plants of virtue rare:
She placed the gifted plants to steep
Within the magic cauldron deep,
Where they a year and day must boil,
'Til three drops crown the matron's toil.

Nine damsels raised the mystic flame;
Gwion the Little near it stood:
The while for simples roved the dame
Through tangled dell and pathless wood.
And, when the year and day had past,
The dame within the cauldron cast
The consummating chaplet wild,
While Gwion held the hideous child.

But from the cauldron rose a smoke
That filled with darkness all the air:
When through its folds the torchlight broke,
Nor Gwion, nor the boy, was there,
The fire was dead, the cauldron cold,
And in it lay, in sleep uprolled,
Fair as the morning-star, a child,
That woke, and stretched its arms, and smiled.

What chanced her labours to destroy,
She never knew; and sought in vain
If 'twere her own misshapen boy,
Or little Gwion, born again:
And, vext with doubt, the babe she rolled
In cloth of purple and of gold,
And in a coracle consigned
Its fortunes to the sea and wind.

The summer night was still and bright,
The summer moon was large and clear,
The frail bark, on the springtide's height,
Was floated into Elphin's weir.
The baby in his arms he raised;
His lovely spouse stood by, and gazed,
And, blessing it with gentle vow,
Cried 'TALIESIN!' 'Radiant brow!'

And I am he: and well I know
Ceridwen's power protects me still;
And hence o'er hill and vale I go,
And sing, unharmed, whate'er I will.
She has for me Time's veil withdrawn:
The images of things long gone,
The shadows of the coming days,
Are present to my visioned gaze.

And I have heard the words of power,
By Ceirion's solitary lake,
That bid, at midnight's thrilling hour,
Eryri's hundred echoes wake.
I to Diganwy's towers have sped,
And now Caer Lleon's halls I tread,
Demanding justice, now, as then,
From Maelgon, most unjust of men.

The audience shouted with delight at the song of Taliesin,
and King Arthur, as President of the Bardic Congress, con-
ferred on him, at once, the highest honours of the sitting.

Where Taliesin picked up the story which he told of himself, why he told it, and what he meant by it, are questions not
easily answered. Certain it is, that he told this story to his contemporaries, and that none of them contradicted it. It may,
therefore, be presumed that they believed it; as anyone who
pleases is mostly heartily welcome to do now.

Besides the single songs, there were songs in dialogue, approaching very nearly to the character of dramatic poetry; and pennillion, or unconnected stanzas, sung in series by different singers, the stanzas being complete in themselves, simple as Greek epigrams, and presenting in succession moral precepts, pictures of natural scenery, images of war or of festival, the lamentations of absence or captivity, and the complaints or triumphs of love. This pennillion-singing long survived among the Welsh peasantry almost every other vestige of bardic customs, and may still be heard among them on the few occasions on which rack-renting, tax-collecting, common-enclosing, methodist-preaching, and similar developments of the light of the age, have left them either the means or inclination of making merry.

CHAPTER XVI

THE JUDGEMENTS OF ARTHUR

Three things to which success cannot fail where they shall justly be: discretion, exertion, and hope.

TRIADS OF WISDOM.[1]

KING ARTHUR had not long returned to his hall, when Queen Gwenyvar arrived, escorted by the Abbot of Avallon and Seithenyn ap Seithyn Saidi, who had brought his golden goblet, to gain a new harvest of glory from the cellars of Caer Lleon.

Seithenyn assured King Arthur, in the name of King Melvas, and on the word of a king, backed by that of his butler, which, truth being in wine, is good warranty even for a king, that the queen returned as pure as on the day King Melvas had carried her off.

'None here will doubt that;' said Gwenvach, the wife of Modred. Gwenyvar was not pleased with the compliment, and, almost before she had saluted King Arthur, she turned suddenly round, and slapped Gwenvach on the face, with a force that brought more crimson into one cheek than blushing had ever done into both. This slap is recorded in the Bardic Triads as one of the Three Fatal Slaps of the Island of Britain. A terrible effect is ascribed to this small cause; for it is said to

have been the basis of that enmity between Arthur and Modred, which terminated in the battle of Camlan, wherein all the
flower of Britain perished on both sides: a catastrophe more
calamitous than any that ever before or since happened in
Christendom, not even excepting that of the battle of Ronces-
valles; for, in the battle of Camlan, the Britons exhausted their
own strength, and could no longer resist the progress of the
Saxon supremacy. This, however, was a later result, and
comes not within the scope of the present veridicous narrative.

Gwenvach having flounced out of the hall, and the tumult
occasioned by this little incident having subsided, Queen
Gwenyvar took her ancient seat by the side of King Arthur,
who proceeded to inquire into the circumstances of her
restoration. The Abbot of Avallon began an oration, in praise
of his own eloquence, and its miraculous effects on King
Melvas; but he was interrupted by Seithenyn, who said, 'The
abbot's eloquence was good and well timed; but the chief
merit belongs to this young bard, who prompted him with
good counsel, and to me, who inspirited him with good
liquor. If he had not opened his mouth pretty widely when I
handed him this golden goblet, exclaiming GWIN O EUR, he
would never have had the heart to open it to any other good
purpose. But the most deserving person is this very promising
youth, in whom I can see no fault, but that he has not the same
keen perception as my friend the abbot has of the excellent
relish of wine from gold. To be sure, he plied me very hard
with strong drink in the hall of Dinas Vawr, and thereby
wormed out of me the secret of Queen Gwenyvar's captivity;
and, afterwards, he pursued us to Avallon, where he persuaded me and the abbot, and the abbot persuaded King
Melvas, that it would be better for all parties to restore the
queen peaceably: and then he clenched the matter with the
very best song I ever heard in my life. And, as my young
friend has a boon to ask, I freely give him all my share of the
merit, and the abbot's into the bargain.'

'Allow me, friend GWIN O EUR,' said the abbot, 'to dispose
of my own share of merit in my own way. But, such as it is, I
freely give it to this youth, in whom, as you say, I can see no
fault, but that his head is brimfull of Pagan knowledge.'

Arthur paid great honour to Taliesin, and placed him on his
left hand at the banquet. He then said to him, 'I judge, from

your song of this morning, that the boon you require from me concerns Maelgon Gwyneth. What is his transgression, and what is the justice you require.'

Taliesin narrated the adventures of Elphin in such a manner as gave Arthur an insight into his affection for Melanghel; and he supplicated King Arthur to command and enforce the liberation of Elphin from the Stone Tower of Diganwy.

Before King Arthur could signify his assent, Maelgon Gwyneth stalked into the hall, followed by a splendid retinue. He had been alarmed by the absence of Rhûn, had sought him in vain on the banks of the Mawddach, had endeavoured to get at the secret by pouncing upon Angharad and Melanghel, and had been baffled in his project by the vigilance of Teithrin ap Tathral. He had, therefore, as a last resort, followed Taliesin to Caer Lleon, conceiving that he might have had some share in the mysterious disappearance of Rhûn.

Arthur informed him that he was in possession of all the circumstances, and that Rhûn, who was in safe custody, would be liberated on the restoration of Elphin.

Maelgon boiled with rage and shame, but had no alternative but submission to the will of Arthur.

King Arthur commanded that all the parties should be brought before him. Caradoc was charged with the execution of this order, and, having received the necessary communications and powers from Maelgon and Taliesin, he went first to Diganwy, where he liberated Elphin, and then proceeded to give effect to Teithrin's declaration, that 'no hand but Elphin's should raise the stone of Rhûn's captivity.' Rhûn, while his pleasant adventure had all the gloss of novelty upon it, and his old renown as a gay deceiver was consequently in such dim eclipse, was very unwilling to present himself before the ladies of Caer Lleon; but Caradoc was peremptory, and carried off the crest-fallen prince, together with his bard of all work, who was always willing to go to any court, with any character, or none.

Accordingly, after a moderate lapse of time, Caradoc reappeared in the hall of Arthur, with the liberated captives, accompanied by Angharad and Melanghel, and Teithrin ap Tathral.

King Arthur welcomed the new comers with a magnificent festival, at which all the beauties of his court were present, and, addressing himself to Elphin, said, 'We are all debtors to this young bard: my queen and myself for her restoration to me; you for your liberation from the Stone Tower of Diganwy. Now, if there be, amongst all these ladies, one whom he would choose for his bride, and in whose eyes he may find favour, I will give the bride a dowry worthy of the noblest princess in Britain.'

Taliesin, thus encouraged, took the hand of Melanghel, who did not attempt to withdraw it, but turned to her father a blushing face, in which he read her satisfaction and her wishes. Elphin immediately said, 'I have nothing to give him but my daughter; but her I most cordially give him.'

Taliesin said, 'I owe to Elphin more than I can ever repay: life, honour, and happiness.'

Arthur said, 'You have not paid him ill; but you owe nothing to Maelgon and Rhûn, who are your debtors for a lesson of justice, which I hope they will profit by during the rest of their lives. Therefore Maelgon shall defray the charge of your wedding, which shall be the most splendid that has been seen in Caer Lleon.'

Maelgon looked exceedingly grim, and wished himself well back in Diganwy.

There was a very pathetic meeting of recognition between Seithenyn and his daughter; at the end of which he requested her husband's interest to obtain for him the vacant post of second butler to King Arthur. He obtained this honourable office; and was so zealous in the fulfilment of its duties, that, unless on actual service with a detachment of liquor, he never was a minute absent from the Temple of Diana.

At a subsequent Bardic Congress, Taliesin was unanimously elected Pen Beirdd,[2] or Chief of the Bards of Britain. The kingdom of Caredigion flourished under the protection of Arthur, and, in the ripeness of time, passed into the hands of Avaon, the son of Taliesin and Melanghel.

CROTCHET
CASTLE

Le monde est plein de fous, et qui n'en veut pas voir,
Doit se tenir tout seul, et casser son miroir.[1]

Crotchet Castle was first published in 1831

CROTCHET CASTLE

Should once the world resolve to abolish
All that's ridiculous and foolish,
It would have nothing left to do,
To apply in jest or earnest to.

BUTLER

Contents of
Crotchet Castle

THE VILLA

Captain Jamy. I wad full fain hear some question 'tween you tway.
                                                    – *Henry V.*

IN ONE OF THOSE beautiful vallies, through which the
Thames (not yet polluted by the tide, the scouring of cities, or
even the minor defilement of the sandy streams of Surrey,)
rolls a clear flood through flowery meadows, under the shade
of old beech woods, and the smoother mossy greensward of
the chalk hills (which pour into it their tributary rivulets, as
pure and pellucid as the fountain of Bandusium,[1] or the wells
of Scamander,[2] by which the wives and daughters of the
Trojans washed their splendid garments in the days of peace,
before the coming of the Greeks); in one of those beautiful
vallies, on a bold round-surfaced lawn, spotted with juniper,
that opened itself in the bosom of an old wood, which rose
with a steep, but not precipitous ascent, from the river to the
summit of the hill, stood the castellated villa of a retired
citizen. Ebenezer Mac Crotchet, Esquire, was the London-
born offspring of a worthy native of the 'north countrie', who
had walked up to London on a commercial adventure, with all
his surplus capital, not very neatly tied up in a not very clean
handkerchief, suspended over his shoulder from the end of a
hooked stick, extracted from the first hedge on his pilgrimage;
and who, after having worked himself a step or two up the
ladder of life, had won the virgin heart of the only daughter of
a highly respectable merchant of Duke's Place, with whom he
inherited the honest fruits of a long series of ingenuous deal-
ings.

Mr Mac Crotchet had derived from his mother the instinct,
and from his father the rational principle, of enriching himself
at the expense of the rest of mankind, by all the recognized
modes of accumulation on the windy side of the law. After
passing many years in the alley,[3] watching the turn of the
market, and playing many games almost as desperate as that
of the soldier of Lucullus,* the fear of losing what he had so

* Luculli miles, &c, HOR. *Ep.* II. 2. 26. 'In Anna's wars, a soldier poor
and bold,' &c.—POPE's *Imitation.* [P.]

righteously gained predominated over the sacred thirst of
paper-money; his caution got the better of his instinct, or
rather transferred it from the department of acquisition to that
of conservation. His friend, Mr Ramsbottom, the zodiacal
mythologist,[4] told him that he had done well to withdraw
from the region of Uranus or Brahma,[5] the maker, to that of
Saturn or Veeshnu,[6] the preserver, before he fell under the eye
of Jupiter or Seva, the destroyer, who might have struck him
down at a blow.

It is said, that a Scotchman returning home, after some
years' residence in England, being asked what he thought of
the English, answered: 'They hanna ower muckle sense, but
they are an unco braw people to live amang'; which would be
a very good story, if it were not rendered apocryphal, by the
incredible circumstance of the Scotchman going back.

Mr Mac Crotchet's experience had given him a just title to
make, in his own person, the last-quoted observation, but he
would have known better than to go back, even if himself, and
not his father, had been the first comer of his line from the
north. He had married an English Christian, and, having none
of the Scotch accent, was ungracious enough to be ashamed of
his blood. He was desirous to obliterate alike the Hebrew and
Caledonian vestiges in his name, and signed himself E. M.
Crotchet, which by degrees induced the majority of his neighbours to think that his name was Edward Matthew. The more
effectually to sink the Mac, he christened his villa Crotchet
Castle, and determined to hand down to posterity the honours
of Crotchet of Crotchet. He found it essential to his dignity to
furnish himself with a coat of arms, which, after the proper
ceremonies (payment being the principal), he obtained, videlicet: Crest, a crotchet rampant, in A sharp: Arms, three
empty bladders, turgescent, to show how opinions are formed;
three bags of gold, pendent, to show why they are maintained;
three naked swords, tranchant, to show how they are administered; and three barbers' blocks, gaspant, to show how
they are swallowed.

Mr Crotchet was left a widower, with two children; and,
after the death of his wife, so strong was his sense of the
blessed comfort she had been to him, that he determined never
to give any other woman an opportunity of obliterating the
happy recollection.

He was not without a plausible pretence for styling his villa

a castle, for, in its immediate vicinity, and within his own enclosed domain, were the manifest traces, on the brow of the
hill, of a Roman station, or *castellum*, which was still called
the castle by the country people. The primitive mounds and
trenches, merely overgrown with greensward, with a few
patches of juniper and box on the vallum, and a solitary ancient
beech surrounding the place of the prætorium, presented
nearly the same depths, heights, slopes, and forms, which the
Roman soldiers had originally given them. From this *castellum*
Mr Crotchet christened his villa. With his rustic neighbours he
was of course immediately and necessarily a squire: Squire
Crotchet of the castle; and he seemed to himself to settle down
as naturally into an English country gentleman, as if his
parentage had been as innocent of both Scotland and Jerusa-
lem, as his education was of Rome and Athens.

But as, though you expel nature with a pitchfork, she will
yet always come back;* he could not become, like a true-born
English squire, part and parcel of the barley-giving earth; he
could not find in game-bagging, poacher-shooting, trespasser-
pounding, footpath-stopping, common-enclosing, rack-renting, and all the other liberal pursuits and pastimes which make
a country gentleman an ornament to the world, and a blessing
to the poor; he could not find in these valuable and amiable
occupations, and in a corresponding range of ideas, nearly
commensurate with that of the great King Nebuchadnezzar,[7]
when he was turned out to grass; he could not find in this
great variety of useful action, and vast field of comprehensive
thought, modes of filling up his time that accorded with his
Caledonian instinct. The inborn love of disputation, which the
excitements and engagements of a life of business had
smothered, burst forth through the calmer surface of a rural
life. He grew as fain as Captain Jamy, 'to hear some airgument
betwixt ony tway;' and being very hospitable in his establishment, and liberal in his invitations, a numerous detachment
from the advanced guard of the 'march of intellect,' often
marched down to Crotchet Castle.

When the fashionable season filled London with exhibitors
of all descriptions, lecturers and else, Mr Crotchet was in his
glory; for, in addition to the perennial literati of the metropolis, he had the advantage of the visits of a number of hardy

* Naturam expellas furcâ, tamen usque recurret. – HOR. *Ep.* I. 10. 24.
[P.]

annuals, chiefly from the north, who, as the interval of their
metropolitan flowering allowed, occasionally accompanied
their London brethren in excursions to Crotchet Castle.

Amongst other things, he took very naturally to political
economy, read all the books on the subject which were put
forth by his own countrymen, attended all lectures thereon,
and boxed the technology of the sublime science as expertly
as an able seaman boxes the compass.

With this agreeable mania he had the satisfaction of biting
his son, the hope of his name and race, who had borne off
from Oxford the highest academical honours; and who,
treading in his father's footsteps to honour and fortune, had,
by means of a portion of the old gentleman's surplus capital,
made himself a junior partner in the eminent loan-jobbing firm
of Catchflat and Company. Here, in the days of paper prosperity, he applied his science-illumined genius to the blowing
of bubbles, the bursting of which sent many a poor devil to
the jail, the workhouse, or the bottom of the river, but left
young Crotchet rolling in riches.

These riches he had been on the point of doubling, by a
marriage with the daughter of Mr Touchandgo, the great
banker, when, one foggy morning, Mr Touchandgo and the
contents of his till were suddenly reported absent; and as the
fortune which the young gentleman had intended to marry
was not forthcoming, this tender affair of the heart was nipped
in the bud.

Miss Touchandgo[8] did not meet the shock of separation
quite so complacently as the young gentleman; for he lost
only the lady, whereas she lost a fortune as well as a lover.
Some jewels, which had glittered on her beautiful person as
brilliantly as the bubble of her father's wealth had done in the
eyes of his gudgeons, furnished her with a small portion of
paper currency; and this, added to the contents of a fairy purse
of gold, which she found in her shoe on the eventful morning
when Mr Touchandgo melted into thin air, enabled her to
retreat into North Wales, where she took up her lodging in a
farmhouse in Merionethshire, and boarded very comfortably
for a trifling payment, and the additional consideration of
teaching English, French, and music to the little Ap-Llymry's.
In the course of this occupation, she acquired sufficient knowledge of Welsh to converse with the country people.

She climbed the mountains, and descended the dingles,

with a foot which daily habit made by degrees almost as steady as a native's. She became the nymph of the scene; and if she sometimes pined in thought for her faithless Strephon,[9] her melancholy was anything but green and yellow; it was as genuine white and red as occupation, mountain air, thyme-fed mutton, thick cream, and fat bacon, could make it: to say nothing of an occasional glass of double X, which Ap-Llymry,* who yielded to no man west of the Wrekin in brewage, never failed to press upon her at dinner and supper. He was also earnest, and sometimes successful, in the recommendation of his mead, and most pertinacious on winter nights in enforcing a trial of the virtues of his elder wine. The young lady's personal appearance, consequently, formed a very advantageous contrast to that of her quondam lover, whose physiognomy the intense anxieties of his bubble-blowing days, notwithstanding their triumphant result, had left blighted, sallowed, and crow's-footed, to a degree not far below that of the fallen spirit who, in the expressive language of German romance, is described as 'scathed by the ineradicable traces of the thunder-bolts of Heaven;' so that, contemplating their relative geological positions, the poor deserted damsel was flourishing on slate, while her rich and false young knight was pining on chalk.

Squire Crotchet had also one daughter, whom he had christened Lemma, and who, as likely to be endowed with a very ample fortune, was, of course, an object very tempting to many young soldiers of fortune, who were marching with the march of mind, in a good condition for taking castles, as far as not having a groat is a qualification for such exploits.† She was also a glittering bait to divers young squires expectant (whose fathers were too well acquainted with the occult signification of mortgage), and even to one or two sprigs of nobility, who thought that the lining of a civic purse would superinduce a very passable factitious nap upon a threadbare title. The young lady had received an expensive and complicated education; complete in all the elements of superficial display. She was thus eminently qualified to be the companion of any masculine luminary who had kept due pace with the 'astounding progress' of intelligence. It must be confessed, that a man who has not kept due pace with it is not very easily

* Llymry. *Anglicé* flummery. [P.]

† 'Let him take castles who has ne'er a groat.' – POPE, *ubi suprà*. [P.]

found; this march being one of that 'astounding' character in which it seems impossible that the rear can be behind the van. The young lady was also tolerably good-looking: north of Tweed, or in Palestine, she would probably have been a beauty; but for the vallies of the Thames, she was perhaps a little too much to the taste of Solomon, and had a nose which rather too prominently suggested the idea of the tower of Lebanon, which looked towards Damascus.

In a village in the vicinity of the castle was the vicarage of the Reverend Doctor Folliott, a gentleman endowed with a tolerable stock of learning, an interminable swallow, and an indefatigable pair of lungs. His pre-eminence in the latter faculty gave occasion to some etymologists to ring changes on his name, and to decide that it was derived from Follis Optimus, softened through an Italian medium into Folle Ottimo, contracted poetically into Folleotto, and elided Anglicé into Folliott, signifying a first-rate pair of bellows. He claimed to be descended lineally from the illustrious Gilbert Folliott, the eminent theologian, who was a bishop of London in the twelfth century, whose studies were interrupted in the dead of night by the devil; when a couple of epigrams passed between them; and the devil, of course, proved the smaller wit of the two.*

* The devil began: (he had caught the bishop musing on politics).

> Oh Gilberte Folliott!
> Dum revolvis tot et tot,
> Deus tuus est Astarot.

> Oh Gilbert Folliott!
> While thus you muse and plot,
> Your god is Astarot.

The bishop answered:

> Tace, daemon: qui est deus
> Sabbaot, est ille meus.

> Peace, fiend; the power I own
> Is Sabbaoth's Lord alone.

It must be confessed, the devil was easily posed in the twelfth century. He was a sturdier disputant in the sixteenth.

> Did not the devil appear to Martin
> Luther in Germany for certain?

when 'the heroic student', as Mr Coleridge calls him, was forced to proceed to 'voies de fait'. The curious may see at this day, on the wall of Luther's study, the traces of the ink-bottle which he threw at the devil's head. [P.]

This reverend gentleman, being both learned and jolly, became by degrees an indispensable ornament to the new squire's table. Mr Crotchet himself was eminently jolly, though by no means eminently learned. In the latter respect he took after the great majority of the sons of his father's land; had a smattering of many things, and a knowledge of none; but possessed the true northern art of making the most of his intellectual harlequin's jacket, by keeping the best patches always bright and prominent.

CHAPTER II

THE MARCH OF MIND

Quoth Ralpho: nothing but the abuse
Of human learning you produce. – BUTLER.

'GOD BLESS MY SOUL, sir!' exclaimed the Reverend Doctor Folliott, bursting, one fine May morning, into the breakfast-room at Crotchet Castle, 'I am out of all patience with this march of mind. Here has my house been nearly burned down, by my cook taking it into her head to study hydrostatics, in a sixpenny tract, published by the Steam Intellect Society, and written by a learned friend who is for doing all the world's business as well as his own, and is equally well qualified to handle every branch of human knowledge. I have a great abomination of this learned friend;[1] as author, lawyer, and politician, he is *triformis*, like Hecate:[2] and in every one of his three forms he is *bifrons*, like Janus;[3] the true Mr Facing-both-ways of Vanity Fair. My cook must read his rubbish in bed; and as might naturally be expected, she dropped suddenly fast asleep, overturned the candle, and set the curtains in a blaze. Luckily, the footman went into the room at the moment, in time to tear down the curtains and throw them into the chimney, and a pitcher of water on her nightcap extinguished her wick: she is a greasy subject, and would have burned like a short mould.'[4]

The reverend gentleman exhaled his grievance without looking to the right or to the left; at length, turning on his pivot, he perceived that the room was full of company, consisting of young Crotchet and some visitors whom he had brought from London. The Reverend Doctor Folliott was introduced to Mr Mac Quedy,* the economist;[5] Mr Skionar,† the transcendental poet;[7] Mr Firedamp, the meteorologist; and Lord Bossnowl, son of the Earl of Foolincourt, and member for the borough of Rogueingrain.

The divine took his seat at the breakfast-table, and began to compose his spirits by the gentle sedative of a large cup of tea, the demulcent of a well-buttered muffin, and the tonic of a small lobster.

THE REV. DR FOLLIOTT. You are a man of taste, Mr Crotchet. A man of taste is seen at once in the array of his breakfast-table. It is the foot of Hercules, the far-shining face of the great work, according to Pindar's doctrine: ἀρχομένου ἔργου, πρόσωπον χρὴ θέμεν τηλαυγές.‡ The breakfast is the πρόσωπον of the great work of the day. Chocolate, coffee, tea, cream, eggs, ham, tongue, cold fowl – all these are good, and bespeak good knowledge in him who sets them forth: but the touchstone is fish: anchovy is the first step, prawns and shrimps the second; and I laud him who reaches even to these: potted char and lampreys are the third, and a fine stretch of progression; but lobster is, indeed, matter for a May morning, and demands a rare combination of knowledge and virtue in him who sets it forth.

MR MAC QUEDY. Well, sir, and what say you to a fine fresh trout, hot and dry, in a napkin? or a herring out of the water into the frying pan, on the shore of Loch Fyne?

THE REV. DR FOLLIOTT. Sir, I say every nation has some eximious virtue; and your country is pre-eminent in the glory of fish for breakfast. We have much to learn from you in that line at any rate.

MR MAC QUEDY. And in many others, sir, I believe. Morals and metaphysics, politics and political economy, the way to make the most of all the modifications of smoke; steam, gas, and paper currency; you have all these to learn from us; in short, all the arts and sciences. We are the modern Athenians.[8]

THE REV. DR FOLLIOTT. I, for one, sir, am content to learn nothing from you but the art and science of fish for breakfast. Be content, sir, to rival the Boeotians,[9] whose re-

---

* Quasi Mac Q. E. D., son of a demonstration. [P.]

† ΣΚΙᾶs ONAP. *Umbrae somnium*. [P.][6]

‡ Far-shining be the face
   Of a great work begun. – PIND. *Ol*. vi. [P.]

deeming virtue was in fish, touching which point you may consult Aristophanes and his scholiast, in the passage of Lysistrata,[10] ἀλλ᾽ ἄφελε τὰς ἐγχέλεις,* and leave the name of Athenians to those who have a sense of the beautiful, and a perception of metrical quantity.

MR. MAC QUEDY. Then, sir, I presume you set no value on the right principles of rent, profit, wages, and currency?

THE REV. DR FOLLIOTT. My principles, sir, in these things are, to take as much as I can get, and to pay no more than I can help. These are every man's principles, whether they be the right principles or no. There, sir, is political economy in a nutshell.

MR MAC QUEDY. The principles, sir, which regulate production and consumption, are independent of the will of any individual as to giving or taking, and do not lie in a nutshell by any means.

THE REV. DR FOLLIOTT. Sir, I will thank you for a leg of that capon.

LORD BOSSNOWL. But, sir, by the by, how came your footman to be going into your cook's room? It was very providential to be sure, but —

THE REV. DR FOLLIOTT. Sir, as good came of it, I shut my eyes, and asked no questions. I suppose he was going to study hydrostatics, and he found himself under the necessity of practising hydraulics.

MR. FIREDAMP. Sir, you seem to make very light of science.

THE REV. DR FOLLIOTT. Yes, sir, such science as the learned friend deals in: everything for everybody, science for all, schools for all, rhetoric for all, law for all, physic for all, words for all, and sense for none. I say, sir, law for lawyers, and cookery for cooks: and I wish the learned friend, for all his life, a cook that will pass her time in studying his works; then every dinner he sits down to at home, he will sit on the stool of repentance.

LORD BOSSNOWL. Now really that would be too severe: my cook should read nothing but Ude.[11]

THE REV. DR FOLLIOTT. No, sir! let Ude and the learned friend singe fowls together; let both avaunt from my kitchen. Θύρας δ᾽ ἐπίθεσθε βεβήλοις.† Ude says an elegant supper may

* Calonice wishes destruction to all Boeotians. Lysistrata answers, 'Except the eels.' Lysistrata, 36. [P.]
† 'Shut the doors against the profane.' Orphica, passim. [P.]

be given with sandwiches. *Horresco referens.*[12] An elegant supper! *Di meliora piis.*[13] No Ude for me. Conviviality went out with punch and suppers. I cherish their memory. I sup when I can, but not upon sandwiches. To offer me a sandwich, when I am looking for a supper, is to add insult to injury. Let the learned friend, and the modern Athenians, sup upon sandwiches.

MR MAC QUEDY. Nay, sir; the modern Athenians know better than that. A literary supper in sweet Edinbroo' would cure you of the prejudice you seem to cherish against us.

THE REV. DR FOLLIOTT. Well, sir, well; there is cogency in a good supper; a good supper, in these degenerate days, bespeaks a good man; but much more is wanted to make up an Athenian. Athenians, indeed! where is your theatre? who among you has written a comedy? where is your attic salt? which of you can tell who was Jupiter's great grandfather? or what metres will successively remain, if you take off the three first syllables, one by one, from a pure antispastic acatalectic tetrameter?[14] Now, sir, there are three questions for you; theatrical, mythological, and metrical; to every one of which an Athenian would give an answer that would lay me prostrate in my own nothingness.

MR MAC QUEDY. Well, sir, as to your metre and your mythology, they may e'en wait a wee. For your comedy, there is the Gentle Shepherd of the divine Allan Ramsay.

THE REV. DR FOLLIOTT. The Gentle Shepherd! It is just as much a comedy as the book of Job.

MR MAC QUEDY. Well, sir, if none of us have written a comedy, I cannot see that it is any such great matter, any more than I can conjecture what business a man can have at this time of day with Jupiter's great grandfather.

THE REV. DR FOLLIOTT. The great business is, sir, that you call yourselves Athenians, while you know nothing that the Athenians thought worth knowing, and dare not show your noses before the civilized world in the practice of any one art in which they were excellent. Modern Athens, sir! the assumption is a personal affront to every man who has a Sophocles in his library. I will thank you for an anchovy.

MR MAC QUEDY. Metaphysics, sir; metaphysics. Logic and moral philosophy. There we are at home. The Athenians only sought the way, and we have found it; and to all this we have added political economy, the science of sciences.

THE REV. DR FOLLIOTT. A hyperbarbarous technology, that no Athenian ear could have borne. Premises assumed without evidence, or in spite of it; and conclusions drawn from them so logically, that they must necessarily be erroneous.

MR SKIONAR. I cannot agree with you, Mr Mac Quedy, that you have found the true road of metaphysics, which the Athenians only sought. The Germans have found it, sir: the sublime Kant, and his disciples.

MR MAC QUEDY. I have read the sublime Kant, sir, with an anxious desire to understand him; and I confess I have not succeeded.

THE REV. DR FOLLIOTT. He wants the two great requisites of head and tail.

MR SKIONAR. Transcendentalism is the philosophy of intuition, the development of universal convictions; truths which are inherent in the organization of mind, which cannot be obliterated, though they may be obscured, by superstitious prejudice on the one hand, and by the Aristotelian logic on the other.

MR MAC QUEDY. Well, sir, I have no notion of logic obscuring a question.

MR SKIONAR. There is only one true logic, which is the transcendental; and this can prove only the one true philosophy, which is also the transcendental. The logic of your modern Athens can prove everything equally; and that is, in my opinion, tantamount to proving nothing at all.

MR CROTCHET. The sentimental against the rational, the intuitive against the inductive, the ornamental against the useful, the intense against the tranquil, the romantic against the classical; these are great and interesting controversies, which I should like, before I die, to see satisfactorily settled.

MR FIREDAMP. There is another great question, greater than all these, seeing that it is necessary to be alive in order to settle any question; and this is the question of water against human woe. Wherever there is water, there is *malaria*, and wherever there is *malaria*, there are the elements of death. The great object of a wise man should be to live on a gravelly hill, without so much as a duck-pond within ten miles of him, eschewing cisterns and water-butts, and taking care that there be no gravel-pits for lodging the rain. The sun sucks up infection from water, wherever it exists on the face of the earth.

THE REV. DR FOLLIOTT. Well, sir, you have for you the authority of the ancient mystagogue, who said, Ἔστιν ὕδωρ ψυχῇ θάνατος.* For my part I care not a rush (or any other aquatic and inesculent vegetable) who or what sucks up either the water or the infection. I think the proximity of wine a matter of much more importance than the longinquity of water. You are here within a quarter of a mile of the Thames; but in the cellar of my friend, Mr Crotchet, there is the talismanic antidote of a thousand dozen of old wine; a beautiful spectacle, I assure you, and a model of arrangement.

MR FIREDAMP. Sir, I feel the malignant influence of the river in every part of my system. Nothing but my great friendship for Mr Crotchet would have brought me so nearly within the jaws of the lion.

THE REV. DR FOLLIOTT. After dinner, sir, after dinner, I will meet you on this question. I shall then be armed for the strife. You may fight like Hercules against Achelous,[15] but I shall flourish the Bacchic thyrsus,[16] which changed rivers into wine: as Nonnus sweetly sings,[17] Οἴνῳ κυματόεντι μέλας κελάρυζεν Ὑδάσπης.†

MR CROTCHET, JUN. I hope, Mr Firedamp, you will let your friendship carry you a little closer into the jaws of the lion. I am fitting up a flotilla of pleasure boats, with spacious cabins, and a good cellar, to carry a choice philosophical party up the Thames and Severn, into the Ellesmere canal, where we shall be among the mountains of North Wales; which we may climb or not, as we think proper; but we will, at any rate, keep our floating hotel well provisioned, and we will try to settle all the questions over which a shadow of doubt yet hangs in the world of philosophy.

MR FIREDAMP. Out of my great friendship for you, I will certainly go, but I do not expect to survive the experiment.

THE REV. DR FOLLIOTT. *Alter erit tum Tiphys, et altera quæ vehat Argo Delectos Heroas.*‡ I will be of the party, though I must hire an officiating curate, and deprive poor Mrs Folliott, for several weeks, of the pleasure of combing my wig.

* Literally, which is sufficient for the present purpose, 'Water is death to the soul.' *Orphica*: Fr. XIX. [P.]

† Hydaspes gurgled, dark with billowy wine. *Dionysiaca*. XXV. 280. [P.]

‡   'Another Tiphys on the waves shall float,
          And chosen heroes freight his glorious boat.'
                                        VIRG. *Ecl.* IV. [P.]

LORD BOSSNOWL. I hope if I am to be of the party, our ship is not to be the ship of fools: He! He!

THE REV. DR FOLLIOTT. If you are one of the party, sir, it most assuredly will not: Ha! Ha!

LORD BOSSNOWL. Pray sir, what do you mean by Ha! Ha!?

THE REV. DR FOLLIOTT. Precisely, sir, what you mean by He! He!

MR MAC QUEDY. You need not dispute about terms; they are two modes of expressing merriment, with or without reason; reason being in no way essential to mirth. No man should ask another why he laughs, or at what, seeing that he does not always know, and that, if he does, he is not a responsible agent. Laughter is an involuntary action of certain muscles, developed in the human species by the progress of civilization. The savage never laughs.

THE REV. DR FOLLIOTT. No, sir, he has nothing to laugh at. Give him Modern Athens, the 'learned friend,'[18] and the Steam Intellect Society. They will develop his muscles.

CHAPTER III

THE ROMAN CAMP

He loved her more than seven yere,
Yet was he of her love never the nere;
He was not ryche of golde and fe,
A gentyll man forsoth was he.
The Squyr of Low Degre[1]

THE REVEREND DOCTOR FOLLIOTT having promised to return to dinner, walked back to his vicarage, meditating whether he should pass the morning in writing his next sermon, or in angling for trout, and had nearly decided in favour of the latter proposition, repeating to himself, with great unction, the lines of Chaucer:

And as for me, though that I can but lite,
On bokis for to read I me delite,
And to 'hem yeve I faithe and full credence,
And in mine herte have 'hem in reverence,
So hertily, that there is gamé none,
That fro my bokis makith me to gone,

> But it be seldome, on the holie daie;
> Save certainly whan that the month of Maie
> Is comin, and I here the foulis sing,
> And that the flouris ginnin for to spring,
> Farewell my boke and my devocion:[2]

when his attention was attracted by a young gentleman who was sitting on a camp stool with a portfolio on his knee, taking a sketch of the Roman Camp, which, as has been already said, was within the enclosed domain of Mr Crotchet. The young stranger, who had climbed over the fence, espying the portly divine, rose up, and hoped that he was not trespassing. 'By no means, sir,' said the divine; 'all the arts and sciences are welcome here: music, painting, and poetry; hydrostatics, and political economy; meteorology, transcendentalism, and fish for breakfast.'

THE STRANGER. A pleasant association, sir, and a liberal and discriminating hospitality. This is an old British camp, I believe, sir?

THE REV. DR FOLLIOTT. Roman, sir; Roman: undeniably Roman. The vallum is past controversy. It was not a camp, sir, a *castrum*, but a *castellum*, a little camp, or watch-station, to which was attached, on the peak of the adjacent hill, a beacon for transmitting alarms. You will find such here and there, all along the range of chalk hills, which traverses the country from north-east to south-west, and along the base of which runs the ancient Ikenild road, whereof you may descry a portion in that long strait white line.

THE STRANGER. I beg your pardon, sir: do I understand this place to be your property?

THE REV. DR FOLLIOTT. It is not mine, sir: the more is the pity; yet is it so far well, that the owner is my good friend, and a highly respectable gentleman.

THE STRANGER. Good and respectable, sir, I take it, mean rich?

THE REV. DR FOLLIOTT. That is their meaning, sir.

THE STRANGER. I understand the owner to be a Mr Crotchet. He has a handsome daughter, I am told.

THE REV. DR FOLLIOTT. He has, sir. Her eyes are like the fishpools of Heshbon, by the gate of Bethrabbim[3]; and she is to have a handsome fortune, to which divers disinterested gentlemen are paying their addresses. Perhaps you design to be one of them.

THE STRANGER. No, sir; I beg pardon if my questions seem impertinent; I have no such design. There is a son, too, I believe, sir, a great and successful blower of bubbles.

THE REV. DR FOLLIOTT. A hero, sir, in his line. Never did angler in September hook more gudgeons.

THE STRANGER. To say the truth, two very amiable young people, with whom I have some little acquaintance, Lord Bossnowl, and his sister, Lady Clarinda, are reported to be on the point of concluding a double marriage with Miss Crotchet and her brother, by way of putting a new varnish on old nobility. Lord Foolincourt, their father, is terribly poor for a lord who owns a borough.

THE REV. DR FOLLIOTT. Well, sir, the Crotchets have plenty of money, and the old gentleman's weak point is a hankering after high blood. I saw your acquaintance Lord Bossnowl this morning; but I did not see his sister. She may be there, nevertheless, and doing fashionable justice to this fine May morning, by lying in bed till noon.

THE STRANGER. Young Mr Crotchet, sir, has been, like his father, the architect of his own fortune, has he not? An illustrious example of the reward of honesty and industry?

THE REV. DR FOLLIOTT. As to honesty, sir, he made his fortune in the city of London; and if that commodity be of any value there, you will find it in the price current. I believe it is below par, like the shares of young Crotchet's fifty companies. But his progress has not been exactly like his father's: it has been more rapid, and he started with more advantages. He began with a fine capital from his father. The old gentleman divided his fortune into three not exactly equal portions: one for himself, one for his daughter, and one for his son, which he handed over to him, saying, 'Take it once for all, and make the most of it; if you lose it where I won it, not another stiver do you get from me during my life.' But, sir, young Crotchet doubled, and trebled, and quadrupled it, and is, as you say, a striking example of the reward of industry; not that I think his labour has been so great as his luck.

THE STRANGER. But, sir, is all this solid? is there no danger of reaction? no day of reckoning, to cut down in an hour prosperity that has grown up like a mushroom?

THE REV. DR FOLLIOTT. Nay, sir, I know not. I do not pry into these matters. I am, for my own part, very well satisfied with the young gentleman. Let those who are not so look to themselves. It is quite enough for me that he came down last night from London, and that he had the good sense to bring with him a basket of lobsters. Sir, I wish you a good morning.

The stranger, having returned the reverend gentleman's good morning, resumed his sketch, and was intently employed on it when Mr Crotchet made his appearance, with Mr Mac Quedy and Mr Skionar, whom he was escorting round his grounds, according to his custom with new visitors; the principal pleasure of possessing an extensive domain being that of showing it to other people. Mr Mac Quedy, according also to the laudable custom of his countrymen, had been appraising everything that fell under his observation; but, on arriving at the Roman camp, of which the value was purely imaginary, he contented himself with exclaiming, 'Eh! this is just a curiosity, and very pleasant to sit in on a summer day.'

MR. SKIONAR. And call up the days of old, when the Roman eagle spread its wings in the place of that beechen foliage. It gives a fine idea of duration, to think that that fine old tree must have sprung from the earth ages after this camp was formed.

MR MAC QUEDY. How old, think you, may the tree be?

MR CROTCHET. I have records which show it to be three hundred years old.

MR MAC QUEDY. That is a great age for a beech in good condition. But you see the camp is some fifteen hundred years, or so, older; and three times six being eighteen, I think you get a clearer idea of duration out of the simple arithmetic than out of your eagle and foliage.

MR SKIONAR. That is a very unpoetical, if not unphilosophical, mode of viewing antiquities. Your philosophy is too literal for our imperfect vision. We cannot look directly into the nature of things; we can only catch glimpses of the mighty shadow in the camera obscura of transcendental intelligence. These six and eighteen are only words to which we give conventional meanings. We can reason, but we cannot feel, by help of them. The tree and the eagle, contemplated in the ideality of space and time, become subjective realities, that rise up as landmarks in the mystery of the past.

MR MAC QUEDY. Well, sir, if you understand that, I wish you joy. But I must be excused for holding that my proposition, three times six are eighteen, is more intelligible than

yours. A worthy friend of mine, who is a sort of amateur in
philosophy, criticism, politics, and a wee bit of many things
more, says, 'Men never begin to study antiquities till they are
saturated with civilization.'*

MR SKIONAR. What is civilization?

MR MAC QUEDY. It is just respect for property: a state in
which no man takes wrongfully what belongs to another, is a
perfectly civilized state.

MR SKIONAR. Your friend's antiquaries must have lived in
El Dorado,[4] to have had an opportunity of being saturated
with such a state.

MR MAC QUEDY. It is a question of degree. There is more
respect for property here than in Angola.[5]

MR SKIONAR. That depends on the light in which things
are viewed.

Mr Crotchet was rubbing his hands, in hopes of a fine discussion, when they came round to the side of the camp where
the picturesque gentleman was sketching. The stranger was
rising up, when Mr Crotchet begged him not to disturb himself, and presently walked away with his two guests.

Shortly after Miss Crotchet and Lady Clarinda, who had
breakfasted by themselves, made their appearance at the same
spot, hanging each on an arm of Lord Bossnowl, who very
much preferred their company to that of the philosophers,
though he would have preferred the company of the latter, or
any company, to his own. He thought it very singular that so
agreeable a person as he held himself to be to others, should
be so exceedingly tiresome to himself: he did not attempt to
investigate the cause of this phenomenon, but was contented
with acting on his knowledge of the fact, and giving himself
as little of his own private society as possible.

The stranger rose as they approached, and was immediately
recognized by the Bossnowls as an old acquaintance, and
saluted with the exclamation of 'Captain Fitzchrome!' The
interchange of salutation between Lady Clarinda and the Captain was accompanied with an amiable confusion on both
sides, in which the observant eyes of Miss Crotchet seemed to
read the recollection of an affair of the heart.

Lord Bossnowl was either unconscious of any such affair,
or indifferent to its existence. He introduced the Captain very
cordially to Miss Crotchet, and the young lady invited him, as

* *Edinburgh Review*, somewhere. [P.]

the friend of their guests, to partake of her father's hospitality; an offer which was readily accepted.

The Captain took his portfolio under his right arm, his camp stool in his right hand, offered his left arm to Lady Clarinda, and followed at a reasonable distance behind Miss Crotchet and Lord Bossnowl, contriving, in the most natural manner possible, to drop more and more into the rear.

LADY CLARINDA. I am glad to see you can make yourself so happy with drawing old trees and mounds of grass.

CAPTAIN FITZCHROME. Happy, Lady Clarinda! oh, no! How can I be happy when I see the idol of my heart about to be sacrificed on the shrine of Mammon?

LADY CLARINDA. Do you know, though Mammon has a sort of ill name, I really think he is a very popular character; there must be at the bottom something amiable about him. He is certainly one of those pleasant creatures whom everybody abuses, but without whom no evening party is endurable. I dare say, love in a cottage is very pleasant; but then it positively must be a cottage ornée[6]: but would not the same love be a great deal safer in a castle, even if Mammon furnished the fortification?

CAPTAIN FITZCHROME. Oh, Lady Clarinda! there is a heartlessness in that language that chills me to the soul.

LADY CLARINDA. Heartlessness! No: my heart is on my lips. I speak just what I think. You used to like it, and say it was as delightful as it was rare.

CAPTAIN FITZCHROME. True, but you did not then talk as you do now, of love in a castle.

LADY CLARINDA. Well, but only consider: a dun is a horridly vulgar creature; it is a creature I cannot endure the thought of: and a cottage lets him in so easily. Now a castle keeps him at bay. You are a half-pay officer, and are at leisure to command the garrison: but where is the castle? and who is to furnish the commissariat?

CAPTAIN FITZCHROME. Is it come to this, that you make a jest of my poverty? Yet is my poverty only comparative. Many decent families are maintained on smaller means.

LADY CLARINDA. Decent families: aye, decent is the distinction from respectable. Respectable means rich, and decent means poor. I should die if I heard my family called decent. And then your decent family always lives in a snug little place: I hate a little place; I like large rooms and large looking-glasses, and large parties, and a fine large butler, with a tinge of smooth red in his face; an outward and visible sign that the family he serves is respectable; if not noble, highly respectable.

CAPTAIN FITZCHROME. I cannot believe that you say all this in earnest. No man is less disposed than I am to deny the importance of the substantial comforts of life. I once flattered myself that in our estimate of these things we were nearly of a mind.

LADY CLARINDA. Do you know, I think an opera-box a very substantial comfort, and a carriage. You will tell me that many decent people walk arm in arm through the snow, and sit in clogs and bonnets in the pit at the English theatre. No doubt it is very pleasant to those who are used to it; but it is not to my taste.

CAPTAIN FITZCHROME. You always delighted in trying to provoke me; but I cannot believe that you have not a heart.

LADY CLARINDA. You do not like to believe that I have a heart, you mean. You wish to think I have lost it, and you know to whom; and when I tell you that it is still safe in my own keeping, and that I do not mean to give it away, the unreasonable creature grows angry.

CAPTAIN FITZCHROME. Angry! far from it: I am perfectly cool.

LADY CLARINDA. Why, you are pursing your brows, biting your lips, and lifting up your foot as if you would stamp it into the earth. I must say anger becomes you; you would make a charming Hotspur. Your every-day-dining-out face is rather insipid: but I assure you my heart is in danger when you are in the heroics. It is so rare, too, in these days of smooth manners, to see anything like natural expression in a man's face. There is one set form for every man's face in female society; a sort of serious comedy, walking gentleman's face; but the moment the creature falls in love, he begins to give himself airs, and plays off all the varieties of his physiognomy, from the Master Slender to the Petruchio; and then he is actually very amusing.

CAPTAIN FITZCHROME. Well, Lady Clarinda, I will not be angry, amusing as it may be to you: I listen more in sorrow than in anger. I half believe you in earnest, and mourn as over a fallen angel.

LADY CLARINDA. What, because I have made up my mind not to give away my heart when I can sell it? I will introduce you to my new acquaintance, Mr Mac Quedy: he will talk to you by the hour about exchangeable value, and show you that no rational being will part with anything, except to the highest bidder.

CAPTAIN FITZCHROME. Now, I am sure you are not in earnest. You cannot adopt such sentiments in their naked deformity.

LADY CLARINDA. Naked deformity: why Mr Mac Quedy will prove to you that they are the cream of the most refined philosophy. You live a very pleasant life as a bachelor, roving about the country with your portfolio under your arm. I am not fit to be a poor man's wife. I cannot take any kind of trouble, or do any one thing that is of any use. Many decent families roast a bit of mutton on a string; but if I displease my father I shall not have as much as will buy the string, to say nothing of the meat; and the bare idea of such cookery gives me the horrors.

By this time they were near the castle, and met Miss Crotchet and her companion, who had turned back to meet them. Captain Fitzchrome was shortly after heartily welcomed by Mr Crotchet, and the party separated to dress for dinner, the captain being by no means in an enviable state of mind, and full of misgivings as to the extent of belief that he was bound to accord to the words of the lady of his heart.

CHAPTER IV

THE PARTY

En quoi cognoissez-vous la folie anticque? En quoi cognoissez-vous la sagesse présente? – RABELAIS.[1]

'IF I were sketching a bandit who had just shot his last pursuer, having outrun all the rest, that is the very face I would give him,' soliloquized the captain, as he studied the features of his rival in the drawing-room, during the miserable half-hour before dinner, when dulness reigns predominant over the expectant company, especially when they are waiting for some one last comer, whom they all heartily curse in their hearts, and whom, nevertheless, or indeed therefore-the-more, they welcome as a sinner, more heartily than all the just persons

who had been punctual to their engagement. Some new
visitors had arrived in the morning, and, as the company
dropped in one by one, the captain anxiously watched the un-
closing door for the form of his beloved; but she was the last
to make her appearance, and on her entry gave him a malicious
glance, which he construed into a telegraphic communication
that she had stayed away to torment him. Young Crotchet
escorted her with marked attention to the upper end of the
drawing-room, where a great portion of the company was
congregated around Miss Crotchet. These being the only
ladies in the company, it was evident that old Mr Crotchet
would give his arm to Lady Clarinda, an arrangement with
which the captain could not interfere. He therefore took his
station near the door, studying his rival from a distance, and
determined to take advantage of his present position, to secure
the seat next to his charmer. He was meditating on the best
mode of operation for securing this important post with due
regard to *bienséance*,[2] when he was twitched by the button by
Mr Mac Quedy, who said to him: 'Lady Clarinda tells me, sir,
that you are anxious to talk with me on the subject of exchangeable value, from which I infer that you have studied
political economy; and as a great deal depends on the definition of value, I shall be glad to set you right on that point.' –
'I am much obliged to you, sir,' said the captain, and was
about to express his utter disqualification for the proposed
instruction, when Mr Skionar walked up, and said: 'Lady
Clarinda informs me that you wish to talk over with me the
question of subjective reality. I am delighted to fall in with a
gentleman who duly appreciates the transcendental philosophy.' – 'Lady Clarinda is too good,' said the captain: and
was about to protest that he had never heard the word transcendental before, when the butler announced dinner. Mr
Crotchet led the way with Lady Clarinda: Lord Bossnowl
followed with Miss Crotchet: the economist and transcendentalist pinned in the captain, and held him, one by each
arm, as he impatiently descended the stairs in the rear of several
others of the company, whom they had forced him to let pass;
but the moment he entered the dining-room he broke loose
from them, and at the expense of a little *brusquerie*, secured his
position.

'Well, captain,' said Lady Clarinda, 'I perceive you can still
manoeuvre.'

'What could possess you,' said the captain, 'to send two unendurable and inconceivable bores, to intercept me with rubbish about which I neither know nor care any more than the man in the moon?'

'Perhaps,' said Lady Clarinda, 'I saw your design, and wished to put your generalship to the test. But do not contradict anything I have said about you, and see if the learned will find you out.'

'There is fine music, as Rabelais observes, in the *cliquetis d'assiettes*,[3] a refreshing shade in the *ombre de salle à manger*,[4] and an elegant fragrance in the *fumée de rôti*,'[5] said a voice at the captain's elbow. The captain turned round, recognized his clerical friend of the morning, who knew him again immediately, and said he was extremely glad to meet him there; more especially as Lady Clarinda had assured him that he was an enthusiastic lover of Greek poetry.

'Lady Clarinda,' said the captain, 'is a very pleasant young lady.'

THE REV. DR FOLLIOTT. So she is, sir: and I understand she has all the wit of the family to herself, whatever that *totum* may be. But a glass of wine after soup is, as the French say, the *verre de santé*.[6] The current of opinion sets in favour of Hock: but I am for Madeira; I do not fancy Hock till I have laid a substratum of Madeira. Will you join me?

CAPTAIN FITZCHROME. With pleasure.

THE REV. DR FOLLIOTT. Here is a very fine salmon before me: and May is the very *point nommé*[7] to have salmon in perfection. There is a fine turbot close by, and there is much to be said in his behalf; but salmon in May is the king of fish.

MR CROTCHET. That salmon before you, doctor, was caught in the Thames this morning.

THE REV. DR FOLLIOTT. Παπαπαῖ![8] Rarity of rarities! A Thames salmon caught this morning. Now, Mr Mac Quedy, even in fish your Modern Athens must yield. *Cedite Graii*.[9]

MR MAC QUEDY. Eh! sir, on its own ground, your Thames salmon has two virtues over all others: first, that it is fresh; and, second, that it is rare; for I understand you do not take half a dozen in a year.

THE REV. DR FOLLIOTT. In some years, sir, not one. Mud, filth, gas dregs, lock-weirs, and the march of mind, developed in the form of poaching, have ruined the fishery. But when we do catch a salmon, happy the man to whom he falls.

MR MAC QUEDY. I confess, sir, this is excellent; but I cannot see why it should be better than a Tweed salmon at Kelso.

THE REV. DR FOLLIOTT. Sir, I will take a glass of Hock with you.

MR MAC QUEDY. With all my heart, sir. There are several varieties of the salmon genus: but the common salmon the *salmo salar*, is only one species, one and the same everywhere, just like the human mind. Locality and education make all the difference.

THE REV. DR FOLLIOTT. Education! Well, sir, I have no doubt schools for all are just as fit for the species *salmo salar* as for the genus *homo*. But you must allow, that the specimen before us has finished his education in a manner that does honour to his college. However, I doubt that the *salmo salar* is only one species, that is to say, precisely alike in all localities. I hold that every river has its own breed, with essential differences; in flavour especially. And as for the human mind, I deny that it is the same in all men. I hold that there is every variety of natural capacity from the idiot to Newton and Shakespeare; the mass of mankind, midway between these extremes, being blockheads of different degrees; education leaving them pretty nearly as it found them, with this single difference, that it gives a fixed direction to their stupidity, a sort of incurable wry neck to the thing they call their understanding. So one nose points always east, and another always west, and each is ready to swear that it points due north.

MR CROTCHET. If that be the point of truth, very few intellectual noses point due north.

MR MAC QUEDY. Only those that point to the Modern Athens.

THE REV. DR FOLLIOTT. Where all native noses point southward.

MR MAC QUEDY. Eh, sir, northward for wisdom, and southward for profit.

MR CROTCHET, JUN. Champagne, doctor?

THE REV. DR FOLLIOTT. Most willingly. But you will permit my drinking it while it sparkles. I hold it a heresy to let it deaden in my hand, while the glass of my *compotator*[10] is being filled on the opposite side of the table. By the bye, captain, you remember a passage in Athenaeus, where he cites Menander on the subject of fish-sauce: ὀψάριον ἐπὶ ἰχθύος.[11] (*The captain was aghast for an answer that would satisfy both his neighbours, when he was relieved by the divine continuing.*) The science of fish sauce, Mr Mac Quedy, is by no means brought to perfection; a fine field of discovery still lies open in that line.

MR MAC QUEDY. Nay, sir, beyond lobster sauce, I take it, ye cannot go.

THE REV. DR FOLLIOTT. In their line, I grant you, oyster and lobster sauce are the pillars of Hercules. But I speak of the cruet sauces, where the quintessence of the sapid[12] is condensed in a phial. I can taste in my mind's palate a combination, which, if I could give it reality, I would christen with the name of my college, and hand it down to posterity as a seat of learning indeed.

MR MAC QUEDY. Well, sir, I wish you success, but I cannot let slip the question we started just now. I say, cutting off idiots, who have no minds at all, all minds are by nature alike. Education (which begins from their birth) makes them what they are.

THE REV. DR FOLLIOTT. No, sir, it makes their tendencies, not their power. Caesar would have been the first wrestler on the village common. Education might have made him a Nadir Shah[13]; it might also have made him a Washington; it could not have made him a merry-andrew, for our newspapers to extol as a model of eloquence.

MR MAC QUEDY. Now, sir, I think education would have made him just anything, and fit for any station, from the throne to the stocks; saint or sinner, aristocrat or democrat, judge, counsel, or prisoner at the bar.

THE REV. DR FOLLIOTT. I will thank you for a slice of lamb, with lemon and pepper. Before I proceed with this discussion – Vin de Grave, Mr Skionar – I must interpose one remark. There is a set of persons in your city, Mr Mac Quedy, who concoct every three or four months a thing which they call a review[14]: a sort of sugar-plum manufacturers to the Whig aristocracy.

MR MAC QUEDY. I cannot tell, sir, exactly, what you mean by that; but I hope you will speak of those gentlemen with respect, seeing that I am one of them.

THE REV. DR FOLLIOTT. Sir, I must drown my inadvertence in a glass of Sauterne with you. There is a set of gentlemen in your city —

MR MAC QUEDY. Not in our city, exactly; neither are they a set. There is an editor, who forages for articles in all quarters, from John O'Groat's house to the Land's End. It is not a board, or a society: it is a mere intellectual bazaar, where A, B, and C bring their wares to market.

THE REV. DR FOLLIOTT. Well, sir, these gentlemen among them, the present company excepted, have practised as much dishonesty as, in any other department than literature, would have brought the practitioner under the cognisance of the police. In politics, they have run with the hare and hunted with the hound. In criticism they have, knowingly and unblushingly, given false characters, both for good and for evil: sticking at no art of misrepresentation, to clear out of the field of literature all who stood in the way of the interests of their own clique. They have never allowed their own profound ignorance of anything (Greek, for instance) to throw even an air of hesitation into their oracular decision on the matter. They set an example of profligate contempt for truth, of which the success was in proportion to the effrontery; and when their prosperity had filled the market with competitors, they cried out against their own reflected sin, as if they had never committed it, or were entitled to a monopoly of it. The latter, I rather think, was what they wanted.

MR CROTCHET. Hermitage, doctor?

THE REV. DR FOLLIOTT. Nothing better, sir. The father who first chose the solitude of that vineyard, knew well how to cultivate his spirit in retirement. Now, Mr Mac Quedy, Achilles was distinguished above all the Greeks for his inflexible love of truth: could education have made Achilles one of your reviewers?

MR MAC QUEDY. No doubt of it, even if your character of them were true to the letter.

THE REV. DR FOLLIOTT. And I say, sir – chicken and asparagus – Titan had made him of better clay.* I hold with Pindar: 'All that is most excellent is so by nature.' $T\grave{o}$ $\delta\grave{e}$ $\phi v\hat{q}$ $\kappa\rho\acute{a}\tau\iota\sigma\tau o\nu$ $\ddot{a}\pi a\nu.$† Education can give purposes, but not powers; and whatever purposes had been given him, he would have gone straight forward to them; straight forward, Mr Mac Quedy.

MR MAC QUEDY. No, sir, education makes the man, powers, purposes, and all.

THE REV. DR FOLLIOTT. There is the point, sir, on which we join issue.

* Juv. xiv. 35. [P.]   † Ol. ix. 152. [P.

Several others of the company now chimed in with their opinions, which gave the divine an opportunity to degustate one or two side dishes, and to take a glass of wine with each of the young ladies.

CHAPTER V

CHARACTERS

Ay imputé a honte plus que mediocre être vu spectateur ocieux de tant vaillans, disertz, et chevalereux personnaiges. – RABELAIS.[1]

LADY CLARINDA (*to the Captain*). I declare the creature has been listening to all this rigmarole, instead of attending to me. Do you ever expect forgiveness? But now that they are all talking together, and you cannot make out a word they say, nor they hear a word that we say, I will describe the company to you. First, there is the old gentleman on my left hand, at the head of the table, who is now leaning the other way to talk to my brother. He is a good tempered, half-informed person, very unreasonably fond of reasoning, and of reasoning people; people that talk nonsense logically: he is fond of disputation himself, when there are only one or two, but seldom does more than listen in a large company of *illuminés*. He made a great fortune in the city, and has the comfort of a good conscience. He is very hospitable, and is generous in dinners; though nothing would induce him to give sixpence to the poor, because he holds that all misfortune is from imprudence, that none but the rich ought to marry, and that all ought to thrive by honest industry, as he did. He is ambitious of founding a family, and of allying himself with nobility; and is thus as willing as other grown children, to throw away thousands for a gew-gaw, though he would not part with a penny for charity. Next to him is my brother, whom you know as well as I do. He has finished his education with credit, and as he never ventures to oppose me in anything, I have no doubt he is very sensible. He has good manners, is a model of dress, and is reckoned ornamental in all societies. Next to him is Miss Crotchet, my sister-in-law that is to be. You see she is rather pretty, and very genteel. She is tolerably accomplished, has her table always covered with new novels, thinks Mr Mac Quedy

an oracle, and is extremely desirous to be called 'my lady.'
Next to her is Mr Firedamp, a very absurd person, who thinks
that water is the evil principle. Next to him is Mr Eavesdrop,[2]
a man who, by dint of a certain something like smartness, has
got into good society. He is a sort of bookseller's tool, and
coins all his acquaintance in reminiscences and sketches of
character. I am very shy of him, for fear he should print me.

CAPTAIN FITZCHROME. If he print you in your own likeness, which is that of an angel, you need not fear him. If he
print you in any other, I will cut his throat. But proceed —

LADY CLARINDA. Next to him is Mr Henbane, the toxico-
logist, I think he calls himself. He has passed half his life in
studying poisons and antidotes. The first thing he did on his
arrival here, was to kill the cat; and while Miss Crotchet was
crying over her, he brought her to life again. I am more shy of
him than the other.

CAPTAIN FITZCHROME. They are two very dangerous
fellows, and I shall take care to keep them both at a respectful
distance. Let us hope that Eavesdrop will sketch off Henbane,
and that Henbane will poison him for his trouble.

LADY CLARINDA. Well, next to him sits Mr Mac Quedy,
the Modern Athenian, who lays down the law about everything, and therefore may be taken to understand everything.
He turns all the affairs of this world into questions of buying
and selling. He is the Spirit of the Frozen Ocean to everything
like romance and sentiment. He condenses their volume of
steam into a drop of cold water in a moment. He has satisfied
me that I am a commodity in the market, and that I ought to
set myself at a high price. So you see he who would have me
must bid for me.

CAPTAIN FITZCHROME. I shall discuss that point with Mr
Mac Quedy.

LADY CLARINDA. Not a word for your life. Our flirtation
is our own secret. Let it remain so.

CAPTAIN FITZCHROME. Flirtation, Clarinda! Is that all
that the most ardent —

LADY CLARINDA. Now, don't be rhapsodical here. Next to
Mr Mac Quedy is Mr Skionar, a sort of poetical philosopher, a
curious compound of the intense and the mystical. He abo-
minates all the ideas of Mr Mac Quedy, and settles everything
by sentiment and intuition.

CAPTAIN FITZCHROME. Then, I say, he is the wiser man.

LADY CLARINDA. They are two oddities; but a little of them is amusing, and I like to hear them dispute. So you see I am in training for a philosopher myself.

CAPTAIN FITZCHROME. Any philosophy, for heaven's sake, but the pound-shilling-and-pence philosophy of Mr Mac Quedy.

LADY CLARINDA. Why, they say that even Mr Skionar, though he is a great dreamer, always dreams with his eyes open, or with one eye at any rate, which is an eye to his gain: but I believe that in this respect the poor man has got an ill name by keeping bad company. He has two dear friends, Mr Wilful Wontsee, and Mr Rumblesack Shantsee,[3] poets of some note, who used to see visions of Utopia, and pure republics beyond the Western deep: but finding that these El Dorados brought them no revenue, they turned their vision-seeing faculty into the more profitable channel of espying all sorts of virtues in the high and the mighty, who were able and willing to pay for the discovery.

CAPTAIN FITZCHROME. I do not fancy these virtue-spyers.

LADY CLARINDA. Next to Mr Skionar, sits Mr Chainmail, a good-looking young gentleman, as you see, with very anti-quated tastes. He is fond of old poetry, and is something of a poet himself. He is deep in monkish literature, and holds that the best state of society was that of the twelfth century, when nothing was going forward but fighting, feasting, and pray-ing, which he says are the three great purposes for which man was made. He laments bitterly over the inventions of gun-powder, steam, and gas, which he says have ruined the world. He lives within two or three miles, and has a large hall, adorned with rusty pikes, shields, helmets, swords, and tattered banners, and furnished with yew-tree chairs, and two long, old, worm-eaten oak tables, where he dines with all his household, after the fashion of his favourite age. He wants us all to dine with him, and I believe we shall go.

CAPTAIN FITZCHROME. That will be something new at any rate.

LADY CLARINDA. Next to him is Mr Toogood, the co-operationist,[4] who will have neither fighting nor praying; but wants to parcel out the world into squares like a chess-board, with a community on each, raising everything for one another, with a great steam-engine to serve them in common for tailor and hosier, kitchen and cook.

CAPTAIN FITZCHROME. He is the strangest of the set, so far.

LADY CLARINDA. This brings us to the bottom of the table, where sits my humble servant, Mr Crotchet the younger. I ought not to describe him.

CAPTAIN FITZCHROME. I entreat you do.

LADY CLARINDA. Well, I really have very little to say in his favour.

CAPTAIN FITZCHROME. I do not wish to hear anything in his favour; and I rejoice to hear you say so, because.—

LADY CLARINDA. Do not flatter yourself. If I take him, it will be to please my father, and to have a town and country-house, and plenty of servants, and a carriage and an opera-box, and make some of my acquaintance who have married for love, or for rank, or for anything but money, die for envy of my jewels. You do not think I would take him for himself. Why he is very smooth and spruce, as far as his dress goes; but as to his face, he looks as if he had tumbled headlong into a volcano, and been thrown up again among the cinders.

CAPTAIN FITZCHROME. I cannot believe, that, speaking thus of him, you mean to take him at all.

LADY CLARINDA. Oh! I am out of my teens. I have been very much in love; but now I am come to years of discretion, and must think, like other people, of settling myself advantageously. He was in love with a banker's daughter, and cast her off on her father's bankruptcy, and the poor girl has gone to hide herself in some wild place.

CAPTAIN FITZCHROME. She must have a strange taste, if she pines for the loss of him.

LADY CLARINDA. They say he was good-looking, till his bubble-schemes, as they call them, stamped him with the physiognomy of a desperate gambler. I suspect he has still a *penchant* towards his first flame. If he takes me, it will be for my rank and connection, and the second seat of the borough of Rogueingrain. So we shall meet on equal terms, and shall enjoy all the blessedness of expecting nothing from each other.

CAPTAIN FITZCHROME. You can expect no security with such an adventurer.

LADY CLARINDA. I shall have the security of a good settlement, and then if *andare al diavolo* be his destiny,[5] he may go, you know, by himself. He is almost always dreaming and *distrait*. It is very likely that some great reverse is in store for him: but that will not concern me, you perceive.

CAPTAIN FITZCHROME. You torture me, Clarinda, with the bare possibility.

LADY CLARINDA. Hush! Here is music to soothe your troubled spirit. Next to him, on this side, sits the dilettante composer, Mr Trillo[6]; they say his name was O'Trill, and he has taken the O from the beginning, and put it at the end. I do not know how this may be. He plays well on the violoncello, and better on the piano: sings agreeably; has a talent at verse-making, and improvises a song with some felicity. He is very agreeable company in the evening, with his instruments and music-books. He maintains that the sole end of all enlightened society is to get up a good opera, and laments that wealth, genius, and energy, are squandered upon other pursuits, to the neglect of this one great matter.

CAPTAIN FITZCHROME. This is a very pleasant fancy at any rate.

LADY CLARINDA. I assure you he has a great deal to say for it. Well, next to him again, is Dr Morbific, who has been all over the world to prove that there is no such thing as contagion; and has inoculated himself with plague, yellow fever, and every variety of pestilence, and is still alive to tell the story. I am very shy of him, too; for I look on him as a walking phial of wrath, corked full of all infections, and not to be touched without extreme hazard.

CAPTAIN FITZCHROME. This is the strangest fellow of all.

LADY CLARINDA. Next to him sits Mr Philpot,[7] the geographer, who thinks of nothing but the heads and tails of rivers, and lays down the streams of Terra Incognita as accurately as if he had been there. He is a person of pleasant fancy, and makes a sort of fairy land of every country he touches, from the Frozen Ocean to the Deserts of Zahara.

CAPTAIN FITZCHROME. How does he settle matters with Mr Firedamp?

LADY CLARINDA. You see Mr Firedamp has got as far as possible out of his way. Next to him is Sir Simon Steeltrap, of Steeltrap Lodge, Member for Crouching-Curtown, Justice of Peace for the county, and Lord of the United Manors of Spring-gun and Treadmill; a great preserver of game and public morals. By administering the laws which he assists in making, he disposes, at his pleasure, of the land and its live stock, including all the two-legged varieties, with and without feathers, in a circumference of several miles round Steeltrap

Lodge. He has enclosed commons and woodlands; abolished cottage-gardens; taken the village cricket-ground into his own park, out of pure regard to the sanctity of Sunday; shut up footpaths and alehouses, (all but those which belong to his electioneering friend, Mr Quassia, the brewer;) put down fairs and fiddlers; committed many poachers; shot a few; convicted one third of the peasantry; suspected the rest; and passed nearly the whole of them through a wholesome course of prison discipline, which has finished their education at the expense of the county.

CAPTAIN FITZCHROME. He is somewhat out of his element here: among such a diversity of opinions he will hear some he will not like.

LADY CLARINDA. It was rather ill-judged in Mr Crotchet to invite him today. But the art of assorting company is above these *parvenus*. They invite a certain number of persons without considering how they harmonize with each other. Between Sir Simon and you is the Reverend Doctor Folliott. He is said to be an excellent scholar, and is fonder of books than the majority of his cloth; he is very fond, also, of the good things of this world. He is of an admirable temper, and says rude things in a pleasant half-earnest manner, that nobody can take offence with. And next to him, again, is one Captain Fitzchrome, who is very much in love with a certain person that does not mean to have anything to say to him, because she can better her fortune by taking somebody else.

CAPTAIN FITZCHROME. And next to him, again, is the beautiful, the accomplished, the witty, the fascinating, the tormenting Lady Clarinda, who traduces herself to the said captain by assertions which it would drive him crazy to believe.

LADY CLARINDA. Time will show, sir. And now we have gone the round of the table.

CAPTAIN FITZCHROME. But I must say, though I know you had always a turn for sketching characters, you surprise me by your observation, and especially by your attention to opinions.

LADY CLARINDA. Well, I will tell you a secret: I am writing a novel.

CAPTAIN FITZCHROME. A novel!

LADY CLARINDA. Yes, a novel. And I shall get a little finery by it: trinkets and fal-lals, which I cannot get from papa. You must know I have been reading several fashionable novels, the fashionable this, and the fashionable that; and I thought to myself, why I can do better than any of these myself. So I wrote a chapter or two, and sent them as a specimen to Mr Puffall, the bookseller, telling him they were to be a part of the fashionable something or other, and he offered me, I will not say how much, to finish it in three volumes, and let him pay all the newspapers for recommending it as the work of a lady of quality, who had made very free with the characters of her acquaintance.

CAPTAIN FITZCHROME. Surely you have not done so?

LADY CLARINDA. Oh, no; I leave that to Mr Eavesdrop. But Mr Puffall made it a condition that I should let him say so.

CAPTAIN FITZCHROME. A strange recommendation.

LADY CLARINDA. Oh, nothing else will do. And it seems you may give yourself any character you like, and the newspapers will print it as if it came from themselves. I have commended you to three of our friends here, as an economist, a transcendentalist, and a classical scholar; and if you wish to be renowned through the world for these, or any other accomplishments, the newspapers will confirm you in their possession for half-a-guinea a piece.

CAPTAIN FITZCHROME. Truly, the praise of such gentry must be a feather in anyone's cap.

LADY CLARINDA. So you will see, some morning, that my novel is 'the most popular production of the day'. This is Mr Puffall's favourite phrase. He makes the newspapers say it of everything he publishes. But 'the day', you know, is a very convenient phrase; it allows of three hundred and sixty-five 'most popular productions' in a year. And in leap-year one more.

CHAPTER VI

THEORIES

But when they came to shape the model,
Not one could fit the other's noddle. – BUTLER.

MEANWHILE, the last course, and the dessert, passed by. When the ladies had withdrawn, young Crotchet addressed the company.

MR CROTCHET, JUN. There is one point in which

philosophers of all classes seem to be agreed; that they only want money to regenerate the world.

MR MAC QUEDY. No doubt of it. Nothing is so easy as to lay down the outlines of perfect society. There wants nothing but money to set it going. I will explain myself clearly and fully by reading a paper. (*Producing a large scroll.*) 'In the infancy of society —'

THE REV. DR FOLLIOTT. Pray, Mr Mac Quedy, how is it that all gentlemen of your nation begin everything they write with the 'infancy of society'?

MR MAC QUEDY. Eh, sir, it is the simplest way to begin at the beginning. 'In the infancy of society, when government was invented to save a percentage; say two and a half per cent —'

THE REV. DR FOLLIOTT. I will not say any such thing.

MR MAC QUEDY. Well, say any percentage you please.

THE REV. DR FOLLIOTT. I will not say any percentage at all.

MR MAC QUEDY. 'On the principle of the division of labour —'

THE REV. DR FOLLIOTT. Government was invented to spend a percentage.

MR MAC QUEDY. To save a percentage.

THE REV. DR FOLLIOTT. No, sir, to spend a percentage; and a good deal more than two and a half per cent. Two hundred and fifty per cent; that is intelligible.

MR MAC QUEDY. 'In the infancy of society' —

MR TOOGOOD. Never mind the infancy of society. The question is of society in its maturity. Here is what it should be. (*Producing a paper.*) I have laid it down in a diagram.

MR SKIONAR. Before we proceed to the question of government, we must nicely discriminate the boundaries of sense, understanding, and reason. Sense is a receptivity —

MR CROTCHET, JUN. We are proceeding too fast. Money being all that is wanted to regenerate society, I will put into the hands of this company a large sum for the purpose. Now let us see how to dispose of it.

MR MAC QUEDY. We will begin by taking a committee-room in London, where we will dine together once a week, to deliberate.

THE REV. DR FOLLIOTT. If the money is to go in deliberative dinners, you may set me down for a committee man and honorary caterer.

MR MAC QUEDY. Next, you must all learn political economy, which I will teach you, very compendiously, in lectures over the bottle.

THE REV. DR FOLLIOTT. I hate lectures over the bottle. But pray, sir, what is political economy?

MR MAC QUEDY. Political economy is to the state what domestic economy is to the family.

THE REV. DR FOLLIOTT. No such thing, sir. In the family there is a *paterfamilias*, who regulates the distribution, and takes care that there shall be no such thing in the household as one dying of hunger, while another dies of surfeit. In the state it is all hunger at one end, and all surfeit at the other. Matchless claret, Mr Crotchet.

MR CROTCHET. Vintage of fifteen, doctor.

MR MAC QUEDY. The family consumes, and so does the state.

THE REV. DR FOLLIOTT. Consumes, sir! Yes: but the mode, the proportions; there is the essential difference between the state and the family. Sir, I hate false analogies.

MR MAC QUEDY. Well, sir, the analogy is not essential. Distribution will come under its proper head.

THE REV. DR FOLLIOTT. Come where it will, the distribution of the state is in no respect analogous to the distribution of the family. The *paterfamilias*, sir: the *paterfamilias*.

MR MAC QUEDY. Well, sir, let that pass. The family consumes, and in order to consume, it must have supply.

THE REV. DR FOLLIOTT. Well, sir, Adam and Eve knew that, when they delved and span.

MR MAC QUEDY. Very true, sir (*reproducing his scroll*). 'In the infancy of society —'

MR TOOGOOD. The reverend gentleman has hit the nail on the head. It is the distribution that must be looked to: it is the *paterfamilias* that is wanting in the state. Now here I have provided him. (*Reproducing his diagram.*)

MR TRILLO. Apply the money, sir, to building and endowing an opera house, where the ancient altar of Bacchus may flourish, and justice may be done to sublime compositions. (*Producing a part of a manuscript opera.*)

MR SKIONAR. No, sir, build *sacella*[1] for transcendental oracles to teach the world how to see through a glass darkly. (*Producing a scroll.*)

MR TRILLO. See through an opera-glass brightly.

THE REV. DR FOLLIOTT. See through a wine-glass, full of claret: then you see both darkly and brightly. But, gentlemen, if you are all in the humour for reading papers, I will read you the first half of my next Sunday's sermon. (*Producing a paper.*)

OMNES. No sermon! No sermon!

THE REV. DR FOLLIOTT. Then I move that our respective papers be committed to our respective pockets.

MR MAC QUEDY. Political economy is divided into two great branches, production and consumption.

THE REV. DR FOLLIOTT. Yes, sir; there are two great classes of men: those who produce much and consume little; and those who consume much and produce nothing. The *fruges consumere nati*[2] have the best of it. Eh, captain! you remember the characteristics of a great man according to Aristophanes: ὅστις γε πίνειν οἶδε καὶ βινεῖν μόνον.[3] Ha! ha! ha! Well, captain, even in these tight-laced days, the obscurity of a learned language allows a little pleasantry.

CAPTAIN FITZCHROME. Very true, sir: the pleasantry and the obscurity go together: they are all one, as it were – to me at any rate. (*aside.*)

MR MAC QUEDY. Now, sir —

THE REV. DR FOLLIOTT. Pray, sir, let your science alone, or you will put me under the painful necessity of demolishing it bit by bit, as I have done your exordium. I will undertake it any morning; but it is too hard exercise after dinner.

MR MAC QUEDY. Well, sir, in the meantime I hold my science established.

THE REV. DR FOLLIOTT. And I hold it demolished.

MR CROTCHET, JUN. Pray, gentlemen, pocket your manuscripts; fill your glasses; and consider what we shall do with our money.

MR MAC QUEDY. Build lecture rooms and schools for all.

MR TRILLO. Revive the Athenian theatre: regenerate the lyrical drama.

MR TOOGOOD. Build a grand co-operative parallelogram, with a steam-engine in the middle for a maid of all work.

MR FIREDAMP. Drain the country, and get rid of *malaria*, by abolishing duck-ponds.

DR MORBIFIC. Found a philanthropic college of anti-contagionists, where all the members shall be inoculated with the virus of all known diseases. Try the experiment on a grand scale.

MR CHAINMAIL. Build a great dining-hall: endow it with beef and ale, and hang the hall round with arms to defend the provisions.

MR HENBANE. Found a toxicological institution for trying all poisons and antidotes. I myself have killed a frog twelve times, and brought him to life eleven; but the twelfth time he died. I have a phial of the drug which killed him in my pocket, and shall not rest till I have discovered its antidote.

THE REV. DR FOLLIOTT. I move that the last speaker be dispossessed of his phial, and that it be forthwith thrown into the Thames.

MR HENBANE. How, sir? my invaluable, and in the present state of human knowledge, infallible poison?

THE REV. DR FOLLIOTT. Let the frogs have all the advantage of it.

MR CROTCHET. Consider, doctor, the fish might participate. Think of the salmon.

THE REV. DR FOLLIOTT. Then let the owner's right-hand neighbour swallow it.

MR EAVESDROP. Me, sir! What have I done, sir, that I am to be poisoned, sir?

THE REV. DR FOLLIOTT. Sir, you have published a character of your facetious friend, the Reverend Doctor F., wherein you have sketched off me; me, sir, even to my nose and wig. What business have the public with my nose and wig?

MR EAVESDROP. Sir, it is all good humoured: all in *bonhomie*: all friendly and complimentary.

THE REV. DR FOLLIOTT. Sir, the bottle, *la Dive Bouteille*,[4] is a recondite oracle, which makes an Eleusinian[5] temple of the circle in which it moves. He who reveals its mysteries must die. Therefore, let the dose be administered. *Fiat experimentum in animâ vili.*[6]

MR EAVESDROP. Sir, you are very facetious at my expense.

THE REV. DR FOLLIOTT. Sir, you have been very unfacetious, very inficete at mine. You have dished me up, like a savory omelette, to gratify the appetite of the reading rabble for gossip. The next time, sir, I will respond with the *argumentum baculinum*.[7] Print that, sir; put it on record as a promise of the Reverend Doctor F., which shall be most faithfully kept, with an exemplary bamboo.

MR EAVESDROP. Your cloth protects you, sir.

THE REV. DR FOLLIOTT. My bamboo shall protect me, sir.

MR CROTCHET. Doctor, doctor, you are growing too polemical.

THE REV. DR FOLLIOTT. Sir, my blood boils. What business have the public with my nose and wig?

MR CROTCHET. Doctor! Doctor!

MR CROTCHET, JUN. Pray, gentlemen, return to the point. How shall we employ our fund?

MR PHILPOT. Surely in no way so beneficially as in exploring rivers. Send a fleet of steamboats down the Niger, and another up the Nile. So shall you civilize Africa, and establish stocking factories in Abyssinia and Bambo.

THE REV. DR FOLLIOTT. With all submission, breeches and petticoats must precede stockings. Send out a crew of tailors. Try if the king of Bambo will invest inexpressibles.

MR CROTCHET, JUN. Gentlemen, it is not for partial, but for general benefit, that this fund is proposed: a grand and universally applicable scheme for the amelioration of the condition of man.

SEVERAL VOICES. That is my scheme. I have not heard a scheme but my own that has a grain of common sense.

MR TRILLO. Gentlemen, you inspire me. Your last exclamation runs itself into a chorus, and sets itself to music. Allow me to lead, and to hope for your voices in harmony.

After careful meditation,
And profound deliberation,
On the various pretty projects which have just been shown,
Not a scheme in agitation,
For the world's amelioration,
Has a grain of common sense in it, except my own.

SEVERAL VOICES. We are not disposed to join in any such chorus.

THE REV. DR FOLLIOTT. Well, of all these schemes, I am for Mr Trillo's. Regenerate the Athenian theatre. My classical friend here, the captain, will vote with me.

CAPTAIN FITZCHROME. I, sir? oh! of course, sir.

MR MAC QUEDY. Surely, captain, I rely on you to uphold political economy.

CAPTAIN FITZCHROME. Me, sir? oh! to be sure, sir.

THE REV. DR FOLLIOTT. Pray, sir, will political economy uphold the Athenian theatre?

MR MAC QUEDY. Surely not. It would be a very unproductive investment.

THE REV. DR FOLLIOTT. Then the captain votes against you. What, sir, did not the Athenians, the wisest of nations, appropriate to their theatre their most sacred and intangible fund. Did not they give to melopoeia,[8] choregraphy, and the sundry forms of didascalics,[9] the precedence of all other matters, civil and military? Was it not their law, that even the proposal to divert this fund to any other purpose should be punished with death? But, sir, I further propose that the Athenian theatre being resuscitated, the admission shall be free to all who can expound the Greek choruses, constructively, mythologically, and metrically, and to none others. So that all the world learn Greek: Greek, the Alpha and Omega of all knowledge. At him who sits not in the theatre, shall be pointed the finger of scorn: he shall be called in the highway of the city, 'fellow without Greek.'

MR TRILLO. But the ladies, sir, the ladies.

THE REV. DR FOLLIOTT. Every man may take in a lady: and she who can construe and metricize a chorus, shall, if she so please, pass in by herself.

MR TRILLO. But, sir, you will shut me out of my own theatre. Let there at least be a double passport, Greek and Italian.

THE REV. DR FOLLIOTT. No, sir; I am inexorable. No Greek, no theatre.

MR TRILLO. Sir, I cannot consent to be shut out from my own theatre.

THE REV. DR FOLLIOTT. You see how it is, Squire Crotchet the younger; you can scarcely find two to agree on a scheme, and no two of those can agree on the details. Keep your money in your pocket. And so ends the fund for regenerating the world.

MR MAC QUEDY. Nay, by no means. We are all agreed on deliberative dinners.

THE REV. DR FOLLIOTT. Very true; we will dine and discuss. We will sing with Robin Hood, 'If I drink water while this doth last;' and while it lasts we will have no adjournment, if not to the Athenian theatre.

MR TRILLO. Well, gentlemen, I hope this chorus at least
will please you:

> If I drink water while this doth last,
> May I never again drink wine:
> For how can a man, in his life of a span,
> Do anything better than dine?
> We'll dine and drink, and say if we think
> That anything better can be;
> And when we have dined, wish all mankind
> May dine as well as we.
>
> And though a good wish will fill no dish,
> And brim no cup with sack,
> Yet thoughts will spring, as the glasses ring,
> To illume our studious track.
> On the brilliant dreams of our hopeful schemes
> The light of the flask shall shine;
> And we'll sit till day, but we'll find the way
> To drench the world with wine.

The schemes for the world's regeneration evaporated in a
tumult of voices.

CHAPTER VII

THE SLEEPING VENUS

> Quoth he: In all my life till now,
> I ne'er saw so profane a show. – BUTLER.

THE LIBRARY OF Crotchet Castle was a large and well-
furnished apartment, opening on one side into an anteroom,
on the other into a music-room. It had several tables stationed
at convenient distances; one consecrated to the novelties of
literature, another to the novelties of embellishment; others
unoccupied, and at the disposal of the company. The walls
were covered with a copious collection of ancient and modern
books; the ancient having been selected and arranged by the
Reverend Doctor Folliott. In the anteroom were card-tables;
in the music-room were various instruments, all popular
operas, and all fashionable music. In this suite of apartments,

and not in the drawing-room, were the evenings of Crotchet
Castle usually passed.

The young ladies were in the music-room; Miss Crotchet at
the piano, Lady Clarinda, at the harp, playing and occasionally
singing, at the suggestion of Mr Trillo, portions of *Matilde di
Shabran*.[1] Lord Bossnowl was turning over the leaves for Miss
Crotchet; the captain was performing the same office for Lady
Clarinda, but with so much more attention to the lady than
the book, that he often made sad work with the harmony, by
turning over two leaves together. On these occasions Miss
Crotchet paused, Lady Clarinda laughed, Mr Trillo scolded,
Lord Bossnowl yawned, the captain apologized, and the per-
formance proceeded.

In the library, Mr Mac Quedy was expounding political
economy to the Reverend Doctor Folliott, who was *pro more*
demolishing its doctrines *seriatim*.[2]

Mr Chainmail was in hot dispute with Mr Skionar, touching
the physical and moral well-being of man. Mr Skionar was
enforcing his friend Mr Shantsee's views of moral discipline;
maintaining that the sole thing needful for man in this world,
was loyal and pious education; the giving men good books to
read, and enough of the hornbook to read them; with a
judicious interspersion of the lessons of Old Restraint, which
was his poetic name for the parish stocks. Mr Chainmail, on
the other hand, stood up for the exclusive necessity of beef and
ale, lodging and raiment, wife and children, courage to fight
for them all, and armour wherewith to do so.

Mr Henbane had got his face scratched, and his finger bitten,
by the cat, in trying to catch her for a second experiment in
killing and bringing to life; and Doctor Morbific was comforting him with a disquisition, to prove that there were only
four animals having the power to communicate hydrophobia,
of which the cat was one; and that it was not necessary that
the animal should be in a rabid state, the nature of the wound
being everything, and the idea of contagion a delusion. Mr
Henbane was listening very lugubriously to this dissertation.

Mr Philpot had seized on Mr Firedamp, and pinned him
down to a map of Africa, on which he was tracing imaginary
courses of mighty inland rivers, terminating in lakes and
marshes, where they were finally evaporated by the heat of the
sun; and Mr Firedamp's hair was standing on end at the bare
imagination of the mass of *malaria* that must be engendered by

the operation. Mr Toogood had begun explaining his diagrams to Sir Simon Steeltrap; but Sir Simon grew testy, and told Mr Toogood that the promulgators of such doctrines ought to be consigned to the treadmill. The philanthropist walked off from the country gentleman, and proceeded to hold forth to young Crotchet who stood silent, as one who listens, but in reality without hearing a syllable. Mr Crotchet senior, as the master of the house, was left to entertain himself with his own meditations, till the Reverend Doctor Folliott tore himself from Mr Mac Quedy, and proceeded to expostulate with Mr Crotchet on a delicate topic.

There was an Italian painter, who obtained the name of *Il Bragatore*, by the superinduction of inexpressibles on the naked Apollos and Bacchuses of his betters. The fame of this worthy remained one and indivisible, till a set of heads, which had been, by a too common mistake of nature's journeymen, stuck upon magisterial shoulders, as the Corinthian capitals of 'fair round bellies with fat capon lined,'[3] but which nature herself had intended for the noddles of porcelain mandarins, promulgated simultaneously from the east and the west of London, an order that no plaster-of-Paris Venus should appear in the streets without petticoats. Mr Crotchet, on reading this order in the evening paper, which, by the postman's early arrival, was always laid on his breakfast-table, determined to fill his house with Venuses of all sizes and kinds. In pursuance of this resolution, came packages by water-carriage, containing an infinite variety of Venuses. There were the Medicean Venus, and the Bathing Venus; the Uranian Venus, and the Pandemian Venus[4]; the Crouching Venus, and the Sleeping Venus; the Venus rising from the sea, the Venus with the apple of Paris, and the Venus with the armour of Mars.

The Reverend Doctor Folliott had been very much astonished at this unexpected display. Disposed, as he was, to hold, that whatever had been in Greece, was right; he was more than doubtful of the propriety of throwing open the classical *adytum*[5] to the illiterate profane. Whether, in his interior mind, he was at all influenced, either by the consideration that it would be for the credit of his cloth, with some of his vice-suppressing neighbours, to be able to say that he had expostulated; or by curiosity, to try what sort of defence his city-bred friend, who knew the classics only by translations, and whose reason was always a little a-head of his knowledge,

would make for his somewhat ostentatious display of liberality in matters of taste; is a question, on which the learned
may differ: but, after having duly deliberated on two full-
sized casts of the Uranian and Pandemian Venus, in niches on
each side of the chimney, and on three alabaster figures, in glass
cases, on the mantelpiece, he proceeded, peirastically, to open
his fire.

THE REV. DR FOLLIOTT. These little alabaster figures on
the mantelpiece, Mr Crotchet, and those large figures in the
niches – may I take the liberty to ask you what they are intended to represent?

MR CROTCHET. Venus, sir; nothing more, sir; just Venus.

THE REV. DR FOLLIOTT. May I ask you, sir, why they are
there?

MR CROTCHET. To be looked at, sir; just to be looked at:
the reason for most things in a gentleman's house being in it
at all; from the paper on the walls, and the drapery of the
curtains, even to the books in the library, of which the most
essential part is the appearance of the back.

THE REV. DR FOLLIOTT. Very true, sir. As great philosophers hold that the *esse* of things is *percipi*, so a gentleman's
furniture exists to be looked at. Nevertheless, sir, there are
some things more fit to be looked at than others; for instance,
there is nothing more fit to be looked at than the outside of a
book. It is, as I may say, from repeated experience, a pure and
unmixed pleasure to have a goodly volume lying before you,
and to know that you may open it if you please, and need not
open it unless you please. It is a resource against *ennui*, if *ennui*
should come upon you. To have the resource and not to feel
the *ennui*, to enjoy your bottle in the present, and your book in
the indefinite future, is a delightful condition of human
existence. There is no place, in which a man can move or sit,
in which the outside of a book can be otherwise than an innocent and becoming spectacle. Touching this matter, there
cannot, I think, be two opinions. But with respect to your
Venuses there can be, and indeed there are, two very distinct
opinions. Now, sir, that little figure in the centre of the mantelpiece – as a grave *paterfamilias*, Mr Crotchet, with a fair nubile
daughter, whose eyes are like the fish-pools of Heshbon – I
would ask you if you hold that figure to be altogether delicate?

MR CROTCHET. The Sleeping Venus, sir? Nothing can be
more delicate than the entire contour of the figure, the flow of

the hair on the shoulders and neck, the form of the feet and fingers. It is altogether a most delicate morsel.

THE REV. DR FOLLIOTT. Why, in that sense, perhaps, it is as delicate as whitebait in July. But the attitude, sir, the attitude.

MR CROTCHET. Nothing can be more natural, sir.

THE REV. DR FOLLIOTT. That is the very thing, sir. It is too natural: too natural, sir: it lies for all the world like – I make no doubt, the pious cheesemonger, who recently broke its plaster fac-simile over the head of the itinerant vendor, was struck by a certain similitude to the position of his own sleeping beauty, and felt his noble wrath thereby justly aroused.

MR CROTCHET. Very likely, sir. In my opinion, the cheesemonger was a fool, and the justice who sided with him was a greater.

THE REV. DR FOLLIOTT. Fool, sir, is a harsh term: call not thy brother a fool.

MR CROTCHET. Sir, neither the cheesemonger nor the justice is a brother of mine.

THE REV. DR FOLLIOTT. Sir, we are all brethren.

MR CROTCHET. Yes, sir, as the hangman is of the thief; the 'squire of the poacher; the judge of the libeller; the lawyer of his client; the statesman of his colleague; the bubble-blower of the bubble-buyer; the slave-driver of the Negro: as these are brethren, so am I and the worthies in question.

THE REV. DR FOLLIOTT. To be sure, sir, in these instances, and in many others, the term brother must be taken in its utmost latitude of interpretation: we are all brothers, nevertheless. But to return to the point. Now these two large figures, one with drapery on the lower half of the body, and the other with no drapery at all; upon my word, sir, it matters not what godfathers and godmothers may have promised and vowed for the children of this world, touching the devil and other things to be renounced, if such figures as those are to be put before their eyes.

MR CROTCHET. Sir, the naked figure is the Pandemian Venus, and the half-draped figure is the Uranian Venus; and I say, sir, that figure realizes the finest imaginings of Plato, and is the personification of the most refined and exalted feeling of which the human mind is susceptible; the love of pure, ideal, intellectual beauty.

THE REV. DR FOLLIOTT. I am aware, sir, that Plato, in his

Symposium, discourseth very eloquently touching the Uranian and Pandemian Venus: but you must remember that, in our Universities, Plato is held to be little better than a misleader of youth; and they have shown their contempt for him, not only by never reading him (a mode of contempt in which they deal very largely), but even by never printing a complete edition of him; although they have printed many ancient books, which nobody suspects to have been ever read on the spot, except by a person attached to the press, who is therefore emphatically called 'the reader'.

MR CROTCHET. Well, sir?

THE REV. DR FOLLIOTT. Why, sir, to 'the reader' aforesaid (supposing either of our Universities to have printed an edition of Plato), or to anyone else who can be supposed to have read Plato, or indeed to be ever likely to do so, I would very willingly show these figures; because to such they would, I grant you, be the outward and visible signs of poetical and philosophical ideas: but, to the multitude, the gross carnal multitude, they are but two beautiful women, one half undressed, and the other quite so.

MR CROTCHET. Then, sir, let the multitude look upon them and learn modesty.

THE REV. DR FOLLIOTT. I must say that, if I wished my footman to learn modesty, I should not dream of sending him to school to a naked Venus.

MR CROTCHET. Sir, ancient sculpture is the true school of modesty. But where the Greeks had modesty, we have cant; where they had poetry, we have cant; where they had patriotism, we have cant; where they had anything that exalts, delights, or adorns humanity, we have nothing but cant, cant, cant. And, sir, to show my contempt for cant in all its shapes, I have adorned my house with the Greek Venus, in all her shapes, and am ready to fight her battle against all the societies that ever were instituted for the suppression of truth and beauty.

THE REV. DR FOLLIOTT. My dear sir, I am afraid you are growing warm. Pray be cool. Nothing contributes so much to good digestion as to be perfectly cool after dinner.

MR CROCHET. Sir, the Lacedaemonian virgins wrestled naked with young men: and they grew up, as the wise Lycurgus had foreseen,[6] into the most modest of women, and the most exemplary of wives and mothers.

THE REV. DR FOLLIOTT. Very likely, sir; but the Athenian virgins did no such thing, and they grew up into wives who stayed at home – stayed at home, sir; and looked after the husband's dinner – his dinner, sir, you will please to observe.

MR CROTCHET. And what was the consequence of that, sir? that they were such very insipid persons that the husband would not go home to eat his dinner, but preferred the company of some Aspasia, or Lais.

THE REV. DR FOLLIOTT. Two very different persons, sir, give me leave to remark.

MR CROTCHET. Very likely, sir; but both too good to be married in Athens.

THE REV. DR FOLLIOTT. Sir, Lais was a Corinthian.[7]

MR CROTCHET. 'Od's vengeance, sir, some Aspasia[7] and any other Athenian name of the same sort of person you like—

THE REV. DR FOLLIOTT. I do not like the sort of person at all: the sort of person I like, as I have already implied, is a modest woman, who stays at home and looks after her husband's dinner.

MR CROTCHET. Well, sir, that was not the taste of the Athenians. They preferred the society of women who would not have made any scruple about sitting as models to Praxiteles;[8] as you know, sir, very modest women in Italy did to Canova[9]: one of whom, an Italian countess, being asked by an English lady, 'how she could bear it?' answered, 'Very well; there was a good fire in the room.'

THE REV. DR FOLLIOTT. Sir, the English lady should have asked how the Italian lady's husband could bear it. The phials of my wrath would overflow if poor dear Mrs Folliott—: sir, in return for your story, I will tell you a story of my ancestor Gilbert Folliott. The devil haunted him, as he did Saint Francis, in the likeness of a beautiful damsel; but all he could get from the exemplary Gilbert was an admonition to wear a stomacher and longer petticoats.

MR CROTCHET. Sir, your story makes for my side of the question. It proves that the devil, in the likeness of a fair damsel, with short petticoats and no stomacher, was almost too much for Gilbert Folliott. The force of the spell was in the drapery.

THE REV. DR FOLLIOTT. Bless my soul, sir!

MR CROTCHET. Give me leave, sir. Diderot —[10]

THE REV. DR FOLLIOTT. Who was he, sir?

MR CROTCHET. Who was he, sir? the sublime philosopher, the father of the encyclopaedia, of all the encyclopaedias that have ever been printed.

THE REV. DR FOLLIOTT. Bless me, sir, a terrible progeny! they belong to the tribe of *Incubi*.

MR CROTCHET. The great philosopher, Diderot —

THE REV. DR FOLLIOTT. Sir, Diderot is not a man after my heart. Keep to the Greeks, if you please; albeit this Sleeping Venus is not an antique.

MR CROTCHET. Well, sir, the Greeks: why do we call the Elgin marbles inestimable? Simply because they are true to nature. And why are they so superior in that point to all modern works, with all our greater knowledge of anatomy? Why, sir, but because the Greeks, having no cant, had better opportunities of studying models?

THE REV. DR FOLLIOTT. Sir, I deny our greater knowledge of anatomy. But I shall take the liberty to employ, on this occasion, the *argumentum ad hominem*.[11] Would you have allowed Miss Crotchet to sit for a model to Canova?

MR CROTCHET. Yes, sir.

'God bless my soul, sir!' exclaimed the Reverend Doctor Folliott, throwing himself back into a chair, and flinging up his heels, with the premeditated design of giving emphasis to his exclamation: but by miscalculating his *impetus*, he over-balanced his chair, and laid himself on the carpet in a right angle, of which his back was the base.

CHAPTER VIII

SCIENCE AND CHARITY

Chi sta nel mondo un par d'ore contento,
Nè gli vien tolta, ovver contaminata,
Quella sua pace in veruno momento,
Può dir che Giove drittamente il guata.
                                        FORTEGUERRI.[1]

THE REVEREND DOCTOR FOLLIOTT took his departure about ten o'clock, to walk home to his vicarage. There was no moon; but the night was bright and clear, and afforded him as much light as he needed. He paused a moment by the Roman

Camp, to listen to the nightingale; repeated to himself a passage of Sophocles; proceeded through the park gate, and entered the narrow lane that led to the village. He walked on in a very pleasant mood of the state called *reverie*; in which fish and wine, Greek and political economy, the Sleeping Venus he had left behind and poor dear Mrs Folliott, to whose fond arms he was returning, passed as in a *camera obscura* over the tablets of his imagination. Presently the image of Mr Eaves-drop, with a printed sketch of the Reverend Doctor F., pre-sented itself before him, and he began mechanically to flourish his bamboo. The movement was prompted by his good genius, for the uplifted bamboo received the blow of a ponderous cudgel, which was intended for his head. The reverend gentleman recoiled two or three paces, and saw be-fore him a couple of ruffians, who were preparing to renew the attack, but whom, with two swings of his bamboo, he laid with cracked sconces on the earth, where he proceeded to deal with them like corn beneath the flail of the thresher. One of them drew a pistol, which went off in the very act of being struck aside by the bamboo, and lodged a bullet in the brain of the other. There was then only one enemy, who vainly struggled to rise, every effort being attended with a new and more signal prostration. The fellow roared for mercy. 'Mercy, rascal!' cried the divine; 'what mercy were you going to show me, villain? What! I warrant me, you thought it would be an easy matter, and no sin, to rob and murder a parson on his way home from dinner. You said to yourselves, doubtless, "We'll waylay the fat parson (you irreverent knave) as he waddles home (you disparaging ruffian), half-seas-over (you calumnious vagabond)."' And with every dyslogistic term, which he supposed had been applied to himself, he inflicted a new bruise on his rolling and roaring antagonist. 'Ah, rogue!' he proceeded; 'you can roar now, marauder; you were silent enough when you devoted my brains to dispersion under your cudgel. But seeing that I cannot bind you, and that I intend you not to escape, and that it would be dangerous to let you rise, I will disable you in all your members; I will contund you[2] as Thestylis did strong-smelling herbs,* in the quality whereof you do most gravely partake, as my nose beareth

* Thestylis . . .
  . . . herbas contundit olentes.
                              VIRG. *Ecl.* ii. 10, 11. [P.]

testimony, ill weed that you are. I will beat you to a jelly, and I will then roll you into the ditch, to lie till the constable comes for you, thief.'

'Hold! hold! reverend sir,' exclaimed the penitent culprit, 'I am disabled already in every finger, and in every joint. I will roll myself into the ditch, reverend sir.'

'Stir not, rascal,' returned the divine, 'stir not so much as the quietest leaf above you, or my bamboo rebounds on your body like hail in a thunderstorm. Confess speedily, villain; are you simple thief, or would you have manufactured me into a subject, for the benefit of science? Ay, miscreant caitiff, you would have made me a subject for science, would you? You are a schoolmaster abroad, are you? You are marching with a detachment of the march of mind, are you? You are a member of the Steam Intellect Society, are you? You swear by the learned friend, do you?'

'Oh, no! reverend sir,' answered the criminal, 'I am innocent of all these offences, whatever they are, reverend sir. The only friend I had in the world is lying dead beside me, reverend sir.'

The reverend gentleman paused a moment, and leaned on his bamboo. The culprit, bruised as he was, sprang on his legs, and went off in double quick time. The doctor gave him chase, and had nearly brought him within arm's length, when the fellow turned at right angles, and sprang clean over a deep dry ditch. The divine, following with equal ardour, and less dexterity, went down over head and ears into a thicket of nettles. Emerging with much discomposure, he proceeded to the village, and roused the constable; but the constable found, on reaching the scene of action, that the dead man was gone, as well as his living accomplice.

'Oh, the monster!' exclaimed the Reverend Doctor Folliott, 'he has made a subject for science of the only friend he had in the world.' 'Ay, my dear,' he resumed, the next morning at breakfast, 'if my old reading, and my early gymnastics (for as the great Hermann says, before I was demulced by the Muses, I was *ferocis ingenii puer, et ad arma quam ad literas paratior* *), had not imbued me indelibly with some of the holy rage of *Frère Jean des Entommeures*, I should be, at this moment, lying on the table of some flinty-hearted anatomist, who would have sliced

---

* 'A boy of fierce disposition, more inclined to arms than to letters.' – Hermann's *Dedication of Homer's Hymns to his Preceptor Ilgen.* [P.]

and disjointed me as unscrupulously as I do these remnants of the capon and chine, wherewith you consoled yourself yesterday for my absence at dinner. Phew! I have a noble thirst upon me, which I will quench with floods of tea.'

The reverend gentleman was interrupted by a messenger, who informed him that the Charity Commissioners requested his presence at the inn, where they were holding a sitting.[3]

'The Charity Commissioners!' exclaimed the reverend gentleman, 'who on earth are they?'

The messenger could not inform him, and the reverend gentleman took his hat and stick, and proceeded to the inn.

On entering the best parlour, he saw three well-dressed and bulky gentlemen sitting at a table, and a fourth officiating as clerk, with an open book before him, and a pen in his hand. The churchwardens, who had been also summoned, were already in attendance.

The chief commissioner politely requested the Reverend Doctor Folliott to be seated; and after the usual meteorological preliminaries had been settled by a resolution, *nem. con.*, that it was a fine day but very hot, the chief commissioner stated, that in virtue of the commission of Parliament, which they had the honour to hold, they were now to inquire into the state of the public charities of this village.

THE REV. DR FOLLIOTT. The state of the public charities, sir, is exceedingly simple. There are none. The charities here are all private, and so private, that I for one know nothing of them.

FIRST COMMISSIONER. We have been informed, sir, that there is an annual rent charged on the land of Hautbois, for the endowment and repair of an almshouse.

THE REV. DR FOLLIOTT. Hautbois! Hautbois!

FIRST COMMISSIONER. The manorial farm of Hautbois, now occupied by Farmer Seedling, is charged with the endowment and maintenance of an almshouse.

THE REV. DR FOLLIOTT (*to the Churchwarden*). How is this, Mr Bluenose?

FIRST CHURCHWARDEN. I really do not know, sir. What say you, Mr Appletwig?

MR APPLETWIG (*parish-clerk and schoolmaster; an old man*). I do remember, gentlemen, to have been informed, that there did stand at the end of the village a ruined cottage, which had once been an almshouse, which was endowed and maintained, by an annual revenue of a mark and a half, or one pound sterling, charged some centuries ago on the farm of Hautbois; but the means, by the progress of time, having become inadequate to the end, the almshouse tumbled to pieces.

FIRST COMMISSIONER. But this is a right which cannot be abrogated by desuetude,[4] and the sum of one pound per annum is still chargeable for charitable purposes on the manorial farm of Hautbois.

THE REV. DR FOLLIOTT. Very well, sir.

MR APPLETWIG. But, sir, the one pound per annum is still received by the parish, but was long ago, by an unanimous vote in open vestry, given to the minister.

THE THREE COMMISSIONERS (*unâ voce*). The minister!

FIRST COMMISSIONER. This is an unjustifiable proceeding.

SECOND COMMISSIONER. A misappropriation of a public fund.

THIRD COMMISSIONER. A flagrant perversion of a charitable donation.

THE REV. DR FOLLIOTT. God bless my soul, gentlemen! I know nothing of this matter. How is this, Mr Bluenose? Do I receive this one pound per annum?

FIRST CHURCHWARDEN. Really, sir, I know no more about it than you do.

MR APPLETWIG. You certainly receive it, sir. It was voted to one of your predecessors. Farmer Seedling lumps it in with his tithes.

FIRST COMMISSIONER. Lumps it in, sir! Lump in a charitable donation!

SECOND AND THIRD COMMISSIONER. Oh-oh-oh-h-h!

FIRST COMMISSIONER. Reverend sir, and gentlemen, officers of this parish, we are under the necessity of admonishing you that this is a most improper proceeding; and you are hereby duly admonished accordingly. Make a record, Mr Milky.

MR MILKY (*writing*). The clergyman and churchwardens of the village of Hm-m-m-m gravely admonished. Hm-m-m-m.

THE REV. DR FOLLIOTT. Is that all, gentlemen?

THE COMMISSIONERS. That is all, sir; and we wish you a good morning.

THE REV. DR FOLLIOTT. A very good morning to you, gentlemen.

'What in the name of all that is wonderful, Mr Bluenose,' said the Reverend Doctor Folliott, as he walked out of the inn, 'what in the name of all that is wonderful, can those fellows mean? They have come here in a chaise and four, to make a fuss about a pound per annum, which, after all, they leave as it was. I wonder who pays them for their trouble, and how much.'

MR APPLETWIG. The public pay for it, sir. It is a job of the learned friend whom you admire so much.[5] It makes away with public money in salaries, and private money in lawsuits, and does no particle of good to any living soul.

THE REV. DR FOLLIOTT. Ay, ay, Mr Appletwig; that is just the sort of public service to be looked for from the learned friend. Oh, the learned friend! the learned friend! He is the evil genius of everything that falls in his way.

The reverend doctor walked off to Crotchet Castle, to narrate his misadventures, and exhale his budget of grievances on Mr Mac Quedy, whom he considered a ringleader of the march of mind.

CHAPTER IX

THE VOYAGE

Οἱ μὲν ἔπειτ' ἀναβάντες ἐπέπλεον ὑγρὰ κέλευθα.

Mounting the bark, they cleft the watery ways. HOMER.

FOUR BEAUTIFUL cabined pinnaces, one for the ladies, one for the gentlemen, one for kitchen and servants, one for a dining-room and band of music, weighed anchor, on a fine July morning, from below Crotchet Castle, and were towed merrily, by strong trotting horses, against the stream of the Thames. They passed from the district of chalk, successively into the districts of clay, of sand-rock, of oolite, and so forth. Sometimes they dined in their floating dining-room, some-times in tents, which they pitched on the dry smooth-shaven green of a newly mown meadow; sometimes they left their vessels to see sights in the vicinity; sometimes they passed a day or two in a comfortable inn.

At Oxford, they walked about to see the curiosities of architecture, painted windows, and undisturbed libraries. The Reverend Doctor Folliott laid a wager with Mr Crotchet 'that in all their perlustrations they would not find a man reading,' and won it. 'Ay, sir,' said the reverend gentleman, 'this is still a seat of learning, on the principle of – once a captain always a captain. We may well ask, in these great reservoirs of books whereof no man ever draws a sluice, *Quorsum pertinuit stipare Platona Menandro?* * What is done here for the classics? Reprinting German editions on better paper. A great boast, verily! What for mathematics? What for metaphysics? What for history? What for anything worth knowing? This was a seat of learning in the days of Friar Bacon. But the friar is gone, and his learning with him. Nothing of him is left but the immortal nose, which when his brazen head had tumbled to pieces, crying "Time's past," was the only palpable fragment among its minutely pulverized atoms, and which is still resplendent over the portals of its cognominal college.[1] That nose, sir, is the only thing to which I shall take off my hat, in all this Babylon of buried literature.'

MR CROTCHET. But, doctor, it is something to have a great reservoir of learning, at which some may draw if they please.

THE REV. DR FOLLIOTT. But, here, good care is taken that nobody shall please. If even a small drop from the sacred fountain, πίδακος ἐξ ἱερῆς ὀλίγη λιβάς,[2] as Callimachus has it, were carried off by anyone, it would be evidence of something to hope for. But the system of dissuasion from all good learning is brought here to a pitch of perfection that baffles the keenest aspirant. I run over to myself the names of the scholars of Germany, a glorious catalogue! but ask for those of Oxford – Where are they? The echoes of their courts, as vacant as their heads, will answer, Where are they? The tree shall be known by its fruit; and seeing that this great tree, with all its specious seeming, brings forth no fruit, I do denounce it as a barren fig.

MR MAC QUEDY. I shall set you right on this point. We do nothing without motives. If learning get nothing but honour, and very little of that; and if the good things of this world, which ought to be the rewards of learning, become the mere gifts of self-interested patronage; you must not wonder if, in

* Wherefore is Plato on Menander piled? HOR. *Sat.* ii. 3, 11. [P.]

the finishing of education, the science which takes precedence of all others, should be the science of currying favour.

THE REV. DR FOLLIOTT. Very true, sir. Education is well finished, for all worldly purposes, when the head is brought into the state whereinto I am accustomed to bring a marrow-bone, when it has been set before me on a toast, with a white napkin wrapped round it. Nothing trundles along the high road of preferment so trimly as a well-biased sconce, picked clean within, and polished without; *totus teres atque rotundus.** The perfection of the finishing lies in the bias, which keeps it trundling in the given direction. There is good and sufficient reason for the fig being barren, but it is not therefore the less a barren fig.

At Godstow they gathered hazel on the grave of Rosamond; and, proceeding on their voyage, fell into a discussion on legendary histories.

LADY CLARINDA. History is but a tiresome thing in itself; it becomes more agreeable the more romance is mixed up with it. The great enchanter has made me learn many things which I should never have dreamed of studying, if they had not come to me in the form of amusement.

THE REV. DR FOLLIOTT. What enchanter is that? There are two enchanters: he of the North,[3] and he of the South.

MR TRILLO. Rossini?

THE REV. DR FOLLIOTT. Ay, there is another enchanter. But I mean the great enchanter of Covent Garden: he who, for more than a quarter of a century, has produced two pantomimes a year, to the delight of children of all ages, including myself at all ages. That is the enchanter for me. I am for the pantomimes. All the northern enchanter's romances put together would not furnish materials for half the southern enchanter's pantomimes.

LADY CLARINDA. Surely you do not class literature with pantomime?

THE REV. DR FOLLIOTT. In these cases I do. They are both one, with a slight difference. The one is the literature of pantomime, the other is the pantomime of literature. There is the same variety of character, the same diversity of story, the same copiousness of incident, the same research into costume, the

* All smooth and round. [P.]

same display of heraldry, falconry, minstrelsy, scenery, monkery, witchery, devilry, robbery, poachery, piracy, fishery, gipsy-astrology, demonology, architecture, fortification, castrametation, navigation; the same running base of love and battle. The main difference is, that the one set of amusing fictions is told in music and action; the other in all the worst dialects of the English language. As to any sentence worth remembering, any moral or political truth, anything having a tendency, however remote, to make men wiser or better, to make them think, to make them even think of thinking; they are both precisely alike: *nuspiam, nequaquam, nullibi, nullimodis.*[4]

LADY CLARINDA. Very amusing, however.

THE REV. DR FOLLIOTT. Very amusing, very amusing.

MR CHAINMAIL. My quarrel with the northern enchanter is, that he has grossly misrepresented the twelfth century.

THE REV. DR FOLLIOTT. He has misrepresented everything, or he would not have been very amusing. Sober truth is but dull matter to the reading rabble. The angler, who puts not on his hook the bait that best pleases the fish, may sit all day on the bank without catching a gudgeon.*

MR MAC QUEDY. But how do you mean that he has misrepresented the twelfth century? By exhibiting some of its knights and ladies in the colours of refinement and virtue, seeing that they were all no better than ruffians, and something else that shall be nameless?

MR CHAINMAIL. By no means. By depicting them as much worse than they were, not, as you suppose, much better. No one would infer from his pictures that theirs was a much better state of society than this which we live in.

MR MAC QUEDY. No, nor was it. It was a period of brutality, ignorance, fanaticism, and tyranny; when the land was covered with castles, and every castle contained a gang of banditti, headed by a titled robber, who levied contributions with fire and sword; plundering, torturing, ravishing, burying his captives in loathsome dungeons, and broiling them on gridirons, to force from them the surrender of every particle of treasure which he suspected them of possessing; and fighting every now and then with the neighbouring lords, his conterminal bandits, for the right of marauding on the boundaries.

* Eloquentiae magister, nisi, tamquam piscator, eam imposuerit hamis escam, quam scierit appetituros esse pisciculos, sine spe praedae moratur in scopulo. Petronius Arbiter. [P.][5]

This was the twelfth century, as depicted by all contemporary historians and poets.

MR CHAINMAIL. No, sir. Weigh the evidence of specific facts; you will find more good than evil. Who was England's greatest hero; the mirror of chivalry, the pattern of honour, the fountain of generosity, the model to all succeeding ages of military glory? Richard the First. There is a king of the twelfth century. What was the first step of liberty? Magna Charta. That was the best thing ever done by lords. There are lords of the twelfth century. You must remember, too, that these lords were petty princes, and made war on each other as legitimately as the heads of larger communities did or do. For their system of revenue, it was, to be sure, more rough and summary than that which has succeeded it, but it was certainly less searching and less productive. And as to the people, I content myself with these great points: that every man was armed, every man was a good archer, every man could and would fight effectively with sword or pike, or even with oaken cudgel: no man would live quietly without beef and ale; if he had them not, he fought till he either got them, or was put out of condition to want them. They were not, and could not be, subjected to that powerful pressure of all the other classes of society, combined by gunpowder, steam, and *fiscality*,[6] which has brought them to that dismal degradation in which we see them now. And there are the people of the twelfth century.

MR MAC QUEDY. As to your king, the enchanter has done him ample justice, even in your own view. As to your lords and their ladies, he has drawn them too favourably, given them too many of the false colours of chivalry, thrown too attractive a light on their abominable doings. As to the people, he keeps them so much in the back-ground, that he can hardly be said to have represented them at all, much less misrepresented them, which indeed he could scarcely do, seeing that, by your own showing, they were all thieves, ready to knock down any man for what they could not come by honestly.

MR CHAINMAIL. No, sir. They could come honestly by beef and ale, while they were left to their simple industry. When oppression interfered with them in that, then they stood on the defensive, and fought for what they were not permitted to come by quietly.

MR MAC QUEDY. If A, being aggrieved by B, knocks down C, do you call that standing on the defensive?

MR CHAINMAIL. That depends on who or what C is.

THE REV. DR FOLLIOTT. Gentlemen, you will never settle this controversy, till you have first settled what is good for man in this world; the great question, *de finibus*,[7] which has puzzled all philosophers. If the enchanter has represented the twelfth century too brightly for one, and too darkly for the other of you, I should say, as an impartial man, he has represented it fairly. My quarrel with him is, that his works contain nothing worth quoting; and a book that furnishes no quotations is, *me judice*,[8] no book — it is a plaything. There is no question about the amusement — amusement of multitudes; but if he who amuses us most, is to be our enchanter κατ᾽ ἐξοχὴν,[9] then my enchanter is the enchanter of Covent Garden.

CHAPTER X

THE VOYAGE, CONTINUED

Continuant nostre routte, navigasmes par trois jours *sans rien descouvrir*. — RABELAIS.[1]

'THERE IS A beautiful structure,' said Mr Chainmail, as they glided by Lechlade church; 'a subject for the pencil, Captain. It is a question worth asking, Mr Mac Quedy, whether the religious spirit which reared these edifices, and connected with them everywhere an asylum for misfortune and a provision for poverty, was not better than the commercial spirit, which has turned all the business of modern life into schemes of profit, and processes of fraud and extortion. I do not see, in all your boasted improvements, any compensation for the religious charity of the twelfth century. I do not see any compensation for that kindly feeling which, within their own little communities, bound the several classes of society together, while full scope was left for the development of natural character, wherein individuals differed as conspicuously as in costume. Now, we all wear one conventional dress, one conventional face; we have no bond of union, but pecuniary interest; we talk anything that comes uppermost, for talking's sake, and without expecting to be believed; we have no nature, no simplicity, no picturesqueness: everything about us is as artificial and as complicated as our steam-machinery: our poetry is a kaleidoscope of false imagery, expressing no real feeling, portraying no real existence. I do not see any compensation for the poetry of the twelfth century.'

MR MAC QUEDY. I wonder to hear you, Mr Chainmail, talking of the religious charity of a set of lazy monks and beggarly friars, who were much more occupied with taking than giving; of whom, those who were in earnest did nothing but make themselves, and everybody about them, miserable, with fastings, and penances, and other such trash; and those who were not, did nothing but guzzle and royster, and, having no wives of their own, took very unbecoming liberties with those of honester men. And as to your poetry of the twelfth century, it is not good for much.

MR CHAINMAIL. It has, at any rate, what ours wants, truth to nature, and simplicity of diction. The poetry, which was addressed to the people of the dark ages, pleased in proportion to the truth with which it depicted familiar images, and to their natural connection with the time and place to which they were assigned. In the poetry of our enlightened times, the characteristics of all seasons, soils, and climates, may be blended together, with much benefit to the author's fame as an original genius. The cowslip of a civic poet is always in blossom, his fern is always in full feather; he gathers the celandine, the primrose, the heath-flower, the jasmine, and the chrysanthemum, all on the same day, and from the same spot: his nightingale sings all the year round, his moon is always full, his cygnet is as white as his swan, his cedar is as tremulous as his aspen, and his poplar as embowering as his beech. Thus all nature marches with the march of mind; but, among barbarians, instead of mead and wine, and the best seat by the fire, the reward of such a genius would have been, to be summarily turned out of doors in the snow, to meditate on the difference between day and night, and between December and July. It is an age of liberality, indeed, when not to know an oak from a burdock is no disqualification for sylvan minstrelsy. I am for truth and simplicity.

THE REV. DR FOLLIOTT. Let him who loves them read Greek: Greek, Greek, Greek.

MR MAC QUEDY. If he can, sir.

THE REV. DR FOLLIOTT. Very true, sir; if he can. Here is the captain, who can. But I think he must have finished his education at some very rigid college, where a quotation, or any other overt act showing acquaintance with classical literature, was visited with a severe penalty. For my part, I make it my boast that I was not to be so subdued. I could not be abated of a single quotation by all the bumpers in which I was fined.

In this manner they glided over the face of the waters, discussing everything and settling nothing. Mr Mac Quedy and the Reverend Doctor Folliott had many digladiations on political economy: wherein, each in his own view, Doctor Folliott demolished Mr Mac Quedy's science, and Mr Mac Quedy demolished Doctor Folliott's objections.

We would print these dialogues if we thought anyone would read them: but the world is not yet ripe for this *haute sagesse Pantagrueline*.[2] We must, therefore, content ourselves with an *échantillon*[3] of one of the Reverend Doctor's perorations.

'You have given the name of a science to what is yet an imperfect inquiry; and the upshot of your so-called science is this, that you increase the wealth of a nation by increasing in it the quantity of things which are produced by labour: no matter what they are, no matter how produced, no matter how distributed. The greater the quantity of labour that has gone to the production of the quantity of things in a community, the richer is the community. That is your doctrine. Now, I say, if this be so, riches are not the object for a community to aim at. I say, the nation is best off, in relation to other nations, which has the greatest quantity of the common necessaries of life distributed among the greatest number of persons; which has the greatest number of honest hearts and stout arms united in a common interest, willing to offend no one, but ready to fight in defence of their own community against all the rest of the world, because they have something in it worth fighting for. The moment you admit that one class of things, without any reference to what they respectively cost, is better worth having than another; that a smaller commercial value, with one mode of distribution, is better than a greater commercial value, with another mode of distribution; the whole of that curious fabric of postulates and dogmas, which you call the science of political economy, and which I call *politicae oeconomiae inscientia*,[4] tumbles to pieces.'

Mr Toogood agreed with Mr Chainmail against Mr Mac Quedy, that the existing state of society was worse than that of the twelfth century; but he agreed with Mr Mac Quedy against Mr Chainmail, that it was in progress to something much better than either – to which 'something much better' Mr Toogood and Mr Mac Quedy attached two very different meanings.

Mr Chainmail fought with Doctor Folliott, the battle of the romantic against the classical in poetry; and Mr Skionar contended with Mr Mac Quedy for intuition and synthesis, against analysis and induction in philosophy.

Mr Philpot would lie along for hours, listening to the gurgling of the water round the prow, and would occasionally edify the company with speculations on the great changes that would be effected in the world by the steam-navigation of rivers: sketching the course of a steam-boat up and down some mighty stream which civilization had either never visited, or long since deserted; the Missouri and the Columbia, the Oroonoko and the Amazon, the Nile and the Niger, the Euphrates and the Tigris, the Oxus and the Indus, the Ganges and the Hoangho; under the overcanopying forests of the new, or by the long-silent ruins of the ancient, world; through the shapeless mounds of Babylon, or the gigantic temples of Thebes.

Mr Trillo went on with the composition of his opera, and took the opinions of the young ladies on every step in its progress; occasionally regaling the company with specimens, and wondering at the blindness of Mr Mac Quedy, who could not, or would not, see that an opera in perfection, being the union of all the beautiful arts – music, painting, dancing, poetry – exhibiting female beauty in its most attractive aspects, and in its most becoming costume – was, according to the well-known precept, *Ingenuas didicisse, etc.*, the most efficient instrument of civilization, and ought to take precedence of all other pursuits in the minds of true philanthropists. The Reverend Doctor Folliott, on these occasions, never failed to say a word or two on Mr Trillo's side, derived from the practice of the Athenians, and from the combination, in their theatre, of all the beautiful arts, in a degree of perfection unknown to the modern world.

Leaving Lechlade, they entered the canal that connects the Thames with the Severn; ascended by many locks; passed by a tunnel three miles long, through the bowels of Sapperton Hill; agreed unanimously that the greatest pleasure derivable from visiting a cavern of any sort was that of getting out of it; descended by many locks again, through the valley of Stroud into the Severn; continued their navigation into the Ellesmere canal; moored their pinnaces in the Vale of Llangollen by the aqueduct of Pontycysyllty; and determined to pass some days in inspecting the scenery, before commencing their home-ward voyage.

The captain omitted no opportunity of pressing his suit on Lady Clarinda, but could never draw from her any reply but the same doctrines of worldly wisdom, delivered in a tone of *badinage*, mixèd with a certain kindness of manner that induced him to hope she was not in earnest.

But the morning after they had anchored under the hills of the Dee – whether the lady had reflected more seriously than usual, or was somewhat less in good humour than usual, or the Captain was more pressing than usual – she said to him, 'It must not be, Captain Fitzchrome; "the course of true love never did run smooth":[5] my father must keep his borough, and I must have a town house and a country house, and an opera box, and a carriage. It is not well for either of us that we should flirt any longer: "I must be cruel only to be kind." [6] Be satisfied with the assurance that you alone, of all men, have ever broken my rest. To be sure, it was only for about three nights in all; but that is too much.'

The captain had *le cœur navré*.[7] He took his portfolio under his arm, made up the little *valise* of a pedestrian, and, without saying a word to anyone, wandered off at random among the mountains.

After the lapse of a day or two, the captain was missed, and everyone marvelled what was become of him. Mr Philpot thought he must have been exploring a river, and fallen in and got drowned in the process. Mr Firedamp had no doubt he had been crossing a mountain bog, and had been suddenly deprived of life by the exhalations of marsh miasmata. Mr Henbane deemed it probable that he had been tempted in some wood by the large black brilliant berries of the *Atropa Belladonna*, or Deadly Nightshade; and lamented that he had not been by, to administer an infallible antidote. Mr Eaves-drop hoped the particulars of his fate would be ascertained; and asked if anyone present could help him to any authentic anecdotes of their departed friend. The Reverend Doctor Folliott proposed that an inquiry should be instituted as to whether the march of intellect had reached that neighbour-hood; as, if so, the captain had probably been made a subject for science. Mr Mac Quedy said it was no such great matter to ascertain the precise mode in which the surplus population was diminished by one. Mr Toogood asseverated that there was no such thing as surplus population, and that the land, properly managed, would maintain twenty times its present inhabitants: and hereupon they fell into a disputation.

Lady Clarinda did not doubt that the captain had gone away designedly: she missed him more than she could have anticipated; and wished she had at least postponed her last piece of cruelty till the completion of their homeward voyage.

CHAPTER XI

CORRESPONDENCE

'Base is the slave that pays.' – ANCIENT PISTOL.[1]

THE CAPTAIN WAS neither drowned nor poisoned, neither miasmatized nor anatomized. But, before we proceed to account for him, we must look back to a young lady, of whom some little notice was taken in the first chapter; and who, though she has since been out of sight, has never with us been out of mind; Miss Susannah Touchandgo, the forsaken of the junior Crotchet, whom we left an inmate of a solitary farm, in one of the deep valleys under the cloudcapt summits of Meirion, comforting her wounded spirit with air and exercise, rustic cheer, music, painting, and poetry, and the prattle of the little Ap Llymrys.

One evening, after an interval of anxious expectation, the farmer, returning from market, brought for her two letters, of which the contents were these:

'*Dotandcarryonetown,*
State of Apodidraskiana :[2]
April 1, 18. .

'MY DEAR CHILD,
'I am anxious to learn what are your present position, in-tention, and prospects. The fairies who dropped gold in your shoe, on the morning when I ceased to be a respectable man in London, will soon find a talismanic channel for transmitting

you a stocking full of dollars, which will fit the shoe, as well as the foot of Cinderella fitted her slipper. I am happy to say, I am again become a respectable man. It was always my ambition to be a respectable man; and I am a very respectable man here, in this new township of a new state, where I have purchased five thousand acres of land, at two dollars an acre, hard cash, and established a very flourishing bank. The notes of Touchandgo and Company, soft cash, are now the exclusive currency of all this vicinity. This is the land in which all men flourish; but there are three classes of men who flourish especially, – Methodist preachers, slave-drivers, and paper-money manufacturers; and as one of the latter, I have just painted the word BANK on a fine slab of maple, which was green and growing when I arrived, and have discounted for the settlers, in my own currency, sundry bills, which are to be paid when the proceeds of the crop they have just sown shall return from New Orleans; so that my notes are the representatives of vegetation that is to be, and I am accordingly a capitalist of the first magnitude. The people here know very well that I ran away from London, but the most of them have run away from some place or other; and they have a great respect for me, because they think I ran away with something worth taking, which few of them had the luck or the wit to do. This gives them confidence in my resources, at the same time that, as there is nothing portable in the settlement except my own notes, they have no fear that I shall run away with them. They know I am thoroughly conversant with the principles of banking; and as they have plenty of industry, no lack of sharpness, and abundance of land, they wanted nothing but capital to organize a flourishing settlement; and this capital I have manufactured to the extent required, at the expense of a small importation of pens, ink, and paper, and two or three inimitable copper plates. I have abundance here of all good things, a good conscience included; for I really cannot see that I have done any wrong. This was my position: I owed half a million of money; and I had a trifle in my pocket. It was clear that this trifle could never find its way to the right owner. The question was, whether I should keep it, and live like a gentleman; or hand it over to lawyers and commissioners of bankruptcy, and die like a dog on a dunghill. If I could have thought that the said lawyers, etc., had a better title to it than myself, I might have hesitated; but, as such title was not

apparent to my satisfaction, I decided the question in my own
favour; the right owners, as I have already said, being out of
the question altogether. I have always taken scientific views of
morals and politics, a habit from which I derive much comfort under existing circumstances.

'I hope you adhere to your music, though I cannot hope
again to accompany your harp with my flute. My last *andante*
movement was too *forte* for those whom it took by surprise.
Let not your *allegro vivace* be damped by young Crotchet's
desertion, which though I have not heard it, I take for granted.
He is, like myself, a scientific politician, and has an eye as
keen as a needle, to his own interest. He has had good luck
so far, and is gorgeous in the spoils of many gulls; but I think
the Polar Basin and Walrus Company will be too much for
him yet. There has been a splendid outlay on credit; and he is
the only man, of the original parties concerned, of whom his
majesty's sheriffs could give any account.

'I will not ask you to come here. There is no husband for
you. The men smoke, drink, and fight, and break more of
their own heads than of girls' hearts. Those among them who
are musical sing nothing but psalms. They are excellent
fellows in their way, but you would not like them.

'*Au reste*, here are no rents, no taxes, no poor-rates, no
tithes, no church-establishment, no routs, no clubs, no rotten
boroughs,[3] no operas, no concerts, no theatres, no beggars,
no thieves, no king, no lords, no ladies, and only one gentleman, videlicet, your loving father,

'TIMOTHY TOUCHANDGO.

'P.S. – I send you one of my notes; I can afford to part with
it. If you are accused of receiving money from me, you may
pay it over to my assignees. Robthetill continues to be my
factotum; I say no more of him in this place: he will give you
an account of himself.'

'*Dotandcarryonetown, etc.*
'DEAR MISS,

'Mr Touchandgo will have told you of our arrival here, of
our setting up a bank, and so forth. We came here in a tilted
waggon, which served us for parlour, kitchen, and all. We
soon got up a log-house; and unluckily, we as soon got it
down again, for the first fire we made in it burned down house
and all. However, our second experiment was more fortunate;

and we are pretty well lodged in a house of three rooms on a floor; I should say the floor, for there is but one.

'This new state is free to hold slaves; all the new states have not this privilege: Mr Touchandgo has bought some, and they are building him a villa. Mr Touchandgo is in a thriving way, but he is not happy here: he longs for parties and concerts, and a seat in congress. He thinks it very hard that he cannot buy one with his own coinage, as he used to do in England. Besides, he is afraid of the regulators, who, if they do not like a man's character, wait upon him and flog him, doubling the dose at stated intervals, till he takes himself off. He does not like this system of administering justice: though I think he has nothing to fear from it. He has the character of having money, which is the best of all characters here, as at home. He lets his old English prejudices influence his opinions of his new neighbours; but I assure you they have many virtues. Though they do keep slaves, they are all ready to fight for their own liberty; and I should not like to be an enemy within reach of one of their rifles. When I say enemy, I include bailiff in the term. One was shot not long ago. There was a trial; the jury gave two dollars damages; the judge said they must find guilty or not guilty; but the counsel for the defendant (they would not call him prisoner), offered to fight the judge upon the point: and as this was said literally, not metaphorically, and the counsel was a stout fellow, the judge gave in. The two dollars damages were not paid after all; for the defendant challenged the foreman to box for double or quits, and the foreman was beaten. The folks in New York made a great outcry about it, but here it was considered all as it should be. So you see, Miss, justice, liberty, and everything else of that kind, are different in different places, just as suits the convenience of those who have the sword in their own hands. Hoping to hear of your health and happiness, I remain,

'Dear Miss, your dutiful servant,
'RODERICK ROBTHETILL.'

Miss Touchandgo replied as follows, to the first of these letters:

'MY DEAR FATHER,
'I am sure you have the best of hearts, and I have no doubt you have acted with the best intentions. My lover, or I should

rather say, my fortune's lover, has indeed forsaken me. I cannot say I did not feel it; indeed, I cried very much; and the altered looks of people who used to be so delighted to see me, really annoyed me so that I determined to change the scene altogether. I have come into Wales, and am boarding with a farmer and his wife. Their stock of English is very small, but I managed to agree with them; and they have four of the sweetest children I ever saw, to whom I teach all I know, and I manage to pick up some Welsh. I have puzzled out a little song, which I think very pretty; I have translated it into English, and I send it you, with the original air. You shall play it on your flute at eight o'clock every Saturday evening, and I will play and sing it at the same time, and I will fancy that I hear my dear papa accompanying me.

'The people in London said very unkind things of you: they hurt me very much at the time; but now I am out of their way, I do not seem to think their opinion of much consequence. I am sure, when I recollect, at leisure, everything I have seen and heard among them, I cannot make out what they do that is so virtuous as to set them up for judges of morals. And I am sure they never speak the truth about anything, and there is no sincerity in either their love or their friendship. An old Welsh bard here, who wears a waistcoat embroidered with leeks, and is called the Green Bard of Cadair Idris, says the Scotch would be the best people in the world if there was nobody but themselves to give them a character; and so, I think, would the Londoners. I hate the very thought of them, for I do believe they would have broken my heart if I had not got out of their way. Now I shall write you another letter very soon, and describe to you the country, and the people, and the children, and how I amuse myself, and everything that I think you will like to hear about: and when I seal this letter, I shall drop a kiss on the cover.

'Your loving daughter,
'SUSANNAH TOUCHANDGO.

'P.S. – Tell Mr Robthetill I will write to him in a day or two. This is the little song I spoke of:

"Beyond the sea, beyond the sea,
 My heart is gone, far, far from me;
 And ever on its track will flee
 My thoughts, my dreams, beyond the sea.

"Beyond the sea, beyond the sea,
    The swallow wanders fast and free:
Oh, happy bird! were I like thee,
    I, too, would fly beyond the sea.

"Beyond the sea, beyond the sea,
    Are kindly hearts and social glee:
But here for me they may not be;
    My heart is gone beyond the sea.'"

CHAPTER XII

THE MOUNTAIN INN

Ὡς ἡδὺ τῷ μισοῦντι τοὺς φαύλους τρόπους
Ἐρημίκ.

How sweet to minds that love not sordid ways
Is solitude! – MENANDER.

THE CAPTAIN WANDERED despondingly up and down hill for several days, passing many hours of each in sitting on rocks; making, almost mechanically, sketches of waterfalls, and mountain pools; taking care, nevertheless, to be always before nightfall in a comfortable inn, where, being a temperate man, he wiled away the evening with making a bottle of sherry into negus.[1] His rambles brought him at length into the interior of Merionethshire, the land of all that is beautiful in nature, and all that is lovely in woman.

Here, in a secluded village, he found a little inn, of small pretension and much comfort. He felt so satisfied with his quarters, and discovered every day so much variety in the scenes of the surrounding mountains, that his inclination to proceed farther diminished progressively.

It is one thing to follow the high road through a country, with every principally remarkable object carefully noted down in a book, taking, as therein directed, a guide, at particular points, to the more recondite sights: it is another to sit down on one chosen spot, especially when the choice is unpremeditated, and from thence, by a series of explorations, to come day by day on unanticipated scenes. The latter process has many advantages over the former; it is free from the disappointment which attends excited expectation, when imagination has outstripped reality, and from the accidents that mar the scheme of the tourist's single day, when the valleys may be drenched with rain, or the mountains shrouded with mist.

The captain was one morning preparing to sally forth on his usual exploration, when he heard a voice without, inquiring for a guide to the ruined castle. The voice seemed familiar to him, and going forth into the gateway, he recognised Mr Chainmail. After greetings and inquiries for the absent, 'You vanished very abruptly, captain,' said Mr Chainmail, 'from our party on the canal.'

CAPTAIN FITZCHROME. To tell you the truth, I had a particular reason for trying the effect of absence from a part of that party.

MR CHAINMAIL. I surmised as much: at the same time, the unusual melancholy of an in general most vivacious young lady made me wonder at your having acted so precipitately. The lady's heart is yours, if there be truth in signs.

CAPTAIN FITZCHROME. Hearts are not now what they were in the days of the old song, 'Will love be controlled by advice?'

MR CHAINMAIL. Very true; hearts, heads, and arms have all degenerated, most sadly. We can no more feel the high impassioned love of the ages, which some people have the impudence to call dark, than we can wield King Richard's battleaxe, bend Robin Hood's bow, or flourish the oaken graff of the Pinder of Wakefield.[2] Still we have our tastes and feelings, though they deserve not the name of passions; and some of us may pluck up spirit to try to carry a point, when we reflect that we have to contend with men no better than ourselves.

CAPTAIN FITZCHROME. We do not now break lances for ladies.

MR CHAINMAIL. No, nor even bulrushes. We jingle purses for them, flourish paper-money banners, and tilt with scrolls of parchment.

CAPTAIN FITZCHROME. In which sort of tilting I have been thrown from the saddle. I presume it was not love that led you from the flotilla.

MR CHAINMAIL. By no means. I was tempted by the sight of an old tower, not to leave this land of ruined castles, without having collected a few hints for the adornment of my baronial hall.

CAPTAIN FITZCHROME. I understand you live *en famille* with your domestics. You will have more difficulty in finding a lady who would adopt your fashion of living, than one who would prefer you to a richer man.

MR CHAINMAIL. Very true. I have tried the experiment on several as guests; but once was enough for them: so, I suppose, I shall die a bachelor.

CAPTAIN FITZCHROME. I see, like some others of my friends, you will give up anything except your hobby.

MR CHAINMAIL. I will give up anything but my baronial hall.

CAPTAIN FITZCHROME. You will never find a wife for your purpose, unless in the daughter of some old-fashioned farmer.

MR CHAINMAIL. No, I thank you. I must have a lady of gentle blood; I shall not marry below my own condition: I am too much of a herald; I have too much of the twelfth century in me for that.

CAPTAIN FITZCHROME. Why then your chance is not much better than mine. A well-born beauty would scarcely be better pleased with your baronial hall, than with my more humble offer of love in a cottage. She must have a town-house, and an opera-box, and roll about the streets in a carriage; especially if her father has a rotten borough, for the sake of which he sells his daughter, that he may continue to sell his country. But you were inquiring for a guide to the ruined castle in this vicinity; I know the way, and will conduct you.

The proposal pleased Mr Chainmail, and they set forth on their expedition.

CHAPTER XIII

THE LAKE – THE RUIN

Or vieni, Amore, e quà meco t'assetta. – ORLANDO INNAMORATO.[1]

MR CHAINMAIL. Would it not be a fine thing, captain – you being picturesque, and I poetical; you being for the lights and shadows of the present, and I for those of the past – if we were to go together over the ground which was travelled in the twelfth century by Giraldus de Barri,[2] when he accompanied Archbishop Baldwin to preach the crusade?

CAPTAIN FITZCHROME. Nothing, in my present frame of mind, could be more agreeable to me.

MR CHAINMAIL. We would provide ourselves with his *Itinerarium*; compare what has been with what is; contemplate in their decay the castles and abbeys which he saw in their strength and splendour; and, while you were sketching their remains, I would dispassionately inquire what has been gained by the change.

CAPTAIN FITZCHROME. Be it so.

But the scheme was no sooner arranged than the captain was summoned to London by a letter on business, which he did not expect to detain him long. Mr Chainmail, who, like the captain, was fascinated with the inn and the scenery, determined to await his companion's return; and, having furnished him with a list of books, which he was to bring with him from London, took leave of him, and began to pass his days like the heroes of Ariosto,[3] who

> — tutto il giorno, al bel oprar intenti,
> Saliron balze, e traversar torrenti.[4]

One day Mr Chainmail traced upwards the course of a mountain-stream, to a spot where a small waterfall threw itself over a slab of perpendicular rock, which seemed to bar his farther progress. On a nearer view, he discovered a flight of steps, roughly hewn in the rock, on one side of the fall. Ascending these steps, he entered a narrow winding pass, between high and naked rocks, that afforded only space for a rough footpath carved on one side, at some height above the torrent.

The pass opened on a lake, from which the stream issued, and which lay like a dark mirror, set in a gigantic frame of mountain precipices. Fragments of rock lay scattered on the edge of the lake, some half buried in the water: Mr Chainmail scrambled some way over these fragments, till the base of a rock, sinking abruptly in the water, effectually barred his progress. He sat down on a large smooth stone; the faint murmur of the stream he had quitted, the occasional flapping of the wings of the heron, and at long intervals the solitary springing of a trout, were the only sounds that came to his ear. The sun shone brightly halfway down the opposite rocks, presenting, on their irregular faces, strong masses of light and shade. Suddenly he heard the dash of a paddle, and, turning his eyes, saw a solitary and beautiful girl gliding over the lake in a coracle; she was proceeding from the vicinity of the point he had quitted towards the upper end of the lake. Her apparel was rustic, but there was in its style something more *recherché*, in its arrangement something more of elegance and precision, than was common to the mountain peasant girl. It had more of the *contadina* of the opera than of the genuine mountaineer[5]; so at least thought Mr Chainmail; but she passed so rapidly, and took him so much by surprise, that he had little opportunity for accurate observation. He saw her land, at the farther extremity, and disappear among the rocks: he rose from his seat, returned to the mouth of the pass, stepped from stone to stone across the stream, and attempted to pass round by the other side of the lake; but there again the abruptly sinking precipice closed his way.

Day after day he haunted the spot, but never saw again either the damsel or the coracle. At length, marvelling at himself for being so solicitous about the apparition of a peasant girl in a coracle, who could not, by any possibility, be anything to him, he resumed his explorations in another direction.

One day he wandered to the ruined castle, on the seashore, which was not very distant from his inn; and sitting on the rock, near the base of the ruin, was calling up the forms of past ages on the wall of an ivied tower, when on its summit appeared a female figure, whom he recognized in an instant for his nymph of the coracle. The folds of the blue gown pressed by the sea breeze against one of the most symmetrical of figures, the black feather of the black hat, and the ringleted hair beneath it fluttering in the wind; the apparent peril of her position, on the edge of the mouldering wall, from whose immediate base the rock went down perpendicularly to the sea, presented a singularly interesting combination to the eye of the young antiquary.

Mr Chainmail had to pass half round the castle, on the land side, before he could reach the entrance: he coasted the dry and bramble-grown moat, crossed the unguarded bridge, passed the unportcullised arch of the gateway, entered the castle court, ascertained the tower, ascended the broken stairs, and stood on the ivied wall. But the nymph of the place was gone. He searched the ruins within and without, but he found not what he sought; he haunted the castle day after day, as he had done the lake, but the damsel appeared no more.

CHAPTER XIV

THE DINGLE

> The stars of midnight shall be dear
> To her, and she shall lean her ear
> In many a secret place,
> Where rivulets dance their wayward round,
> And beauty, born of murmuring sound,
> Shall pass into her face. – WORDSWORTH.

MISS SUSANNAH TOUCHANDGO had read the four great poets of Italy, and many of the best writers of France. About the time of her father's downfall, accident threw into her way *Les Rêveries du Promeneur Solitaire*; and from the impression which these made on her, she carried with her into retirement all the works of Rousseau. In the midst of that startling light which the conduct of old friends on a sudden reverse of fortune throws on a young and inexperienced mind, the doctrines of the philosopher of Geneva struck with double force upon her sympathies: she imbibed the sweet poison, as somebody calls it, of his writings, even to a love of truth; which, every wise man knows, ought to be left to those who can get anything by it. The society of children, the beauties of nature, the solitude of the mountains, became her consolation, and, by degrees, her delight. The gay society from which she had been excluded remained on her memory only as a disagreeable dream. She imbibed her new monitor's ideas of simplicity of dress, assimilating her own with that of the peasant girls in the neighbourhood; the black hat, the blue gown, the black stockings, the shoes tied on the instep.

Pride was, perhaps, at the bottom of the change; she was willing to impose in some measure on herself, by marking a contemptuous indifference to the characteristics of the class of society from which she had fallen,

> 'And with the food of pride sustained her soul
>   In solitude.'[1]

It is true that she somewhat modified the forms of her rustic dress: to the black hat she added a black feather, to the blue gown she added a tippet, and a waistband fastened in front with a silver buckle; she wore her black stockings very smooth and tight on her ancles, and tied her shoes in tasteful bows, with the nicest possible ribbon. In this apparel, to which, in winter, she added a scarlet cloak, she made dreadful havoc among the rustic mountaineers, many of whom proposed to 'keep company' with her in the Cambrian fashion, an honour which, to their great surprise, she always declined. Among these, Harry Ap-Heather, whose father rented an extensive sheepwalk, and had a thousand she-lambs wandering in the mountains, was the most strenuous in his suit, and the most pathetic in his lamentations for her cruelty.

Miss Susannah often wandered among the mountains alone, even to some distance from the farmhouse. Sometimes she descended into the bottom of the dingles, to the black rocky beds of the torrents, and dreamed away hours at the feet of the cataracts. One spot in particular, from which she had at first shrunk with terror, became by degrees her favourite haunt. A path turning and returning at acute angles, led down a steep wood-covered slope to the edge of a chasm, where a pool, or resting-place of a torrent, lay far below. A cataract fell in a single sheet into the pool; the pool boiled and bubbled at the base of the fall, but through the greater part of its extent lay calm, deep, and black, as if the cataract had plunged through it to an unimaginable depth without disturbing its eternal repose. At the opposite extremity of the pool, the rocks almost met at their summits, the trees of the opposite banks inter-mingled their leaves, and another cataract plunged from the pool into a chasm on which the sunbeams never gleamed. High above, on both sides, the steep woody slopes of the dingle soared into the sky; and from a fissure in the rock, on which the little path terminated, a single gnarled and twisted oak stretched itself over the pool, forming a fork with its boughs at a short distance from the rock. Miss Susannah often sat on the rock, with her feet resting on this tree: in time, she made her seat on the tree itself, with her feet hanging over the abyss; and at length she accustomed herself to lie along upon its trunk, with her side on the mossy boll of the fork, and an arm round one of the branches. From this position a portion of the sky and the woods was reflected in the pool, which, from its bank, was but a mass of darkness. The first time she reclined in this manner, her heart beat audibly; in time, she lay down as calmly as on the mountain heather: the perception of the sublime was probably heightened by an intermingled sense of danger;[2] and perhaps that indifference to life, which early disappointment forces upon sensitive minds, was necessary to the first experiment. There was, in the novelty and strangeness of the position, an excitement which never wholly passed away, but which became gradually subordinate to the influence, at once tranquillizing and elevating, of the mingled eternity of motion, sound, and solitude.

One sultry noon, she descended into this retreat with a mind more than usually disturbed by reflections on the past. She lay in her favourite position, sometimes gazing on the cataract; looking sometimes up the steep sylvan acclivities into the narrow space of the cloudless ether; sometimes down into the abyss of the pool, and the deep bright-blue reflections that opened another immensity below her. The distressing recollections of the morning, the world, and all its littlenesses, faded from her thoughts like a dream; but her wounded and wearied spirit drank in too deeply the tranquillizing power of the place, and she dropped asleep upon the tree like a ship-boy on the mast.

At this moment Mr Chainmail emerged into daylight, on a projection of the opposite rock, having struck down through the woods in search of unsophisticated scenery. The scene he discovered filled him with delight: he seated himself on the rock, and fell into one of his romantic reveries; when suddenly the semblance of a black hat and feather caught his eye among the foliage of the projecting oak. He started up, shifted his position, and got a glimpse of a blue gown. It was his lady of the lake, his enchantress of the ruined castle, divided from him by a barrier, which, at a few yards below, he could almost overleap, yet unapproachable but by a circuit perhaps of many hours. He watched with intense anxiety. To listen if she breathed was out of the question: the noses of a dean and chapter would have been soundless in the roar of the torrent.

From her extreme stillness, she appeared to sleep: yet what creature, not desperate, would go wilfully to sleep in such a place? Was she asleep then? Nay, was she alive? She was as motionless as death. Had she been murdered, thrown from above, and caught in the tree? She lay too regularly and too composedly for such a supposition. She was asleep then, and in all probability her waking would be fatal. He shifted his position. Below the pool two beetle-browed rocks nearly overarched the chasm, leaving just such a space at the summit as was within the possibility of a leap; the torrent roared below in a fearful gulf. He paused some time on the brink, measuring the practicability and the danger, and casting every now and then an anxious glance to his sleeping beauty. In one of these glances he saw a slight movement of the blue gown, and, in a moment after, the black hat and feather dropped into the pool. Reflection was lost for a moment, and, by a sudden impulse, he bounded over the chasm.

He stood above the projecting oak; the unknown beauty lay like the nymph of the scene; her long black hair, which the fall of her hat had disengaged from its fastenings, drooping through the boughs: he saw that the first thing to be done was to prevent her throwing her feet off the trunk, in the first movements of waking. He sat down on the rock, and placed his feet on the stem, securing her ancles between his own: one of her arms was round a branch of the fork, the other lay loosely on her side. The hand of this arm he endeavoured to reach, by leaning forward from his seat; he approximated, but could not touch it: after several tantalizing efforts, he gave up the point in despair. He did not attempt to wake her, because he feared it might have bad consequences, and he resigned himself to expect the moment of her natural waking, determined not to stir from his post, if she should sleep till midnight.

In this period of forced inaction, he could contemplate at leisure the features and form of his charmer. She was not one of the slender beauties of romance; she was as plump as a partridge; her cheeks were two roses, not absolutely damask, yet verging thereupon; her lips twin-cherries, of equal size; her nose regular, and almost Grecian; her forehead high, and delicately fair; her eyebrows symmetrically arched; her eyelashes long, black, and silky, fitly corresponding with the beautiful tresses that hung among the leaves of the oak, like

clusters of wandering grapes.* Her eyes were yet to be seen;
but how could he doubt that their opening would be the
rising of the sun, when all that surrounded their fringy portals
was radiant as 'the forehead of the morning sky'?

CHAPTER XV

THE FARM

Da ydyw'r gwaith, rhaid d'we'yd y gwir,
Ar fryniau Sir Meirionydd;
Golwg oer o'r gwaela gawn
Mae hi etto yn llawn llawenydd.

Though Meirion's rocks, and hills of heath
    Repel the distant sight;
Yet where, than those bleak hills beneath,
    Is found more true delight?

AT LENGTH THE young lady awoke. She was startled at the
sudden sight of the stranger, and somewhat terrified at the
first perception of her position. But she soon recovered her
self-possession, and, extending her hand to the offered hand of
Mr Chainmail, she raised herself up on the tree, and stepped
on the rocky bank.

Mr Chainmail solicited permission to attend her to her
home, which the young lady graciously conceded. They
emerged from the woody dingle, traversed an open heath,
wound along a mountain road by the shore of a lake, descended
to the deep bed of another stream, crossed it by a series of
stepping stones, ascended to some height on the opposite
side, and followed upwards the line of the stream, till the
banks opened into a spacious amphitheatre, where stood, in
its fields and meadows, the farmhouse of Ap-Llymry.

During this walk, they had kept up a pretty animated conversation. The lady had lost her hat; and, as she turned towards Mr Chainmail, in speaking to him, there was no envious
projection of brim to intercept the beams of those radiant
eyes he had been so anxious to see unclosed. There was in

* Ἀλήμονα βότρυν ἐθείρας. – NONNUS. [P.]³

them a mixture of softness and brilliancy, the perfection of the beauty of female eyes, such as some men have passed through life without seeing, and such as no man ever saw, in any pair of eyes, but once; such as can never be seen and forgotten. Young Crotchet had seen it; he had not forgotten it; but he had trampled on its memory, as the renegade tramples on the emblems of a faith which his interest only, and not his heart or his reason, has rejected.

Her hair streamed over her shoulders; the loss of the black feather had left nothing but the rustic costume, the blue gown, the black stockings, and the ribbon-tied shoes. Her voice had the full soft volume of melody which gives to common speech the fascination of music. Mr Chainmail could not reconcile the dress of the damsel with her conversation and manners. He threw out a remote question or two, with the hope of solving the riddle; but, receiving no reply, he became satisfied that she was not disposed to be communicative respecting herself, and, fearing to offend her, fell upon other topics. They talked of the scenes of the mountains, of the dingle, the ruined castle, the solitary lake. She told him that lake lay under the mountains behind her home, and the coracle and the pass at the extremity saved a long circuit to the nearest village, whither she sometimes went to inquire for letters.

Mr Chainmail felt curious to know from whom these letters might be; and he again threw out two or three fishing questions, to which, as before, he obtained no answer.

The only living biped they met in their walk was the unfortunate Harry Ap-Heather, with whom they fell in by the stepping-stones, who, seeing the girl of his heart hanging on another man's arm, and, concluding at once that they were 'keeping company', fixed on her a mingled look of surprise, reproach, and tribulation; and, unable to control his feelings under the sudden shock, burst into a flood of tears, and blubbered till the rocks re-echoed.

They left him mingling his tears with the stream, and his lamentations with its murmurs. Mr Chainmail inquired who that strange creature might be, and what was the matter with him. The young lady answered, that he was a very worthy young man, to whom she had been the innocent cause of much unhappiness.

'I pity him sincerely,' said Mr Chainmail; and, nevertheless, he could scarcely restrain his laughter at the exceedingly original figure which the unfortunate rustic lover had presented by the stepping-stones.

The children ran out to meet their dear Miss Susan, jumped all round her, and asked what was become of her hat. Ap-Llymry came out in great haste, and invited Mr Chainmail to walk in and dine: Mr Chainmail did not wait to be asked twice. In a few minutes the whole party, Miss Susan and Mr Chainmail, Mr and Mrs Ap-Llymry, and progeny, were seated over a clean homespun tablecloth, ornamented with fowls and bacon, a pyramid of potatoes, another of cabbage, which Ap-Llymry said 'was poiled with the pacon, and as coot as marrow', a bowl of milk for the children, and an immense brown jug of foaming ale, with which Ap-Llymry seemed to delight in filling the horn of his new guest.

Shall we describe the spacious apartment, which was at once kitchen, hall, and dining-room – the large dark rafters, the pendent bacon and onions, the strong old oaken furniture, the bright and trimly arranged utensils? Shall we describe the cut of Ap-Llymry's coat, the colour and tie of his neckcloth, the number of buttons at his knees – the structure of Mrs Ap-Llymry's cap, having lappets over the ears, which were united under the chin, setting forth especially whether the bond of union were a pin or a ribbon? We shall leave this tempting field of interesting expatiation to those whose brains are high-pressure steam engines for spinning prose by the furlong, to be trumpeted in paid-for paragraphs in the quack's corner of newspapers: modern literature having attained the honourable distinction of sharing with blacking and macassar oil, the space which used to be monopolized by razor-strops and the lottery, whereby that very enlightened community, the reading public, is tricked into the perusal of much exemplary nonsense; though the few who see through the trickery have no reason to complain, since as 'good wine needs no bush', so, *ex vi oppositi*, these bushes of venal panegyric point out very clearly that the things they celebrate are not worth reading.

The party dined very comfortably in a corner most remote from the fire; and Mr Chainmail very soon found his head swimming with two or three horns of ale, of a potency to which even he was unaccustomed. After dinner, Ap-Llymry made him finish a bottle of mead, which he willingly accepted, both as an excuse to remain, and as a drink of the dark ages, which he had no doubt was a genuine brewage, from uncorrupted tradition.

In the meantime, as soon as the cloth was removed, the children had brought out Miss Susannah's harp. She began, without affectation, to play and sing to the children, as was her custom of an afternoon, first in their own language, and their national melodies, then in English; but she was soon interrupted by a general call of little voices for 'Ouf! di giorno'. She complied with the request, and sang the ballad from Paër's Camilla: *Un dì carco il mulinaro.** The children were very familiar with every syllable of this ballad, which had been often fully explained to them. They danced in a circle with the burden of every verse, shouting out the chorus with good articulation and joyous energy; and at the end of the second stanza, where the traveller has his nose pinched by his grandmother's ghost, every nose in the party was nipped by a pair of little fingers. Mr Chainmail, who was not prepared for the process, came in for a very energetic tweak, from a chubby girl that sprang suddenly on his knees for the purpose, and made the roof ring with her laughter.

So passed the time till evening, when Mr Chainmail moved to depart. But it turned out on inquiry that he was some miles from his inn, that the way was intricate, and that he must not make any difficulty about accepting the farmer's hospitality till morning. The evening set in with rain: the fire was found agreeable; they drew around it. The young lady made tea; and afterwards, from time to time, at Mr Chainmail's special request, delighted his ear with passages of ancient music. Then came a supper of lake trout, fried on the spot, and thrown, smoking hot, from the pan to the plate. Then came a brewage, which the farmer called his nightcap, of which he insisted on

* In this ballad, the terrors of the Black Forest are narrated to an assemblage of domestics and peasants, who, at the end of every stanza, dance in a circle round the narrator. The second stanza is as follows:

> Una notte in un stradotto
> Un incauto s'inoltrò;
> E uno strillo udí di botto
> Che l'orecchio gl'intronò:
> Era l'ombra di sua nonna,
> Che pel naso lo pigliò.
> Ouf! di giorno nè di sera,
> Non passiam la selva nera.
> (*Ballano in Giro.*) [P.]¹

Mr Chainmail's taking his full share. After which the gentleman remembered nothing, till he awoke, the next morning,
to the pleasant consciousness that he was under the same roof
with one of the most fascinating creatures under the canopy of
heaven.

CHAPTER XVI

THE NEWSPAPER

Ποίας δ' ἀποσπασθεῖσα φύτλας
Ὀρέων κευθμῶνας ἔχει σκιοέντων;

Sprung from what line, adorns the maid
These valleys deep in mountain shade?

PIND. *Pyth* IX.

MR CHAINMAIL forgot the captain and the route of Giraldus
de Barri. He became suddenly satisfied that the ruined castle
in his present neighbourhood was the best possible specimen
of its class, and that it was needless to carry his researches
further.

He visited the farm daily: found himself always welcome;
flattered himself that the young lady saw him with pleasure,
and dragged a heavier chain at every new parting from Miss
Susan, as the children called his nymph of the mountains.
What might be her second name, he had vainly endeavoured
to discover.

Mr Chainmail was in love; but the determination he had
long before formed and fixed in his mind, to marry only a
lady of gentle blood, without a blot on her escutcheon, repressed the declarations of passion which were often rising to
his lips. In the meantime, he left no means untried, to pluck
out the heart of her mystery.

The young lady soon divined his passion, and penetrated his
prejudices. She began to look on him with favourable eyes;
but she feared her name and parentage would present an
insuperable barrier to his feudal pride.

Things were in this state when the captain returned, and
unpacked his maps and books in the parlour of the inn.

MR CHAINMAIL. Really, captain, I find so many objects of
attraction in this neighbourhood, that I would gladly postpone
our purpose.

CAPTAIN FITZCHROME. Undoubtedly, this neighbour-hood has many attractions; but there is something very inviting in the scheme you laid down.

MR CHAINMAIL. No doubt, there is something very tempting in the route of Giraldus de Barri. But there are better things in this vicinity even than that. To tell you the truth, captain, I have fallen in love.

CAPTAIN FITZCHROME. What! while I have been away?

MR CHAINMAIL. Even so.

CAPTAIN FITZCHROME. The plunge must have been very sudden, if you are already over head and ears.

MR CHAINMAIL. As deep as Llyn-y-dreiddiad-vrawd.

CAPTAIN FITZCHROME. And what may that be?

MR CHAINMAIL. A pool not far off: a resting-place of a mountain stream, which is said to have no bottom. There is a tradition connected with it; and here is a ballad on it, at your service:

LLYN-Y-DREIDDIAD-VRAWD

THE POOL OF THE DIVING FRIAR

GWENWYNWYN withdrew from the feasts of his hall;
He slept very little, he prayed not at all;
He pondered, and wandered, and studied alone;
And sought, night and day, the philosopher's stone.

He found it at length, and he made its first proof
By turning to gold all the lead of his roof:
Then he bought some magnanimous heroes, all fire,
Who lived but to smite and be smitten for hire.

With these, on the plains like a torrent he broke;
He filled the whole country with flame and with smoke;
He killed all the swine, and he broached all the wine;
He drove off the sheep, and the beeves, and the kine;

He took castles and towns; he cut short limbs and lives;
He made orphans and widows of children and wives:
This course many years he triumphantly ran,
And did mischief enough to be called a great man.

When, at last, he had gained all for which he had striven,
He bethought him of buying a passport to heaven;
Good and great as he was, yet he did not well know
How soon, or which way, his great spirit might go.

He sought the grey friars, who, beside a wild stream,
Refected their frames on a primitive scheme;
The gravest and wisest Gwenwynwyn found out,
All lonely and ghostly, and angling for trout.

Below the white dash of a mighty cascade,
Where a pool of the stream a deep resting-place made,
And rock-rooted oaks stretched their branches on high,
The friar stood musing, and throwing his fly.

To him said Gwenwynwyn, 'Hold, father, here's store,
For the good of the church, and the good of the poor';
Then he gave him the stone; but, ere more he could speak,
Wrath came on the friar, so holy and meek:

He had stretched forth his hand to receive the red gold,
And he thought himself mocked by Gwenwynwyn the Bold;
And in scorn of the gift, and in rage at the giver,
He jerked it immediately into the river.

Gwenwynwyn, aghast, not a syllable spake;
The philosopher's stone made a duck and a drake:
Two systems of circles a moment were seen,
And the stream smoothed them off, as they never had been.

Gwenwynwyn regained, and uplifted, his voice:
'Oh friar, grey friar, full rash was thy choice;
The stone, the good stone, which away thou hast thrown,
Was the stone of all stones, the philosopher's stone!'

The friar looked pale, when his error he knew;
The friar looked red, and the friar looked blue;
And heels over head, from the point of a rock,
He plunged, without stopping to pull off his frock.

He dived very deep, but he dived all in vain,
The prize he had slighted he found not again:
Many times did the friar his diving renew,
And deeper and deeper the river still grew.

Gwenwynwyn gazed long, of his senses in doubt,
To see the grey friar a diver so stout:
Then sadly and slowly his castle he sought,
And left the friar diving, like dabchick distraught.

Gwenwynwyn fell sick with alarm and despite,
Died, and went to the devil, the very same night:
The magnanimous heroes he held in his pay
Sacked his castle, and marched with the plunder away.

No knell on the silence of midnight was rolled,
For the flight of the soul of Gwenwynwyn the Bold:
The brethren, unfeed, let the mighty ghost pass,
Without praying a prayer, or intoning a mass.

The friar haunted ever beside the dark stream;
The philosopher's stone was his thought and his dream:
And day after day, ever head under heels
He dived all the time he could spare from his meals.

He dived, and he dived, to the end of his days,
As the peasants oft witnessed with fear and amaze:
The mad friar's diving-place long was their theme,
And no plummet can fathom that pool of the stream.

And still, when light clouds on the midnight winds ride,
If by moonlight you stray on the lone river-side,
The ghost of the friar may be seen diving there,
With head in the water, and heels in the air.

CAPTAIN FITZCHROME. Well, your ballad is very pleasant: you shall show me the scene, and I will sketch it; but just now I am more interested about your love. What heroine of the twelfth century has risen from the ruins of the old castle, and looked down on you from the ivied battlements?

MR CHAINMAIL. You are nearer the mark than you suppose. Even from those battlements a heroine of the twelfth century has looked down on me.

CAPTAIN FITZCHROME. Oh! some vision of an ideal beauty. I suppose the whole will end in another tradition and a ballad.

MR CHAINMAIL. Genuine flesh and blood; as genuine as Lady Clarinda. I will tell you the story.

Mr Chainmail narrated his adventures.

CAPTAIN FITZCHROME. Then you seem to have found what you wished. Chance has thrown in your way what none of the gods would have ventured to promise you.

MR CHAINMAIL. Yes, but I know nothing of her birth and

parentage. She tells me nothing of herself, and I have no right to question her directly.

CAPTAIN FITZCHROME. She appears to be expressly destined for the light of your baronial hall. Introduce me: in this case, two heads are better than one.

MR CHAINMAIL. No, I thank you. Leave me to manage my chance of a prize, and keep you to your own chance of a —

CAPTAIN FITZCHROME. Blank. As you please. Well, I will pitch my tent here, till I have filled my portfolio, and shall be glad of as much of your company as you can spare from more attractive society.

Matters went on pretty smoothly for several days, when an unlucky newspaper threw all into confusion. Mr Chainmail received newspapers by the post, which came in three times a week. One morning, over their half-finished breakfast, the captain had read half a newspaper very complacently, when suddenly he started up in a frenzy, hurled over the breakfast table, and, bouncing from the apartment, knocked down Harry Ap-Heather, who was coming in at the door to challenge his supposed rival to a boxing-match.

Harry sprang up, in a double rage, and intercepted Mr Chainmail's pursuit of the captain, placing himself in the doorway, in a pugilistic attitude. Mr Chainmail, not being disposed for this mode of combat, stepped back into the parlour, took the poker in his right hand, and displacing the loose bottom of a large elbow chair, threw it over his left arm, as a shield. Harry, not liking the aspect of the enemy in this imposing attitude, retreated with backward steps into the kitchen, and tumbled over a cur, which immediately fastened on his rear.

Mr Chainmail, half-laughing, half-vexed, anxious to overtake the captain, and curious to know what was the matter with him, pocketed the newspaper, and sallied forth, leaving Harry roaring for a doctor and a tailor, to repair the lacerations of his outward man.

Mr Chainmail could find no trace of the captain. Indeed, he sought him but in one direction, which was that leading to the farm; where he arrived in due time, and found Miss Susan alone. He laid the newspaper on the table, as was his custom, and proceeded to converse with the young lady: a conversation of many pauses, as much of signs as of words. The young lady took up the paper, and turned it over and over, while she listened to Mr Chainmail, whom she found every day more and more agreeable, when, suddenly, her eye glanced on something which made her change colour, and dropping the paper on the ground, she rose from her seat, exclaiming, 'Miserable must she be who trusts any of your faithless sex! Never, never, never, will I endure such misery twice.' And she vanished up the stairs. Mr Chainmail was petrified. At length, he cried aloud, 'Cornelius Agrippa[1] must have laid a spell on this accursed newspaper;' and was turning it over, to look for the source of the mischief, when Mrs Ap-Llymry made her appearance.

MRS AP-LLYMRY. What have you done to poor dear Miss Susan? She is crying, ready to break her heart.

MR CHAINMAIL. So help me the memory of Richard Cœur-de-Lion, I have not the most distant notion of what is the matter!

MRS AP-LLYMRY. Oh, don't tell me, sir; you must have ill-used her. I know how it is. You have been keeping company with her, as if you wanted to marry her; and now, all at once, you have been trying to make her your mistress. I have seen such tricks more than once, and you ought to be ashamed of yourself.

MR CHAINMAIL. My dear madam, you wrong me utterly. I have none but the kindest feelings and the most honourable purposes towards her. She has been disturbed by something she has seen in this rascally paper.

MRS AP-LLYMRY. Why, then, the best thing you can do is to go away, and come again tomorrow.

MR CHAINMAIL. Not I, indeed, madam. Out of this house I stir not, till I have seen the young lady, and obtained a full explanation.

MRS AP-LLYMRY. I will tell Miss Susan what you say. Perhaps she will come down.

Mr Chainmail sate with as much patience as he could command, running over the paper, from column to column. At length, he lighted on an announcement of the approaching marriage of Lady Clarinda Bossnowl with Mr Crotchet the younger. This explained the captain's discomposure, but the cause of Miss Susan's was still to be sought; he could not know that it was one and the same.

Presently the sound of the longed-for step was heard on the stairs; the young lady reappeared, and resumed her seat: her eyes showed that she had been weeping. The gentleman was now exceedingly puzzled how to begin, but the young lady relieved him by asking, with great simplicity, 'What do you wish to have explained, sir?'

MR CHAINMAIL. I wish, if I may be permitted, to explain myself to you. Yet could I first wish to know what it was that disturbed you in this unlucky paper. Happy should I be if I could remove the cause of your inquietude!

MISS SUSANNAH. The cause is already removed. I saw something that excited painful recollections; nothing that I could now wish otherwise than as it is.

MR CHAINMAIL. Yet, may I ask why it is that I find one so accomplished living in this obscurity, and passing only by the name of Miss Susan?

MISS SUSANNAH. The world and my name are not friends. I have left the world, and wish to remain for ever a stranger to all whom I once knew in it.

MR CHAINMAIL. You can have done nothing to dishonour your name.

MISS SUSANNAH. No, sir. My father has done that of which the world disapproves, in matters of which I pretend not to judge. I have suffered for it as I will never suffer again. My name is my own secret; I have no other, and that is one not worth knowing. You see what I am, and all I am. I live according to the condition of my present fortune; and here, so living, I have found tranquillity.

MR CHAINMAIL. Yet, I entreat you, tell me your name.

MISS SUSANNAH. Why, sir?

MR CHAINMAIL. Why, but to throw my hand, my heart, my fortune, at your feet, if —

MISS SUSANNAH. If my name be worthy of them.

MR CHAINMAIL. Nay, nay, not so; if your hand and heart are free.

MISS SUSANNAH. My hand and heart are free; but they must be sought from myself, and not from my name.

She fixed her eyes on him, with a mingled expression of mistrust, of kindness, and of fixed resolution, which the far-gone *innamorato* found irresistible.

MR CHAINMAIL. Then from yourself alone I seek them.

MISS SUSANNAH. Reflect. You have prejudices on the score of parentage. I have not conversed with you so often, without knowing what they are. Choose between them and me. I too have my own prejudices on the score of personal pride.

MR CHAINMAIL. I would choose you from all the world, were you even the daughter of the *exécuteur des hautes œuvres*,[2] as the heroine of a romantic story I once read turned out to be.

MISS SUSANNAH. I am satisfied. You have now a right to know my history; and, if you repent, I absolve you from all obligations.

She told him her history; but he was out of the reach of repentance. 'It is true,' as at a subsequent period he said to the captain, 'she is the daughter of a moneychanger; one who, in the days of Richard the First, would have been plucked by the beard in the streets; but she is, according to modern notions, a lady of gentle blood. As to her father's running away, that is a minor consideration: I have always understood, from Mr Mac Quedy, who is a great oracle in this way, that promises to pay ought not to be kept; the essence of a safe and economical currency being an interminable series of broken promises. There seems to be a difference among the learned as to the way in which the promises ought to be broken; but I am not deep enough in their casuistry to enter into such nice distinctions.'

In a few days there was a wedding, a pathetic leave-taking of the farmer's family, a hundred kisses from the bride to the children, and promises twenty times reclaimed and renewed, to visit them in the ensuing year.

CHAPTER XVII

THE INVITATION

A cup of wine, that's brisk and fine,
And drink unto the leman mine.
MASTER SILENCE.[1]

THIS VERIDICOUS history began in May, and the occurrences already narrated have carried it on to the middle of autumn. Stepping over the interval to Christmas, we find ourselves in our first locality, among the chalk hills of the Thames; and we discover our old friend, Mr Crotchet, in the act of accepting an invitation, for himself, and any friends who might be with him, to pass their Christmas-day at Chainmail Hall, after the fashion of the twelfth century. Mr Crotchet had assembled about him, for his own Christmas-festivities, nearly the same party which was introduced to the reader in the spring. Three of that party were wanting. Dr Morbific, by inoculating himself once too often with non-contagious matter, had explained himself out of the world. Mr Henbane had also departed, on the wings of an infallible antidote. Mr Eavesdrop, having printed in a magazine some of the after-dinner conversations of the castle, had had sentence of exclusion passed upon him, on the motion of the Reverend Doctor Folliott, as a flagitious violator of the confidences of private life.

Miss Crotchet had become Lady Bossnowl, but Lady Clarinda had not yet changed her name to Crotchet. She had, on one pretence and another, procrastinated the happy event, and the gentleman had not been very pressing; she had, however, accompanied her brother and sister-in-law, to pass Christmas at Crotchet Castle. With these, Mr Mac Quedy, Mr Philpot, Mr Trillo, Mr Skionar, Mr Toogood, and Mr Firedamp, were sitting at breakfast, when the Reverend Doctor Folliott entered and took his seat at the table.

THE REV. DR FOLLIOTT. Well, Mr Mac Quedy, it is now some weeks since we have met: how goes on the march of mind?

MR MAC QUEDY. Nay, sir; I think you may see that with your own eyes.

THE REV. DR FOLLIOTT. Sir, I have seen it, much to my discomfiture. It has marched into my rick-yard, and set my stacks on fire, with chemical materials, most scientifically compounded. It has marched up to the door of my vicarage, a hundred and fifty strong; ordered me to surrender half my tithes; consumed all the provisions I had provided for my audit feast, and drunk up my old October. It has marched in through my back-parlour shutters, and out again with my silver spoons, in the dead of night. The policeman, who was sent down to examine, says my house has been broken open on the most scientific principles. All this comes of education.

MR MAC QUEDY. I rather think it comes of poverty.

THE REV. DR FOLLIOTT. No, sir. Robbery perhaps comes of poverty, but scientific principles of robbery come of education. I suppose the learned friend has written a sixpenny treatise on mechanics, and the rascals who robbed me have been reading it.

MR CROTCHET. Your house would have been very safe, doctor, if they had had no better science than the learned friend's to work with.

THE REV. DR FOLLIOTT. Well, sir, that may be. Excellent potted char.[2] The Lord deliver me from the learned friend.

MR CROTCHET. Well, doctor, for your comfort, here is a declaration of the learned friend's that he will never take office.

THE REV. DR FOLLIOTT. Then, sir, he will be in office next week. Peace be with him! Sugar and cream.

MR CROTCHET. But, doctor, are you for Chainmail Hall on Christmas-day?

THE REV. DR FOLLIOTT. That am I, there will be an excellent dinner, though, peradventure, grotesquely served.

MR CROTCHET. I have not seen my neighbour since he left us on the canal.

THE REV. DR FOLLIOTT. He has married a wife, and brought her home.

LADY CLARINDA. Indeed! If she suits him, she must be an oddity: it will be amusing to see them together.

LORD BOSSNOWL. Very amusing. He! he!

MR FIREDAMP. Is there any water about Chainmail Hall?

THE REV. DR FOLLIOTT. An old moat.

MR FIREDAMP. I shall die of *malaria*.

MR TRILLO. Shall we have any music?

THE REV. DR FOLLIOTT. An old harper.

MR TRILLO. Those fellows are always horridly out of tune. What will he play?

THE REV. DR FOLLIOTT. Old songs and marches.

MR SKIONAR. Amongst so many old things, I hope we shall find Old Philosophy.

THE REV. DR FOLLIOTT. An old woman.

MR PHILPOT. Perhaps an old map of the river in the twelfth century.

THE REV. DR FOLLIOTT. No doubt.

MR MAC QUEDY. How many more old things?

THE REV. DR FOLLIOTT. Old hospitality, old wine, old ale – all the images of old England; an old butler.

MR TOOGOOD. Shall we all be welcome?

THE REV. DR FOLLIOTT. Heartily; you will be slapped on the shoulder, and called old boy.

LORD BOSSNOWL. I think we should all go in our old clothes. He! he!

THE REV. DR FOLLIOTT. You will sit on old chairs, round an old table, by the light of old lamps, suspended from pointed arches, which, Mr Chainmail says, first came into use in the twelfth century; with old armour on the pillars, and old banners in the roof.

LADY CLARINDA. And what curious piece of antiquity is the lady of the mansion?

THE REV. DR FOLLIOTT. No antiquity there; none.

LADY CLARINDA. Who was she?

THE REV. DR FOLLIOTT. That I know not.

LADY CLARINDA. Have you seen her?

THE REV. DR FOLLIOTT. I have.

LADY CLARINDA. Is she pretty?

THE REV. DR FOLLIOTT. More — beautiful. A subject for the pen of Nonnus, or the pencil of Zeuxis.[3] Features of all loveliness, radiant with all virtue and intelligence. A face for Antigone. A form at once plump and symmetrical, that, if it be decorous to divine it by externals, would have been a model for the Venus of Cnidos.[4] Never was anything so goodly to look on, the present company excepted, and poor dear Mrs Folliott. She reads moral philosophy, Mr Mac Quedy, which indeed she might as well let alone; she reads Italian poetry, Mr Skionar; she sings Italian music, Mr Trillo; but, with all this, she has the greatest of female virtues, for she superintends the household, and looks after her husband's dinner. I believe she was a mountaineer: παρθένος οὐρεσίφοιτος, ἐρημάδι σύντροφος ὕλῃ,* as Nonnus sweetly sings.

CHAPTER XVIII

CHAINMAIL HALL

Vous autres dictes que ignorance est mere de tous maulx, et dictes vray: mais toutesfoys vous ne la bannissez mye de vos entendemens, et vivez en elle, avecques elle, et par elle. C'est pourquoy tant de maulx vous meshaignent de jour en jour. — RABELAIS, l. 5. c. 7.[1]

* A mountain-wandering maid,
Twin-nourished with the solitary wood. [P.]

The party which was assembled on Christmas-day in Chainmail Hall, comprised all the guests of Crotchet Castle, some of Mr Chainmail's other neighbours, all his tenants and domestics, and Captain Fitzchrome. The hall was spacious and lofty; and with its tall fluted pillars and pointed arches, its windows of stained glass, its display of arms and banners intermingled with holly and mistletoe, its blazing cressets and torches, and a stupendous fire in the centre, on which blocks of pine were flaming and crackling, had a striking effect on eyes unaccustomed to such a dining-room. The fire was open on all sides, and the smoke was caught and carried back, under a funnel-formed canopy, into a hollow central pillar. This fire was the line of demarcation between gentle and simple, on days of high festival. Tables extended from it on two sides, to nearly the end of the hall.

Mrs Chainmail was introduced to the company. Young Crotchet felt some revulsion of feeling at the unexpected sight of one whom he had forsaken, but not forgotten, in a condition apparently so much happier than his own. The lady held out her hand to him with a cordial look of more than forgiveness; it seemed to say that she had much to thank him for. She was the picture of a happy bride, *rayonnante de joie et d'amour*.[2]

Mr Crotchet told the Reverend Doctor Folliott the news of the morning. 'As you predicted,' he said, 'your friend, the learned friend, is in office; he has also a title; he is now Sir Guy de Vaux.'[3]

the rev. dr folliott. Thank heaven for that! he is disarmed from further mischief. It is something, at any rate, to have that hollow and wind-shaken reed rooted up for ever from the field of public delusion.*

* I may here insert, as somewhat germane to the matter, some lines which were written by me, in March, 1831, and printed in the *Examiner* of August 14, 1831. They were then called 'An Anticipation:' they may now (1837), be fairly entitled 'A Prophecy fulfilled.'

THE FATE OF A BROOM: AN ANTICIPATION[4]

Lo! in Corruption's lumber-room,
The remnants of a wondrous broom;
That walking, talking, oft was seen,
Making stout promise to sweep clean;
But evermore, at every push,
Proved but a stump without a brush.

MR CROTCHET. I suppose, doctor, you do not like to see a great reformer in office; you are afraid for your vested interests.

THE REV. DR FOLLIOTT. Not I, indeed, sir; my vested interests are very safe from all such reformers as the learned friend. I vaticinate what will be the upshot of all his schemes of reform. He will make a speech of seven hours' duration, and this will be its quintessence: that, seeing the exceeding difficulty of putting salt on the bird's tail, it will be expedient to consider the best method of throwing dust in the bird's eyes. All the rest will be

> Τιτιτιτιτιμπρό.
> Ποποποί, ποποποί.
> Τιοτιοτιοτιοτιοτιοτίγξ.
> Κικκαβαῦ, κικκαβαῦ.
> τοροτοροτοροτορολιλιλίγξ.*

as Aristophanes has it; and so I leave him, in Nephelococcygia.†

Mr Mac Quedy came up to the divine as Mr Crotchet left him, and said: 'There is one piece of news which the old gentleman has not told you. The great firm of Catchflat and Company, in which young Crotchet is a partner, has stopped payment.'

> Upon its handle-top, a sconce,
> Like Brahma's, looked four ways at once,
> Pouring on king, lords, church, and rabble,
> Long floods of favour-currying gabble;
> From four-fold mouth-piece always spinning
> Projects of plausible beginning,
> Whereof said sconce did ne'er intend
> That anyone should have an end;
> Yet still, by shifts and quaint inventions,
> Got credit for its good intentions,
> Adding no trifle to the store,
> Wherewith the devil paves his floor.
> Worn out at last, found bare and scrubbish,
> And thrown aside with other rubbish,
> We'll e'en hand o'er the enchanted stick,
> As a choice present for Old Nick,
> To sweep, beyond the Stygian lake,
> The pavement it has helped to make. [P.]

* Sounds without meaning; imitative of the voices of birds. From the Ὄρνιθες of Aristophanes. [P.]

† 'Cuckoo-city-in-the-clouds.' From the same comedy. [P.]

THE REV. DR FOLLIOTT. Bless me! that accounts for the young gentleman's melancholy. I thought they would over-reach themselves with their own tricks. The day of reckoning, Mr Mac Quedy, is the point which your paper-money science always leaves out of view.

MR MAC QUEDY. I do not see, sir, that the failure of Catch-flat and Company has anything to do with my science.

THE REV. DR FOLLIOTT. It has this to do with it, sir, that you would turn the whole nation into a great paper-money shop, and take no thought of the day of reckoning. But the dinner is coming. I think you, who are so fond of paper promises, should dine on the bill of fare.

The harper at the head of the hall struck up an ancient march, and the dishes were brought in, in grand procession.

The boar's head, garnished with rosemary, with a citron in its mouth, led the van. Then came tureens of plum-porridge; then a series of turkeys, and, in the midst of them, an enormous sausage, which it required two men to carry. Then came geese and capons, tongues and hams, the ancient glory of the Christmas pie, a gigantic plum-pudding, a pyramid of minced pies, and a baron of beef bringing up the rear.

'It is something new under the sun,' said the divine, as he sat down, 'to see a great dinner without fish.'

MR CHAINMAIL. Fish was for fasts, in the twelfth century.

THE REV. DR FOLLIOTT. Well, sir, I prefer our reformed system of putting fasts and feasts together. Not but here is ample indemnity.

Ale and wine flowed in abundance. The dinner passed off merrily; the old harper playing all the while the oldest music in his repertory. The tables being cleared, he indemnified himself for lost time at the lower end of the hall, in company with the old butler and the other domestics, whose attendance on the banquet had been indispensable.

The scheme of Christmas gambols, which Mr Chainmail had laid for the evening, was interrupted by a tremendous clamour without.

THE REV. DR FOLLIOTT. What have we here? Mummers?

MR CHAINMAIL. Nay, I know not. I expect none.

'Who is there?' he added, approaching the door of the hall.

'Who is there?' vociferated the divine, with the voice of Stentor.

'Captain Swing,' replied a chorus of discordant voices.[5]

THE REV. DR FOLLIOTT. Ho, ho! here is a piece of the dark ages we did not bargain for. Here is the Jacquerie.[6] Here is the march of mind with a witness.

MR MAC QUEDY. Do you not see that you have brought disparates together? the Jacquerie and the march of mind.

THE REV. DR FOLLIOTT. Not at all, sir. They are the same thing, under different names. Πολλῶν ὀνομάτων μορφὴ μία.* What was Jacquerie in the dark ages, is the march of mind in this very enlightened one – very enlightened one.

MR CHAINMAIL. The cause is the same in both; poverty in despair.

MR MAC QUEDY. Very likely; but the effect is extremely disagreeable.

THE REV. DR FOLLIOTT. It is the natural result, Mr Mac Quedy, of that system of state seamanship which your science upholds. Putting the crew on short allowance, and doubling the rations of the officers, is the sure way to make a mutiny on board a ship in distress, Mr Mac Quedy.

MR MAC QUEDY. Eh! sir, I uphold no such system as that. I shall set you right as to cause and effect. Discontent increases with the increase of information.† That is all.

THE REV. DR FOLLIOTT. I said it was the march of mind. But we have not time for discussing cause and effect now. Let us get rid of the enemy.

And he vociferated at the top of his voice, 'What do you want here?'

'Arms, arms,' replied a hundred voices. 'Give us the arms.'

THE REV. DR FOLLIOTT. You see, Mr Chainmail, this is the inconvenience of keeping an armoury, not fortified with sand bags, green bags,[7] and old bags of all kinds.

MR MAC QUEDY. Just give them the old spits and toasting irons, and they will go away quietly.

MR CHAINMAIL. My spears and swords! not without my life. These assailants are all aliens to my land and house. My

*   'One shape of many names.'
                                   Æschylus, Prometheus. [P.]
   † This looks so like caricature (a thing abhorrent to our candour), that we must give authority for it. 'We ought to look the evil manfully in the face, and not amuse ourselves with the dreams of fancy. The discontent of the labourers in our times is rather a proof of their superior information than of their deterioration.' Morning Chronicle: December 20, 1830. [P.]

men will fight for me, one and all. This is the fortress of beef and ale.

MR MAC QUEDY. Eh! sir, when the rabble is up, it is very indiscriminating. You are e'en suffering for the sins of Sir Simon Steeltrap, and the like, who have pushed the principle of accumulation a little too far.

MR CHAINMAIL. The way to keep the people down is kind and liberal usage.

MR MACQUEDY. That is very well (where it can be afforded), in the way of prevention; but in the way of cure, the operation must be more drastic. (*Taking down a battle-axe*). I would fain have a good blunderbuss charged with slugs.

MR CHAINMAIL. When I suspended these arms for ornament, I never dreamed of their being called into use.

MR SKIONAR. Let me address them. I never failed to convince an audience that the best thing they could do was to go away.

MRMACQUEDY. Eh! sir, I can bring them to that conclusion in less time than you.

MR CROTCHET. I have no fancy for fighting. It is a very hard case upon a guest, when the latter end of a feast is the beginning of a fray.

MR MAC QUEDY. Give them the old iron.

THE REV. DR FOLLIOTT. Give them the weapons! *Pessimo, medius fidius, exemplo.** Forbid it the spirit of *Frère Jean des Entommeures!* No! let us see what the church militant, in the armour of the twelfth century, will do against the march of mind. Follow me who will, and stay who list. Here goes: *Pro aris et focis!*[8] that is, for tithe pigs and fires to roast them!

He clapped a helmet on his head, seized a long lance, threw open the gates, and tilted out on the rabble, side by side with Mr Chainmail, followed by the greater portion of the male inmates of the hall, who had armed themselves at random.

The rabble-rout, being unprepared for such a sortie, fled in all directions, over hedge and ditch.

Mr Trillo stayed in the hall, playing a march on the harp, to inspirit the rest to sally out. The water-loving Mr Philpot had diluted himself with so much wine, as to be quite *hors de combat*. Mr Toogood, intending to equip himself in purely

* A most pernicious example, by Hercules! – Petronius Arbiter. [P.]

defensive armour, contrived to slip a ponderous coat of mail over his shoulders, which pinioned his arms to his sides; and in this condition, like a chicken trussed for roasting, he was thrown down behind a pillar, in the first rush of the sortie. Mr Crotchet seized the occurrence as a pretext for staying with him, and passed the whole time of the action in picking him out of his shell.

'Phew!' said the divine, returning; 'an inglorious victory: but it deserves a devil and a bowl of punch.'

MR CHAINMAIL. A wassail-bowl.

THE REV. DR FOLLIOTT. No, sir. No more of the twelfth century for me.

MR CHAINMAIL. Nay, doctor. The twelfth century has backed you well. Its manners and habits, its community of kind feelings between master and man, are the true remedy for these ebullitions.

MR TOOGOOD. Something like it: improved by my diagram: arts for arms.

THE REV. DR FOLLIOTT. No wassail-bowl for me. Give me an unsophisticated bowl of punch, which belongs to that blissful middle period, after the Jacquerie was down, and before the march of mind was up. But, see, who is floundering in the water?

Proceeding to the edge of the moat, they fished up Mr Firedamp, who had missed his way back, and tumbled in. He was drawn out, exclaiming, 'that he had taken his last dose of *malaria* in this world.'

THE REV. DR FOLLIOTT. Tut, man; dry clothes, a turkey's leg and rump, well devilled, and a quart of strong punch, will set all to rights.

'Wood embers,' said Mr Firedamp, when he had been accommodated with a change of clothes, 'there is no antidote to *malaria* like the smoke of wood embers; pine embers.' And he placed himself, with his mouth open, close by the fire.

THE REV. DR FOLLIOTT. Punch, sir, punch: there is no antidote like punch.

MR CHAINMAIL. Well, doctor, you shall be indulged. But I shall have my wassail-bowl nevertheless.

An immense bowl of spiced wine, with roasted apples hissing on its surface, was borne into the hall by four men, followed by an empty bowl of the same dimensions, with all the materials of arrack punch,[9] for the divine's especial brewage. He accinged[10] himself to the task, with his usual heroism; and having finished it to his entire satisfaction, reminded his host to order in the devil.

THE REV. DR FOLLIOTT. I think, Mr Chainmail, we can amuse ourselves very well here all night. The enemy may be still excubant:[11] and we had better not disperse till daylight. I am perfectly satisfied with my quarters. Let the young folks go on with their gambols; let them dance to your old harper's minstrelsy; and if they please to kiss under the mistletoe, whereof I espy a goodly bunch suspended at the end of the hall, let those who like it not, leave it to those who do. Moreover, if among the more sedate portion of the assembly, which, I foresee, will keep me company, there were any to revive the good old custom of singing after supper, so to fill up the intervals of the dances, the steps of night would move more lightly.

MR CHAINMAIL. My Susan will set the example, after she has set that of joining in the rustic dance, according to good customs long departed.

After the first dance, in which all classes of the company mingled, the young lady of the mansion took her harp, and following the reverend gentleman's suggestion, sang a song of the twelfth century.

FLORENCE AND BLANCHFLOR*

Florence and Blanchflor, loveliest maids,
    Within a summer grove,
Amid the flower-enamelled shades
    Together talked of love.

A clerk sweet Blanchflor's heart has gained;
    Fair Florence loved a knight:
And each with ardent voice maintained,
    She loved the worthiest wight.

Sweet Blanchflor praised her scholar dear,
    As courteous, kind, and true;
Fair Florence said her chevalier
    Could every foe subdue.

* Imitated from the Fabliau, *De Florance et de Blanche Flor*, *alias Jugement d'Amour*. [P.]

And Florence scorned the bookworm vain,
    Who sword nor spear could raise;
And Blanchflor scorned the unlettered brain
    Could sing no lady's praise.

From dearest love, the maidens bright
    To deadly hatred fell;
Each turned to shun the other's sight,
    And neither said farewell.

The king of birds, who held his court
    Within that flowery grove,
Sang loudly: ''Twill be rare disport
    To judge this suit of love.'

Before him came the maidens bright,
    With all his birds around,
To judge the cause, if clerk or knight
    In love be worthiest found.

The falcon and the sparrow-hawk
    Stood forward for the fight:
Ready to do, and not to talk,
    They voted for the knight.

And Blanchflor's heart began to fail,
    Till rose the strong-voiced lark,
And, after him, the nightingale,
    And pleaded for the clerk.

The nightingale prevailed at length,
    Her pleading had such charms;
So eloquence can conquer strength,
    And arts can conquer arms.

The lovely Florence tore her hair,
    And died upon the place;
And all the birds assembled there,
    Bewailed the mournful case.

They piled up leaves and flowerets rare,
    Above the maiden bright,
And sang: 'Farewell to Florence fair,
    Who too well loved her knight.'

Several others of the party sang in the intervals of the dances. Mr Chainmail handed to Mr Trillo another ballad of the twelfth century, of a merrier character than the former. Mr Trillo readily accommodated it with an air, and sang –

THE PRIEST AND THE MULBERRY TREE*

Did you hear of the curate who mounted his mare,
And merrily trotted along to the fair?
Of creature more tractable none ever heard,
In the height of her speed she would stop at a word;
And again with a word, when the curate said Hey,
She put forth her mettle, and galloped away.

As near to the gates of the city he rode,
While the sun of September all brilliantly glowed,
The good priest discovered, with eyes of desire,
A mulberry tree in a hedge of wild briar;
On boughs long and lofty, in many a green shoot,
Hung large, black, and glossy, the beautiful fruit.

The curate was hungry and thirsty to boot;
He shrunk from the thorns, though he longed for the fruit;
With a word he arrested his courser's keen speed,
And he stood up erect on the back of his steed;
On the saddle he stood, while the creature stood still,
And he gathered the fruit, till he took his good fill.

'Sure never,' he thought, 'was a creature so rare,
So docile, so true, as my excellent mare.
Lo, here, how I stand' (and he gazed all around,)
'As safe and as steady as if on the ground,
Yet how had it been, if some traveller this way,
Had, dreaming no mischief, but chanced to cry Hey?'

He stood with his head in the mulberry tree,
And he spoke out aloud in his fond reverie:
At the sound of the word, the good mare made a push,
And down went the priest in the wild-briar bush.
He remembered too late, on his thorny green bed,
Much that well may be thought, cannot wisely be said.

* Imitated from the Fabliau, *Du Provoire qui mengea des Môres*. [P.]

Lady Clarinda, being prevailed on to take the harp in her turn, sang the following stanzas:

> In the days of old,
> Lovers felt true passion,
> Deeming years of sorrow
> By a smile repaid.
> Now the charms of gold,
> Spells of pride and fashion,
> Bid them say good morrow
> To the best-loved maid.
>
> Through the forest wild,
> O'er the mountains lonely,
> They were never weary
> Honour to pursue:
> If the damsel smiled
> Once in seven years only,
> All their wanderings dreary
> Ample guerdon knew.
>
> Now one day's caprice
> Weighs down years of smiling,
> Youthful hearts are rovers,
> Love is bought and sold:
> Fortune's gifts may cease,
> Love is less beguiling;
> Wiser were the lovers,
> In the days of old.

The glance which she threw at the Captain, as she sang the last verse, awakened his dormant hopes. Looking round for his rival, he saw that he was not in the hall; and, approaching the lady of his heart, he received one of the sweetest smiles of their earlier days.

After a time, the ladies, and all the females of the party, retired. The males remained on duty with punch and wassail, and dropped off one by one into sweet forgetfulness; so that when the rising sun of December looked through the painted windows on mouldering embers and flickering lamps, the vaulted roof was echoing to a mellifluous concert of noses, from the clarinet of the waiting-boy at one end of the hall, to the double bass of the Reverend Doctor, ringing over the empty punch-bowl, at the other.

CONCLUSION

FROM THIS eventful night, young Crotchet was seen no more on English mould. Whither he had vanished, was a question that could no more be answered in his case than in that of King Arthur, after the battle of Camlan.[12] The great firm of Catchflat and Company figured in the Gazette and paid sixpence in the pound[13]; and it was clear that he had shrunk from exhibiting himself on the scene of his former greatness, shorn of the beams of his paper prosperity. Some supposed him to be sleeping among the undiscoverable secrets of some barbel-pool in the Thames; but those who knew him best were more inclined to the opinion that he had gone across the Atlantic, with his pockets full of surplus capital, to join his old acquaintance, Mr Touchandgo, in the bank of Dotand-carryonetown.

Lady Clarinda was more sorry for her father's disappointment than her own; but she had too much pride to allow herself to be put up a second time in the money-market; and when the Captain renewed his assiduities, her old partiality for him, combining with a sense of gratitude for a degree of constancy which she knew she scarcely deserved, induced her, with Lord Foolincourt's hard-wrung consent, to share with him a more humble, but less precarious fortune, than that to which she had been destined as the price of a rotten borough.

NOTES
HEADLONG HALL
Thomas Peacock

CHAPTER I

1 '*I cannot tell . . .*' The *Lay of the Last Minstrel*. Walter Scott.
2 'μειζονος δ' αλλον τινος' – And of something better as well.
3 '*Mr Foster, the perfectibilian . . . Mr Escot . . . Mr Jenkison . . .*'
Mr Foster and Mr Escot represent extreme expressions of ideas
that both Peacock and P. B. Shelley (the young Shelley of 'Queen
Mab') held, i.e. the possibility of the perfectability of human kind,
and, by contrast, the reality of its present state of deterioration and
degradation. Mr Jenkison (a character based on T. J. Hogg's
attitude) represents the eternal compromise.

CHAPTER II

1 '*Silenus*'. A satyr pictured as a fat old jolly man with a bald
head and pug-nose.
2 '*Achates*'. Friend of Aeneas (Virgil).
3 '*Prometheus*'. Stole fire from Zeus for mankind's use and was
as punishment chained to a rock where his liver was eaten daily –
being restored each night – by an eagle. Subject of Shelley's
Prometheus Unbound.
4 '*Jehu*'. A king of the Old Testament with a reputation for
driving his chariot furiously.

CHAPTER III

1 '*Mr Milestone*'. Based on Humphrey Repton, landscape garden
designer.
2 '*Mr Gall . . . Mr Nightshade, Mr Mac Laurel . . .*' Jeffrey,
Campbell, and Southey – editor and contributors to the *Edinburgh
Review*.
3 '*Sir Patrick O'Prism*'. Based on Sir Uvedale Price who wrote
An Essay on the Picturesque.
4 '*Miss Philomela Poppyseed*'. Based on Mrs Amelia Opie, the
novelist, whom the *Edinburgh Review* treated very kindly.
5 '*Mr Panscope*'. Based on S. T. Coleridge (cf. Mr Flosky of
Nightmare Abbey, Mr Skionar of *Crotchet Castle*).

Chapter IV

1 '. . . *Jason sailed through the Cyanean Symplegades* . . .' The Cyanean Symplegades were islands near the entrance to the Black Sea, that were fabled to close together on ships that tried to pass between them. Jason succeeded in passing them and from then on they became fixed islands.

2 '. . . *the battle of Salamis* . . .' I.e. 480 BC when off its coast the fleet of Xerxes, the Persian, was defeated by the Greeks.

3 '*Trusty comrades*' – Homer.

Chapter V

1 '*No heeltaps* . . .' The liquor left at the bottom of the glass.

2 '*As to skylight* . . .' The space between the liquid and the top of the glass.

3 '. . . *featherless biped* . . .' I.e. man.

4 '*Memento mori* . . .' A reminder of death.

5 'ΟΜΑΔΟΣ ΚΑΙ ΔΟΥΠΟΣ ΟΡΩΡΕΙ!' A bustle and a din broke forth. – Homer.

Chapter VI

1 '. . . *mastigophoric* . . .' Bearing a whip.

Chapter VII

1 '. . . *les premices des dépouilles* . . .' The first fruits of the spoils.

2 '. . . *to the embankment* . . .' An embankment with which Shelley had concerned himself and for which he collected money.

3 '. . . *continuò auditae voces* . . .' Together with this, were heard the voices of children crying loudly, the weeping spirits of babies who, on the very threshold of life, had had no share in the sweetness of living, and whom black day had snatched from the breast, and plunged into bitter death.

4 '. . . *le droit du plus fort* . . .' The right of the strongest (i.e. might is right).

Chapter VIII

1 '. . . *Com' era scritto* . . .' (*Peacock's note*). As it was written in some of his own personal diaries, he had killed with his own hands an infinite number of animals. Five thousand and fifteen pheasants, six thousand hares, eighty-three wild boars, and even thirteen dogs by accident.

Chapter IX

1 '... *like Ladurlad in the Curse of Kehama* ...' The Curse of
Kehama – a poem by Southey (pub. 1810) where Ladurlad, a
peasant, kills the son of Kehama, the great Raja of the World, to
protect his own daughter and is cursed by Kehama.

2 '... *forgotten what the inside of a church was made of* ...' Falstaff
in *Henry IV*, Part I, iii. 3 – Shakespeare

3 '... *pensa que fut un diableteau* ...' Thought it was a devil.

4 '... *'orlt* ...' World.

5 '... *Nunc Tandem* ...' Now at last.

Chapter XI

1 '*dies albâ cretâ notandos* ...' Well-known days painted white,
i.e. outstanding days.

2 '... *qui par engin mirificque* ...' Who, with a miraculous engine,
threw the houses out of the windows – Rabelais.

3 '*the songs of Hoel and Cyveilioc* ...' Hoel is Hywel ab Owain
Gwynedd (1140–70), a court poet. Cyveilic is Cyfeiliog, Prince
Owain, ruler over Powys (1149–95) and a poet.

4 '... *osteosarchaematosplanchnochondroneuromuelous*' 'Osseocarni-
sanguineovixcericartilaginonervomedullary'. I.e. the complete body.

Chapter XII

1 '*At the gallows first* ...' Massinger – *The Bondman*.

2 '... *with edge of penny cord and vile reproach* ...' *Henry V*, iii. 5 –
Shakespeare.

Chapter XIII

1 '... *romantic Meirion* ...' Merionethshire.

2 '... *Caractacus* ...' King of the Silures in the west of Britain,
first century AD.

3 '... *like Llugwy* ...' The River Llugwy.

4 '*elixion and assation* ...' Boiling and roasting.

5 'συμμισγεται τη επιτυχουση' – Lies with the first woman he
meets. – Origin uncertain.

6 '*Condillac* ...' Etienne de Condillac (1715–80), French philosopher. In his *Traité des Sensations* he imagines man as a statue
whose sense impressions he unlocks one by one starting with the
sense of smell.

7 '... *with twenty mortal murders on his crown* ...' Macbeth, iii. 4.

8 '... *army of blue devils* ...' The devils of melancholy (see also
Nightmare Abbey Ch. I Note 2).

CHAPTER XIV

1 '... *cataballitive* ...' A down (cata) hurling (ballitic) quality.

2 '... *Quod victus fateare* ...' Because you are defeated you must allow this.

CHAPTER XV

1 '... *humani nihil alienum puto* ...' There is no part of humanity that I think alien to me.

2 '... *garments of Nessus or Medea* ...' Nessus is Hercules to whom Deianira, in order to win back his love, sent a cloak smeared with the Centaur's blood, which had become poisoned and caused Hercules great suffering. Medea was the daughter of the King of Colonis – and famed for her use of magic.

NIGHTMARE ABBEY
Thomas Peacock

CHAPTER I

1 '*Ay esleu gazouiller* ...' I have dared to chirp and whistle like a goose, as the proverb says, amongst swans, rather than, amongst so many pleasant poets and eloquent orators, to be thought by all to be quite dumb.

2 '... *blue devils* ...' The devils of melancholy (see *Headlong Hall* Ch. XIII Note 8).

3 '*Sir Leoline in Christabel* ...' *Christabel* – S. T. Coleridge.

4 '*had christened Scythrop* ...' The character of Scythrop (from the Greek meaning 'sad-faced') expresses the ideas of the young P. B. Shelley (see *Headlong Hall* Ch. I Note 1).

5 '... *tandem and random* ...' A conveyance where three horses are harnessed one behind the other.

6 '... *seraglio* ...' A walled palace suitable for a sultan's harem.

7 '*was Mr Flosky* ...' The character is based on S. T. Coleridge (cf. Mr Panscope, p. 34, *Headlong Hall*).

8 '... *perdu* ...' Lost.

9 '... *ignis fatuus* ...' Stupid fire.

10 '... *God save King Richard* ...' 'And some ten voices cried, God save King Richard', *Richard III*, iii. 7 – Shakespeare.

11 '... *polemic theology* ...' Theological beliefs arrived at by argument and discussion.

12 '... *Mr Toobad, the Manichaean Millenarium* ...' The Manichaeans believed that God and Satan were co-eternal. Toobad is based on J. F. Newton – a vegetarian who blamed the increasing

wretchedness of society on to its bad (i.e. carnivorous) diet. The young Shelley was much influenced by him, and Newton was one of the group who stayed with the Shelleys at Bracknell in 1812.

CHAPTER II

1 '... *his cogitative faculties* ...' Quoted from the *Most Tragical Tragedy – Chrononhotonthologos* – (1744), a burlesque by Henry Carey.

2 '... *Sorrows of Werter* ...' *The Sorrows of Young Werther* (1744) – Goethe.

3 '... *illuminati* ...' A secret society founded by Adam Weishaupt in 1776 for people claiming special powers.

4 '... *Horrid Mysteries* ...' A German story told by Carlos, Marquis of Grosse and translated by P. Will (1796). (See *Nightmare Abbey* Ch. III Note 4.)

5 '... *eleutherachs* ...' Those with a mad zeal for freedom.

CHAPTER III

1 '... *The Honourable Mr Listless* ...' A character based on Sir Lumley Skeffington (1771–1850), a friend of Shelley, a fop and a playwright.

2 '... *Miss Marionetta Celestina O'Carroll* ...' A portrait, particularly in its physical details, of Shelley's first wife – Harriet Shelley.

3 '... *I prithee deliver* ...' Falstaff in *Henry IV*, Part 2, v. 3 – Shakespeare.

4 '... *Do as Rosalie does with Carlos* ...' See *Nightmare Abbey* Ch. II Note 4.

CHAPTER IV

1 '... *ancestor's skull* ...' See *Headlong Hall* Ch. X p. 60.

2 '... *antithalian* ...' Thalia was the muse of comedy – hence anti-thalian – opposed to comedy.

3 '*Thalia – Melpomene* ...' The muses of comedy and tragedy.

CHAPTER V

1 '... *zitti, zitti* ...' 'Hush, hush, quietly quietly, Let us not cause confusion.' *The Barber of Seville* – Rossini.

2 '... *Nina pazza per amore* ...' An opera, *Nina,* by Giovanni Paisiello (1741–1816).

3 '... *Bath and Cheltenham* ...' Spa watering-places with their social seasons.

4 '... *Devilman* ...' Refers to William Godwin's book *Mandeville* (1817)

5 '... *Paul Jones* ...' John Paul Jones (1747–92), slave trader and smuggler who joined the American and later the French navies.

6 '... *The Red Book* ...' *The Red Book of Hergest* – Welsh manuscript of the fourteenth to fifteenth centuries. See *The Misfortunes of
Elphin* Ch. III Note 1.

7 '... *Roderick Sackbut* ...' Robert Southey, who, as Poet
Laureate, received a butt of sack.

Chapter VI

1 '*Emmanuel Kant Flosky* ...' After Emmanuel Kant (1724–1804),
the philosopher. Coleridge named two of his children after philosophers – Hartley and Berkeley.

Chapter VII

1 '... *à priori, à posteriori* ...' Before, behind, and strongly.

2 '... *sleeking her soft alluring locks* ...' *Comus* – Milton.

3 '... *Don Feijoo* ...' A Spanish Benedictine – Don Benito
Jeronimo Feijoo y Montenegro (1675–1764). Regarded as an initia-
tor of educational reform in Spain.

4 '... *à révérendissime père Jean* ...' Frère Jean des Entommeures –
Rabelais.

5 '... *genus Marauder* ...' The family (genus) Pilferers.

6 '... *Berkeley* ...' George Berkeley (1685–1753), philosopher.

7 '... *A subtle question* ...' *Hudibras* – S. Butler.

8 '... *Macedon and Monmouth* ...' Fluellen in *Henry V*, iv. 7 –
Shakespeare.

Chapter VIII

1 '... *his eye in a fine* ...' *A Midsummer Night's Dream*, v. 1 –
Shakespeare.

2 '... *hyperoxysophistical paradoxology* ...' An over-sophisticated
determination to contradict.

3 '... *such stuff as* ...' *The Tempest*, iv. 1 – Shakespeare.

4 '... *five hundred lines* ...' A reference to Coleridge's writing of
Kubla Khan (1816).

Chapter IX

1 '... *comme il faut* ... Quite correct.

2 '... *toute autre chose* ...' Quite another thing.

Chapter X

1 '... *A stranger, muffled* ...' Celinda, the stranger, is based on
Mary Godwin, Shelley's second wife, and William Godwin's
daughter.

2 '. . . *I guess 'twas* . . .' 'Christabel' – S. T. Coleridge.

3 '. . . *Our immaculate laureate* . . .' Robert Southey (see *Nightmare Abbey* Ch. V Note 7).

4 '. . . *Mr Burke's graduated* . . .' Edmund Burke's *A Philosophical Inquiry into the Sublime and the Beautiful* was published in 1756.

5 '. . . *Stella* . . .' Goethe's *Stella*, translated 1798.

6 '. . . *They alone are subject* . . .' From *A Vindication of the Rights of Women*, by Mary Wollstonecraft, Mary Godwin's mother.

7 '. . . *Lord C. and the Alien Act* . . .' Lord Castlereagh and . . . Lord S. . . .' Lord Sidmouth. The Alien Act (1816) which permitted the government to deport aliens suspected of treacherous acts or intentions.

8 '*Spartacus Weishaupt* . . .' See *Nightmare Abbey* Ch. II Note 3.

Chapter XI

1 '. . . *Mr Cypress* . . .' Based on Lord Byron.

2 '. . . *Hic non bibitur* . . .' Here you will not drink.

3 '. . . *Certainly, ancient* . . .' *Henry V*, iii. 5 – Shakespeare.

4 '. . . *The false knave* . . .' 'The knave is mine honest friend', from *Henry IV*, Part 2, v. 1 – Shakespeare.

5 'καλος καγαθος' – Fair and good.

6 '. . . *alembic* . . .' Apparatus formerly used in distilling.

7 '. . . *Helen of Zeuxis* . . . *the virgins of Crotona* . . .' Zeuxis was a Greek painter. Crotona, a town on the East coast of South Italy.

8 '. . . *The Norfolk Tragedy* . . .' *The Children in the Wood* – an old ballad (*c.* 1595), which is the story of the Babes in the Wood.

9 '. . . *Harry Gill* . . .' *Goody Blake and Harry Gill* by William Wordsworth.

Chapter XII

1 '. . . *Sacré – Cochon – Bleu* . . .' Holy – Pig – Blue.

2 '. . . *Sunt geminae* . . .' There are twin gates of sleep.

3 '. . . *M. Swebach* . . .' A Flemish Painter.

4 '. . . *to consult Tillotson* . . .' John Tillotson (1630–94), who became Archbishop of Canterbury, and wrote sermons of remarkable clarity of style.

5 '. . . *palpable to feeling* . . .' A misquotation from *Macbeth*, ii. 1 – Shakespeare.

THE MISFORTUNES OF ELPHIN
Thomas Peacock

Much of the Welsh legend material Peacock used in this story came from unreliable sources. Iolo Morganwg (Edward Williams) for example, who took a prominent part in the revival of interest in

Welsh legends at the end of the eighteenth and beginning of the nineteenth centuries, and who formulated the beginnings of the Gorsedd of Bards, could be over-enthusiastic. Many of the Triads (a form of old Welsh poetry where the subjects are arranged in groups of three, e.g. Ch. II p. 179) printed in the Myvyrian Archailogy, on which Peacock based a lot of his information, were not old Welsh ones but written by Iolo himself. In addition, many of the songs Peacock uses, although there are Old Welsh poems on the same subject (e.g. 'The Battle of Catraeth' by Aneurin) are neither translations nor adaptations. They are romantic pieces from Peacock's own imagination.

Peacock's Welsh spelling also tends to be unreliable. It is very probable he based it on the work of Owen Pughe, who like Iolo, was a somewhat over-enthusiastic 'scholar', and who tried to clarify the Welsh language. It is often hard to tell whether Peacock is using a legendary character or inventing one. Notes, therefore, are given only about legendary characters who can be traced – when the spelling allows this.

1 '... *Quod non exspectes* ...' See Peacock's own rendering of the Latin lines.

Chapter I

1 '... *Uther Pendragon* ...' King Arthur's father.
2 '... *Gwythno* ...' A Celtic hero (nicknamed Longshanks) possessor of the magic cauldron – one of the treasures of Britain.
3 '... *Cymry* ...' The Welsh.
4 '... *Caer Lleon* ...' Caerleon on Usk in Monmouthshire where King Arthur's court was.
5 '... *Prince Seithenyn ap Seithyn* ...' 'ap' meaning 'son of'.
6 '... *Mochres* ...' The point of Mochres in Cardigan Bay.
7 '... *Caredigion* ...' Cardiganshire.
8 '... *Elphin* ...' Elffin, friend of Taliesin.

Chapter II

1 '... *The three immortal* ...' The Triads, see above.
2 '... *The Circling of the Mead Horns* ...' The original is from the Hirlas of Owain Cyfeilog, Prince in Powys, d. 1197.
3 '... *Decay is one thing* ...' Seithenyn's attitude satirizes that of the opponents to Reform – see p. x, Introduction.

Chapter III

1 'The Englynion of Llywarch Hen' ... – contained in the *Red Book of Hergest* (see *Nightmare Abbey* Ch. V Note 6). They are now thought to be about him, not by him.

2 '... *tremendous crash* ...' In Celtic myth, Llyon-Llion, the Lake of Waves, overflowed, causing the Deluge from which Dwyvant and Dwyvach (a Welsh Noah and his wife) escaped.

Chapter V

1 '... *Weave a circle* ...' 'Kubla Khan' – Coleridge.

2 '... *Taliesin* ...' According to legend, the son whom Ceridwen bore after swallowing Gwion (she was in the form of a hen, he a grain of corn, at the time). This possibly describes an early initiation ritual for a bard.

Chapter VI

1 '... *The three objects* ...' *The Triads*, see p. 368.

2 '... *eidouranion* ...' A clockwork model of the planetary system.

3 '... *Odinism* ...' A belief in Odin, the Norse hero.

4 '... *the seven sleepers of Ephesus* ...' Seven young Christians who were walled up in a cave by their persecutor, Emperor Decius (AD 250) and were found 187 years later still alive, having, it appeared, merely been asleep.

5 '... *funipendulous* ...' Cord-hanging.

6 '... *autochthonal* ...' Earliest known.

7 '... *kakistocracy* ...' Government by the worst people.

8 '... *Bardd Braint* ...' In the time of Hywel Dda (d. *c.* 950) there were three bardic groups according to records – pencerdd (chief of song), teuluwr (household bard), cerddor (minstrel). The system mentioned here, however, is obviously based on Iolo Morganwg's own system for the setting up of the Gorsedd of Bards (*c.* 1780) which is the one that is still, to a large degree, followed today at the Gorsedd.

Chapter VII

1 '... *Maelgon* ...' Maelon (?) – a young chief whom Branwen loved.

2 '... *the Castle of Diganwy* ...' Castle of Deganwy.

3 '... "*nowle*" was "*tottie of the must*" ...' His head was dizzy with new wine – *Faerie Queene* Bk. VII, Canto vii, st. 39 – Spenser.

4 '... *Tarquin* ...' Who set out to rape Lucrece.
5 '... *Merion* ...' Merionethshire.

CHAPTER VIII

1 '... *The Three Chaste Kisses* ...' *The Triads* – see p. 368.

CHAPTER IX

1 '*Three things that will* ...' *The Triads* – see p. 368.

CHAPTER XI

1 '... *schistous* ...' Split into layers.
2 '... *King Melvas* ...' Melwas (?) was, according to Cornish legend, the dark god of the underworld who carried Gwynhwyvar off to his palace.

CHAPTER XII

1 '... *The three principal cities* ...' *The Triads* – see p. 368.
2 '... *Barlow* ...' Bishop of St David's (1536–49), who despaired of forcing his convictions on the wild Welsh there and transferred his see to Carmarthen; to prevent his successors returning to St David's, he had the lead stripped from the episcopal palace roof.
3 '... *Plautus* ... *Terence* ...' Roman playwrights.
4 '... *Ross of Warwick* ...' John Rous or Ross (1411 ?–91) antiquary of Warwick buried in St Mary's church there, to which he left his library.
5 '... *Giraldus* ...' Giraldus Cambrensis (1146 ?–1220), churchman and author of *Itinerarium* – a description of the topography of Wales.
6 '... *The Battle of Badon hill* ...' A battle (518 AD), described in the *Annales Cambriae*, in which Arthur carried the cross of Jesus Christ.
7 '... *Enid* ...' Wife to Geraint, one of Arthur's knights, and daughter to Earl Iniol.
8 '... *Caradoc* ...' Or Caractacus, King of the Silures in West Britain.
9 '... *Llywarch Hen* ...' See *The Misfortunes of Elphin* Ch. III Note 1.
10 '... *Aneurin* ...' A sixth-century poet at the court of Mynyddwg Mwynvawr at Edinburgh, who celebrated the Battle of Catraeth where three hundred youths of the nobility were killed attacking an English stronghold.

11 '... *Merddin Gwyllt* ...' Myrddin, or Merlin the Wild, a sixth-century poet who subsequently acquired a reputation for magic and prophesy.

12 '... *King Bedwyr* ...' Sir Bedivere.

Chapter XIII

1 '... *poco piu* ...' All the world lives more or less by deceiving; and the brave-hearted man dissimulates when necessary, is merry when he can be, believes what he wants to believe, laughs at fools, and creates a world to his liking.

2 '... *Scourge of the Pelagians* ...' Followers of Pelagus, a British monk, of the fourth to fifth centuries whose doctrines were condemned by the Pope in 418.

3 '... *Richard Whiting* ...' Abbot of Glastonbury (d. 1539) imprisoned in the Tower and later executed at Glastonbury.

4 '... *I'd be a butterfly* ...' Popular song of the day.

Chapter XIV

1 '... *The three triumphs* ...' Triads – see p. 368.

2 '... *accinged* ...' To brace oneself to.

Chapter XV

1 '... *The three dignities* ...' Triads – see p. 368.

2 '*Prince Cei* ...' Sir Kay, one of Arthur's knights.

Chapter XVI

1 '... *Three things to which* ...' Triads – see p. 368.

2 '... *Pen Beirdd* ...' Chief Bard – see *The Misfortunes of Elphin* Ch. VI Note 8.

CROTCHET CASTLE
Thomas Peacock

1 '... *Le monde* ...'
The world is full of fools, and who doesn't want to see one
Must shut himself up alone and break his mirror.

CHAPTER I

1 '... *Bandusium* ...' Bandusia, a fountain celebrated by Horace.

2 '... *Scamander* ...' A river of Asia Minor, joining the sea near Troy.

3 '... *alley* ...' Change Alley, near the Stock Exchange, London.

4 '... *Ramsbottom* ...' J. F. Newton – see *Nightmare Abbey* Ch I Note 12.

5 '... *Uranus or Brahma* ...' The most ancient gods – Uranus of Greece, personifying the sky; Brahma of India, born from a golden egg.

6 '... *Saturn or Veeshnu* ...' Saturn, a mild god who dethroned Uranus; Veeshnu (Vishnu) one of the original Great Triad with Brahma and Siva, who gradually became the most popular of the three.

7 '... *Nebuchadnezzar* ...' King of Babylon 605–562 BC who went mad.

8 '... *Miss Touchandgo* ...' A heroine resembling in many ways Jane Gryffydh whom Peacock married.

9 '... *Strephon* ...' A shepherd whose lament for his lost Urania opens Sidney's *Arcadia* – eventually a conventional name for a rustic lover.

CHAPTER II

1 '... *learned friend* ...' Lord Brougham – Baron of Brougham and Vaux (1778–1868). One of the founders, with Jeffrey and Sidney Smith, of the *Edinburgh Review*. He also founded the Society for the Diffusion of Useful Knowledge (1825).

2 '... *Hecate* ...' A moon goddess with three bodies or three heads.

3 '... *Janus* ...' The two-faced god of the old and new year.

4 '... *short mould* ...' A candle made in a mould.

5 '... *Mac Quedy* ...' John Ramsay MacCulloch (1789–1846), political economist, and from 1818 to 1828 a regular contributor to the *Edinburgh Review*.

6 '*Umbrae somnium*'. The dream of a shadow. Pindar.

7 '... *Skionar* ...' A character representing S. T. Coleridge (cf. Mr Panscope of *Headlong Hall*, and Mr Flosky of *Nightmare Abbey*).

8 '... *modern Athenians* ...' Athenaeus (*c*. AD 230) wrote Deipnosophistae – Banquet of the Learned – which contained anecdotes from ancient writers on various subjects, particularly gastronomy.

9 '... *Boeotians* ...' People from Boeotia, a district of Greece, famed for their dull wits.

10 '... *Lysistrata* ...' Aristophanes' play *Lysistrata*.

11 '... *Ude* ...' Chef to Louis XVI at one time, and author of *The French Cook adapted to the use of English families*.

12 '... *Horresco referens* ...' Recalling it, I shudder.

13 '... *Di meliora piis* ...' May God give right-minded people better fare.

14 '... *antispastic acatalectic tetrameter* ...' Flowing unshortened four-footed verse.

15 '... *Hercules against Achelous* ...' Hercules fought Achelous, the god of the river Achelous, in Greece, and won.

16 '... *Bacchic thyrsus* ...' The wand carried by the followers of Bacchus.

17 '... *Nonnus* ...' Greek poet sixth century AD, whose epic poem was *Dionysaca*.

18 '... *learned friend* ...' Lord Brougham, see *Crochet Castle* Ch. II Note 1.

Chapter III

1 '... *He loved her more* ...' From *A Squire of Low Degree* – a four-teenth-century metrical romance.

2 '... *And as for me, though* ...' From *The Legend of Good Women* – Chaucer.

3 '... *Heshbon, by the gate of Bethrabbin* ...' From *The Song of Solomon*.

4 '... *El Dorado* ...' The name of the Great and Golden City of Manoa believed by Sir Walter Raleigh and the Spaniards to exist on the banks of the Amazon or the Orinoco.

5 '... *Angola* ...' A general name for the Portuguese possessions in West Africa south of the Equator.

6 '... *a cottage ornée* ...' A cottage plus.

Chapter IV

1 '... *En quoi* ...' Where do you find yesterday's foolishness? Where do you find today's wisdom?

2 '... *bienséance* ...' Decorum.

3 '... *cliquetis d'assiettes* ...' Clattering of plates.

4 '... *ombre de salle à manger* ...' The shade of the dining-room.

5 '... *the fumée de rôti* ...' The smell of roasting.

6 '... *verre de santé* ...' The glass for good health.

7 '... *point nommé* ...' Nominated season.

8 '*Παπαπαι!*' Amazing!

9 '... *Cedite, Graii* ...' Yield, men of Greece.

10 '... *compotator* ...' Drinking companion.

11 '*ὀψάριον ἐπί ἰχθύος*'. Literally means 'tasty food'. Here refers to fish.

12 '... *sapid* ...' Savoury flavouring.

13 '... *Nadir Shah* ...' Nadir opposite to zenith – i.e. the lowest point in a career.

14 '... *a review* ...' The *Edinburgh Review*, see *Crotchet Castle* Ch. II Notes 1 and 5.

Chapter V

1 '... *Ay imputé* ...' I considered it more than a little shameful to be seen the useless spectator amongst so many valiant, eloquent, and chivalrous people – Rabelais.

2 '*Mr Eavesdrop* ...' Leigh Hunt who was, according to Peacock, a reporter of private affairs and gossip.

3 '... *Mr Wilful Wontsee* ...' William Wordsworth.
   '... *Mr Rumbleshack Shantsee* ...' Robert Southey.

4 ... *Mr Toogood* ...' Robert Owen (1771–1868), reformer and Socialist who agitated for factory reform.

5 '... *andare al diavolo* ...' To go to the devil.

6 '... *Trillo* ...' Thomas Moore (1779–1852), Irish poet and song-writer who also sang his own songs.

7 '... *Mr Philpot* ...' MacGrigor Laird, a friend of Peacock's.

Chapter VI

1 '... *sacella* ...' Small shrines.

2 '... *Fruges consumere* ...' Born to consume the produce.

3 'ὅσεις γε πίνειν οἶδε καὶ βινεῖν μόνον – A man who's no good at anything but tippling and coupling.

4 '... *La Dive Bouteille* ...' The divine bottle.

5 '... *Eleusinian* ...' Eleusin was an ancient city in Attica famous for the worship of Ceres – the goddess of the crops.

6 '... *Fiat experimentum* ...' Let us experiment in cheap souls.

7 '... *argumentum oaculinum* ...' The argument stick, i.e. the exemplary bamboo.

8 '... *melopoeia* ...' Song-making.

9 '... *didascalics* ...' Teachings.

Chapter VII

1 '... *Matilde di Shabran* ...' A comic opera by Rossini.

2 '... *pro more* ...' – As is his wont. '... *seriatim* ...' – one by one.

3 '... *fair round bellies* ...' 'Fair round belly with good capon lined' – *As You Like It*, ii, 7 – Shakespeare.

4 '... *Uranian Venus. ... Pandemian Venus* ...' Venus as worldly or profane love and as heavenly or sacred love.

5 '... *adytum* ...' The holiest of holies.

6 '... *Lycurgus* ...' Legendary legislator of Sparta.

7 '... *Aspasia. ... Lais* ...' Greek courtesans.

8 '... *Praxiteles* ...' A Greek sculptor of *c.* 390 BC.

9 '... *Canova* ...' Antonio Canova (1757–1822), Marquis of Ischia and a sculptor patronized by Pope Clement XIV.

10 '... *Diderot* ...' French philosopher, dramatist, and critic (1713–84).

11 '... *argumentum ad hominem* ...' The argument applied to real people.

CHAPTER VIII

1 '... *Chi sta* ...' The man who spends a couple of hours happily in the world and when his peace is never snatched from him or disturbed at any moment, he can say that the gods are smiling on him.

2 '... *I will contund* ...' Bruise, pound to pieces.

3 '... *Charity Commissioners* ...' In 1818 there was set up a Commission of Enquiry on Education Charities and in 1819 a Commission of Enquiry on Charities for the Poor in England and Wales. Both came about through the auspices of Lord Brougham. Their work was not completed until 1838.

4 '... *abrogated by desuetude* ...' Desuetude = passing into disuse.

5 '... *learned friend* ...' Lord Brougham – see *Crotchet Castle* Ch. II Note 1.

CHAPTER IX

1 '... *immortal nose* ...' In Friar Bacon and Friar Bungay, a comedy (c. 1594) by Greene, the two friars make a head of brass, which, with the help of the devil, is given speech. It only speaks six words while Bacon sleeps – Time is, Time was, Time is past – and on the last falls to pieces.

2 'πίδκκος ἐξ ἱερῆς ὀλίγη λιβὰς' – A small stream springing from the holy fountain.

3 '... *he of the North* ...' Sir Walter Scott.

4 '... *nuspiam, nequaquam* ...' On no occasion, by no means, nowhere, in no way.

5 '... *Eloquentiae magister* ... (note by Peacock)*'. Unless the teacher of the art of speaking, like the fisherman, baits his hook with food that he knows to be to the fish's liking, he will remain on his rock with no hope of a catch.

6 '... *fiscality* ...' Public revenue.

7 '... *de finibus* ...' The ultimate.

8 '... *me judice* ...' In my opinion.

9 'κατ 'ἐξοχὴν'. Pre-eminent.

CHAPTER X

1 '... *Continuant nostre routte* ...' Continuing our way, we navigated three days without discovering anything.

2 '... *haute sagesse Pantagrueline* ...' Great high-spirited wisdom.

(Rabelais defines Pantagruelism as 'a certain gaiety of spirit steeped in disregard of things fortuitous'.)

3 '. . . *échantillon* . . .' Example.

4 '. . . *politicae oeconomiae inscientia* . . .' Science of political economy.

5 '. . . *the course of true love* . . .' *A Midsummer Night's Dream*, I, i – Shakespeare.

6 '. . . *I must be cruel* . . .' *Hamlet*, III, 4 – Shakespeare.

7 '. . . *le cœur navré* . . .' Broken-hearted.

CHAPTER XI

1 '. . . *Base is the slave* . . .' *Henry V*, II, 1 – Shakespeare.

2 '. . . *Apodidraskiana* . . .' The State of the Runaway.

3 '. . . *no rotten boroughs* . . .' An area which, although it had a very small population, still returned an MP.

CHAPTER XII

1 '. . . *a bottle of sherry into negus* . . .' Negus: a hot toddy.

2 '. . . *Pinder of Wakefield* . . .' The pinder looked after the pound where in the days of strip farming, straying animals were impounded.

CHAPTER XIII

1 '. . . *Or vieni, Amore* . . .' Come now, Love, and sit here with me. From *Orlando Innamorato*, a poem by Boiardo on the subject of falling in love.

2 '*Giraldus de Barri* . . .' Giraldus Cambransis – see *The Misfortunes of Elphin* Ch. XII Note 5.

3 '. . . *Ariosto* . . .' Ariosto (1474–1533), author of *Orlando Furioso*.

4 '. . . *tutto il giorno* . . .' All the day, intent on good deeds, they climbed the hills and crossed the torrential streams.

5 '. . . *contadina* . . .' Italian peasant girl.

CHAPTER XIV

1 '. . . *And with the food of pride sustained her soul* . . .' From 'Lines left upon a Yew Tree Seat'. In the original 'sustained his soul'.

2 '. . . *the perception of the sublime* . . .' This parallels very closely both the sentiment and the words of *Tintern Abbey* by Wordsworth.

3 '*Ἀλήμονα βότρυν ἐφείρας*' – Her hair's errant tendrils.

Chapter XV

1. '... *Una notte in un stradotto* ...' (*in Peacock's note*). One night a foolhardy man was strolling down a lane, when suddenly a scream re-echoed in his ear; there was his grandmother's shadow which tweaked him by the nose. Oh! let us neither by night nor day venture through the black forest (Dance in a circle).

Chapter XVI

1 '... *Cornelius Agrippa* ...' Henry Cornelius Agrippa von Nettesheim (1486–1535) who wrote *De Occulta Philosophia* – a book about magic.

2 '... *executeur des hautes œuvres* ...' Executioner.

Chapter XVII

1 '... *A cup of wine* ...' *Henry IV*, Part II, v. 3 – Shakespeare.

2 '... *Excellent potted char* ...' Char is a hill trout from Wales.

3 '... *pencil of Zeuxis* ...' See *Nightmare Abbey* Ch. II Note 7.

4 '... *the Venus of Cnidos* ...' The most celebrated statue to Venus was that by Praxiteles in her temple at Cnidos.

Chapter XVIII

1 '... *Vous autres dictes* ...' You others say that ignorance is the mother of all evils, and say truly; but despite that, you do not banish it from your existence, but live in it, with it, and by it. That is why so much evil envelops you from day to day.

2 '... *rayonnante de joie* ...' Radiant with joy and love.

3 ... '*Sir Guy de Vaux* ...' Lord Brougham – see *Crotchet Castle* Ch. II Note 1.

4 '... *The Fate of a Broom* ...' A play on sound – Broom and Brougham.

5 '... *Captain Swing* ...' An imaginary person to whom were attributed in 1830–3 a number of risings against farmers using agricultural machinery.

6 '... *the Jacquerie* ...' A peasant rebellion in North France in 1358 caused by their sufferings as a result of the English invasion. The nickname for a French peasant was Jacques Bonhomme, hence La Jacquerie.

7 '... *green bags* ...' Brief bags carried by barristers.

8 '... *Pro aris et ficis* ...' For hearth and home.

9 '... *of arrack punch* ...' Arrack = a distillation from coco-palm or rice and sugar.

10 '... *accinged himself to the task* ...' Accinged = applied himself.

11 '... *may be still excubant* ...' Excubant = from the Latin to keep watch.

12 '... *the battle of Camlan* ...' In the battle of Camlan according to the Annales Cambriae, in 539, Arthur and Medraut fell.

13 '... *figured in the Gazette* ...' *The London Gazette* was a record of, amongst other things, notices of bankruptcies.

Thomas Love Peacock: Bibliography

NOVELS

HEADLONG HALL	1816	(Anonymous)
MELINCOURT (3 vols.)	1817	
NIGHTMARE ABBEY	1818	
MAID MARION	1822	By the author of
THE MISFORTUNES	1829	HEADLONG HALL
OF ELPHIN		
CROTCHET CASTLE	1831	
GRYLL GRANGE	1860	

First collected edition (1875) ed. Sir Henry Cole (3 vols) with useful biographical notes by Peacock's grand-daughter Edith Nicolls.

The definitive modern edition is *Thomas Love Peacock*, *THE COMPLETE NOVELS* (2 vols) ed. David Garnett, Hart-Davis.

Biography: *Thomas Love Peacock*, by J. B. Priestley, Macmillan.

Pan Classics

Each volume is completely unabridged and contains an analytic introduction and text notes

Pan Classics (cont.)

Pan Reference Books